TANTAMOUNT

THOMAS J. RADFORD

TANTAMOUNT

Thomas J. Radford

TYCHE BOOKS LTD.

TANTAMOUNT

Published by Tyche Books Ltd.
www.TycheBooks.com

Copyright © 2013 Thomas J. Radford
First Tyche Books Ltd Edition 2014

Print ISBN: 978-0-9918369-9-4
Ebook ISBN: 978-1-928025-00-9

Cover Art by James F. Beveridge
Cover Layout by Lucia Starkey
Interior Layout by Ryah Deines
Editorial by M. L. D. Curelas

Author photograph by Devin Hart

CIP data has been requested

The publisher does not have any control over and does not assume any responsibility for author or third party websites or their content.

This is a work of fiction. All of the characters, organizations and events portrayed in this story are either the product of the author's imagination or are used fictitiously.

Any resemblance to persons living or dead would be really cool, but is purely coincidental.

Dedication

This novel is dedicated to my grand-father, Phil Wright,
who inspired my love of story telling. He doesn't read fantasy.
But he said he might read this one.

CONTENTS

Chapter 1

Kitchen cutlery burst through the wall, rupturing it and showering splinters across the room on the other side. A knife struck the wall, digging into the wood only inches above where Nel's head rested in her hammock. Her eyes focused in shock on the blade, still shaking with momentum, arms grabbing for the sides of the hammock and fighting the urge to sit bolt upright in bed. She rolled to the side, got tangled in the hammock and hung upside down for a moment before dropping to the cabin floor. Yells streamed through the wooden panels of her cabin walls. Or what was left of them. Swearing aloud herself, Nel got her hands to the floor under her and started to stand up. Another projectile rocketed through the hole in the wall and Nel dropped back to the floor, sprawling ungracefully with her face against dust and grit. She spat it out furiously, her eyes going to the unwelcome addition to her cabin. A fork.

A fork. The tines were embedded in the wall, the handle still quivering from the force of the impact. A fork. That made sense, the galley was right next to Nel's cabin, sandwiched between her own and the captain's. Nel stared at it, eyes narrowing.

"Gabbi!" she shouted pulling her legs up and crawling towards the cabin door. The yelling continued unabated; she could make out at least three distinct voices, all of them intertwined and trying to drown out the others, rising higher and higher in an effort to be heard.

Nel stumbled out onto the deck as the ship pitched under her feet. She had to grab for the frame of the cabin doorway. More yelling and screaming outside, the crew grabbing for lines and purchase as the ship heaved, tossing them from their posts. The deck rolled under Nel's feet, tilting and shuddering. The whole horizontal plane shifted for a moment and Nel thought the ballast in the hold was going to go. She looked up at the stars, the sparkling pinpricks of light in the inky miasma that was deep space and waited for the world to turn topsy-turvy. However, the ballast and its artificial gravity held, keeping them all from being thrown overboard.

Gravity was a damned convenient thing to have in space. Murder to sail a ship without it.

Another crash came from the galley. Nel turned and glared that way. It sounded like every pot and pan inside the narrow room was being thrown around, which likely was not too far from the truth. However, if Gabbi's little temper tantrum was rocking the ship the way it felt like it was then Nel was going to put a stop to it. If that meant putting the boot into her cook then so much the better.

She took a step and the ship swayed again, pitching the other way and ending on a lean. The ballast was definitely shifting now, the ship's gravity plane with it. Nel made a dive for the galley and hooked the entry, pulling herself in and taking her first look at the commotion that had woken her.

The ship's cook, Gabbi, faced off against Nel's navigator. Gabbi was a small woman, dark and petite, if you were being polite. Rotund and stout if you weren't and chubby if you were being honest. Right now Gabbi's puffed up cheeks were red, but not from any sort of good humour—she was enraged and brandished a soup ladle in one hand to prove it. The ladle was making threatening motions towards her crewmate.

The crewmate in question was Loveland Quill, an unfortunate name that the navigator was sensitive about. Being a Kelpie, one of the non-human misfits on the *Tantamount's* roster, the snake-skinned Quill literally wasn't the most likeable crewman aboard. This also wasn't the first time someone had turned violent on him. Right now Gabbi was trying to cram all of the ship's cooking utensils down the navigator's throat. Half a dozen long-handled copper pots circled around Gabbi's head, kept there by the sheer force of her will.

Bloody thaumatics, Nel thought grimly. Thaumatics was what people like Quill used to propel ships through air and space. Combined with the still shifting ballast in the ship's hull, thaumatics was what made travel between worlds possible. People who were strong enough used it to propel ships. People like Quill. People like Gabbi, who weren't quite that strong, could still move smaller things at a fair decent clip. Things like pots, pans, and the entire cutlery drawer embedded in Nel's wall.

All the smaller ammunition in the galley had already been expended, cutlery was scattered around the room, here and there, driven into the wall, the tables, even the floor. One of the long table benches floated in front of Quill, studded with sharp, pointy projectiles. While Quill didn't possess the thaumatic nuance to manage dozens of items like Gabbi, he could heft significantly larger and heavier objects, hence his responsibility for launching and landing the ship planet-side and keeping it moving in the void.

The pots circling Gabbi picked up speed, a dizzying spiral of cooking implements that began to peel off one by one and fly towards Quill. The navigator threw the bench in the way, pots ricocheting off the hardwood furniture.

"Stand fast!" Nel bellowed at the top of her lungs. Her order startled the two combatants so sufficiently that Gabbi lost her concentration; pots, pans and the odd surviving spoon dropped out of the air. Quill kept his defences up, peering cautiously out around his improvised shield. Across the galley, a bald and wrinkly head popped up from behind the range, framed by two oversized ears. Jack, Korrigan Jack, Gabbi's burly kitchen assistant.

"Skipper," Gabbi started to say. There was a crash as Quill released his grip on the bench and it fell to the floorboards. The noise it made was thunderous, but hardly enough to shake the whole ship. Nel's gaze focused on it, feeling sick inside.

It wasn't Gabbi and Quill that had been making the ship rock.

"You two . . ." Nel left the threat unfinished, unwilling to waste any more time on them. She turned away from the aerial battlefield that was the galley and began to sprint the length of the ship, heading for the bridge, passing confused crew members on the way. She didn't stop to ask any of them what was going on; she needed to see for herself.

Nel found the bridge just as confused as the rest of the ship, but at least the captain was there. Horatio Phelps turned at the arrival of his first officer. His dishwater grey hair was a mess and he was still in his nightclothes, the overlong shirt flapping around his knees. He had been roused as surely as Nel herself and looked none the wiser for it. His baggy and sleep-ridden eyes seized on Nel with a sudden urgency she found deflating. Horatio obviously had no idea what was going on either.

"What's going on, Nel?" he called out, confirming her suspicions.

Nel shook her head, manhandling her captain aside to take over his vantage point. From the elevated bridge they could see the length of the ship. They could see for countless leagues in any direction, in fact, but being as they were in the deep void of space between planets there shouldn't have been anything to see at all. Unless they'd hit a freak solar storm. Some stray satellite maybe? No, such an impact would have been tossing the *Tantamount* like a bathtub toy or ripping a new hole in its hull. What then?

Debris. She could see it now. Flotsam. The mangled wreckage of what had once been another ship of the void. Like a fireside story, more details gradually emerged, becoming visible in the black misty miasma they sailed through. Shredded sails floated in the airless void, not stirred by so much as a flutter of breeze, broken spars splintered into jagged stakes, a mast broken in two but with some of its rigging still attached. Bits and pieces of the ship's paraphernalia hung off the rigging, pulleys and locks, hawsers and nets, like some mad artist's inertialess sculpture of a spider web.

"Hells," Nel whispered. The ship she was looking at wasn't just dead and adrift—it had been smashed, utterly smashed, almost down to the last boards and nail. For the crew who had manned her, the ship might as well have been in one of the nine hells. The void was often considered one of them.

The *Tantamount* shuddered again as a large piece of debris nudged it before ricocheting off into the deep, spinning slowly.

"Why wasn't anyone on watch?" Horatio demanded indignantly. "Where was Quill?"

"The galley," Nel said shortly, not caring to explain right now. She had just seen something else in the wreckage. The crew.

She could make out a dozen or so bodies, scattered amongst the timbers of what had once been their vessel. They hung limp and motionless, drifting with the rest of the debris. They made Nel think of puppets, marionettes with severed strings. Some bodies were snagged in the wastrels, others floated free, grotesquely drifting through the midnight skies that were the void.

"There could be survivors," the captain said, not sounding as though he believed it himself.

"Not likely," Nel said. "This could have happened days ago. Weeks . . . months even."

It could have happened years ago. Nothing decayed in the void; it just drifted, frozen and cold until it encountered something else. Then, depending just what was encountered, the flotsam could burn up, crash, or get dragged into orbit. In some parts of the void, where the lanes were treacherous, there were whole leagues of wrecked ships. They were graveyards built up over centuries of collected disasters, held together as huge, floating mausoleums.

"Wreckage isn't dispersed enough," Horatio said, sounding

sure of himself now. "This isn't so old."

"Still not likely to find anyone." Nel sought to head off what she saw as a pointless exercise.

"We're looking," Horatio said firmly. "Get to it."

Nel grimaced. "Aye aye, Captain."

She snapped out orders to the milling crew. Quill had surfaced from the galley. It was hard to read his scaly-faced moods but he didn't look particularly chastened to find the ship in such a state during his watch. Nel knew she would be having words with Quill later, about several things.

For now, she let him take the helm, bringing the ship to a stop clear of most of the debris. Quill was the navigator and an officer for good reason. It was his abilities that propelled the *Tantamount* through the void and you didn't keep that post without being good at it. It was why Nel and the captain tolerated the confrontational Kelpie. In the same way as he and Gabbi had hurled pots and pans at each other, he now put his abilities to better use steering the ship clear of any further damage.

Without people like Quill, it was impossible to break free of a planetary surface or to navigate the void. Even if a ship could be launched without navigators to guide them and adjust their course, they would continue on a straight lined course until something caused them to stop, like another planet. And it would be a sudden and fiery stop without a navigator.

Under Nel's orders the crew rushed to launch the tenders, or "bubbles" as most people referred to them. There was no breathable air in space, gases and solar currents aplenty, but nothing most humanoids could survive in. Space was just that, empty apart from the miasma, a misty black cloud found wherever ships sailed.

A ship carried its own atmosphere, its own gravity and air inside an envelope surrounding the ship, kept there by the same etheric ballast that kept the crew's feet planted to the deck. Bigger ships resulted in bigger envelopes, but when a situation required someone to leave the ship the normal procedure was to "bubble up" and float out from the ship in what was essentially an oversized fish bowl.

"Coming out, Skipper?" one of the crewmembers, a man named Cyrus, asked, holding the hatch to one of the bubbles open. The bubble was a glass structure, roughly spherical in shape, like its name suggested, with a flattened base so it could be stored more easily when not in use.

Nel grimaced, but nodded.

"Just the two of us, Skipper?" Cyrus asked her. Nel followed his sideways glance to the gangly figure at his side.

"Violet," Nel acknowledged the ship's cabin girl.

"Skipper," the teenager's voice sounding thin in that awkward adolescent stage of development where nothing was ever in sync. "Do you need any help . . . ?" she left the question hanging hopefully. "Out there?"

Nel frowned. "You been out in a tender yet?"

"No, Skipper." Violet shook a tangled head of fairy locks. "But Piper's been teaching me."

"Maybe now's not the time . . . ," Nel started to say. Cyrus coughed into his hand.

"Sorry, Skipper," he apologised, catching her eye. "Got something in my throat."

Nel looked at him for a moment longer, her crewman gave her a shrug back, a slight roll of his shoulders.

He's right, she thought, *just like I told the captain. We're not going to find anyone alive out there.*

"All right, Vi," Nel agreed. "You're coming, but this isn't a game. You do what I tell you, when I tell you."

"Aye, aye, Skipper," Violet responded with an enthusiastic salute. The girl was beaming, tail practically wagging. Nel sighed at the sight. Damned misfits, the whole crew.

"Get in." The skipper shook her head at Violet, pointing to the bubble. Then to Cyrus: "Go and find Gabbi, see if she needs any help. And tell Jack I'm going to be bringing him some patients."

"Aye, Skipper." Cyrus nodded as Violet clambered into the

bubble. "As you say."

"As I say," Violet heard the skipper mutter as she climbed into the bubble herself. The flattened base gave them both something to stand on as they swung the hatch shut behind them. It made a squelching sound as it sealed in place. At a wave from Cyrus, the ship's crane then hoisted them up, just enough to clear the ship's railing before it swung them out into the void.

Cyrus winked at Violet before he gave the signal; she could feel herself grinning back. It would be her first real time out in a tender, a bubble. Cyrus dropped his arm and the crane released them.

Violet felt her stomach drop as they fell out of the *Tantamount's* envelope, the deck of the *Tantamount* disappearing from sight. In a moment it was replaced by the utter emptiness of space as weightlessness caught them. It went on forever and ever, pure black void and the duller black mist broken by distant stars. The only sound was the faint hiss from the hose piping air into the bubble. That and a wire-wrapped cable were the only things linking Violet and the skipper to the ship. Away from the *Tantamount's* gravity-well the weightlessness of the void reasserted itself; both of them started to float freely within the bubble. Fortunately the controls inside were sturdy and robust, the turn-wheels and levers doubled as handholds during missions away from the ship, though they had to brace themselves between the controls and the bubble to operate both.

Violet worked the controls for the exterior valves that controlled their movement at the skipper's instructions. It was hard work. Without a sense of weight Violet had to brace herself against the interior of the bubble to turn a wheel or pull a lever. She concentrated hard, trying to remember everything Piper had told her about controlling the tender.

The valves she worked released tightly controlled bursts of air from the bubble that nudged them in the right direction. The skipper watched carefully as Violet worked. Air was precious and to be used sparingly in space. The bubble was a finicky and cumbersome contraption. Violet found it difficult to steer and now that they were out here amongst this mess of debris she thought it worryingly fragile. The walls were made from thick, toughened glass but they were still glass. Gradually though, Violet worked them through the field, moving in close enough to the crew of the shattered ship.

The crew. The dead, frozen bodies floated listlessly around them.

"What do you think happened here, Skipper?" Violet asked. Her voice sounded shaky even to her and the skipper glanced over. Violet kept her eyes away from the bodies, focusing on the remains of the other ship and the working of the tender instead.

"Something ploughed right through their ship," the skipper said, eyeing the bodies. One drifted in perfect slow motion past the bubble. There was a slight thump as it collided with the curved glass wall. Violet flinched, the involuntary motion causing her to drift back to the other side of the bubble. The impact of the body stuck the deceased sailor to the bubble for a moment, before their momentum shoved it off and sent the dead man spinning slowly in another direction. It was a macabre sight but Violet found herself focusing on the details. Not the cloudy, crystallised eyes or the curious hook of stiff fingers, but material details, the cut and colour of the uniforms all the dead wore. The cloth was a deep blue, almost black in colour, with white trim.

"Like an asteroid, Skipper?" Violet asked while their momentum took them deeper into the debris field. "Think someone was asleep at the helm?"

"Nothing like that around here," the skipper told her. The woman's face darkened and Violet remembered the whispers and shouts of shipboard gossip. Even in the brief moments before they'd launched the tender she'd heard Quill's name mentioned. It was enough to make her regret her flippant comment. If the wreckage hadn't been as demolished as it was, with most of the ship broken into tiny fragmented pieces, the

Tantamount would have been in serious trouble. She was already dreading the return trip to the ship, seeing first-hand how much damage had been done.

"See those cannons?" The skipper pointed to where the iron castings floated freely, anchored to a scrap of decking by a fraying rope. "High calibre, military issue."

"You saying this was an Alliance ship?" Violet looked at the uniformed bodies again and immediately wished she hadn't. Her stomach wanted to climb back up from wherever it had dropped to.

"Air-corps," the skipper confirmed. "You can't tell from the uniforms?"

"Never saw a lot of them back home, Skipper," Violet mumbled, covering her mouth with her hand. "Seen them less since I've been with you."

The skipper didn't press on the subject. Maybe she was regretting bringing Violet out here—she could hardly be blamed.

"Sorry, Skipper," Violet managed to say. She gripped the wheel tightly with clammy hands.

"It's fine," the skipper said, and sounded like she meant it.

When Violet felt she could safely look up again she found the skipper still studying their surroundings. The skipper used to be in the Alliance—that was more shipboard gossip but something Violet heard often enough to believe it was genuine. What was it like for her, seeing her former fellows out here like this? If the woman felt anything, she didn't give it away. Tough woman, the skipper. She'd been around— Violet could read that from the tattooed sleeve on one arm. A Kitsune girl like Violet from a backwater rock just didn't compare.

"Alliance ship, military protocols," the skipper mused aloud. "They weren't going to get hit by a stray asteroid. Not even out here."

"So what did happen?" Violet asked, because it felt like she was expected to.

"They were rammed."

"Rammed?" Violet blinked, startled.

The skipper nodded grimly. "This was a ship that was maybe twenty-eight gun, lightweight, frigate class. Whatever attacked them was much bigger. Heavy, massive envelope ran straight through them. The change in pressure from the bigger ship's envelope would have ripped them apart. That's what happened."

Violet studied their surroundings. "You asked Jack to get ready for patients."

A shrug. "Wanted him to feel useful. There was a ruckus in the galley just before."

"You don't think we're going to find any survivors, do you, Skipper?"

"Captain says we look. We're looking."

"Aye, Skipper," Violet said quietly.

The bubble drifted at its leisurely pace through the remains of the alliance ship. Every time they came to a body they would inspect it, moving around stray bits of timber and canvas, checking the obvious places a survivor might be. All they found were more cold bodies.

"Something odd about these bodies, Skipper," Violet said eventually.

The skipper turned back to face her, eyebrows raised quizzically. There was precious little light out here amongst the mist and debris. Much of the skipper's face was shadowed, giving the woman a foreboding look. That look fit with what Violet had been feeling since they got out here. Something was wrong.

"They look dead, Skipper, a long time dead."

"How so?" the skipper pushed for her to explain.

"Seen bodies before, Skipper," Violet shivered at the memories. "They . . . usually they all look the same out here. Frozen. Cold. These," Violet turned her head to follow another corpse, "they look like they were left in the sun to dry. Or maybe someone buried them for a week."

Violet shuddered, rubbing at her wrist as she did so. There

was a tattoo there, braided rope looped around the wrist and up into the palm, protection against being lost overboard, so she would always have something to hold fast. Most sailors had tattoos—the rope was Violet's first and only. Piper had taken her out to get it the first time she'd made planetfall with the *Tantamount*.

"You think it was a corpse ship, Skipper? Maybe taking their dead back from some battle out in the Lanes?"

The idea had been sitting at the back of her mind for some time now. Too many bodies out here, too far gone. It wasn't normal.

"No," the skipper said quietly, "that's not what the Alliance does with its dead."

"You'd be one to know, Skipper. But then what . . . ?" Violet gestured. She didn't finish her question.

"Draugr," the skipper said. "They're Draugr. Air-corps run with them these days,"

"Oh." It was a long time before Violet tried to make conversation again.

She'd heard of Draugr before. Most everyone had. They were supposed to be common around the Alliance Lanes, but not out in the backwaters. Labourers, servants, slaves, Violet wasn't quite sure. She didn't even know if they were even alive or some sort of animation, just that they were becoming more and more common in the High Lanes. She hadn't expected to see something like that out in the Free Lanes.

The thoughts washed away when she looked ahead of them. Part of the hull, more or less intact. The reinforced section around the keel of the ship; where heavier cargo would have been stored. It might even have maintained something of an envelope.

"Skipper," Violet called, pointing.

"All right," the skipper said. "Take us over. Nice and easy."

"Only speed we've got, Skipper," Violet said, adjusting the angle of their approach. The bubble drifted leisurely towards the broken hull, which yawned dark even against the black. But not so dark Violet couldn't see it.

"There's someone in there." Violet's voice rose to a high pitch. She twisted around to face the skipper with wide eyes. "They look like they could still be alive."

The skipper's face creased into her habitual frown, hand straying to her side but grasping at air. Often the skipper carried a wand there, especially when they were ashore, less often aboard.

"Hells."

"Skipper?"

"Nice and easy," the skipper repeated through clenched teeth.

With white-knuckled hands Violet manoeuvred the bubble right to the edge of the hull wreckage until the empty space between them started to twist and fray. Violet eyed the distorted air warily, for that disruption meant there was air of some sort between them. There was an envelope present and it was reacting to the pressure of the air inside the bubble.

"Skipper," Violet called out, pointing.

"Keep us out here," the skipper cautioned her. "That's a fractured envelope, a different atmosphere from us. We won't take any chances here."

Violet shivered. This close and she could just about see inside the darkened recess. A figure huddled up as far inside the hull as it was possible. No uniform that she could see, the man wore drab colours that seemed to blend into his environment. The head shifted, appearing to lift to regard them. There was no other sign the survivor was aware of them.

"Signal the ship," the skipper said. "Tell them we've found someone."

Violet reached out and grabbed the signaller with one hand. She stared at it, struggling.

"Skipper ...," she said after a moment, her voice drying up.

The skipper took her attention away from the survivor for a moment.

"What do I send them?" Violet asked quietly.

"You don't know?" the skipper asked sternly.

Violet bit down on her bottom lip, shook her head.

"Two white flashes, one red," she was told shortly. "Survivors found. Send it 'til you get an answer."

Violet felt her face burning as she went to operate the signaller. A triangular fixture with three different faces of coloured glass, the faces could be flashed in coded sequences to relay messages. Violet took a long look at the survivor while she worked. The man was becoming more animated now, like a machine shaking off cobwebs and dust and starting up after a long downtime.

The survivor didn't try to speak, not that he would have been able to make himself heard across the envelopes anyway. He appeared to be waiting, gauging the skipper and Violet.

"Violet?" the skipper called, "what does the ship say?"

Violet jerked her head back. She'd missed the ship's answering signal, had to wait for it to repeat. "Two green flashes, one white, Skipper."

"And that means what, Violet?"

"Come back to the ship," she said quickly.

"Come back to the ship with cargo." The skipper glanced over her shoulder reprovingly.

Violet flushed. "I knew that, Skipper."

"Then say so. All right, Captain says we bring him in, we bring him in. It's one more than I thought we'd find."

The keel of the wrecked ship would have been filled with ether, Violet thought. The amber coloured rock that all ships of the void used as ballast. Ether was what provided both gravity and envelopes in space, keeping the miasma out and the breathable air in. Enough of it seemed to have survived to keep an envelope, and the survivor, alive.

"Get ready to open the hatch, Violet. Stand back."

"You're not going to mesh the envelopes?" Violet asked, referring to the process of merging two different atmospheres. Strictly speaking the bubble didn't have an envelope as it lacked the induced gravity to hold it in, but it still had its own air, so long as the hatch remained shut. A hatch the skipper had just said she intended to open.

"We can't mesh. The bubble won't fit in there."

"It might!" Violet protested.

"And if we get stuck in their gravity?" The skipper shook her head. "No, we're doing this the hard way."

Violet was incredulous at the plan so Nel ignored the girl. If she stopped to think about it she would realise how stupid it was. Taking a moment to clip a safety cord to a carabineer on her belt, she took a firm grip on the valve release wheel that held the hatch shut. Nel twisted the wheel slowly, counter-clockwise, and grit her teeth as the hiss of leaking atmosphere grew louder. They only had a few minutes before the hatch would have to be shut again, minutes before the air inside the bubble became too thin to breathe as it was vented into space.

Nel took a firm grip on hatch, bracing her feet against the interior wall in the weightless bubble and pulled. The hiss became a rush as the atmosphere was sucked out of the bubble. Unlike a ship like the *Tantamount*, the bubble didn't have the gravity to keep the air where it was meant to be and now it was making good its escape from the glass confines.

With a clear run to the other envelope now, Nel braced herself for what she knew would be bitter, freezing cold. When her fingers and toes wrapped around the edge of the hatch opening, ready to pull herself through, she looked at her bare skin and swore. In the rush since she'd woken up in her hammock, she hadn't realized she was wearing little more than her nightshirt and breeches. No gloves or boots, no coat, very little at all to protect herself from the void. All back in her cabin, along with her sidearm. She could already feel the icy touch in the square of the hatch.

"Skipper?" Violet asked again. "You sure about this?"

That quiet voice of reason. Irritating. No, Nel wasn't sure about this at all.

"It's fine." Nel clenched her jaw, gauging the distance to the other envelope. Not more than a few feet really. She could do this. Just a few feet.

She braced herself, crouching down in the flow of air as it rushed out of the bubble. Her legs uncoiled beneath her as she launched herself across the gap.

The cold hit her like a slap, a vicious blow the size of a breaking wave, washing over every inch of her skin. It lasted only a few seconds and then she was inside the dead ship's envelope, which felt like a furnace by comparison. Gravity reasserted its presence, some hangover from the original ship and she hit the deck hard on her knees. Nel's whole body was shivering; sweat had formed on her skin and turned to an icy hoarfrost, a second bodily layer her shivering shook off like an animal shedding its skin. She managed to get her feet up and under, rising shakily, not looking forward to the return trip she'd have to make in a moment.

"Can you move at all?" she asked of the survivor, who hadn't made a move towards her. Up close she got her first good look at him.

Probably early thirties, square jawed like so many other Alliance corpsmen Nel had seen aboard ships of the line. Close cropped practical haircut, barely a finger's width of black follicles remained and the beard on his face appeared to be only a couple of days old. Had he been here that long? She could find out later. The survivor was gaunt and tired but otherwise healthy, though she didn't like the way he studied her with those dark eyes. It felt like she was being judged.

"Yes," he said in a voice hoarse from thirst and disuse.

"Good," Nel said, unclipping her safety cord and pulling two lengths of rope through her carabineer. "Loop this round your waist and tie it off. Is there anyone else with you?"

"No." The survivor followed her instructions, finishing by clicking the sprung gate over the cord. He pulled on it once or twice, testing the lock before inclining his head at

Nel. She frowned back at him, hand on her carabineer. The knot he'd tied was a good one, just not one a sailor would have chosen. She expected more conversation, if not outright questions. Her survivor was taking this all a bit too calmly for her liking.

She turned, shuffling the carabineer round to the other side of her belt so as not to be caught up in the loose rope. Violet gave her a wave and slowly cranked the hand winch Nel's safety rope was attached to until it was taut. Nel looked back at her passenger.

"We're going to jump, same way I came in, and Violet is going to reel us in at the same time. It's going to be cold so brace yourself and don't even think about missing the hatch. I won't be coming back out to get you."

The survivor ducked his head. "I understand."

"Good." Nel scowled. "You got a name?"

"Sharpe. Castor Sharpe."

"Hold on to your breeches, Castor Sharpe. On the count of three then, one . . . two . . . three!"

Nel took another leap out into the void, experiencing that flash of vertigo as gravity vanished and sub-zero temperatures took over. She realised she should have waited longer between exposures, too much haste, but that realisation came a second too late. Her vision was tinged with red now. In all likelihood she'd done some damage by not letting her body recover. She clutched at her lifeline with frost-tinged fingers, trusting in Violet to get her back inside the bubble. She was dimly aware of something large looming up ahead of her and could assume it was the bubble. A current hit her, pushing her back and all but killing her momentum; the air gushing out of the bubble. Then the line went taut again as the winch caught up and took over. Hands were pulling her inside and she felt the flush of warmth on her limbs. Not as fierce as the last time, suggesting that the bubble's atmosphere was still leaking out faster than it could be pumped in.

Struggling to see through the red haze that was her vision, Nel pushed herself towards where she guessed the hatch was.

"I've got it, Skipper," Violet called over the roar of air being sucked out.

"The hells you do." Nel could see her tangled up with the survivor and the rope they'd both been pulled in on. She gasped as her own frozen hands touched the cold metal wheel and stuck but she managed to brace herself and pull the hatch towards her, fighting against the outgoing flow of air. For a moment she wasn't sure she was going to be able to finish the job, then someone else grabbed the wheel and between them they forced it close. The wheel locked solidly into place. Exhausted, Nel just held onto it, not quite leaning—that was impossible floating inside the bubble— but she took a moment to collect herself. Carefully she pried her fingers off the metal, leaving skin behind.

She pushed herself around, expecting to see Violet, but it was Castor Sharpe instead. Just past him she saw Violet, who winced at her expression.

"Thank you," Nel said to Sharpe. She put a hand to her face; it came away with the faintest smear of red. She must have burst a blood vessel out there. That explained the red haziness then.

"Take us back, Violet," she ordered, still looking at the blood. "Think you can manage that?"

"Aye, Skipper." Violet quickly busied herself with the signaller, telling the *Tantamount* to reel the bubble back in, much as Nel and Sharpe had themselves been. At least Violet remembered the signal for that.

"Good," Nel said. Using the wheel to push against, she turned herself around to face Sharpe. He was shaky after their ordeal, not as bad as she imagined she herself looked, but he might have had trouble standing in actual gravity.

"That was impressive how quickly you recovered from the exposure," Sharpe said, his voice still sounding raw and disused.

"You managed all right yourself," Nel replied. She'd recovered because the hatch needed to be shut, simple as that. Sharpe had moved a little too quickly for her liking, though maybe it had just been the adrenaline. He looked ragged now.

"Once my surgeon looks you over you can tell your story to the captain," Nel told Sharpe. "No sense in you telling it twice, let's do it once and do it right."

Sharpe's head pivoted on his thick neck to regard Violet, who was busy with the signaller and didn't notice. With her back to them her bushy foxtail was plainly visible. As always it moved with a mind of its own, snapping back and forth.

"Kitsune," Sharpe commented.

Violet's head jerked round, her skin flushed. "What about it?" she demanded.

"Nothing." Sharpe shrugged. "Tails are supposed to be good luck, that's all."

Violet drew her tail back behind her protectively. "What about my tail?"

"Turned out to be my lucky day, that's all I'm saying," Sharpe told her. "I don't mean anything by it, little princess."

"Princess." Nel shook her head. "Watch your name-calling. You'll make the girl's head puff up to match that tail."

"Skipper!" Violet protested.

"Skipper," Sharpe repeated. "But you say you aren't the captain?"

"First officer to you," Nel corrected. "Or Nel. The crew call me Skipper but Horatio Phelps is the *Tantamount*'s captain."

Sharpe nodded slowly. "I see."

Nel scowled, wondering if he was humouring her. She chewed on that as the bubble made its slow journey back to the ship. Sharpe didn't offer any more conversation and she was happy to leave it at that. A small crowd waited for them at the *Tantamount*'s railing, including Jack and the captain. Getting a bubble back onto a ship involved reeling it back into a cradle. It was a finicky process that had to be done properly if the bubble wasn't to come crashing down on deck when it re-entered the ship's envelope and gravity. After what seemed an eternity, Cyrus and the crew working the crane wrestled the bubble into place and swung it back onto the ship.

Nel felt weight returning as suddenly as it had left, a not altogether pleasant sensation that made her feel like she'd been overindulging in Gabbi's cooking. When the hatch opened she was the first through it, though that too was a drawn out process as they had to wait for the pressure inside the bubble to be adjusted to match the *Tantamount*'s.

"Found one after all, did you?" Horatio stood before her on the deck. He'd managed to find time to dress himself she noticed, was clad in his threadbare best coat and boots sorely in need of polishing. A battered captain's hat topped the ensemble. Not exactly dressed to receive guests but somehow she doubted Sharpe would care.

Behind her Nel could hear Sharpe and Violet exiting the bubble, feet hitting the tar stained deck. She leaned in close to whisper to Horatio.

"I don't like this. Is he really the only one we found?"

"You were the one who didn't expect to find anyone alive, Nel," the captain reminded her.

"That's what I don't like about it. You have to be strong to survive what happened out there. As far as I'm concerned that makes him dangerous."

"I understand what you're saying, Nel. We'll talk to him, find out." Horatio cocked an eyebow at her. "Do you want to get dressed or should we get started now?"

Nel glanced round at the crew. She wasn't exactly undressed and they'd all seen her in less and she them. Being roused during an emergency didn't leave time for propriety and anyone who dithered to take the time wouldn't last long on her ship. But her aching body was crying out for gloves and boots and other fleece-lined clothes. She decided she could spare the time to get changed.

"Jack can give him the once over."

Horatio nodded. "We'll meet in the chart room then."

"I'll be there," Nel said.

She retreated to her cabin, hobbling a little and realising just how frostbitten her feet were. She could barely feel heels or toes as she walked the short distance. It was with relief that she shut the door behind her and sank into the lone chair in the room. Away from the eyes of crew.

She didn't allow herself more than a few minutes rest though. Her body ached and felt slow and ponderous, but her mind was racing along. An Alliance ship, smashed to pieces, one survivor. It felt like a bad tavern tale, the sort that ended in tragedy or at least with a cruel joke. She wanted no part of it. Not on her ship.

With that thought overriding all other concerns she stood and grabbed clothes from corners of her cabin. For working on the ship during her watch she preferred fingerless gloves and calf high boots. Linen breeches replaced the ones she was wearing and a sleeveless leather jerkin completed the outfit. Her eyes fixed on one last item as she laced up the jerkin: her holster slung over a hook in the wall. A wall still studded with kitchen utensils, some embedded an inch or more deep, but what hung from the hook was more dangerous.

It was simple and effective, though at first glance it appeared innocuous. A wand, her wand, not much more than a bronze hued rod in appearance, engraved, but not as intricately as some, the only exotic part the silver patterned basket-hilt above the grip. It didn't look dangerous, not being sharp or even heavy enough to bludgeon with, but the wand was thaumatically charged to a near lethal level. Nel didn't often want for her sidearm aboard the ship with only the crew she knew so well, but with a shipwrecked survivor aboard, then yes, she felt the need. She hitched the holster round her waist on the way to the chart room.

"If this were a tavern brawl, you ain't coming drinking with me ever."

Nel heard Jack's voice as she entered the room. It was hard not to hear Jack's voice. Like the rest of him it was large, crude, and simple. It was useful having crew members who could pull double duty, but as Jack's double duties combined the roles of Gabbi's butchery assistant with that of ship's surgeon his approach to the latter was blunt and direct.

"No," Horatio insisted, "this wasn't a tavern brawl, Jack. The man survived a shipwreck. Be gentle with him."

It was quite the sight, the grey haired and knobbly kneed stick of a captain getting right up in the face of Korrigan Jack, interposing himself between the butcher-turned-surgeon and his latest patient. It reminded Nel that there was at least one world where Korrigan Jack always stayed aboard ship, a place where he'd done hard time. For a Korrigan, Jack was short but broad. Each of Jack's ears was fully half the size of his flattened face, which made him seem even wider. Most of his hair was tied back into three scraggly braids, one behind each flapping ear and a third atop his head. That and his walnut coloured skin made him look wizened like an old oak tree, all in all not someone whose appearance inspired trust.

Sharpe for his part regarded both Jack and the captain somewhat warily. The man had taken a seat atop the chart table, which had been cleared of its normally heaped up contents to serve as a makeshift examination table. He'd been stripped of his shirt and his chest was marred by blue and grey mottling. Broken ribs, most likely. Nel agreed with Jack. Sharpe could have just come through a rather vicious tavern brawl.

"I've been in a shipwreck," Jack snorted. "Piper has too, and he got the rings to prove it. Didn't neither of us get banged up like this one."

"It's nothing, Captain," Sharpe said in an attempt to alleviate the tension, running his hands down his ribs gingerly. "A few stiff drinks in front of a warm fire and I'll be fine. Your first officer got worse than I did."

"Foolish woman," Horatio said. "Should have taken her time, no need to go getting exposed like that. No need at all."

"I heard that." Nel strode into the scene, trying to ignore the pain in her feet that accompanied each step. "Just wrap his ribs, Jack. Captain's orders."

Jack shook his head doubtfully. "Soft, Skipper," he said. "Soft folks don't make good crew."

"Not our problem if he is, Jack, 'cause this man's not crew, so don't be judging him like he is. Just wrap his ribs up good 'til we can drop him off at the next port."

Jack considered this before nodding in agreement. He turned to Sharpe and held up his scalpel suggestively. "I'll go get some bandages. We'll get you wrapped up then. You wait." He made it sound like a threat.

"Sure," Sharpe agreed, leaning back on the table. "How about something to drink while you're at it? All this talk about taverns has got me thirsty."

That got a grin from Jack. "Yeah, I could do that. Brandy should do it. Captain's got some brandy."

"I do?" Horatio winced.

"Yeah, you do."

"Well, I . . . ," Horatio mumbled.

"It's medicinal," Jack growled.

"Yes, but it's very strong medicine, Jack," the captain stressed.

"Yeah?" Jack said. He laughed at Sharpe and nodded. "Yeah, you're right. He's a bit soft, like I said. Aye, Captain, don't worry. I'll be testing it before I give him any."

"That wasn't quite what I —"

"Be right back," Jack rumbled, lumbering towards the door to collect his brandy and bandages.

"Hurry back, Jack," Horatio called after him. "And check on the rest of the crew, make sure there aren't any more injuries."

"Crew's fine," Jack hollered back. "They ain't soft. Except that damned Kelpie."

"Go check on the crew, Jack." Nel pushed him out the door. "What was that about injuries, Captain?"

"We may have a couple of bumps and bruises," Horatio explained. "Some of that debris knocked a few holes in the ship. Ripped a few sails, that sort of thing."

"That sort of thing?" Nel shook her head. She'd forgotten to take a look at the ship as they came in on the bubble, not that she'd been able to see much with her bloodshot vision. "How bad is it? And what does Quill have to say about all this?"

"Yes, well, with things being as they are I haven't gotten around to talking to him yet," Horatio admitted.

"I found him and Gabbi trying to tear a few holes in the ship themselves," Nel told him.

"He's still on the bridge," the captain said. "We can talk to him later."

"Later," Nel agreed, turning to their unexpected guest.

Sharpe returned their regard unfazed. "Your ship's doctor is rather . . . direct."

"He knows what he's doing," Horatio defended his crew quickly. *More out of habit*, Nel thought, *than any real desire to defend Jack.*

"Most of the time," Nel couldn't help muttering.

Jack knew anatomy extensively from his work in the galley, so as far as fixing broken bones and patching up cuts and tears to the *Tantamount*'s crew he was competent. It was his bedside manner that needed work. Korrigan Jack didn't have a lot of respect for anyone who wasn't tougher than he was. And if you got injured you weren't as tough as he was.

Nel noticed Sharpe give her the once over, noticed that his eyes lingered on the wand holstered at her waist. He didn't show any reaction to it, but he definitely knew she was armed now. She took the time to have a closer look at him.

With sailors it was usually easy to read them—they had their life stories written proudly on their own bodies. Hoops through the ears for years in the void, tattoos for ports and planets visited. Nel had some of her own, though she'd kept them confined to just a sleeve on one arm. But she knew how to match crooked dice to a sailor who had spent time at Vice or a manta-ray for someone who had traversed beyond the periphery and out into the Deep Lanes. But Sharpe didn't have any markings, not ink nor jewellery. Not so much as a good luck charm to keep him from being lost overboard. That was odd. Even the Alliance had their own brand of markings.

"Thank you for the rescue, Captain Phelps," Sharpe said.

"You were timely."

"Yes, well, glad we could help, my boy." The captain straightened his clothing as he spoke, beaming. "We were hoping you could tell us what happened out there. You were attacked, obviously."

"Who was it?" Nel asked directly.

Sharpe's gaze shifted to her. "I'm afraid I can't help you with that. I was below deck when we were attacked. Got buried under the water casks and never got a good look at them."

"That's an Alliance ship out there." Nel watched him carefully. "A warship at that, one that's had something big and solid driven right through it. You were rammed, Sharpe."

"Seems the way of it," Sharpe agreed.

"And you don't know who did it?" Nel said.

He shrugged. "I'm not Alliance. I was just a passenger."

"What was the name of your ship?" Nel asked.

"The *Falchions Rise*."

"And how many souls aboard her?" Horatio inquired.

Sharpe sighed. "Over a hundred, Captain."

Over a hundred. The number hung in the air with an ugly sense of reality. The *Tantamount* ran with less than twenty, Alliance ships ran heavy it was true, but the number still sounded high. Nel had counted maybe two dozen bodies during her expedition. That left at least four score unaccounted for. Floating out there in the void.

"A tragedy," Horatio said uncomfortably. He motioned for Nel to continue the conversation.

"Where were you bound? What port?" she asked.

"Marching, on Thatch," Sharpe told her.

The port he'd named was on a distant planet and not one aligned with the Alliance. Lawless was too strong a word, independent might be closer. It wasn't the sort of place an Alliance vessel would go without a good reason.

Nel was about to ask what sort of person could get passage aboard an Alliance warship when they were interrupted by a piping, high pitched voice.

"Captain!"

The thin voice belonged to Violet. The girl's hair was still a tangle of fairy locks and half undone braids, like she'd just climbed out of her hammock.

"Captain, oh, Skipper!" Violet stared as she realised that Nel was present too. She didn't pay Sharpe so much as a second look, probably still ignoring him for that quip about her tail.

"Piper sent me to find you, he needs to see one of you. Says it's urgent!"

"Urgent, is it?" Horatio repeated. "Well, we'd best see about that then."

"I'll go," Nel offered. "I want to see what's been going on while I was out in that damned bubble."

"As you say, Nel," Horatio agreed. "I'd like a few more words with our guest in any case."

Nel hesitated. There was something about Sharpe she didn't like, but on consideration it wasn't likely he would do anything while aboard the *Tantamount*.

"Take me to Piper," she said.

Chapter 2

Sharpe had given Nel the impression of being dangerous, but if impressions were what to go by then Piper had dangerous written all over him. That writing took the literal form of extensive, intricate tattoos that ran from the backs of his hands to the balls of his feet, even making forays up one side of his face. Tattoos marking every port he'd ever sailed into; rays, dragons, cuttlefish, and other more obscure creatures Nel didn't even know the names for. On one shoulder he had the constellation surrounding his home planet, a map home if he ever needed it. Hoops ran up the top length of one ear, one for every five years a sailor. The opposite ear held a black pearl, evidence, as Jack said, that Piper had once survived a shipwreck, and a silver stud to pay for his burial, should he not survive a second one.

Stripped down to not much more than shorts, there was plenty of bare skin to display Piper's artwork. The sweaty sheen on his arms and shaved head suggested he'd been working hard at something. Nel and Violet found him involved in an animated discussion with his constant companion, Bandit, in the deepest recesses of the ship. Piper was doing most of the talking.

"Didn't I tell you to get rid of that thing?" Nel interrupted the one sided debate.

Piper turned to her, his heavy features drawing down into a sulk. "No," he claimed.

"No? You know damn well I did, Piper. Why is it still on board?"

Her problem with Bandit was simple. She detested rodents. And the foot-high, furry mongrel was definitely a rodent. The animal, called a loompa, looked like a cross between a monkey and a raccoon, with a monkey's tail and ambidextrous limbs. The raccoon-like slitted mask of fur over his eyes was what Bandit got his name from. Uninspired, given the creative artwork covering his owner.

"No, Bandit stays," Piper told her firmly. "If Bandit goes, Piper goes. And right now we have to fix the ship so we can't go."

Nel groaned. This was all Horatio's fault; the man was forever picking up strays. The scamp at her side that looked up to her with calf eyes and the deranged engineer in front of her were only two of the many that made up the misfit crew.

"Vi," she said. "Go keep an eye on the captain for me. If you see anything suspicious from our guest you come get me straight away. Got it?"

"Aye aye, Skipper." The cabin girl fired off another over-exaggerated salute and turned, disappearing with a flick of the bushy fox-tail she flashed every time she turned around. The tail made Nel shake her head.

Misfits, all of them.

"Something amiss, Skipper?" Piper asked.

"You been teaching our girl signalling?" Nel said pointedly.

"Yes," Piper said slowly.

"Teach her better."

Piper exchanged a long look with his pet but said nothing.

Nel leaned wearily against the curved hull. "What's wrong with my ship, Piper?"

"She is full of holes, Skipper."

"How?" Nel said. "Where?"

Piper gestured around the hold. "Bits hit us. Big bits, Bandit says. They woke him up. Bandit tried to plug the holes but the holes are big and Bandit is so small."

Bandit scampered down from the rafters and onto Piper's shoulders, chattering constantly. The loompa held a mallet in its dark, wiry hand and Nel wouldn't have put it past the thing to have banged out the holes itself.

"You're saying the hull is breached?" Nel concluded. "How badly?"

"Badly," Piper pointed at a pile of crates. Nel stared. What at first had looked like haphazard storage she now realised was, in fact, covering a gaping hole in the side of the ship.

"There are more," Piper said. "Bandit can crawl through most of them, all the way to the outside. We should watch where we step."

"Can she still fly?" Nel asked, pushing one of the crates aside to get a better look at the damage. It was bad—she could see straight through the breach to the outside, the swirling emptiness of dust and misty miasma. Bandit wasn't the only one who could have fit through the hole; Violet could, and with a bit of squeezing Nel herself probably could have too. Not good, not good at all.

"There is more," Piper said.

Nel braced herself. "Show me."

Piper took her deeper into the hold, near the prow where the planks of the ship curved in. Driven through those curves was a massive log. Piper couldn't have put his arms around it if he'd tried. It appeared to be part of a mast, with rigging and hawsers still attached. Probably it was the other half of the mast she'd seen when out in the bubble.

"Hells," Nel said anyway. "Is that what I think it is?"

"Somewhere out there is a ship without a mast," Piper confirmed sagely. "Here there is a mast without a ship and we have one more mast than the ship needs. Too many masts is not a good thing, Bandit thinks."

"Can we fly with that thing sticking out of us? Will it just do more damage?"

Piper hesitated. "Fly yes, but Bandit says we should be stopping soon. Stop soon, fix ship. Sooner is better."

"I asked you, not that overgrown swamp rat," Nel snapped.

"You will hurt Bandit's feelings," Piper said sternly. "Bandit knows this ship, every nook and cranny. The ship is hurt. Fix her soon, or she will not be flying. Bandit knows."

"Fine," Nel waved a hand wearily. "We need to make some repairs. Can we do that here? Or while we sail?"

Piper glanced questioningly at the loompa. Nel made a sound of disgust. Their ship was impaled. She trusted Piper's knowledge on the matter, in spite of the loompa obsession, but she didn't really need to hear it. Her ship was hurt and hurt bad. So was he really going to ask the damned rodent's opinion on that?

It turned out he was.

"No," Piper said firmly. "We cannot. We can patch and sew, perhaps, but fix? No, we cannot fix. The ship must be set down, big repairs. This will take a while."

"And cost a fortune," Nel sighed, running a hand through her hair, tugging a red strand in front of her eyes. It was getting long again, almost down to her shoulders. One more thing to attend to.

"How far can we get with the ship like this?" she asked. "*Your* opinion, Piper. If that swamp rat says anything else I'm going to hang him over the side as bait."

Bandit squawked in alarm and took off into the rafters. Nel watched him go, surprised but satisfied at the same time.

"Is a good thing Bandit likes you," Piper said crossly. "Anyone else would get bitten."

"Piper, how long can the damned ship fly?"

"A week, maybe more, maybe less. But not much. The ship needs fixing."

"A week, fine," Nel said. "We'll set down. Has to be somewhere nearby we can go. Do what you can down here,

Piper, grab whoever you need. Get Jack to help you with the heavy stuff, at least."

She looked up the loompa still cowering in the rafters. "And when we get to wherever we're going, we're getting rid of some excess ballast, you understand?"

Piper glanced up. "Bandit hopes you are not talking about him."

"Bandit can hope all he likes. Just fix the ship, Piper."

"We will do what we can, Skipper."

"Someone want to explain how in the hells this happened?" Nel folded her arms in disgust.

Quill and Gabbi stood ill at ease in front of the tribunal of two. Nel and Horatio had sequestered them on the bridge, away from the prying eyes of the rest of the crew. Violet had taken Sharpe to find somewhere to hang a spare hammock, with orders from Nel to make sure it wasn't too private. She still couldn't put a finger on the source of her unease but with a ship full of holes she wouldn't lose sleep over caution.

Now her feelings were leaning towards angry. She wanted an explanation from Quill as to why he hadn't been on the bridge and another from both him and Gabbi as to why they'd been firing cutlery into her room.

"I've just been down to the hold," Nel said. "Piper showed me what's left of the mast of that ship out there. The *Tantamount*'s been skewered like a harvest festival pig. How the hells did that happen?"

Quill and Gabbi were chastised into silence for perhaps a heartbeat before both of them burst out talking. Talking quickly escalated into shouting, then degenerated into abusive name-calling as the two stopped trying to explain themselves and turned on each other.

". . . psychotic lizard-freak!"

"Incompetent scullery wench!"

". . . of all the . . . ! You ungrateful snake-skinned bigot!"

"Grateful?! You tried . . ."

"... half a mind to ..."

"... poison me! Repulsive gluttonous meat bag ..."

"I'll turn you into a meat bag!"

Sparks were on the verge of flying again, thaumatic ones. The very air was alive and crackling, blue arcs of free-flowing energy writhing between them and coiling around clenched fists. Quill's tail lashed, Gabbi stamped her foot, and the deck creaked. Nel stepped in at that point.

"Enough, both of you!" she yelled. "One more move out of either of you and I'll have you scraping fungus off the underside of the hull."

Nel glared at both of them until they quieted down, though both still simmered angrily.

"One at a time, if you please," Horatio suggested. "Mister Quill, why weren't you at your post tonight?"

"I was until she poisoned me!" Quill pointed an accusing finger at Gabbi.

"I never!" Gabbi retorted. "Don't be blaming me if your slimy stomach is giving you problems."

"Gabbi, please." Horatio held up a hand. "You'll get your chance. Quill, go on."

The Kelpie navigator might have smirked; it was hard to read his cold blooded features. "I took my evening meal before I started my watch. Two bells later I was face down in the head. It was her cooking; it couldn't have been anything else."

"It was the same slop as you eat every night, Loveland," Gabbi retorted, emphasising the first name he detested so much. "Damned Kelpies and your bland cuisine. It was raw meat, minced! There's no way to screw it up."

"Then you put something in it." Quill glared down at the diminutive cook.

"Get in my face and say that!" Gabbi glared back up at him.

"You see?" Quill appealed to his captain. "When I went to confront her about it she attacked me."

"He started it," Gabbi countered.

"Either of you starts anything more and I'll be the one to finish it," Nel warned them. "You could have damaged the ship, to say nothing of the dereliction of duty."

"Easy, Nel," Horatio said with a pained expression. "This isn't an Alliance ship, we don't flog our crew."

"Maybe we should start," she suggested darkly.

"Humans," Quill muttered.

"Damned Kelpie," Gabbi matched him tone for tone.

"All right, that really is quite enough, all of you," the captain said. "Gabbi, do a check of our stores, make sure we haven't taken on anything bad and that nothing's spoiled since we left port. It sounds like we'll be making an unscheduled stopover soon anyway."

"Where?" Quill asked quickly.

"Excuse me?" Horatio blinked.

"Where are we stopping over?" Quill repeated his question. "I'm still the navigator. Where am I navigating to?"

Nel spread out a star chart over the map table. Originally they'd been on a cargo run, a simple and legitimate expedition for an independent ship like theirs. They were still several weeks from their intended destination. With luck they'd be able to make up the time later but now they needed a stopover. Somewhere close, accessible, and, if Nel was being honest with herself, someplace that wouldn't ask too many questions.

The choices were limited.

Quill came over and gave the charts a critical looking over. Knowing the charts as well as he did, he didn't have to contemplate long before coming to a conclusion.

"Cauldron," he pronounced. "It's the only place anywhere near that might have what we need."

Nel pursed her lips. She agreed but had been searching hard for an alternative. The problem being there wasn't one.

Horatio came up, squinting at the map unhappily.

"What about Settler's Landing?" he suggested.

"Too much of a backwater," Nel said heavily.

"Gateway." Horatio pointed to a spot on the map, back the way they'd come.

"An Alliance port," Quill reminded him. "The last one before we hit the High Lanes and tolled space."

Which wasn't necessarily a bad thing. Within the High Lanes, Alliance patrols provided security but, between the tolls and the competition that safety engendered, it was hard for a ship like the *Tantamount* to scrounge out a living.

The Alliance, being the loose collection of disparate parties that it was, had come about more or less by an accident of mutual interest. It was badly managed and over bureaucratised, with different groups often ending up competing against one another. The worst, as far as Nel was concerned, were the trading companies, some of which bordered on being nations unto themselves.

"Tamil?" She could hear the wistfulness in Horatio's voice.

"Too small, Captain," Nel said. "We took a lot of damage out there, sir. Rope, sails, timber, maybe stores. We need some place with all of that and we need it cheap. We'll be lucky to break even on this run now."

Horatio grimaced at the mention of money. Nel's suspicions started again.

"It'll have to be Cauldron." She rolled up the chart when the captain didn't add anything else, ending the conversation. "Figure two or three days at a safe speed?"

"About that, yes." Quill took the proffered chart from her.

"Well, get to it, navigator," she said. "And when I say safe I mean safe. We have a damned mast sticking out the wrong side of the ship."

Gabbi and Quill left to attend to their duties. When they were alone, Nel said to Horatio, "Captain, tell me we don't have debts waiting for us on Cauldron."

"A rigged game," Horatio assured her all too quickly. "It'll never stand up."

"It will on Cauldron." Nel folded her arms. "You're going to tell me you weren't cheating yourself?"

"Nel," the captain scowled. "You're fussing."

It's my job, Nel thought. "Captain . . ."

"Don't worry about it, Nel," her captain assured her. "It's a small debt, trifling really. Likely we won't even run into the creditors in any case."

"Let's hope so, sir," Nel said neutrally. "About our passenger, now."

"What about him?"

"I think he should get off at Cauldron."

Horatio frowned. "Do you?"

"Yes," Nel said firmly. "There's something not right about him."

"Not right how?"

"He's too calm for one," Nel stated. "No one who's been through what he has should be that relaxed. It's like he was just waiting for us to come along and rescue him."

"Seemed a reasonable sort to me, Nel."

"Did he now?" Nel asked suspiciously.

"Indeed," Horatio nodded. "We had a chat, him and I, after you left."

"Really, Captain." Nel bit down on her lower lip. "About what?"

"All sorts, Nel, all sorts. I rather like him actually. In fact, I think you're just letting your prejudices get in the way."

"My prejudices?" Nel exclaimed.

"Because he was on an Alliance ship," Horatio said. "You can take the girl out of the service but—"

"Captain," Nel interrupted.

"Well, service left its mark on you, you can't deny that. In any case, Sharpe told us he wasn't part of the Alliance. Didn't you ever carry non-service personnel?"

"None I'd want on this ship," Nel said pointedly.

"Hardly a reason to abandon him on Cauldron though. Terrible place, Cauldron, awful. Can't believe I'm going there myself, ourselves, I mean all of us. Together."

"What else are we supposed to do with him then?" Nel asked. "He was on his way to Thatch, that's weeks out of our way. You want to take him all the way to the drop off on Vice with the rest of our cargo?"

"There's plenty of places we could let him off along the way, Nel."

"Cauldron is the first such place, sir."

"We'll talk about it," Horatio said, which meant that they wouldn't. "We have a couple of days before we arrive, in any case."

Nel sighed. The conversation was taking on an all too familiar pattern. Horatio was a soft touch for strays, always had been. If she wasn't careful, or pushed this too much, she'd end up with another misfit crew member on her roster. The best she could say about Sharpe so far was that he was human and that didn't mean much.

"I hope you do, sir," she said. "Think about it, that is. And try and remember that creditor's name while you're at it."

"You know I hate to think about those sorts of things, Nel," the captain dismissed her concerns.

"I know, sir. That's why you have me."

The first thing Nel did after she left the captain was go back below deck to check on their cargo. She'd been too concerned about the state of the ship itself to pay it any mind when she'd been down before. The captain, and by extension the crew, was already going to be out of pocket fixing the ship. If they forfeited on this run because of damaged goods, they might find themselves patching the ship only to hand it over to their creditors.

Sharpe was standing by one of the breaches in the hull, deep in the belly of the *Tantamount* where the heavier cargo was stored during flight. That cargo came down from above, hoisted via cranes into the hold. During flight the gap was covered by a wooden mesh, a criss-crossed lattice of timber that let very little light in. Light above deck was provided by glowstones, a gemlike substance that only lit up in the midst of the void, surrounded by all that nothing. They had to be close to that open airless void to glow, to the miasma, so they were less effective inside cabins and below decks. The glowstones put out a silvery hue, like white light in that it provided both visibility and a degree of colour, but left everything tinged with shade, looking faded.

Sharpe, on the other hand, was carrying one of the ship's oil lamps, the flickering of which cast both him and the hold in inconsistent, twitching shadows. He had his back to Nel, but turned at her approach.

"What are you doing down here?" Nel asked him, keeping her eyes averted from the oil lamp. Down here in the dark it was overly bright, almost painful to the eyes.

Sharpe gestured to the jagged hole behind him. "Heard you took some damage," he said. "Wanted to see for myself."

"That so? Look like something you can fix then?"

Sharpe frowned. "Not really my speciality, Skipper."

"Then why bother looking?"

"Because if the ship I'm on is full of holes, I want to know how bad it is."

"My ship, my problem," Nel said. "But since we've come to it, what is your speciality?"

Sharpe shrugged, then turned at the sound of something skittering along wood. A quick-fire scrapping and scratching sign and then a fist-sized shadow shot between two crates, a larger clutch of darkness in hot pursuit.

"The hells was that?" Sharpe lifted the lantern higher.

"Bandit." Nel made a face.

Sharpe rocked back on his heels, swaying. "Part of your crew?"

"Not if ever I catch him," Nel muttered.

"Looked like he was trying to do the catching. Every ship needs a rat-catcher. Didn't look much like a cat though," Sharpe observed.

"Loompa."

"That's different." Sharpe mused. "Didn't know loompa were carnivorous. You sure he eats what he catches?"

"—don't care if it walks off the plank after them. I want him off my ship."

The skipper's voice carried to Violet as she descended the stairs into the hold, cradling a steaming bowl of soup between her hands. She hadn't bothered with a light; the hold was easy enough to navigate though she knew some of the crew had trouble. She followed the sound of the skipper's voice, pausing when a small bodied form ran up to her out of the shadows.

"Don't be letting the skipper see you, Bandit," Violet whispered. "She'll break out that plank like she's been threatening."

The loompa peered up at her with big eyes. A garbled sound emerged from his throat, muffled by the limp form of his latest catch. He scurried off into the depths of the hold again, presumably to devour his prize. Violet was just glad she'd never had to clean up whatever he didn't finish eating.

Holding the soup out in front of her, Violet made her way towards the sound of voices. Rounding a stack of crates, she found herself staring down a bright, angry red glare. She squeezed her eyes down to the barest slits, trying to hold still and not spill the soup.

"Skipper?" Violet called out uncertainly. "That you?"

"What is it, Vi?" The skipper's voice came from behind the glare.

"Nothing, Skipper." Violet felt her tail going into a slow, nervous spin behind her. "Wasn't even looking for you. Gabbi thought Mister Sharpe might like something to eat. Thought he was down here with you."

"It's just Sharpe," she heard the man they'd rescued say. The light, a lantern, dimmed. She could make out Sharpe and the skipper, though she had blotches in her vision. "No mister. You say mister I'm gonna start looking around for my old man and none of us wants that fellow here. So just Sharpe, or Castor."

"I got some soup here, Mister . . . Sharpe, Castor." Violet held out the bowl.

"Thank you." Sharpe took the bowl in his free hand,

hanging the lantern up on a nearby hook. He gave the soup a sniff.

"Don't mean to be rude, miss," he said apologetically, "but I did hear something about your cook poisoning someone just before I came on board."

The skipper snorted, reminding Violet of the accusations Quill had been throwing about.

"That was just Quill," Violet said, giving her tail a savage whip. "He was just venting. Gabbi never poisoned nobody. I've been helping her out in the galley."

"You seem to be everywhere on this ship," Sharpe observed. "Should be running it someday."

"Skipper runs the ship, Mister Sharpe," Violet said.

"And you do the running. I see," Sharpe nodded. He looked down at the bowl of soup. "This might be easier if I had a spoon."

"Sorry." Violet grinned at him. "Skipper's got all the spoons still. Haven't had time to go dig them out yet."

"Dig them out?" Sharpe repeated. "Dig them out of what?" He cocked an eyebrow at the skipper in confusion.

The skipper ignored him. "Maybe you should get to that," she suggested to Violet. "The digging."

Violet's eyesight was coming back, and for the first time she got a good look at the damage to the *Tantamount*. "The ship sure took a hammering, Skipper." She scampered up to one of the breaches and knelt down beside it. The hole was big enough to fit her head and shoulders through. She could see through to the edge of the *Tantamount*'s envelope. This close she could see something she'd never noticed before, how the miasma broke and roiled like surf on a beach before it reached the wooden hull.

"All that black mist outside, how come it doesn't come through?" she asked, looking back at the skipper. "We got more holes in us than Gabbi's galley even and the miasma's just floating out there."

"The ether keeps it out," Sharpe said, blowing on his soup.

"How?" Violet asked him.

Sharpe glanced at the skipper. "You mind?" he asked. "She's your crew; you don't mind me educating her some?"

The skipper raised her eyebrows. "Not at all." She leaned against a post and folded her arms. "Seems she could do with some educating."

"Skipper!" Violet protested.

"You should know this already, Violet."

Sharpe spoke up before she could answer that rebuke. "You know how ships like this fly, right? Pack the hull and the keel full of ether and get a navigator to push the thing out into space. Going through the atmosphere is like taking a breath before you go swimming, the ship drags some of the air out with it."

"Yeah." Violet fidgeted impatiently. "I know all that. What's it got to do with keeping the mist out?"

"That black mist, that miasma, is like ether. Or ether is like a solid form of mist, they repel each other like a couple of magnets. You get the opposing magnets and they push each other apart, same with mist and ether, the mist is trying to get in but the ether keeps it out."

"It's a balancing act," the skipper added. "Too much ether in the hold and the ship won't fly, it pushes all the miasma away. You sink. Too little and you don't have an envelope, so you can't trap any air."

"Exactly," Sharpe nodded. "The pressure of the mist trying to get in is what keeps your feet stuck to the floor. In fact," he added conspiratorially, "since there's no other gravity out here, up and down is all relative to where you put the ether in your ship. That's why it goes in the keel and the bottom of the hull."

"So?" Violet glanced down. "What does that mean?"

"It means if you went out through that hole," Sharpe pointed, "and climbed down underneath the ship, your feet would stick to the hull of the ship."

"Really?" Violet took half a step towards the breach. "You mean it? I'd be upside down then?"

"Sort of, well no, only from our point of view, from yours

you'd still be right ways up." Sharpe gestured vaguely with one hand, then looked at the still steaming bowl of soup. "It's like this," he said, pointing at the bowl. Holding the bowl one handed he swung it back and over his head, upside down, before quickly bringing his arm back down and holding the soup out on the flat of his hand in front of him.

"It's like that," he said. "The force of me swinging it keeps it in the bowl even when it's upside down. Same with the ether and flying this ship. If you climbed through that hole then to me and the skipper you'd be upside down but to you it would seem like normal. They call it void walking and . . ."

And if it works for a bowl of soup . . .

"Don't!" the skipper snapped, when Violet put a hand to the edge of the breach. The skipper glared at both of them. "That's enough planar theory for one day. Go get those spoons, Vi, I don't want to find any in my cabin when I turn in tonight."

"Aye, Skipper," Violet sighed, disappointed, but she moved quickly. She gave Sharpe a grin as she went.

Void walking, have to remember that for when the skipper's not around. Maybe talk to Piper . . .

"Sweet girl," was Sharpe's observation, taking another cautious sip from the bowl. "You know, this soup's not that bad, actually. My compliments to your cook. I'm almost willing to forget all those nasty rumours I heard about her."

"You can compliment her all you like," Nel replied. "I won't stop you and neither will she. But unless you want to be face deep in that soup you like so much that's the last time you put any ideas about void walking in my cabin girl's head."

"Educating, Skipper." Sharpe smiled. "And I did ask first. Maybe I made my first friend aboard this ship."

"Violet's a good kid," Nel said. "She doesn't need someone like you . . ."

"Someone like me?" Sharpe interrupted, grinning.

"Watch yourself," Nel said. "And get yourself above deck. I don't like having oil lamps down here. Fire hazard."

"Aye, Skipper," Sharpe mockingly echoed Violet's words. "As you say."

"Gabbi," Violet called. "Where do you want these?"

"What?" Gabbi turned, waving a hand to see through the cloud of steam that was filling the galley. The cook eventually spotted Violet with her armful of cutlery.

"Is that from Nel's cabin?" Gabbi flushed at the sight of half a serving set in Violet's arms. "Put it in the tub. I'll wash it down before anyone eats with it."

"Skipper's wall looks like a dartboard," Violet said. She'd had to chip at the timbers to get the utensils free, bending more than a few and picking up splinters in the process.

"Lost my temper," Gabbi muttered, turning back to her pots. "Quill . . . damned Kelpie."

She gestured and a box skidded across the floor, stopping at her feet. The way Gabbi and Quill made things move like that tugged at Violet.

"How do you do that?" she asked wistfully.

"Thaumatics," Gabbi said.

"Yeah, but how?"

"Just do." Gabbi asked, "How do you move that tail of yours, then?"

"My tail?" Violet twitched her tail, grabbing a self-conscious handful of bushy fur. "I dunno, I just do. It's a tail, what else?"

"See, you can't explain that?" Gabbi shrugged. "Make your head hurt just thinking about it. Same for thaumatics. Some folks have 'em, some don't."

That didn't seem like enough of an explanation. "Mister Sharpe and the skipper were explaining ether to me before," she said. "It's gotta be something like that."

"Mister Sharpe?" Gabbi grinned at her. "He that one you brought aboard then? Not bad looking, that one."

"Bandit and I think there might be too much steam in your eyes, cook," Piper rumbled, appearing at the doorway with armfuls of sailcloth. Bandit was perched on his shoulders carrying a hammer and mouthful of nails.

"You just focus on fixing that wall, Piper." Gabbi pointed at the holes in the wall separating the galley from the skipper's cabin. What was left of it, anyway. "Skipper's mad enough without having holes in her cabin."

Piper opened his mouth to say something then thought better of it. He grinned at Violet and handed her one corner of the cut down sail he was carrying.

"This will have to do for now," he said. "The skipper will manage. The skipper also tells me we need to work on our signalling, little one. Something about your sojourn to rescue our new friend."

Violet flushed. "I . . . might have forgotten a few."

"We will work on them," Piper assured her. "These things cannot be rushed."

"Piper, explain thaumatics to me," Violet changed the subject as they stretched the sailcloth over the wall, covering the holes Gabbi and Quill's fight had left.

"Thaumatics?" Piper frowned, taking the hammer and starting to nail the sailcloth into the wall. "Ah, wizardry. Alas, little one, that one I cannot explain."

"Why?"

"It's not wizardry, Piper," Gabbi said.

"I cannot explain because I am not a wizard like our friends Gabbi and Quill." Gabbi snorted at Quill's name but Piper didn't seem to notice. "How would you explain sound to a deaf man, sight to the blind? No, I do not think it is for us to know, little one. Leave it to the wizards."

"Piper, it's not wizardry," Gabbi repeated. "You'll confuse the girl."

"Then explain it to me," Violet said, exasperated. "Why is that so hard?"

"Later," Gabbi said, shaking an empty box critically. "Right now I need more salted meat for the slush fund."

The slush fund. That was one of Violet's least favourite duties. Boiling salted meat until it was a sickly grey colour produced an excess of fat and grease. Gabbi collected that grease and sold it when the *Tantamount* made port. The slush fund, as the crew called it.

"Go find Jack for me, Violet," Gabbi said. "I don't know where he's been storing the meat lately."

"Are we done here, Piper?" Violet asked.

Piper stepped back from the wall, studying their work critically. The sail covered the holes into the skipper's quarters but it wouldn't do much to stop noise coming through. *Still*, Violet thought, *quieter than slinging a hammock with the rest of the crew below decks.*

"It appears so." On his shoulder, Bandit chirped. Piper turned his head towards his pet.

"Bandit wishes to go with you." He looked thoughtful. "Very well, but hurry back, the both of you. We will have lessons later."

Violet held out an arm and the loompa jumped, transferring to her. He ran up her arm and settled on her shoulder, clinging to her hair.

"Don't pull," she warned him, feeling his small hands becoming tangled. Bandit squawked a reply. Violet laughed at his small, screwed up face. She didn't believe Bandit talked in quite the way Piper made out but she could read his moods well enough.

"Where's Jack, Bandit?" she said to him once they made their way down the ship. The loompa didn't jump off her shoulder and lead her to the sailor, as Violet had secretly hoped he would, but tightened his claws on her shoulder. Violet saw why.

At the other end of the ship, atop the bridge, Quill had fixed his gaze on them. Violet shuddered as the Kelpie's cold regard swept over them. It was clear the ship's navigator was still fuming.

The ship started to bank at that point, tilting to one side as Quill pushed the sails to make a change in their course. Violet heard a snapping sound and out of the corner of her eye caught sight of a water barrel starting to lean. It passed the tipping point and crashed to the deck, rolling straight for her.

Violet heard a yelp, unsure if it was from her or Bandit and jumped, catching hold of the railing leading to the forecastle. She swung her legs up just in time—the barrel hit the side banister and ruptured, water flooding over the deck and Violet.

"The hells was that, Quill?" Violet yelled one of the skipper's favourite expressions at the navigator, who appeared unconcerned. She was soaked, the light downy fur on her arms and legs was sodden, to say nothing of the tail which soaked up the water in sponge-like quantities. Violet had to resist the urge to shake and ring it out.

Quill shrugged, barely deigning to look at her. "The water barrel was unsecured."

"Yeah?" Violet said. "It just happened to almost crush me? You just happened to have to turn the ship just as I was in the way?"

"I wouldn't waste the barrel," Quill dismissed her accusation. He turned his attention away from her. "Make sure that is cleaned up."

Violet bristled at the order, knowing she'd actually have to do it. Quill outranked her, hells, everybody on the ship outranked her. And she still had to find Jack!

A chirp from above caught her attention. Bandit was up in the rigging—she hadn't even noticed he was gone. *Jumped ship at the first sign of danger, the little rat.*

"Get down from there," she called.

Bandit ignored her and darted higher up the ratlines. Violet tracked him and saw him frolic amongst the sailors in the rigging. Mostly they ignored the critter as they trimmed sails and pulled lines. He settled on the shoulder of one sailor at the extreme end of the yard. Jack.

"Oh, hells," Violet whispered. She thought to call out but knew he wouldn't hear her. She'd have to climb up.

Gingerly she set bare feet to cordage. Ratlines, thin cords strung between the shrouds formed ladders up into the sails. Violet used her legs to propel herself up into those sails. And the higher up she climbed the more the mast swayed, every slight adjustment Quill made to their course amplified. When she reached the spar where the *Tantamount*'s sailors were working, Violet paused, hugging the mast to steady herself. She felt the first touch of nausea and she'd yet to step out onto the footrope. Glancing down she could see Quill staring up at her.

I'm just imagining that smile, Violet thought as the ship twitched again.

"All right there, lass?"

"Fine, Cyrus," Violet told the sailor closest to her as she hugged the mast.

"What do you need?" Cyrus grinned. "Come up for a spell in the nest?"

Violet shuddered at the idea. The crow's nest was the worst place to be on the ship. Even seasoned crew got motion sickness whilst up there. Most saw it as a form of punishment.

"Need to talk to Jack," she said.

Cyrus jerked his head. "He's out on the horse."

"I can see," Violet said unhappily.

Cyrus chuckled. "Off you go then, lass."

The spar ran out from the side of the mast, extending over the edge of the ship. A footrope ran the length of the spar so the crew had something to stand on. Near the far end where it was attached it became too steep to find purchase, so a second and shorter rope, the horse, was hung. Two footropes provided an unstable purchase, so it was the most experienced sailors who found themselves out on the far end. Sailors like Jack, who Violet needed to get to.

She edged round Cyrus first, which meant leaning out behind him and swinging round to the other side. Not ideal.

Cyrus leaned in towards the spar to help her. The second sailor was not so helpful, annoyed at having his work interrupted. Violet almost missed her footing and might have got into trouble. Jack's gnarled hand launched out and closed on her upper arm, hauling her back in.

"Not so lucky up here," Jack rumbled at her.

"What?"

"Saw that barrel miss you down there."

"It didn't miss me, I jumped."

"Yeah, lucky."

"What's luck got to do with it?"

"Kitsune tails. Lucky," Jack stated.

"My tail ain't lucky, Korrigan Jack," Violet snapped.

"You got it wet," Jack said critically. "Maybe it's no good wet."

"Stop looking at my tail!"

"Don't look right wet," Jack grunted. "Why's the Kelpie looking at us all angry?"

"Because he's a Kelpie," Violet muttered, glaring down at Quill. The navigator's head jerked away, determinedly trying to act busy. "What is his problem?"

"Weak stomach," Jack chuckled. "Now what do you want, girl?"

Violet remembered why she'd come up in the first place. "Gabbi needs to know where you put the salted meat. She can't find anything the way you pack the hold."

"Couldn't wait for me to be done with the sails? Why didn't you just signal me from down below?"

Violet started to say something, before realising Jack was right. She could have signalled him from the deck. Except she couldn't remember how. She turned away from Jack instead, starting the shuffle back towards the ratlines.

With Jack and Bandit trailing her she made the journey back to the main deck. The wood was wet underfoot, causing Jack to stop and stare at his feet.

"That tail of yours ain't the only thing that got wet."

Violet shrugged. "Quill said it weren't tied off proper."

"'Course it weren't. Look at all this. Find a mop and bucket."

"Don't tell me what to do, Jack." Violet was annoyed at the way he was talking to her. First her tail and now with the orders. She'd been sent to get him to do his job, not to be fobbed off herself.

"Why not?" Jack said. "You got better stuff to do? You're getting mouthy girl, but we all still get to tell you what to do. So get to mopping."

He left her there, seething. Violet stomped the deck for a moment before relenting, as if she had a choice. She found a mop and began to push the puddles of water around the deck with it. She squeezed the handle of the mop as she worked, grinding her hands, then winced suddenly as she caught some of the splinters she'd got from digging out cutlery in the skipper's cabin. She'd forgotten about those.

"Having fun there?"

Violet had been so engrossed in her sulk she hadn't heard Sharpe come up. He was in annoyingly cheerful spirits, though he was moving somewhat gingerly and holding one hand to his injured ribs.

"Does this look like fun?" Violet planted the mop on the deck and leaned on it, glad for the excuse to avoid the job.

"I was a cabin boy once," Sharpe recalled, sweeping a gaze along the length of the ship. "*Litany of Gabrielle*, that was my first ship. I rubbed my knuckles raw scrubbing her deck and my feet down to nubs running orders from one end to the other."

Violet fidgeted with her own hands, the palms rough and callused from hard labour.

"Been here a while then?" Sharpe commented. "Long enough to thicken your skin."

"Years," Violet said, starting to work at the splinters.

"Tell that one to the marines." Sharpe winked. "Either you mean Kitsune years or you're the worst cabin girl ever."

"Feels like years," Violet muttered.

"On the *Falchions* they had Draugr do stuff like that." Sharpe pointed at the still present puddle of water. "Not always a good thing when you're out here in the Free Lanes and might end up needing to drink that same water."

Violet recalled the frozen creatures out in the ship wreckage. "What are Draugr?" she said. That and thaumatics had been tagging at her mind for explanations of late. Violet figured Sharpe was more likely to answer than the crew. He owed her and the skipper for his rescue. "Skipper said the Alliance runs with them on their ships."

"Skipper used to be Alliance, didn't she?" Sharpe said.

Violet shrugged. The last thing she needed right now was for the skipper to come along and catch Violet talking about her.

"It's all right," Sharpe said, "I can figure things out for myself. What was I saying, then? Draugr? No easy answer there, little princess."

"That's what everyone says." Violet made a face. "About everything."

Sharpe chuckled. "But I'm not everyone. Didn't say I minded if things weren't easy. Here, look." He knelt down on the edge of the water spill and started drawing patterns with his finger.

"This is where we are." He sketched a wide circle near the middle of the pool. "Way out in the Free Lanes, sparsely populated, unregulated, a big free for all with lots of opportunity for people who are smart and capable and trouble for those who aren't. Here," he pointed to the centre, "we have the High Lanes."

Sharpe made a number of patterns, zigzagging his finger back and forth only for the water to quickly flood back in. "Dense, lots of people, lots of rules and laws. It's all Alliance territory. There are trade routes all over the place, industry and more. It takes a lot of labour, a lot of manpower, to make a machine like that. The Alliance is made up of nations, planets, guilds, and companies. A lot of those . . . members use Draugr as labour. They don't sleep, don't complain, and don't ask for pay. Half the High Lane trade routes are built off the backs of Draugr labour. To some people they're the perfect workers."

"To some people," Violet repeated.

Sharpe waggled his finger at her. "Yes, some people. Don't make the same mistake most do. Don't look at a group, especially a big group like the Alliance, and assume they're all working together. Most . . . they're like this ship."

"What about this ship?" Violet said quickly.

"Well, there's you," Sharpe pointed. "Everybody always telling you what to do. And," he said before she could interrupt, "your cook and your navigator, always at each other's throats. Why doesn't your captain do something about it?" Sharpe waved towards the hold, covered by latticework. "Your friend Jack there has had enough whippings to be married to the gunner's daughter. He's got the scars that prove it, but I don't think he got them on this ship."

"Captain doesn't like flogging," Violet told him. "Says it don't prove anything."

"And is the captain the one in charge?" Sharpe folded his arms across his chest. "Because it looks like Nel is running this ship. Why does she put up with some of this crew?"

The thing of it was, he wasn't wrong. Violet hadn't been on a lot of ships, only the *Tantamount*, to be honest. But from the moment the captain brought her aboard it had been clear that Nel was the one who ran the ship, even if she deferred to the captain. But if it were up to the skipper, Violet could imagine a lot of the crew getting the boot the next time they made port. It was the captain that had decided Violet could stay aboard in the first place.

"Why don't you ask them?" Violet told Sharpe. It wasn't her job to explain to him why the *Tantamount* worked the way it did.

Sharpe thought about it. He grinned suddenly. "Maybe I will. Thanks, princess." He turned to go.

"Hey!" Violet called after him. Sharpe turned.

"You never explained what Draugr are," she reminded him.

Sharpe grinned at her and winked. "That's right, I didn't."

Violet stared at his departing back, then gave a small scream of frustration and pitched the mop after him.

"I hate you!" she yelled. Her only answer was a laugh drifting across the deck. So much for gratitude.

Sharpe liked to talk. That much had been obvious to Nel from the moment he'd regained his voice. His first lesson to Violet wasn't the last. Over the next few days Nel would often come across the two of them, Sharpe telling ever more outlandish tales, Violet torn between fascination and frustration. And if he wasn't with her he was with the captain, playing endless rounds of cards. Conveniently, that kept him from helping out in any other manner, but it seemed to please Horatio, so Nel didn't object. Much.

What Nel hadn't figured on was how much the rest of her crew liked to listen to Sharpe as well. Boredom was a factor on long voyages, an odd, blissful boredom that crews on shore leave started to long for. But they never remembered that longing during the boredom—they craved novelty and entertainment only to quickly tire of it in turn. For now, Sharpe was that novelty.

Nel had been looking for Jack to ask about the results of his inventory. She'd found Sharpe holding court on the main deck, Jack being one of the few not present. The crew had been asking about the Draugr, Cyrus in particular, who'd had to man the forecastle and push some of them away from the ship while Nel had been amidst the wreckage. He had the shakes every time he talked about one getting caught on his boat hook and almost ending up aboard.

"This one time," Sharpe leaned forward from his perch on a water barrel outside the galley, "we were out on the Lanes, been at sail for a few days, three bells after the midnight watch. There I was asleep in my hammock, dead to the world, when someone starts to climb in with me."

He grinned round at the crew. "Well, you all know what that's like, your hammock is the only thing on a ship that's yours, your own little haven and you don't let nobody in it. Unless it's cold."

The crew laughed.

"As it happens it was a cold night and I was feeling a bit lonely so I didn't object at first. I roll over and start snuggling up the way you do and I'm relieved to find out my new friend is a lady, if I can use the term."

More laughter.

Sharpe grinned, getting into his own story. "At this point in my dreamy state I'm thinking to myself, Castor, there's some mighty fine women on this ship and we all love a woman in uniform, don't we, lads? Yeah, that's what I thought. So I start to get things warmed up and plant a kiss on the old girl."

He leaned back, shaking his head. "Her breath, let me tell you . . . well, no, don't let me. It was awful, but us beggars can't be choosers. Then I'm starting to wake up a bit, I realise maybe it's not just her breath, I'm thinking her skin's a bit rough and I start thinking this isn't as good as I thought it would be and I'm trying to figure out who's in my hammock."

Nel snorted, shaking her head. She'd heard enough tavern tales to recognise this one. Enough of the crew were wide eyed and slack jawed though. Sharpe had them.

"So I open my eyes and there she is, in all her glory. We called her Gammy on account of her having no teeth. One of the ship's Draugr and she must have been feeling lonesome as even those lot do. And it was then that I realised something."

"What?" Violet demanded when Sharpe didn't say anything else. "What?"

Sharpe blinked at her, as if it were obvious. "That was when I realised that it wasn't even my hammock."

The crew roared with laughter, except for Violet. She looked annoyed at the punch line, then indignant as Sharpe tousled her already tangled hair.

"Back to work, all of you," Nel called out, allowing the crew a moment to have their joke. They jumped when they heard her, leaving with a mix of grins and backslapping. Gabbi ushered Violet away, the girl's frown deepening. Gabbi was shaking her head in answer to whatever questions had been raised by the indignant, young Kitsune.

"Skipper," Sharpe greeted her from his perch. He held two steaming mugs in his hands. "Coffee?"

Nel took the proffered mug, a quick sniff confirmed the contents. She grinned at Sharpe. "So who's hammock was it?"

"It was my mate Stoker's," Sharpe said, shaking his head. "I figured he might have been mad about me sleeping in his hammock so I never told him. He came back and found Gammy snoring away, happy as you please."

He raised the mug, drinking deep from the piping contents. Nel raised hers too, but didn't sip, watching Sharpe. His expression changed, becoming uncertain, then pained. She watched him consider his options, the discomfort becoming more evident. Finally he swallowed, reluctantly.

"That," he coughed into his hand, "was different."

Nel smirked. "Too hot?"

"That's not like any coffee I've ever had before," Sharpe said diplomatically.

"Got it from Jack, didn't you?"

Sharpe made a face.

"Next time ask Gabbi," Nel advised. "Jack sometimes . . . experiments."

She walked over to the edge of the ship, flinging the contents of her own untouched mug over the side. The hot liquid flash froze into a storm of dark snow the moment it hit the edge of the envelope.

"What was that?" Sharpe followed her example. "Or would I rather not know?"

"Probably the latter."

"Could have been worse, I suppose."

"Probably could."

Sharpe grimaced. Nel was content to let him suffer.

"Your navigator, the Kelpie," he said.

"What about him?"

"Watches me a lot."

"Makes a change," Nel muttered. "You have a problem with Quill?"

"Not Quill as such, no."

"Kelpies in general then?"

Sharpe hesitated. "No, least, not on this ship. Was just saying, feels like he's watching me."

"Then stop distracting my crew," she told him. "They've got work to do."

"Aye, Skipper," Sharpe told her, all smiles now. "Whatever you say."

"And make yourself useful."

"How?" Sharpe grinned. "I already admitted to getting lost on the way to my own hammock. How do you think I can be of service, Skipper?"

"Take these back to the galley," Nel tossed her mug in his direction. His hand jumped out and caught it. Nel frowned at that—the man was fast.

"Such a waste of my talents," he sighed. "If you had another mug, I could juggle. But you don't, so I can't. To the galley then."

A moment after Sharpe was gone Nel realised that much as he liked to talk Sharpe said very little about who he was or where he was from. Even what his talents were, as he put it. She wanted a word with Horatio.

The captain's cabin was the largest private accommodation on the *Tantamount*, the great cabin as such things were called, spanning the width of the stern of the *Tantamount*, with large windows covering the back wall, providing a vista out into the void. The cabin covered the same area as the galley and the two cabins above it, one of which was Nel's, the other Quill's. Unlike their cabins, Horatio's was as spacious as the layout of the ship allowed, divided into two sections: the chartroom and Horatio's private quarters. And unlike Nel's cabin both of those rooms had actual doors. Both Nel and Quill were on call as first officer and navigator respectively, at all times, and their cabins reflected that. Personal accomodation yes, but directly underneath the bridge and open to the deck.

The captain was counting coins. Stacks of them balanced atop ledgers and receipts, a precarious construction of towers that threatened to topple over at any second. What concerned Nel was the small denomination of most of the currency.

She grabbed a second chair by the neck, slamming it down backwards on the other side of the small counting table. Coins shuddered, then fell like gleaming dominoes, a cascade of money that spread out over the table. She straddled the chair, resting her arms over the back as her captain looked at the mess she'd made of his collection.

"I was counting those," he said plaintively.

"They don't need counting," Nel said. "There's not enough of them to need counting."

Horatio sighed, pushing loose coins towards the pile. "There's never enough, Nel. Join me in a drink?"

Nel nodded and retrieved the iced brandy from Horatio's liquor cabinet.

"What happened to the advance for this run?" she said, pouring two tumblers of golden liquor over ice.

"This is the advance."

Nel froze, the brandy halfway to her lips. "You're joking."

Horatio shook his head sadly. "This is my last bottle of brandy too. Sheridan, the good stuff."

Nel took a sip from her glass. Horatio was right, it was the good stuff. Burning all the way down and spreading out from there.

"That's what happens when you pay off debts, Nel," the captain said disapprovingly. "You run out of money."

"We'd have more money if you'd stop getting us into debt," Nel countered.

"I'll get us out when we reach Cauldron," the captain predicted. "I know some places, easy money. Never fails."

"I've heard that before."

"This time will be different," he promised.

"I've heard that before as well." Nel drained her glass, dropping it down on the table. "Captain, I wanted a word about . . ."

"Hear something?" Horatio lifted his head, and then a slow

grin spread over his face.

"Rays," he pronounced.

The two rose from the table, Horatio still carrying his drink. A loud crooning came from outside the cabin, from outside the ship in fact. Both had heard the sound before and knew it well. Following the song they found more crew above deck, looking out to the side of the ship. At the rays.

A whole school of them. The void going variant of their sea dwelling cousins, only much bigger. Most of them measured ten feet in body with that much again in tail. Some were bigger; the pack leader was almost as big as the *Tantamount*. Its white underbelly blocked out the expanse as it banked towards the ship, coming in for a closer look, one massive yellow eye studying the tiny crew scurrying about on the deck.

"Mister Quill," Horatio called out. "Take us a few points to starboard."

On the bridge above them Quill raised both hands, hands encompassed in blue as he used his power to turn the ship to starboard. The sails filled out, creaking as they adjusted to the sudden strain. Without wind in space the ship needed Quill to fill those sails and he needed those sails as something to push against, something to push and prod, simulating the currents on an actual sea to help the ship sail through a solar sea. The ship cut away from the rays, flying parallel to the pack. The leader banked away, taking the point position.

The crooning continued. Nel wondered what the rays heard outside of the envelope—sound wasn't supposed to exist outside of the area around a ship, though she had no idea how anyone would have gone about testing that. It sounded too philosophical for her—if a ray sings in space and there's no one to hear it, was it really singing? Nel would have just asked the ray, if rays could talk. All roundabout nonsense that didn't matter, the sort of thing scholars and sages used to justify their pursuits.

"Rays are like albatross," Horatio commented.

"Supposed to foreshadow good luck."

"Superstition, Captain," Nel chuckled. "Isn't that a bit late-night-fireside?"

"Doesn't mean it's not true, Nel."

"Doesn't make it true, either."

Horatio swirled his brandy, casting admiring glances at the rays. One banked away from them, all but disappearing as it showed its topside, a skin as black as the void. Others drifted in and out of the miasma that followed all ships sailing the stars.

"They're beautiful, aren't they, Nel." Horatio sighed happily. "Even you have to admit that."

"I like their singing," Nel admitted grudgingly. "Makes a change from the silence."

"What do you think they're singing about then?"

Someone laughed. "That there's no good fishing around here."

"You speak ray, then?" Nel put the question to Sharpe, standing at the lower deck below Horatio's cabin.

He coughed, covering his mouth. "Sorry, throat's still a bit raw, must have been something I drank. And course I do, Skipper," Sharpe grinned up at them, hands in his pockets now. "Doesn't everyone?" He winked, turned, and started walking towards the prow of the ship. Nel scowled at the man's back.

"Nel?" Horatio asked. "Everything ok?"

"I don't like him," Nel said, watching Sharpe move along the ship. He seemed sure footed enough, probably no stranger to sailing. There was something military in his background, of that she was sure. He was too fit, had come through the destruction of his ship too well. You wouldn't know what he'd been through to look at him. He claimed he wasn't Alliance, but had been on one of their ships. That didn't sit well with her.

"Any reason?" Horatio sighed.

"Not yet."

Horatio struggled for something to say. Horatio was an optimist when it came to the people aboard the *Tantamount*. Nel considered herself a realist.

"Well, we'll see when we get to Cauldron." He brightened.

"At least we know I'm going to have a good run at the tables now."

Nel turned. "We don't know anything like that."

Horatio gestured expansively. "That's a lot of rays out there."

"Captain," Nel sighed in irritation.

"Oh, be positive, Nel. Agree with me for once. You saw the rays."

Nel looked hard at her captain. Sometimes she wondered.

"Let me have a chat with our guest, Nel. Man to man. I'll soon discover if he's got anything to hide."

"Man to man?" Nel eyed her captain sceptically.

"Aye, that's what I said, Nel. You'd be surprised at what a man will tell you after a few drinks and a few friendly hands of Freehold Poker."

"Fine, just don't lose the rest our advance, Captain."

"Rays, Nel. You saw the rays. And one day you'll come around to my way of thinking," Horatio predicted. "One day you'll know what it's like to be in charge of a ship like this."

"I like things just the way they are, Captain," Nel said.

Horatio grinned. "Me too, Nel." He waggled a finger at her. "But nothing lasts forever. Don't forget that."

His words reminded her of something. "Speaking of which, Captain, I need to go find Jack."

Jack was meant to have been doing a stock take of all the stores on the ship, like the captain had ordered, working out if anything had spoiled, in an attempt to get to the truth of the matter that had affected Quill. Nel wasn't optimistic about a resolution to the mystery but going through the motions was better than nothing.

Jack wasn't doing just nothing when she found him. He was eyeing up the rays, particularly a smallish one that had drifted close to the ship. Jack seemed to be weighing up whether it was within harpoon range. He held one ready in his hands. His big, burly hands with their scar tissue wrist bands. Scar tissue that came from manacles and fetters, a signature from time incarcerated. Everyone had a past and Nel didn't hold Jack's scars against him. Scars to Jack were like tattoos to Piper—they held hidden stories. Nel had never asked about most of those stories, they just reminded her that he was capable of violence.

"Don't even think about it, Jack," Nel warned, stamping her boots as she walked to make sure he knew she was there. Jack turned his big head to regard her with small dark eyes.

Jack had things in common with Piper, as far as first impressions went. They were both big men, large and imposing, and both had strange ways of talking. Both were good sailors, earning their keep on the *Tantamount*. Jack had done hard time and Piper looked like he had. But that was where the similarities ended, Nel thought. Piper was . . . deranged, but his actions always followed a strange sort of logic. Most could be traced back to Bandit. Jack was just plain crazy, in a colder-than-Quill sort of way.

"Skipper," he said in his coarse, gravelly voice.

"What are you doing with that harpoon, Jack?"

Jack looked at the harpoon; his big hands easily encircled the shaft even though it was nearly twice his height.

"We need fresh meat. Those rays look like they got enough on them."

"There's also a lot of them out there, Jack."

"So?"

"You kill one of them, the rest will attack," Nel pointed out.

Jack's head bobbed as he counted the breadth of the pack. "I don't got enough space for them all, especially not that big one."

Nel frowned. That hadn't been her point. "We'll be at Cauldron soon. You can pick up supplies there."

"Won't be as fresh," Jack argued.

"Crew's used to that."

"Yeah, but we got fresh meat flying right alongside us. Waste not to take advantage of that."

"Didn't Gabbi give you another job to do?"

"Yeah."

"And?"

"And what?"

"Did you do it?"

"Course I did," Jack growled.

"So?" Nel didn't budge. She wasn't about to let Jack intimidate her, not on her own ship. "Find anything wrong with the stores?"

"The meat ain't fresh. Rest of it tasted all right."

"You shouldn't have to taste everything to check if it's gone bad, Jack."

"That's how you know if it's gone bad."

"Fine," she sighed. "So what made Quill sick?"

"Kelpie's got a weak stomach."

"He eats raw meat, Jack. That's rarer than what you like, and I've seen you at mess."

"Kelpies," Jack grunted dismissively. "You sure you don't want me to hook one of those rays? They're just floating there. Asking for it."

"They're swimming, Jack."

"In what?" Jack shook his head. "Fine. I got work to do."

"Then get to it. Where's Gabbi?"

"Where a woman should be, in the galley."

"You looking to be scraping the hull, Jack?"

Jack shrugged. "If it needs scraping get your cabin girl to do it."

"Get off my deck, Jack." Nel shook her head in disgust. She went searching for Gabbi next, doubting she could handle any more male company.

Shards of ice flew as Violet chipped away at the hull's frozen covering. She stepped back and eyed the bucket at her side speculatively. *That ought to be enough*, she thought. The metal pail was about two-thirds full, anymore and she'd just be digging out the dirty ice, not the clean hoarfrost she wanted.

Violet shivered, rubbing at her arms. It was cold in this

part of the ship, deep in the hold. This close to the edge of the envelope ice would form, so it was where perishable stores were kept. And once every few days the captain would send Violet down to fetch ice.

Violet hefted the pail, carrying it awkwardly with two hands and started the climb out of the hold. There was more than one level to climb and her shoulders had started to ache by the time she reached the main deck.

She could hear voices before she reached the captain's cabin, mostly laughter. Mostly the captain.

"Violet." Sharpe was downcast as he faced her. "Your captain is killing me."

"Experience, my boy," the captain chortled as Violet set the bucket of ice down near to him. "Years and years of experience. Thank you, Violet, that's just what we needed."

He started to fill his and Sharpe's glasses with handfuls of ice.

"I didn't realise your ship ran cold, Captain," Sharpe said as he accepted his glass.

"Perks of the trade, my boy," the captain beamed. "Can't make a proper brandy without ice."

"It's better than the coffee, I must say," Sharpe agreed, setting his glass aside as he considered his cards.

"Tried Jack's coffee, didn't you, Mister Sharpe?" Violet grinned.

"Just Sharpe, princess, I told you. And yes, gods help me, I did. Nel didn't even warn me, evil woman that she is."

"Aye, she's got a mean streak to her, no doubt." The captain nodded conspiratorially. "You don't want to get on her bad side, you'll never get off it. Holds grudges, that woman."

"I believe you." Sharpe took another card, scrutinising the captain over his hand. The captain returned a dead pan stare, ignoring his own cards. Sharpe sighed and leaned over towards Violet.

"Put me out of my misery, princess. What was in that coffee?"

Violet fought back a smile. "Toast," she admitted.

Sharpe blinked. "Toast?" he repeated.

"Burnt toast," Violet confirmed, watching the distaste grow on Sharpe's face with amusement. *Maybe the skipper isn't the only one with a mean streak.*

"A run," the captain announced loudly, laying down his cards. "Queen high."

"Queen?" Sharpe exclaimed. He stared at the cards on the table before throwing his own away. "I give up, Captain. Your whole crew's against me. I can't compete."

"Ah, well, more's the pity," the captain said, looking over his winnings.

"Your captain's cleaned me out, princess," Sharpe confided to Violet.

"I can see." Violet grinned, eyeing her captain's newly acquired collection of matchsticks and buttons. "Barely a stitch to your name, Mister Sharpe."

"Aye, he left me that dignity, barely," Sharpe grumbled. "How did a sweet girl like you end up crewing for a crooked poker player like Captain Phelps?"

Violet shrugged. "Not much of a story there."

"I recall it involved a tavern brawl," the captain mused.

"All the best stories do," Sharpe said.

"Nel had been drinking," the captain said, his eyes becoming distant. "She didn't do that often but after Thyme got stabbed she started again."

"Again?" Sharpe said, his eyes narrowing. "Who was Thyme?"

"He was . . . before me," Violet told him. She looked unhappily at the captain. Sometimes . . . he got confused. This was the first time Violet had seen it happen without the skipper or someone else around.

"Captain," she said, touching his shoulder.

"I sent Quill to go find Nel, can't sail the ship without a skipper," the captain rambled, like he hadn't heard. "And we found Violet on the way. Found her on the way and . . ."

The captain looked at both of them, seeming to notice Violet's touch. "What was I saying? Something about a tavern brawl?"

Sharpe reached out and carefully gathered the cards from the table.

"Another hand, Captain?"

The galley was in better shape than the last time Nel had visited. Pots and pans were still flying around but not as vigorously as when Quill had been their target. Gabbi stood in the middle of the galley, directing her utensils like a pudgy choirmaster. There was a queued up procession for the stove, brimming pots cycling over it as they were required. Gabbi's control wasn't quite fine enough to manage tasks like cutting and dicing ingredients but she could haul the heavier items in the kitchen around, cutting down on the number of assistants she needed. Mostly she just made do with Jack. He'd learnt to duck after the first day on the job. They dented less pots that way.

"Jack was looking to bring you a side of manta ray," Nel announced her presence dryly. "Freshly caught."

"Ray?" Gabbi's head came up, shaking. "I saw them before, pretty things, if you don't annoy them. Shooting them full of harpoons annoys them. Besides, those things are tough and dry. Taste terrible."

"You should try them battered and fried in oil," Nel suggested, though she was pleased Gabbi agreed with her.

"I'm trying to teach Jack more than butchery," Gabbi said. "But that boy is pure hunter-gatherer. If you can't skin it and fillet it, he doesn't want it."

"At least he's easily amused. Unlike some."

Gabbi cast Nel a cock-eyed glance. "Watch this," she said, taking a cracked walnut shell out of a box on the table. She tossed it into the air, catching it with her power and floating it out the door. Nel watched as Gabbi guided the nut case down the deck towards the back of the ship, towards the bridge. Quill stood there, feet splayed, and tail swaying. He seemed to be on edge.

With a flick of her wrist Gabbi sent the shell skittering across the deck right behind Quill, sliding off the back of the ship and out into space. Quill turned like someone had prodded him with a lightning rod, trying to spot where the sound came from. Nel could hear his snarl of frustration all the way from the galley.

"Been doing that long?" she asked her.

"Day or two," Gabbi admitted. "He's been jumpy lately. Still thinks I tried to poison him."

"Did you?"

"Skipper," Gabbi protested.

"Ok, ok."

"He'd be dead if I had, anyways."

Nel raised an eyebrow.

Gabbi shrugged. "Just saying."

"Ease off on him, Gabbi. The ship's in rough shape enough, don't need Quill twisting us apart because you scared the scales off him."

Gabbi snickered at the idea.

"Gabbi," Nel warned.

"Aye, Skipper, I hear you. No more tricks."

CHAPTER 3

It was bells that woke her from a comfortable but dreamy sleep this time. Jack had tried to spear one of the giant rays and it had taken him for a ride, doing loops around the *Tantamount* while Jack clung to the harpoon. Gabbi threw giant walnuts to try and knock him free while the crew cheered and for some reason Sharpe stood on the bridge waving a flag to conduct the aerial display. And then, as so often happened in her dreams, clouds of ash and dust erupted to cover the scene, cloaking the *Tantamount* and all aboard her in choking billows. Nel woke to the sound of her crew shouting landfall amidst the pealing bells.

"Landfall," she muttered, rolling out of her hammock and reaching for her boots. It was a gross exaggeration. She stood, trying to ignore the sheen of sweat that often accompanied her bad dreams. And the best way to do so was to join her crew on the deck, as Cauldron grew larger on the forward plane.

Cauldron was so named because it was settled in the bowl-shaped crater of a giant asteroid, one that could have made a case for being a small planetoid, but not a planet itself. The active, volcanic vents and flaming geysers were fuelled by underground gas chambers that provided heat and light to an otherwise desolate rock.

Old Smoky was what some of the locals called the biggest

vent, a miniature volcano that rose in the centre of the crater. Much of the industry on Cauldron was powered by steam, rather than ether like it would have been on a more developed world. Huge machines could be found around most of the vents, mills and wheels powered by the constant gush, with clusters of buildings around the contraptions, the only places on the rock it was warm enough to live. Cauldron was cold and generally miserable but survived because it happened to be roughly in the middle of two intersecting trade routes. Accessible but still off the high traffic lanes, a place where less than legitimate exchanges could happen and where not too many questions would be asked.

Having begun as a bare and airless rock, breathing came at a premium on Cauldron. Piers extended out from the rim of the crater to which ships could dock, or alternatively they could tie up to the floating moorings left adrift in space above Cauldron and lower bubbles down to the township. Either way would be met with eager toll collectors.

"Used to be they shipped air in the hard way," Nel explained to Violet, leaning over the railing as Quill brought the ship to one of the piers. She would have preferred a mooring for the lesser expense and detachment it offered but repairs necessitated a proper berth. They needed scaffolding and skilled labour. They were going to have to bring materials onto the ship and there was no way they could do that with just bubbles and the ship's cranes. Not if they wanted to make their delivery within the next month. And they still had to get that damned mast out of the hull— it was already drawing attention. She could see people on the docks staring and pointing.

"How'd they do that?" Violet looked over the township with fascination. The girl always got fidgety whenever they made landfall. Nel put it down to youth; Violet had the attention span of any other teenager. She'd be over Cauldron soon enough once she got an idea of the place. Nel just had to keep her out of trouble 'til then.

"Brought it in by ship," Nel explained. "All bottled up. Or

sometimes they'd just siphon it straight out of the bigger ships once they'd put an envelope around this dust ball."

"How'd they do that, Skipper? Put an envelope around a big rock like this."

"Same way we do it on the ship, fill the hull full of ballast."

"You mean ether," Violet said, trying to appear knowledgeable.

"Right," Nel grinned, ruffling the girl's hair. "That thing that throws up a field around the ship. The more ballast, the bigger the field and envelope, and the more gravity there is. You can do the same for stations like this, just takes a lot more ballast."

"Sounds expensive."

"It was. It is. So they keep telling us. There's enough stunted shrubbery in this crater now to keep pumping out the air but the tolls are still here."

"What are those?" Violet asked, pointing at a group of lumbering figures across the docks.

Nel squinted. "Golems. Steam powered."

The golems were roughly man-shaped, boxy constructs made of wood and metal, gushing steam from various orifices. They had the same crudely painted symbol she could see all over Cauldron, a spider's web. She knew it for the sign of the group who controlled Cauldron. The Spider's Web, mercenaries, the strong arm employed by whichever shady trading company had set up the first trading posts on Cauldron, back before it had been called that.

Nel knew the Web for a big group, as far as mercenaries went, that used to have something of a reputation. Over time the mercs had taken over more and more of the day-to-day operations of running Cauldron until eventually they'd just cut out the middlemen altogether. They administered the tolls to anyone who stepped foot on the surface proper and made sure they got a piece of whatever else went on in their territory. The fees were high but not enough to drive people away. It was part of the price of doing business on Cauldron.

The golems Nel could see were mules; made to handle heavy lifting and transport at the docks—for a price of course. They'd probably started off as siege engines, war machines, and run on things other than steam. But mercenaries, being the most practical of people, could never justify anything that didn't bring in coin. Steam was cheaper than everything else on Cauldron and the golems were free labour sitting idle. So they'd been put to work.

Smart, Nel conceded. Their presence everywhere reminded everyone who ran Cauldron.

"How do they work, those golem things?" Violet twisted round to ask.

"I don't know," Nel said. The girl had endless questions, answer one and half a dozen more were blurted out. "Go ask Piper if you're so curious, maybe he'll tell you."

On cue the lesson was interrupted by Piper's arrival. Bandit crouched on his shoulders, black clawed hands gripping the sides of Piper's bald head for balance. The loompa's own head turned excitedly left to right and then back again as it steered Piper towards Nel and Violet.

"Skipper." Piper nodded, causing Bandit to squawk in alarm and almost lose his balance.

"Piper," Nel said, "either kick that disgusting creature over the railings or tie it up somewhere out of sight. But for goodness sake don't cart it around like it's the one in charge."

"I'll take him," Violet declared, extending one arm to the loompa. Bandit chirped and transferred himself to the girl, scampering along her arm and taking a perch on her shoulder. He peered around with interest from his new vantage.

"Don't fall." Piper appeared concerned for his pet. Bandit turned his head to regard him, then went back to Violet. He seemed crestfallen that his new transport was so much shorter, until he discovered the handholds Violet's tangled hair provided.

"He won't fall," Violet assured Piper, giggling as Bandit played with her hair. "He likes me too."

"The two of you are probably related." A clicking on the

coarse deck planking announced Quill's arrival. Like all Kelpies his legs bent backwards at the knee and ended in two hoof-like toes, so he rarely wore boots, going barefoot aboard the ship same as the rest of the crew. More of the crew were starting to appear now they were planetside.

"We're docked," Quill told Nel, "and the vultures are gathering. Or should that be monkeys? Kin of yours, yes? Close cousins perhaps." He eyed the loompa meaningfully.

"You might want to stow the attitude, Quill," Nel said. "You're part of the reason we're here."

"I was poisoned," Quill was quick to remind her. "We should find ourselves a new cook while we're here, one who cooks more than she eats."

Bandit made a chattering sound, drawing suspicious looks from both Nel and Quill.

"What does that thing want?" the Kelpie hissed.

"Bandit should not use language like that," Piper shook his finger. "Where did you learn such things? What? From the skipper?" He turned to Nel, poised to start lecturing. She wasn't in the mood.

"Don't even start, Piper," she warned him off.

"I'm feeling peckish," Quill muttered. "Perhaps a bite of monkey might go down well. What do you say, Skipper? Get rid of the fur and the thing might make good eating."

Bandit bared sharp teeth in a high pitched growl, taking refuge behind Violet.

"You leave him alone," the cabin girl snapped. "Just cause something got under your scales—"

"My scales?" Quill sounded surprised. "Insolent brat."

"Touch them and I will hammer your tail into the anchor, wizard," Piper warned Quill when the Kelpie took a step forward.

"That's navigator, oaf," Quill snarled. "Navigator, not wizard!"

Piper snorted. "They are the same thing."

"Gods below," Nel exclaimed, "quiet, all of you. We've got a ship to fix. None of you are helping. Quill, I'm going ashore, you're in charge 'til I or the captain gets back. You two," she pointed at Piper and Violet, "are coming with me."

"Where is the captain?" Violet asked, looking around. She stood on her tiptoes to scan the ship which made Bandit imitate her atop her shoulders. "Shouldn't he be here?"

"The captain likes the games," Piper told her. "The captain is not good at the games, but likes them all the same."

"He was the first one ashore," Nel said dryly. "Always is at a place like this. He'll be back when he runs out of money."

"Shouldn't he be . . . ," Violet hesitated.

"What?" Nel asked.

The girl hesitated. "I don't know, running stuff? Instead of letting you do all the work all the time?"

Quill laughed. Nel glared at him.

"The captain is the captain. Nel is the skipper," Piper told Violet. "This is how things are. This is what works. Even the wizard knows this."

"Navigator," Quill repeated irritably.

"Horatio has his quirks, but he's a good captain," Nel told the girl. "We've all had worse, believe me."

Violet looked unconvinced but it wasn't Nel's job to change her mind. They had a long list of repairs that needed to be made and standing around wasn't getting them done.

"Where's our guest?" Nel asked, casting her eye up and down the crew starting to line the rail. Violet wasn't the only one with a short memory and attention span. Sailors had an odd fascination with terra firma; they were always glad to see it but grew restless soon after.

"Anyone seen Sharpe?" she asked those around her. She received shaken heads from all of them.

"Maybe he went ashore with the captain," Violet suggested.

"Or without him," Quill muttered.

"You don't think he left, do you?" Violet was crestfallen. She'd been spending time with him since they picked him up, Nel recalled.

Nel shrugged. "We can hope."

"Skipper!" Violet protested.

"He was never going to stay, Violet," Nel said. "He wasn't part of the crew."

"And he was Alliance," Quill said.

"No he wasn't," Violet protested. "He said he wasn't."

Quill snorted. "Doesn't matter what he said, he was on an Alliance ship."

"What's wrong with Alliance, anyway?" Violet asked the navigator.

"They're Alliance." Quill shrugged.

"So?"

Quill shook his head. "Idiot girl." He looked at Nel. "Haven't you taught her anything yet?"

"Watch your tone, navigator," Nel said.

"Children shouldn't be allowed on ships, bad luck." He glared at Bandit. "Neither should rodents."

Violet turned her back on Quill, flicking her tail upwards at him. Bandit kept facing the navigator and shook his tiny fist at the Kelpie, screeching.

"Disgusting creatures, both of them," Quill said.

"Quill, go up to the bridge," Nell ordered. "You're on watch, remember? Try and find out where Sharpe got to, though I can't say as I'll miss him if he has jumped."

"Aye," Quill muttered. "And I won't shed any tears if you choose to lose a few more crew members ashore." He made the word crew sound like an insult.

Piper laughed.

"What?" Quill said suspiciously.

"Your joke," Piper said. "It was funny."

"What joke? There was no joke!"

"Kelpies cannot shed tears," Piper said. "So you will be crying on the inside, yes?"

Quill spluttered indignantly.

"You try very hard to pretend. Bandit was getting worried."

Quill stared. "This is not funny," he hissed. He appealed to

Nel. "This is not funny!"

Nel thought it was funny.

But she didn't let on.

Violet noticed how hard the skipper avoided looking at Quill whilst they were leaving the ship. Quill had retreated to the bridge and was being given a wide berth by the crew remaining on the ship. She'd already checked that all the water barrels were tightly lashed. Nel led Piper and Violet ashore and straight to the toll collectors barring the way out of the docks.

"Chanel," the man in charge of the check point leered. "Long time no see."

"Oh, hells," Violet heard the skipper mutter. "Just my luck."

Violet tried not to stare. She hadn't been paying attention to where they were headed, eager to take in the sights and sounds of their latest port. She'd been hoping for a closer peek at those golems and how they worked. But she could count the number of times she'd heard anyone use Nel's full name on one hand and hadn't expected today to be one of those times. Personally she could never think of Nel as anything but the skipper. Anything else struck her as disrespectful, something someone like Quill might do.

"Brawn," the skipper sighed, rocking back on her heels in front of the strapping man who blocked their path. *The skipper doesn't look happy*, Violet thought. The man who'd greeted her was big, almost as big as Piper, with pale eyes and dark hair slicked back with oil. His arms were bare and sporting a sailor's tattoos. Violet picked out the ones that mentioned naval service and trips to the Far Lanes. Most prominent was the web-like design Violet had been seeing since they got to Cauldron. It covered one shoulder and much of his upper arm.

"You looked better last time," the skipper told him. "When I'd been drinking."

"You were a mess," Brawn replied, to the amusement of the others at the checkpoint.

The skipper scowled. "Didn't put you off."

"Nothing puts me off."

"Pity."

"Isn't it just?"

Piper leaned in close to the skipper. "Bandit will bite him if you give the words," he whispered loud enough for Violet to hear. On her shoulder Bandit tensed, shuffling around.

The skipper appeared to seriously consider it for a moment. But she shook her head.

"That your ship?" Brawn gestured towards the *Tantamount* with his ledger.

"You know it is," the skipper frowned.

Brawn scribbled a note on his ledger. "Where's Captain Phelps?"

"What's it to you?" the skipper countered.

"Like to say hi to the captains when they pass through," Brawn grinned. "Touch bases, familiar faces, that sort of thing. Phelps hasn't been this way in a time."

"Try the poker tables," was all the skipper suggested.

Brawn chuckled. "Yeah, I'll do that. Man loves his games. He's already ashore then?"

A shrug. "Didn't say that."

"Didn't have to. Now what's wrong with your ship?"

"Nothing's wrong with my ship."

"It's got a tree sticking out of it. You let the cabin girl steer or something?"

"It's a mast," Violet told him, annoyed. "We found a smashed up ship out there."

"You found what?" Brawn sounded surprised.

"Shush, Violet," the skipper said, shaking her head slightly. Violet bit down on her tongue at the chastisement.

Brawn eyed her speculatively. "New kid, Chanel? She got something to say?"

"Not to you she doesn't."

"When you say a smashed ship?" Brawn inquired with a

frown.

"I mean something hit them and pieces of them hit us," the skipper told him simply.

"What, right after it happened? You picking fights out there?" Brawn's eyes narrowed. "People think they can hide out on Cauldron. Doesn't mean we like them doing it. Not if folks are likely to come to Cauldron looking for them. You ought to remember that."

"We were late to what happened out there," the skipper said. "Got caught in the aftermath, that's all."

"Sloppy work, girl," Brawn mocked her. "Your pilot asleep on the watch?"

The skipper flinched slightly at that comment, though Violet doubted anyone else would notice. Still aboard and Quill was still causing the skipper grief.

"We done catching up, Brawn?" the skipper said. "Just tell me the toll so we can get this over with."

"Well, now," Brawn mused laconically. He gestured at the ship again. "There's a lot to consider. Landing fees, docking fees. Shore tax, that air you're sucking down ain't free, Chanel. You know that, right? Then there's the protection levy . . ."

"The what?" Violet could hear anger in the skipper's voice.

"Oh, yeah," Brawn grinned. "Protection levy. You know what Cauldron's like, girl, all sorts of bad trouble just waiting to happen."

The skipper's face darkened. It was clear even to Violet the man was trying to shake them down for coin, and not even being subtle about it. Whatever history the two had, Brawn was clearly enjoying his position of authority now.

"Real shame your captain ain't here, Chanel. He owes me for his last big win. All down to me that one was." The man leered.

"I doubt that."

Brawn chuckled. "And here was me thinking he sent you to settle his affairs for him. Now that'd be ironic. But you and me, we already had our fun. I've gone up in the world since the last time you were here."

Bandit chose that moment to dig his claws into Violet's shoulder, causing her to cry out a little. She twisted, trying to make the loompa stop. He grabbed on with all four limbs and stared with wide, almost manic eyes at the toll collector. It was enough to draw his attention.

"Pretty young thing you got with you there, Chanel." Brawn reached out and caressed Violet's hair with the back of his hand. Violet flinched away from that hand, feeling like something dirty had just touched her.

"Can't be too careful, why—"

He didn't get to finish as the skipper's knee came up sharply and connected with his groin. Brawn gave a sort of squeak and sunk to his knees in front of Violet. His men stared for a moment before reaching for weapons. Piper balled his fists expectantly, but Nel ignored them, not bothering to reach for the wand at her side.

The skipper spoke quietly, but loud enough for all to hear her. "You don't touch my crew. Not a one of them. Not ever."

She crouched down beside Brawn, holding up a handful of dominions, trading currency. Coins that were taken anywhere and everywhere, usually at a favourable exchange rate.

"This is all you're getting," she told him. "You want more, go pick on someone who doesn't know you like I do."

She dropped the coins next to Brawn and gave him a shove. Brawn collapsed sideways, still clutching at his groin.

"Move," the skipper said, glaring at his men.

They moved out of her way, some giving dark looks but none seemed willing to incite more trouble.

"Skipper? What was —" Violet started to say.

"Keep walking." The skipper took a firm grip on the girl's elbow, dragging her along.

But Violet wasn't about to let it go. She rubbed at her face where the man had touched her. "Did you know that guy? Who was he?"

"Local muscle, appropriately named," the skipper muttered,

not slowing.

"He called you Chanel," Violet exclaimed.

The skipper made a face, kept walking.

"Not even the captain calls you that," Violet said aloud.

"So don't start," the skipper warned her. The grip the skipper had on her arm tightened once reflexively.

"But . . ."

"He was a mistake, Vi." They stopped, the skipper speaking plainly. "He and I. He was a mistake I made. He was drunk, hells, so was I. Really drunk. It was a bad time. Sometimes . . . everyone makes mistakes, all right?"

Violet brushed hair away from her face, staring up at the skipper. For once the skipper didn't meet her eyes. She was . . . upset.

"You could have done better," Piper said.

"Nobody asked you," the skipper said angrily.

"You are setting a bad example for us all," Piper added. "Next time Bandit will do the biting."

"Piper," the skipper growled.

"If you continue to make such poor choices in life, I will have Quill do the biting as well," Piper threatened. "It would not be the first either, he will do it."

The skipper glared at him. "Stow it, Piper." But there was just the hint of a smile at the edge of her mouth. Violet felt a grin spreading over her face. Then the image of Quill attached by his teeth to Brawn popped into her head and she couldn't hold it back.

"Oh, shut up, the both of you." The skipper turned her back on them. "Move."

"Aye, Skipper, as you say," Piper called, striding after her. Violet hastened to catch up.

The skipper took them all the way to the commissioning office, through the warehouse district and a shanty market. Like everywhere else on Cauldron, there was a web emblem above the door.

"These guys are everywhere," Violet commented as the skipper studied the outside of the building. There was no one else around but the path was well beaten, indicating heavy traffic.

"Like cockroaches," Piper agreed. "They need a good stomping."

"Would you two behave while we're here," the skipper muttered.

"You were the one who beat up that guy at the checkpoint," Violet said.

For the reminder she earned herself a vicious glare. "You should have taken notes."

"Who should have? What notes?" Violet complained.

Piper reached out and enfolded Violet in one burly, tattooed arm, ruffling her hair affectionately. She pulled her head away.

"What?" she complained, looking up at Piper. He smiled and she settled down into a sulk.

"Let the skipper do the talking," he said. "This is one of those times."

"Fine," Violet muttered. *Shut up and listen. Be quiet and take notes. It's too hard to explain. Always the same.*

The skipper stared at the two of them. She didn't seem happy about what she saw. "Keep quiet," she repeated before opening the door.

"Actually," the skipper said before stepping into the office. "Just stay out here. And keep quiet."

Violet sighed. *Always the same.*

The clerk at the desk inside the commissioning office barely looked up at Nel's entrance.

"Name?" he asked, not missing a beat as he ran a quill back and forth along a ream of parchment.

"Nel Vaughn —"

"Not yours," the clerk interrupted. "Ship, company, office, faction. Something I might actually have heard of."

"*Tantamount*," Nel said shortly. "That's a ship, in case you're wondering."

"*Tantamount, Tantamount*," the man muttered, turning,

and opened a filing cabinet behind him. The wooden drawer stuck and he tugged on it viciously. It came out with a swirl of dust. The clerk waved a hand to clear the air. "Equivalent, synonymous, as in equal to or near enough. That was *Tantamount* with a T?"

"Yes."

The man plucked a file out of the drawer, swivelling back and laying it over his desk.

"What can I do for you?" the clerk asked, starting to page through the file.

"My ship needs repairs," Nel said. "Hull breaches, decking, sails."

"That will be expensive."

"Surprise me."

"Your ship has debt loaded against it," the clerk pushed the file away. Nel scowled. That hadn't been the surprise she'd been hoping for. To be honest, it wasn't even much of a surprise.

She frowned. "You have that on file?"

"On the wall behind you, next to the door."

Nel turned. Next to the door was a list of names. People, ships, organisations. All of them in bold red ink, meaning indebted. About halfway down the list was the captain's name.

"My ship's name isn't on that list," she said, not willing to make the obvious mistake. There was a reason she hadn't used Horatio's name.

"Your captain's is," the clerk said. He held up the file. "His name is in here, so is your ship's."

Bloody Cauldron, Nel thought.

"You keep papers on every gambling debt?"

The clerk shrugged. "Only the ones wowed to our members. You won't be able to commission materials or labour until the debt is settled."

Who expected a smuggler's nest to keep detailed records? That was the thing about mercenaries though; they were meticulous about who owed them money. Nel winced when she saw the other name next to Horatio's. Brawn hadn't been kidding—the captain really did owe him money.

"How much is the debt?" Nel grimaced.

The clerk told her. She started swearing. Loudly.

"Skipper?" Piper stuck his head in the door, looking round the room carefully.

Nel took a breath. "It's fine, Piper," she said. "Go wait outside."

The clerk scribbled out a note, handed it to her. "The interest on the debt will be added to your docking fees. I suggest you settle it quickly."

"I already paid my docking fee," Nel objected.

"You'll pay this before you're allowed to leave."

Nel took the paper reluctantly. She managed to resist the urge to crumple it until she was outside the office. She and Horatio were going to have words when she next laid eyes on him.

"Problems?" Piper asked when she emerged. He and Violet looked up from some discussion.

"We need to go somewhere else," Nel said. "Some place without a damned web over the door."

Piper glanced up at the mercenary logo. "The captain is going to be needing a big win, yes?" he guessed. Piper had been with the captain almost as long as Nel had.

"The captain has done enough, Piper. Find me a salvage shop. Next to a bar, one that serves beer. Cheap beer. In fact, forget the salvage shop."

Ebon stared at the cards on the table. It was a favourable hand. A very favourable hand in fact. The problem was that it wasn't his. The hand belonged to the man opposite him, a battered middle aged man sporting a just as battered captain's hat. The two of them were the only ones left in the game. In fact the other man, the captain, had been taking all the other players for whatever they were worth for the past few bells. A good run, the sort that made management suspicious. The captain was being watched closely, but as far as Ebon could tell he was playing it straight. The man was just lucky. It didn't make any sense. Nobody was that lucky. Not on Cauldron.

"Out." Ebon threw down his cards in disgust. The captain chortled gleefully, raking in his winnings. Ebon retired to the bar, ordering a drink with a wave of his hand. It was embarrassing, getting fleeced by a visitor on his home grounds.

"Losing your touch, Ebon," his server chuckled.

Ebon glared up at the man, recognising him. He'd just lost a considerable amount of coin and wasn't in the mood to be ribbed about it. "You tend bar now?" he muttered. "Thought you had better things to do. Last I saw you were running jobs for the Web."

"The bar was empty and I couldn't miss a chance to chat with an old friend." The bartender chuckled again. "Seems Captain Phelps took you for a ride, Ebon."

Ebon snorted, reaching for his drink. "You said he was a lousy player. He's taken me and everyone else here for all we own."

The bartender shrugged. "Guess he was due, but you were the one who wanted a ship. The *Tantamount* was bound for Vice before she had to stop here. She can run cold cargo and that's what you need."

"What I need is a way to get my money back," Ebon growled.

"Suppose I staked you in the next round. And suppose I confide to you some of Captain Phelps' tells."

Ebon glared at the man. "Now you mention his tells?"

The bartender leaned down, grinning. He lowered his voice to a whisper. "Ebon, this ship is perfect for your run. The crew as well."

"You remember what'll happen at the end of this run, right? Why this ship? What'd Captain Phelps ever do to you?"

"Ain't Phelps so much as his first officer."

Ebon stared, then chuckled, remembering the table talk. "Phelps' first officer is a woman."

"And a hard one at that," the bartender muttered, running a hand through short hair. "So, are we doing this or not?"

Ebon took a long look at Captain Phelps. The man was busy ordering another drink and poring over his winnings. A fair amount of that coin had been Ebon's until recently. The skinny, frail looking old human looked out of place amongst Cauldron's motley inhabitants. *Don't see too many like him out in the Free Lanes*, Ebon thought.

"All right," he said, "tell me everything you know about Captain Phelps."

"Who's got my spendings?" Gabbi asked, looking round at her party. Jack didn't answer, looking round at Cauldron's milling populace. They'd come to the markets, a place where if it could be moved, it was for sale. That included anything and everyone, so it was not a place Gabbi would have come alone. That was why Jack and the other two crew heavies were with her.

Aldy and Orim were Free Lanes muscle, no other words for it. If it was a dangerous job or heavy lifting then they were the first in line. Like most sailors they got antsy staying in one place too long so were always volunteering, if volunteering would get the ship underway any quicker. Aldy didn't have the sense to string more than two sentences together, but he knew ships and sailing well enough. Given his ropes and a heading, he was happy. Everything a trader wanted in a sailor. Orim was a lousy hand at poker and dice which made him a favourite amongst the rest of the crew.

She wouldn't have trusted either with cold coin which was why Jack was holding onto the ship's slush fund. She had money for the provisions—that came from the ship's running costs, which was worked out between the officers. But the slush fund was gravy, so to speak, for all those extra luxuries that kept the crew happy and in line.

Jack had insisted on carrying it.

"This is hardly bulk." The bearded Domovoi grocer she'd been buying from seemed bored by the lot. "Goods are in back, you can take 'em when you pay me up front. No discount."

"You don't have much," Gabbi said. "For once in my life I've money to spend and naught to spend it on."

The shelves in this store and many others were thin. Not bare, but the bulk produce was mostly gone. The stuff that remained wasn't as good as Gabbi would have liked, the perishables looking older and wilted more than what she herself would have put on display.

"Just what you've seen."

"And no liquor?"

"Not to be had here."

And that wasn't going to sit well with the crew. Wasn't even going to be able to keep that from them neither, not once Aldy and Orim got back and started running their mouths. Only thing worse than sailors with liquor was sailors without it. Worse than crying babes they became.

"Jack, what's this then?" Aldy was asking her assistant. They were over at the meat racks. Jack didn't do greens; it was a wonder he had any teeth left at all. Meat was all her assistant desired out of the galley.

"Furred trout," Jack responded after careful consideration.

"Looks like what we had for mess the other week," Aldy complained. "Where'd you go getting furred trout?"

"Didn't."

"So what was we eating the other week then?"

"Loompa."

"Loompa? Couldn't have been, saw Bandit when we left the ship, with Piper like always. Ain't no other loompas on the *Tantamount*, Jack."

"Looked like a loompa," Jack grunted, tugging at his topknot. "Only smaller."

"Smaller?" Aldy sounded disturbed.

"Yeah, smaller. Not as big."

"Jack," Gabbi called. "Found anything we need?"

Jack waved over at her. "They got furred trout, Gabbi."

"We don't need no trout, Jack. Furred nor otherwise."

"That's what they got."

"In some places that would be a delicacy," the grocer said.

"Ain't no delicacies on Cauldron," Jack told him.

"We'll take the dry goods," Gabbi said. "Meat and perishables can be shipped to the docks, right? Cold storage?"

"Aye," the grocer shrugged, "we can manage that well enough. Gonna be trail mix, though."

"Don't like trail mix," Jack grumbled.

"Can't do anything else," he was told. "We've been cleaned out as you can plainly see."

"Cleaned out?" Gabbi narrowed her eyes. "Why's everyone so short?"

The grocer leaned over his counter, smirking down at her. Gabbi resolved that if he made a joke about her height she'd brain the lout.

"Alliance group came through a few weeks ago, bought everything they could buy up, then took off again."

"Alliance? Here?" Gabbi thought to the blasted ship they'd been holed by. But that had been a single ship, not a group. They were well clear of the High Lanes, but Alliance ships wouldn't have left one of their own in such a state. "What's that lot doing out this way?"

"War, or like as such," the grocer shrugged. "Not here, not even Alliance. Thatch is brewing, they say, bit of a hotspot. And there's always Vice. Someone in the Alliance wants to play hero, I figure, sail around putting out fires."

"Ain't nothing wrong with Vice," Gabbi asserted. "We was on a run to there, we would have heard if there was."

"Must be Thatch then." The grocer shrugged again.

Gabbi snorted. "Figures, bloody Alliance, always putting their end in."

"Aye," the grocer agreed. "Here, I'll show you how they paid for their goods, seeing as you'll be seeing them yourself shortly.

Follow me."

Curious, Gabbi followed the man, getting Jack to come with them as well. It was safer and he would have like as done it anyway. The grocer led them back into the meat locker, where hoarfrost covered the walls and cuts of meat hung on hooks along the room. It wasn't empty. There were two men there, but they weren't working. They just stood at one end against the wall, not so different from the other meat.

"Best workers I've ever had," the grocer proclaimed. "Don't eat, don't slack, don't complain, just do as they told until you tell 'em not too. Good lads, really."

Gabbi couldn't suppress a shudder at the grocer's "good lads." They were Draugr, grey skinned and unmoving, with that empty, dead look they all had.

"That's how they paid you?" she asked quietly.

"Aye," the man chuckled. "Didn't have no trading coins, just that Alliance chit. Can you believe it? I was a bit sceptical myself, but they wouldn't give me no choice. Thought I was getting shafted by the uniformed prats but these boys," he nodded towards the Draugr, "worth their weight, they are. Work day in and day out, don't have to feed 'em, don't have to do nothing but tell 'em what to do."

"That's it?" Gabbi shivered. "They just do what they're told?"

"Yeah, simple stuff. Can't do the books, though I wish they could, least they'd be honest about it. Loading and carrying and fetching stuff, can't beat them. Couple of times someone tried to make off with one or the other, put 'em to work in their own business. But the Kelpie who handed them over fixed it so they just end up back here. Brilliant, ain't it?"

"Guess so," Gabbi agreed. She had to look away from the Draugr. She'd seen them before, but never so close. They were like anybody else, anybody who'd been dead a couple of days. Draugr were . . . hells nobody was quite sure what they were. She hadn't had a good answer when Violet asked her and she didn't have one now. Some said they were golems, flesh and blood or clay made to look like people, though supposedly their skin felt like carved hardwood to the touch. Gabbi couldn't bring herself to find out, even given the chance. Some people said they were what happened to Alliance sailors after they died, that they signed a contract to come back and keep serving. Witched up to keep on going, come hells or void water. Gabbi couldn't imagine anyone ever agreeing to something like that. Maybe that was why people like the skipper left the Alliance.

"These two'll bring your cold goods over," the grocer grinned. "Don't worry. Like I said, they're reliable."

Looking at the pair, Gabbi could only shudder.

"Let's go," Jack rumbled, putting one hand on her shoulder and steering her out. His hand felt warm in the chilled room and she clasped it, scars and all. Jack let her.

"Keep them coming," Nel said, staring at the counter top. She didn't look up as a pint of foaming beer was pushed under her nose, just dropped a handful of coins off to the side.

"Where's mine?" Violet complained. The girl leaned with her back against the bar, eyeing the other patrons unhappily. She held her tail in one hand, keeping it clear of the floorboards. Despite that the appendage was covered in dust and cobwebs.

"You get yours when you can pay for it yourself," Nel said.

"When do I get paid then?" Violet asked indignantly.

"When you start pulling your weight."

That sent Violet into another sulk.

"Hate Cauldron," Nel muttered. "Hate it. Sooner we're out of here the better. Bloody Cauldron."

"Hey."

Someone pushed their way to the bar, shoving Violet out of the way, drawing an indignant squawk out of her. Nel did her best to ignore the newcomer. Vodyanoy, she noted out of the corner of her eye. This one was like a walrus crossed with a skin. The flat, whiskered face and bulging eyes were out of place on Cauldron. Normally they stuck to wet planets. Smoke filled holes like Cauldron dried them out.

"You're Horatio Phelps' first mate. Nel Vaughn, if I'm not mistaken," the Vodyanoy said, showing an impressive grasp of the trader's tongue. Not easy with that mouth.

Nel took a deep drink. She hadn't heard anything that warranted her attention yet.

"I'm Ebon Masaius." He held out a hand. Nel ignored it.

"Do I know you?" she conceded the words grudgingly.

Ebon withdrew the unshaken hand, whiskers twitching with annoyance. "No, but I know your captain."

Nel shrugged. "Good for you."

"Former master of the *Tantamount*."

Nel's hand automatically went to her side, but she stopped herself, fingers just curling under the guard of her weapon.

"Why former?" she asked, pushing her beer away. Eyes narrowing she took a closer look at the Vodyanoy; there was no sign of a spider's web tattoo or sigil. Nor had the *Tantamount*'s debt been anywhere near enough to have it seized, even with the interest.

What was this Ebon on about then? Did Horatio have other debts she didn't know about? Stupid question, of course he did. Most of the time Nel was happier not knowing.

Ebon smiled, a broad smile that nearly split his face in half. Nel figured this wasn't going to be one of those times. "Because he lost it to me."

Nel turned away from the Vodyanoy. "You're full of it."

"Recognise this?" Ebon held up something. Nel glanced at the deed of property. It was familiar all right, official looking with the *Tantamount*'s name embossed large in the header. A deed of title that appeared for all the world to be genuine. Nel knew for a fact that Horatio always carried those papers on his person.

Violet gasped. "Hells, Skipper."

"Watch your mouth," Nel warned her. To the man with the deed, "How'd you get that?"

"Won it, fair and legal." Ebon turned the deed over in his hands, admiring it.

"I doubt that," Nel retorted. "Horatio's never played fair in his life. He wouldn't put up the ship if he thought he could lose."

That grin again. "He didn't have much of a choice."

"You threatened my captain then?" Nel asked quietly.

"He was on a good run," Ebon told her, redirecting the question. "A very good run. And then it went bad and he was in deep. The ship was his last card."

"Am I supposed to care about any of this?" Nel went back to her beer. Next time she told Piper to find a bar that sold cheap beer she'd have to leave out the cheap part. That could have gone without saying on Cauldron. The stuff she was downing was more head than the swill it claimed to be, which was saying something.

And Ebon wasn't even letting her enjoy that much. "You're supposed to tell me where the *Tantamount* is berthed. Phelps ran out on us last time before we could collect."

"Sounds like your problem is with my captain." Nel shrugged. "Go bother him. You're not even the first person who's been asking about him."

"You're here. He's not."

"I'm drinking, you're distracting me. Get lost."

Ebon leaned back. "Not the best attitude for someone in your position."

"I said I'm drinking," Nel growled. "Go away."

"Nothing in this charter that says I have to let the current crew stay. You should be nicer."

"The hells I should."

"Fine." Ebon folded up the deed and put it away carefully. "I'll find Phelps without you then. And then I'll find your ship."

"Yeah, good luck with that."

Ebon smiled, scaly lips pressed into a thin line, but left without another word.

Nel waited a minute, counting silently. She finished her drink as well. She could feel the watered down liquid sloshing in the pit of her stomach, churned up into its own little swell. No smooth sailing tonight.

"Violet," she said, just loud enough to be heard in the bar.

"What're we gonna do, Skipper?" Violet asked anxiously. The girl had heard every word of the exchange with Ebon and except for that one outburst had kept her quiet. She was learning. If they were lucky, all of the *Tantamount*'s new majority shareholder's attention had been focused on Nel.

"In a minute we're going to walk out of here. Once we're out I'm going to go find Piper," Nel explained.

She'd sent Piper off to the salvage yards by himself. Himself and Bandit. Piper had seemed happy enough with the arrangement and Nel hadn't been in the mood to do any more negotiating. As long as Piper kept names, both the ship and captain's, out of the equation he should have been fine.

"You want me to go find the captain, then?" Violet said eagerly.

"Captain can take care of himself," Nel said. "No, you go back to the ship. At a run."

"Is that a good idea?" Violet was doubtful. "If someone's looking for the *Tantamount* couldn't they follow me back to it?"

"Don't let them."

"But—"

Nel cut her off. "Someone wants to find our ship, it's not going to be that hard for them. Cauldron's not that big. Plenty of people who could tell them, wouldn't even take that long to go through all the ships docked here right now. No, they're going to find us, can't help that."

Violet looked dismayed. "So what do you want me to do?"

"Get back. Let Quill and the others know. Don't let anyone on board, no matter what. That happens we're proper sunk, understand, Vi?"

"Yes, Skipper."

"Good girl." Nel stood up. "Let's go."

They made their way through the crowded and smoky tap room. Outside Violet glanced once at Nel for confirmation and then disappeared into the streets, vanishing like the street urchin she was. Nel scowled for a minute, remembering how difficult it was to find Violet when she didn't want to be found. The first few days Violet had been aboard the *Tantamount* Nel had chased her from one end to the other. Violet wasn't meant to have been aboard and both Nel and Quill had been trying to throw the girl over the side. Violet had good incentive to hide back then. Inevitably it had been the captain who had found her first, curled up inside of a barrel. After that, throwing her overboard had become less of an option, though Quill still suggested it occasionally.

Nel found Piper on his way out of a second-hand salvage shack. The front yard was littered with scrap metal and wood, bits and pieces of ships in various stages of being dismantled and recycled to be sold for profit. The leavings were of what might have once been proud and functional vessels, things with soul and purpose that had fallen on hard times and would never recover from them. The shack itself was a lean-to affair built from scrap but at least it didn't have a web on it. Of course the whole yard was falling apart. Maybe there had been a sign and it had fallen down. More likely it had been sold itself, maybe to a less legitimate business to lend it the veneer of officialdom. Or maybe the dusty cobwebs adorning corner nooks and crannies were meant to represent the mercenaries' logo. Spiders specially imported for just such a purpose. Stranger things happened.

Piper had what was probably a sheaf of promissory notes clutched in his hands and was passing them up to Bandit. The loompa examined one such paper carefully before screwing it up and stuffing it into Piper's pack with overstated deliberation.

"What are those?" Nel asked, bringing her ship's engineer to a stop.

"Consents," Piper answerred, passing one up to Bandit.

"Requests, requisitions. For the ship."

He examined another he was holding. "This one is for nails."

"Are they important?"

"Very," Piper assured her. "Nails generally are."

"Then stop giving them to the monkey," Nel said through gritted teeth. Bandit stared at her, midway through crumpling another requisition. Perhaps the creature was finally starting to understand her dislike for it. Bandit still finished his filing but did it very slowly and carefully, almost reverently, carefully watching her to determine if there was going to be some sort of reaction.

"We have problems," Nel said, trying not to glare at the loompa. "Start walking, we're going back to the ship."

Piper fell into step with her. Though she wasn't short, Nel had to take three steps for every two of Piper's. As he walked, the big man folded the remaining papers in half and stuffed them into his pack. He swung it round in front of him to do so and his actions required a feat of acrobatics from Bandit to keep his seat. The loompa squawked his protest, but for once was ignored.

"What has the captain gone and done this time?" Piper asked with a familiar wariness.

"Apparently he bet the ship in a game," Nel said.

"Betting the ship is not a problem. Losing the ship is."

"Captain always loses, Piper."

Piper nodded. "This is true." He sighed hugely. "So we will be running, yes? Before the ship is getting her new legs even?"

"Haven't got to that part, Piper," Nel admitted. "Right now I just want to get back to her before someone else does. I sent Violet back to warn Quill."

"Ah." Piper rumbled approvingly. Nel grinned in reply. For once the xenophobic Kelpie's prejudices were going to work in their favour. Quill barely tolerated his crewmates; neither of them had any doubts as to what the navigator would do to anyone trying to take possession of the

Tantamount on his watch.

All the same they hurried back to the ship, Piper's tree trunk legs chewing up the distance and Nel hustling to keep pace. She was slightly out of breath by the time they reached the docks and saw the first signs of trouble.

There was a crowd. Crowds were bad—people would congregate to watch festivals, performances, and circuses, but they were drawn in much more quickly by the spontaneity of bad things. Crashes, executions, brawls. Crowds loved a spectacle. A ship given over in a gambling debt and its repossession being contested by the original crew qualified as a spectacle. Given that they were on Cauldron, Nel half expected to see stands being erected and an admission fee being charged.

"Hells," Nel muttered as they started to push their way through the crowd. She let Piper go first. His bulk made it easier going and anyone who protested usually thought better of it. Especially once they got a good look at the tattooed man with the loompa riding his shoulders. Big tattooed men were scary, but not that unusual. Sailors liked tattoos and plenty of ships made up their crew's numbers with ex-cons and less-than-savouries. It was the eccentric ones people were wary of. People missing body parts—eyes, a leg, hands—folk who talked to themselves and held conversations with people no one else could see. Or one's with strange fashion sense; like a man Nel had once met who wore skin-tight smocks over his head likes a mask, or others who used souvenir body parts as accessories.

Mascots, which most people assumed Bandit was, were not uncommon aboard ships and plenty of crews were possessive and protective of their mascots. Again, Nel knew more than one ship that had been burned to the gunnels after incidents involving another ship's mascot. Most people looking at the loompa cautiously made that association.

In Piper's case they were probably right. He was both possessive and protective, and the fact that Nel and a majority of her crew would have happily pitched the loompa overboard in mid-voyage wasn't relevant today. Still, Bandit screamed and shook his tiny fist at anyone who still didn't get the hint. Nel was like an unseen shadow at their backs compared to that spectacle, too normal and unremarkable to register.

There was a commotion up ahead. Nel couldn't see over Piper and the crowd, but Bandit's squawk of alarm made her try anyway. The sound of something smashing, a cloud of dust kicking up while people screamed in alarm.

"Piper?" Nel called out.

"Quill," he replied without preamble.

"Get us over there, Piper, now."

Piper gave a huge roar at the top of his lungs, scattering the people in front of him. They couldn't move fast enough to get out of the tattooed giant's way and Piper ploughed straight through the gap, Nel following in his wake. They reached the edge of the crowd, just shy of the pier leading to the *Tantamount*.

And found themselves behind an armed group. On Cauldron they could only be mercenaries. All were taking refuge behind a stack of crates, clouds of dust and splinters were still settling overhead. The group was a mixture of men, women, and non-human. It seemed to Nel that someone wasn't particular about who they recruited. She saw all shapes and sizes, a seven foot woman with tattoos covering one side of her face, a reedy looking man with glasses, a diminutive Korrigan that looked to be reamed in scars and more Vodyanoy. From that last Nel deduced the group answered to one Ebon Masaius.

Beyond them on the raised deck of the *Tantamount* stood Quill, the Kelpie's tail lashing violently behind him. That and the blue electricity arcing between his fingertips were bad signs. A shipping crate hovered ominously close above him. Ranged behind him along the ship's gunwales were the rest of the crew, brandishing boathooks and other makeshift weapons, all looking equally mean and evil.

Nel wasn't fooled though. Whatever show the crew might put on, they would be no match for a group of armed mercenaries. Self-preservation was holding them back right now, and a healthy respect for Quill's thaumatic abilities, but it wouldn't take them long to get over that and find a way to counter him. Thaumaturgy looked flashy but it was nothing new and couldn't stand up to an armed group by itself.

"I do not see the captain," Piper rumbled.

"Me neither," Nel admitted.

"It is up to you then, Skipper."

"Yeah," Nel muttered. "Hey!" she yelled, causing the group of mercs to turn and face her as she strode to close the distance. She picked Ebon Masaius out from the other Vodyanoy and made straight for him, hand on her sidearm.

Ebon's brows rose when he saw her bearing down on him, but to his credit he didn't flinch, motioning for his group to stay their arms as well.

"First officer Vaughn, I expected we'd be seeing you here. Looks like we arrived before you."

"For all the good it did you." Nel glared at him. "Ugly friends you've got here, Ebon."

"Watch your mouth," the giant woman told her, towering over her employer.

Nel craned her neck upwards. "Hells, Ebon, what are you feeding this woman? Whatever it is, stop. She's too damned big. Big don't make ugly any better."

The woman nudged past Ebon, who looked pathetically small in contrast, before leaning down to shove her face in front of Nel's. "Are you stupid?"

"Just sober," Nel said.

Ebon frowned. "I don't think—"

His reluctance was lost or came too late—the woman raised one meaty fist to pound Nel into the ground. Nel didn't hesitate with her sidearm. There was a flash of light as the wand discharged with a concussive shock and a yell from the woman. The ground shook again as the woman staggered and fell, clutching her foot.

"What?" Nel shrugged at Ebon, who was shaking his head. "I didn't hurt her . . . much. Piper, help the lady up." She gestured.

Piper stooped to help up the woman, who swatted his hands aside angrily, making it back to her feet but clearly favouring the one Nel hadn't shot. Nel was amused to see she was marginally taller than Piper.

"If there's not going to be any more misunderstandings," Nel asked, holding tight onto her wand. Nearby, one of Ebon's minions spun a similar weapon lazily through his fingers, making a show of it. He caught her look and leered.

The discharge from a flick of Nel's wand scattered splinters and loose grit from the dock, blowing the wand clear out of the man's grasp. He grabbed for it, missed, and had to chase after the weapon.

Nel inclined her head towards Ebon. "Like I said."

"Idiot," Ebon muttered, neither flinching nor looking around. The man had nerve, Nel conceded. His lackey stumbled back into position, shamefaced.

"I was hoping to avoid this when I saw you in the bar," Ebon told her. "This could have proceeded much smoother than it has."

"You're trying to take my ship," Nel stated grimly. "Nothing is going to go smoothly about that."

"My ship," Ebon corrected her.

"Horatio Phelps' ship," she corrected Ebon. "I've only your word you won that docket from him. Any transfer of an independent vessel in a neutral port takes place on the vessel and requires the presence of the current and acting captain as well as the new owner."

Ebon's yellow eyes narrowed at her.

"Want to try me on that one?" she asked him. "Places like Cauldron take this sort of stuff seriously. Can't do business off the map if everyone is hijacking everyone else's ships all the time. Fact of the matter is I'm surprised we haven't got the taxman's goons breathing down our necks already. All I see so far are those misfit dropouts you've got working for you."

Nel smiled coolly at Ebon's consternation. "Until my captain turns up, that pretty piece of paper of yours is just that. So why don't we all just sit here nice and quiet like, 'til Horatio deigns to honour us with his presence. I'm going aboard my ship. Don't follow me."

She didn't wait for an answer, leaving Ebon and his goons to stew on the dock. She felt Piper at her back as she strode up the gangway to join the rest of their crew.

"What's going on?" Quill asked, barely concealed irritation in his voice. The rest of the crew crowded round, jeering and making obscene gestures towards the dock.

"I just bought us some time," Nel said, glancing back over her shoulder. Ebon's group hadn't moved from the dock, he seemed to be addressing them. "They can't legally take possession of the ship until the captain gets back. Legally."

"What?" Gabbi exclaimed. "What do you mean, take the ship?"

"Nobody is taking the ship." Quill snapped his sharp teeth.

Nel swept her gaze over the crew. They shouldn't have been surprised at that bit of news. "Where's Violet?" she asked.

"She was with you," Jack rumbled. He had his butchery apron on—it was bloody and so were his hands up to the elbows. He held a savage looking meat cleaver in one hand and looked to be begging for an excuse to use it. Typical Jack.

"I sent her back to warn you."

"She's not here," Jack grunted.

"Then she didn't make it." Nel had to look around to place that voice. It was Sharpe, leaning innocuously in the shadow of the mast beside the rigging stowed against it. She was sure he'd left them. Had he been on the ship the whole time?

"I spotted the group out there," Sharpe went on to say. "They looked ready for trouble and we're the only ship docked out here."

Nel turned to Quill. "And you didn't bother to find out what they wanted?"

Quill shrugged.

"What do we do now, Skipper?" Gabbi piped up.

Nel considered their options. New owners on the dock; bitter, resentful crew aboard a ship not safe to fly. Two crew members missing including the captain, though it was Violet Nel was most worried about. A lot of things could happen to a girl in a place like Cauldron.

She glanced down at the docks. The spectators had dispersed and there was a clear reason why. The tax collectors had arrived with golems in tow. A group of steam gushing constructs led by a member of the Spider's Web. They spent a few minutes talking to Ebon's group before a spokesperson detached himself from the group and made his way up to the *Tantamount*. Quill's tail lashed as the messenger approached.

He called out, "Which one of you is in charge?"

"I am," Nel told him, stepping up to the railing.

The messenger nodded. He didn't ask who she was—possibly he didn't care, more likely it just didn't matter who he delivered his message to. "I represent the Spider's Web, meaning the people who are in charge of this miserable rock. Let me explain to you that it's our miserable rock and you're making a mess of it. There will be no more . . . violence on the docks over your dispute."

"How about violence regarding other people's disputes?" Sharpe said coyly.

Quill laughed. Nobody else did. The messenger did not look amused.

The messenger pointed. "See those golems?" He didn't elaborate.

"Tell them to keep to their side of the dock," Nel said, pointing to Ebon's group.

"They have been told." The messenger frowned. "Ebon Masaius, a person known to us here on Cauldron, offers you the following arrangement. A meeting at one of his warehouses to finalise the arrangements for the transfer of this ship."

"Ain't gonna be no transfer," Jack growled.

"Final transfer requires the presence of the captain," Nel said.

"Ebon Masaius has . . . ," the messenger considered his

next words, ". . . assured us your captain will be present at the meet."

Gabbi scowled. "Ebon Masaius can go jump off the bloody pier."

"He also says you can collect your captain once he has collected his ship." The messenger paused to let that sink in.

There was a rigid silence from the crew.

"You saying Ebon has our captain?" Jack took a step forward.

"Funny," Nel said. "I remember him saying Horatio skipped out before they could complete the transfer. Now we're supposed to believe he's waiting at the warehouse?"

"His words," the messenger said. "You can make what you like of it, as long as there are no more outbursts on our dock."

"One of my crew is missing," Nel said. "A girl."

"A fox-girl," Piper put in.

"She has a tail," Gabbi added, talking over Piper. "A bushy one."

Nel glared round at her crew. "Would all of you be quiet?" She turned back to the messenger. "Her name's Violet, my cabin girl. She's a Kitsune."

"You can post a flyer at any office," the Spider's Web messenger said. "For all the good it will do. People who go missing here tend to end up being put to work, doing one thing or another . . ."

"Skipper," Gabbi whispered, alarmed.

"I know, Gabbi, I know," Nel muttered. Dammit, what had happened to the girl? It wasn't even that far from the ship to the bar. Put to work. That could mean slavery or it could mean worse. Hells. For all she knew Cauldron used Kitsune tails for dusters.

She waved for someone to show the messenger off the ship, not bothering to see who it was.

"What's the plan, Skipper?" Gabbi asked, her round face anxious. "We need to get Violet and the captain back."

"We should take off," Quill snorted. "Take off and leave this place while we still have a ship to leave with."

Gabbi whirled on the Kelpie. "You unfaithful, dried out little skink! Don't you even think that! We are not leaving Violet, or the captain."

"Dead weight, both of them," the Kelpie asserted.

"The only dead weight around here is going to be that fat tail of yours when I chop it off and serve it to you on a skewer!" Gabbi shook her finger at him.

"I would get more meat out of your squelching behind," Quill retorted.

Gabbi's eyes bulged. "Squelching? Squelching!?"

"Stow it, the both of you," Nel said sharply. She didn't issue any more warnings, turning her back on the crew to go stand by the railing. Looking out over Cauldron's bowl, into the heart of the steaming settlement. Somewhere out there were Violet and Horatio. And a whole bunch of other people.

Sharpe settled himself on the railing, his back to Cauldron and facing the crew. He watched Quill and Gabbi's rant with interest. Nel's orders hadn't kept the peace for more than a few moments. The crew was tense. "Those two fight like an old married couple."

"If an old married couple could kill each other just by thinking about it, sure," Nel muttered.

"Maybe she really did try and poison him?" Sharpe suggested.

"Probably did." Right now Nel didn't care if Gabbi really had.

"This meet, you realise it's a trap," Sharpe said. "And an obvious one at that."

"Probably is."

Sharpe chuckled. "Audacious. I like that. Want me to go with you?"

"You?" Nel paused. "Why?"

He shrugged. "I owe you a rescue." He grinned. "And I'm not bad in a fight either."

"Jack thinks otherwise."

"What about what you think?"

"What's your angle, Sharpe?" Nel folded her arms.

"You're not part of this crew, you could have cut and run the minute we made planetfall. Hells, I thought you had."

Sharpe glanced over his shoulder, back at Cauldron. "Not my kind of place, Skipper. Places I'd rather be, people I'd rather be with. Prefer it if I wasn't stuck here. That means sticking with you a bit longer."

"I've got problems, Sharpe. Don't need you being one of them."

"I'm hoping the captain feels differently about me," Sharpe said.

"Why should he?"

"Got to know him a bit during the trip here. Good man. Lousy card player though."

Nel raised an eyebrow. "That's why you want to help?"

"Let's be honest, Skipper," Sharpe said. "Even if you get your captain back, you still have to fix this tub and get your papers."

"Unless we just leave without them," Nel said.

Sharpe shook his head. "Without what? You already vetoed leaving without your captain and your cabin girl. If you leave with someone else holding papers on this ship you'll be declared rogue. That puts you outside the law, not what you want. You can't trade, can't run cargo, and you'll be fair game for anyone and everyone. This ship and this crew aren't built for a life of piracy."

"Know something about that? Piracy?" Nel said pointedly.

"I know ruthless," Sharpe corrected her. "You've got some issues on this crew, that Kelpie navigator and your . . . doctor." Sharpe flexed his fingers, no doubt remembering Jack's no-frills treatment. "But you're not ruthless, not pirate ruthless. Don't think you're gonna cut and run over some bad gambling debt."

Nel stared at him. "Who are you Sharpe? Seems to me we never got around to that part."

He shrugged, rolling muscular shoulders like it just wasn't important. "Who are you, Skipper? We've all got a past, most of it don't make no difference to here and now. I'm here and it's now. You're in trouble, I'm offering to help. You want me or not?" He tried the grin again. *A flash of white teeth, a little charm, a whole lot of man-pretty*, Nel thought. Most people probably said yes to him.

"No."

Nel wasn't most people. She had to admit, she enjoyed the way his face dropped at her answer.

"Gabbi," she called loudly.

"Yeah, Skipper?" her cook answered.

"I'm heading back out," Nel said.

"You just got here," Gabbi objected. "What if those guys come back?"

"Throw stuff at them. Not forks, we need those. I'm going to find the captain."

"And Violet?"

Nel hesitated. "Her too. We ain't leaving anyone. We . . ."

The truth was she had no idea what had happened to the girl and didn't like to think about what could have. But she wasn't losing any of her crew. Not this time.

"Piper," she called, hitching the belt for her sidearm into a more comfortable position. "Here, now."

The big mate emerged from the crew to make his way to her side. "Skipper?"

"Repairs. Details. Gimme," Nel ordered.

"Trolls."

Nel winced. "You hired Troll labour?"

Piper nodded. "Best there is, Skipper. Cheap too."

"There's a reason for that, Piper," Nel said. "They're smelly, disgruntled, they break stuff, what they don't break they eat—"

"You are a very hard woman to please, Skipper," Piper said disapprovingly. "Not as bad as Quill, but very hard."

"You should be used to that by now, Piper. Look, just get the ploughing ship fixed."

Piper looked at her disapprovingly. "Swearing, Skipper."

Nel ignored that. "I'm going to go get the captain."

"By yourself?"

"Yes."

"That is a bad idea."

"The hells it isn't."

Piper frowned. "I am confused. Do you agree it is a bad idea?"

Nel shrugged. "Most of the ideas that come out of this ship are bad, Piper. Mine are just a wee bit little less bad."

"You shouldn't go alone, Skipper. Bandit thinks it is a trap. You should have someone with you for when it gets to the violent part."

"I want everyone to stay here, make sure we don't get boarded or nothing while I'm gone. I don't want to come back and find my ship boarded, Piper, we clear? Don't let no boardings be happening whilst I'm gone."

"Aye, Skipper," Piper sighed.

Nel left her crew, stomping back onto the dock. It was now mostly empty. The crowd had dispersed when it became obvious there wasn't going to be any more fun. She did see the first of the Trolls to arrive, a five foot, greyish-blue skinned individual in a workman's harness and a loincloth. She stepped aside as it ambled up to the gangway.

She shook her head. "Captain's gonna love this."

Chapter 4

The bars and taverns on Cauldron were all alike. Dark, shuttered common rooms that were smoky and badly lit. The light came from the fires in the corners of the room and the smoke gushed from the fires. Those four fires cast unusual shadows across the room and the smoke added to the obscurity.

It was that obscurity that Sharpe moved through, flitting from one table to another. He didn't like Cauldron, he hadn't been lying about that, but there was work that needed to be done and it could only be done out amongst the locals.

He moved from table to table, palming the odd drink when no one was looking. No one noticed; they rarely did.

Here and there in snatches of conversation Sharpe pieced together the local set of affairs. Cauldron was aptly named, a melting pot of people and species, trades and things best left under the table. Things that were whispered about in huddled corners. Things shouted across the room. And things not talked about at all unless you knew what to listen for.

He heard rumours of unrest, skirmishes between factions, races, planets, all the same. People with too little getting desperate, people with too much becoming paranoid, nothing new, nothing that hadn't happened a hundred times before.

The rumours about Grange were interesting. Insurrection,

raiding, and pillaging the neighbour's yard. Poor Thatch. How fortunate there were Alliance forces nearby to quell the situation. What would a couple of border colonies do without someone to step in and save them?

The skipper had surprised him. Her back was up against the wall and she'd still turned down his help. Tough woman. He liked that, made her worth knowing. Didn't mean he was going to just stay aboard the ship and sit by though. The ship wasn't going anywhere without its missing people. And he needed a ride off of Cauldron—he had places to be.

"If I was to go looking for work," he said to Harlem, a man he'd offered a pilfered drink to, "who would be the best person to ask?"

Harlem, a Korrigan like Jack, grubby and unshaven like most others in the den, squinted near-sightedly at him.

"Depends," he grunted. "What sort of work you in the market for?"

Sharpe shrugged evasively. "This and that."

Harlem belched loudly, swathing Sharpe in a cloud of noxious fumes that reeked of stale beer and rotting teeth. Outwardly he didn't react, inwardly he cringed. *Never thought I'd be missing Jack.*

"Gotta be more specific," Sharpe was told. "You want work? So do most who come here. What sort? You a sailor, a workman, a labourer? You don't look the type. You got a trade to sell? Say so 'cause I'm thinking you don't."

Sharpe leaned back, covering his surprise. Two surprises in less than a day, first the skipper and now this guy. Maybe he was losing his touch? He'd picked Harlem because of the stream of people he'd seen coming and going from the man's corner table. Corner tables usually meant someone in authority, or at least well known—they were accessible without being private, meaning you wanted to be seen but needed a modicum of privacy. He'd figured his mark for some sort of middleman. He hadn't counted on the man actually being that smart.

"Everyone has a trade," Sharpe said.

"What's yours then?" Harlem blinked beady eyes at him.

"Getting things done."

"What sort of things?"

Sharpe frowned. "Things people don't want talked about."

Then Harlem squinted at him. "You move stuff?"

"Can do."

"How 'bout fetching?"

"Sometimes."

"Disposal?"

"Been known to happen."

"Look around the room, tell me who you'd be afraid of."

Sharpe didn't look. "Nobody."

"You're either brave or stupid then."

"Neither," Sharpe said. "There's a guy two tables over with a brace of throwing knives under his coat, got no chance of hitting anyone in a place this packed. There's two heavies sitting behind us who kept looking your way every time you talked to someone. Now they don't look smart enough to tie their own shoes without help so they're probably waiting on you to tell 'em what to do. The barman's got some sort of weapon under the bar, probably something with a charge to knock sense into anyone who gives him grief. He keeps reaching for it every time someone gets frisky, dead giveaway."

Harlem blinked. "And?"

"And what?" Sharpe growled, playing up his role as a tough guy. "Every motherless wannabe in this room has got some sort of weapon hidden away, the ones I mentioned are just lousy at hiding 'em."

"All right, so you're observant, I'll give you that. The two behind you, how would you go about dealing with them?" Harlem grinned, showing blackened teeth. "If you had to?"

Sharpe was halfway up and turned around before the man had finished speaking. He saw the two heavies he'd marked out earlier coming towards him. He didn't have to guess about their intent: one had a club out and the other was cracking his knuckles, a gleeful expression filling an otherwise dim face.

Sharpe hooked the stool he'd been sitting on with one ankle, flinging it forward towards the two. Knuckles became tangled up in it, tripped, went down flat on his face to the filthy floor, bellowing. Club paused to look at what had happened to his friend and Sharpe didn't miss the opportunity. He jumped the man, grabbing the club and dragging it down, hooking the man across the face then back again with the elbow. Club swayed on his feet, stunned, but was in no danger of going down. Sharpe hit him again before taking the club from his slackened grip, bringing it down hard on Knuckles' head as the man tried to rise. He went down and stayed down.

Club was still swaying on his feet. Sharpe glared at him, starting to wonder if the man was doped up on something. He was taking more hurt than a Draugr. Sharpe rammed the end of the club into his stomach, doubling him over, before socking it to his chin. Slowly, like a tree toppling, Club collapsed, sprawling on top of Knuckles. Sharpe nodded in satisfaction, observing that what little attention the fight had garnered was now gone. He tossed the club away in the direction of the bartender, a goodwill gesture to the man who still had one hand under the bar, presumably on his own peacemaker. The bartender glowered but his attention wasn't fully focused on Sharpe, rather somewhere past him. Sharpe turned back to Harlem.

To find him floating in the air just above his table, arms flailing helplessly, still glued to his stool.

"Well, ain't that something?" Sharpe said aloud, looking at Harlem curiously.

"Put me down! Put me down this instant!" Harlem bellowed, his face flushing a deep red. The man's windmilling arms tipped him over and he would have fallen if his seat hadn't pitched to swing him the other way. Harlem shrieked.

"Ain't my doing," Sharpe said, chuckling.

"It's mine," a sibilant voice said, the shadow of someone new stepping up beside Sharpe. He was only mildly surprised to see the Kelpie navigator standing next to him.

"You didn't say there was more than one of you," Harlem spluttered.

"Didn't know there was," Sharpe admitted. "You following me, Kelpie?"

"Yes," was Quill's short-tempered reply.

"Appreciate the honesty," Sharpe said.

"This one attacked you. Why?" Quill demanded.

Sharpe shrugged. "Little bit of a test, unless I'm mistaken. I ain't mistaken, am I, Harlem?"

"Put me down!" Harlem shrieked.

"I think he wants you to put him down, Mister Navigator," Sharpe chuckled.

Quill looked at him with contempt. "I dislike Korrigans."A gesture, a snap of blue sparks dissipating, and Harlem sank down with his chair. Quill unceremoniously dropped him the last foot or so, landing Harlem sharply on his chair, off which he promptly fell.

"Didn't think you could float folks like that," Sharpe whispered. "Living folk, I mean."

Quill shrugged.

"Couldn't have done that to the other two a bit earlier, could you?" Sharpe commented.

"Yes," Quill replied.

"Why didn't you?"

"You managed." Quill snorted. "Well enough, anyway."

Sharpe shrugged.

"Yes." Harlem struggled back to his seat, an air of wounded dignity about him. "You can handle yourself, no doubt about that."

"You could have just asked." Sharpe took a seat at the table. Quill remained standing, scowling. *Miserable bunch, that crew from the* Tantamount.

"I recommend you, you need to be the real thing." Harlem shook his head, trying to regain his composure. "Can't take your word for it."

Sharpe glanced back over his shoulder at the motionless Club and Knuckles. "You must go through guys like these weekly."

Harlem grunted. "You'd be surprised." He gathered himself, shooting a resigned look at his two lackeys lying bruised and broken on the common room floor.

"You a two-for-one act then?" he asked brusquely, giving the new arrival a once over. Quill's tailed snapped irritably under the survey, knocking a nearby stool back until its travels were interrupted by a couple of unconscious bodies.

Sharpe could see the man's thinking clear enough. Quill had rattled him and he was trying to get his bearings, work out how much he could risk pushing them, how much of his own cut he could bleed off.

Money, always the bottom line.

Quill turned his scaled head to Sharpe.

"Two for one?" he repeated and Sharpe's stomach sank. The Kelpie was going to screw everything up.

"I am no double act with this fleshy meat bag," Quill ground out through his pointed teeth. "This human does not speak for me."

"Hey, let's not be too hasty here," Sharpe tried to interrupt, fearing whatever was coming next. Harlem was already leaning back, brow creasing in furrows of suspicion.

"In fact," Quill hissed, "if you can have me, what would you want this pathetic monkey for?" The Kelpie glared at the table, shuffling around to face the stool he'd dispatched just moments ago. He gestured and the stool slid back across the floor in a trail of blue sparks. He sat, placing his scaly forearms across the table, clawed fingers interlinking, with a derisive flick of the tongue in Sharpe's direction.

So that's how he did it, clever.

"Missed you too, partner," Sharpe muttered. On the inside he heaved a sigh of relief, a sigh which threatened to turn into hysterical laughter as Harlem took the insults for what it appeared to be: banter between two people jaded enough with each other's company that they no longer even bothered pretending. Those sorts of partnerships persisted for only one reason. They worked.

The Kelpie was quick on his feet after all.

"Well," Harlem leaned forward conspiratorially, "I don't know about that. Seems to me I can think of just the job for two such . . . capable persons such as yourself."

"Capable," Quill repeated, turning to Sharpe. "Yes, yes, the human is quite . . . capable."

"Don't overdo the praise, Kelpie," Sharpe said with a strained smile, trusting Quill would catch his meaning. "Let the man talk."

There were guards outside of the warehouse. There was no other way to describe the group of burly, over-eaters posted outside Ebon's warehouse. They were big, ugly, and bad-tempered, another misfit collection that made Nel think better of her own crew. They were clearly there to scare off trouble as they certainly didn't look capable of chasing it down should it come to that. Their chosen spokesman sauntered and wheezed his way up to Nel, flanked and trailed by his own sycophants. The man was bursting out of his boiled leather outfit, the jerkin ties and material stretched taut over his protruding stomach, a bulge threatening escape at any second.

"You Vaughn?" he demanded.

Nel felt that flicker of distaste she experienced every time she heard her last name spoken. Didn't like her last name, hated her first name, didn't like people who addressed her with either.

She ignored the question. "Where's Ebon?"

"Inside," the goon grunted. "I'm to take your weapon before you see him."

"Not gonna happen."

"Wasn't a question."

The guards stepped forward to relieve Nel of her weapons. They froze when they found her wand pointed directly at them.

"Wasn't a debate either. I'm not giving up my wand," she said quietly.

Sweat beaded on the brow of Ebon's lackey, his eyes

squirming on the tip of Nel's wand.

"I need to take it," he repeated, stubbornly.

"So tell me where you want to take it, then?"

"Come now, there's no need for all this," Ebon's voice broke the deadlock. Nel's target swung his head wildly to look for his boss. She didn't move her eyes.

"Miss Vaughn," Ebon said in his slick, oily voice. "Every time I see you you're threatening one of my employees."

"Hire smarter ones," Nel said, watching the hired help back up to an invisible line behind Ebon. She slung her wand back into its holster. "They keep doing stupid stuff."

"Yes, well," Ebon didn't disagree, "good help is hard to find. Maybe we can help each other out in that regard."

"Doubt that."

Ebon sighed. "I think you disagree with me just to disagree . . . with me."

"Got that, did you?"

"Could we perhaps continue this inside?" Ebon motioned to the warehouse behind him. "There's some things I wish to show you."

"In there?" Nel said pointedly.

Ebon rolled his eyes in irritation, the first genuine emotion he'd displayed. "Miss Vaughn, you've already shown me you're more than ready to shoot first and forget about asking questions. This warehouse has goods, most of them owned by me. They're fragile, valuable, and I don't want them damaged. Believe me when I tell you that inviting you inside poses just as much risk for me as you feel it does you."

Nel smiled, patting the wand at her side. "So long as that's understood."

"It better be." Ebon glared round at his people. "Nobody start anything, understand."

He made sure it wasn't a question.

Ebon led Nel inside the warehouse. Rows and rows of crates were stacked high to the ceiling with barely breathing room between them. The corridors were narrow, just barely wide enough to accommodate the merchandise. Labourers strained with small, wooden wheeled carts to move still more crates about. Space at a premium then. The crates for the most part were wooden shipping boxes, stamped with symbols. Medical symbols, Nel realised.

In one corner of the warehouse on a raised platform, squeezed back from the storage shelves was a makeshift office, with chairs and a desk piled high with papers. Seated in one of those chairs was Horatio, twisting this way and that to try and get away from the guard positioned behind him.

"Nel!" he called, trying to rise. He was shoved back down into his chair.

"Captain." Nel rushed her steps to reach him, only to find herself restrained by a hand to her shoulder. She was spun around, coming face to face with Ebon. Her first instinct was to go for her wand.

"Easy," he anticipated her response, holding up his other hand placatingly. "Your captain is just fine, you can see that for yourself. Now it's time for us all to talk business."

"Take your hand off me," Nel said. "Now."

Ebon waited a moment then with deliberate slowness took his hand off her shoulder. "Can we dispense with the idle threats now?"

Nel was tempted to hit the man. "They're not idle."

"They're really not," Horatio chimed in.

"As you say," Ebon said. "But we have the matter of the transfer of your ship into my hands to settle."

"You're not getting my ship," Horatio hollered. "I'll scuttle her first."

"Ship's beat pretty bad," Nel told Ebon. "You must have seen for yourself. Gonna cost us just to get her back up again. You take her off us, those debts land on you. I'm not paying for you to fly away and leave my crew in this sinkhole."

Ebon smiled. "She's a good ship with a good reputation. She'll fly again."

"Reputation's only as good as the crew and the captain. You take her over and they're both gone," Nel warned.

Ebon considered this. "You're not doing yourself any favours here, Vaughn."

"Not looking for favours, Ebon. And stop using my last name. I don't like having it and I like hearing it less."

"Chanel, then." Ebon switched to her given name.

Nel gave him a flat look. "No."

Ebon shrugged.

"I see my captain but I'm still down one more crew member." Nel narrowed her eyes at Ebon. "You want this discussion to go anywhere you tell me where she is."

Ebon stared at her. "I have no idea what you're talking about."

If it wasn't genuine confusion on his face it played the part well. Nel hesitated. She'd been sure Ebon must have grabbed Violet on her way back to the ship. He'd surely had people watching the tavern where he first hit her up about the *Tantamount*. It was what she would have done.

"Nel," Horatio called, "what are you talking about?"

"Our cabin girl, Violet, went missing after I sent her back to the ship to warn them about you." She punctuated the accusation with a stabbing finger in Ebon's direction, since she was speaking more for his benefit. Horatio couldn't help her right now.

"That had nothing to do with me," Ebon said. "What sort of operation do you think I'm running here?"

"You're holding my captain," Nel reminded him with a growl, tapping her wand hilt for emphasis.

"He tried to run out on a debt."

"I want my crew back," Nel said. "All of my crew."

"And I'm not in the business of kidnapping children."

"And I should believe that?" Nel scoffed. "This is Cauldron."

"And things like that happen here—the Spider's Web control is not as absolute as they'd have us believe—but they are not my doing," Ebon insisted. "If I had the girl she'd be of more use to me in this negotiation than any other I could think of. But I assure you, my operations do not involve such deplorable actions."

"Don't try and sell me on your operation. Are you forgetting I saw that rabble you tried to take my ship with?" Nel said.

"Security," Ebon said.

"What rabble?" Horatio yelped. "What happened? Nel, is the ship all right?"

Nel ignored her captain. "Security has restraint, you had a bunch of hired thugs."

"You get what you pay for, and around here you pay for what you can get." Ebon shrugged. "Do you believe me concerning the girl or not? If not, then we have a problem."

Nel looked to Horatio. He shook his head in a negative. "I haven't seen her, Nel."

Which meant Violet was still out there, alone.

"I believe you," Nel said. "For now. But we still have a problem."

"Which brings me to my next point." Ebon walked over to Horatio and took a seat behind the desk, motioning for Nel to take the remaining chair. She declined and chose to remain standing. Ebon frowned in annoyance but then dismissed the guard standing behind Horatio. The captain squirmed in his chair, finally free to get up but now seeming compelled to stay, at least for a moment.

Ebon pulled a tattered paper out from his pocket, the deed to the *Tantamount* he'd produced at the drinking hole. Nel and Horatio watched as he placed it on the desk in front of him.

"These," he said distastefully, "are fake."

Nel and Horatio exchanged a look.

"But you two already knew that."

Nel folded her arms. The captain laughed manically, almost giggling.

Ebon's eyes narrowed in him. "You tried to hustle me."

"Can't lose what you don't have," the captain chortled. "Besides, you stacked the deck. I saw it."

Ebon pinched the fake papers between his fingers like he was about to rip them in two. "It would be a lot harder to claim your ship now."

"Much harder," the captain agreed.

"It's a difficult decision for me to make," Ebon went on, "as to whether I'd lose more face trying to pursue a claim based on forged papers."

He looked at Nel. "Or letting a gambling debt like this slide. People might think I'd gone soft. I can't have that."

Nel waited. There was an offer coming, one that would have hooks and barbs in it, something difficult to swallow but slightly more palatable than trying to settle a challenge for ownership of the *Tantamount* through Cauldron's convoluted legal system. She knew they were going to have to take it, Ebon knew it, hells, probably even Horatio knew it. They still had to go through the set piece.

"So here's my offer," Ebon started. "You have a ship, I have a claim on it. You do a job for me, I forget about that claim."

"What sort of job?" Nel asked.

"A delivery. I need a cargo sent somewhere that strictly speaking . . . it shouldn't be going."

Nel glared. "Why's that?"

"It wouldn't be . . . to my advantage to be seen playing sides in this matter. Or attracting the wrong kind of attention."

"Why us?" Nel glanced at her captain. "Of all the dubious captains and runabout ships in all the ports . . ."

"Nel," Horatio complained.

"You're currently set for Vice." Ebon leaned back in his chair. "Fully loaded, correct?"

Nel didn't answer. Horatio did, and she sighed. She glared at him but he didn't seem to notice.

"Vice is a peculiar market, very needy," Ebon mused, as though talking to himself. "They like a discreet crew who take good care of their cargo. They like it to arrive . . . unsampled."

"They have the biggest narcotic trade this side of the Free Lane Rimworlds. Let's not be stepping around that," Nel said.

"And you were headed there with an undisclosed cargo," Ebon added.

"Nothing illegal or undisclosed about our cargo," Nel said.

"Legal is a vague term out this way." Ebon shrugged. "Else we wouldn't be having this conversation."

"Got a point?" Nel growled. "Get to it."

"Your ship is thin-hulled for a trader, correct?" Ebon said.

"Seems you know a lot about my ship, Ebon."

"I know she runs cold, good for long runs with perishable cargo."

"There's a war going on near Grange," Nel said, her eyes narrowing. "Thatch. Civil war, messy stuff, bad politics. Lots of money for someone there."

Ebon tapped his hands together softly in admiration. "Very good, first officer," he said approvingly. "Very, very good."

"What?" Horatio said. "What's going on?"

"Take a look around us, Captain," Nel said quietly. "What do you see?"

Horatio arched his neck, trying to look everywhere at once. It popped, loud enough to be heard. "Ow," he exclaimed, reaching up to cradle the back of his neck.

Ebon shook his head. "He doesn't get it."

"Get what?" Horatio complained. "All I see is a bunch of crates."

"Explain something to me," Ebon addressed his question to Nel. "From our first conversation, the way you talked about the *Tantamount* anyone would think it was your own personal property. The crew refer to you as Skipper. And yet," he looked at Horatio with something like contempt, "this man is the captain. A captain who as it turns out walks around with forged ownership papers. He strikes me as less than competent. How has he remained such?"

"Well, see, I have this hat," Horatio started mumbling.

"Captain," Nel interrupted. Horatio shrugged, leaning back on his chair so just the back feet were on the ground.

"We have an arrangement," Nel told Ebon.

"And I have this hat," Horatio repeated, starting to rock his chair and pointing at his head.

Nel sighed, shaking her own head. "It suits both of us."

"Perhaps you and I could come to an arrangement," Ebon suggested.

"Which part of suits both of us was unclear?" Nel retorted.

"Think about it." Ebon smiled.

"Thought about it. Still no," Nel said shortly.

Ebon smiled thinly. "Loyalty, how quaint."

"The devil you know, Masaius."

"Devil," he glanced at Horatio, who smiled back. "Yes. To our delivery then."

"What delivery?" Horatio said in exasperation.

"Medical supplies," Nel told him. "To Thatch." She glared at her captain. "Thatch, imagine that?"

"Grange, actually," Ebon corrected. "Was there something about Thatch . . . Skipper?"

Horatio broke in. "Medical supplies? Which ones? And why Grange? You just said there's a war going on there."

"There is," Nel confirmed.

Horatio turned to Nel, then to Ebon, then threw up his hands. "Fine," he muttered.

"Do we have a deal?" Ebon asked.

"What's the catch?" Nel asked. "Everything comes with a catch."

"Yes, the catch here being that we're going to have to establish some trust for this to work," Ebon agreed. "Now how do you suggest we go about doing that?"

"You've got some suggestions, no doubt," Nel muttered.

Ebon's thin smile was back. Nel was starting to hate it. "How would you feel about leaving your captain here?"

Nel made a face. There was no way she was leaving without the captain. Neither would most of the crew—they'd mutiny at the idea. Most of them hadn't had anywhere to go before the captain had taken them on. *Except Quill*, she thought, grimacing. *Quill and maybe Jack*. They'd probably leave Horatio, Violet, and herself without much more than a second thought. Maybe Quill even fancied himself as captain. He'd hate the job—too much people work involved—but likely he hadn't thought about that. If he had thought about it his solution probably involved long walks off the short end of the ship.

"No deal," she said.

Ebon nodded like he'd expected that. "Then if you won't leave someone here, I'll have to send someone with you."

Nel stared at him, considering the options. "Sure. Why don't you come along then?"

Her response sparked a smile out of Ebon, not a nice one. She didn't think he had those. "Too soon, first officer. You'd have me over the side once we cleared the envelope."

"Oh, she would not," Horatio told him.

"I don't like blackmail," Nel said.

"Nor do I." Ebon shrugged. "Let's not forget I have a legitimate claim to your ship here."

"Not with those papers, you don't."

"The intent was to gamble the ship. The papers, fake or not, are a promissory note." Ebon stared Nel down, daring her to claim otherwise. She dropped her gaze first.

"All right then," she said. "You're sending somebody with us. Tell me about them."

"Of course. But in exchange why don't you tell me about just whose name I might find on the real papers to the *Tantamount*?"

Nel smiled. "Not yours, Ebon, never yours."

It sounded almost like bells but it wasn't. It was the clinking of links of chain against each other. Links that weighted down Violet's arms and legs, made her hands and feet hurt. They'd been put on tight—she thought her hands at least had taken on a darker tinge but it was hard to tell in the dim lighting. Her head hurt and she could still taste something coppery, blood, in her mouth. That might not have been hers though. She'd bitten the hand that covered her mouth as hard as she could when they'd grabbed her. Bitten someone hard enough to make them scream. Scream and hit her 'til she blacked out. There was a painful sort of satisfaction to that last memory.

She'd woken alone and hadn't seen anyone since. But she could hear people moving around. Somewhere outside and she could only tell there was an outside because of cracks of light seeping into her room. Enough to tell there was a wooden door blocking the exit. A wooden door, four stone walls, and nothing else but mouldy straw and her.

But outside she could hear other chains, suggesting she wasn't alone. That first time it really had sounded like the *Tantamount*'s bells and Violet had to repress a sob at the thought. The *Tantamount* seemed far away now. Far away and maybe gone for good—she hadn't gotten anywhere near the ship with the skipper's message. Hadn't been able to warn Quill and the others.

She hadn't even got close, barely more than a street before someone had plucked her off it. How long ago was that now? It was hard to measure time, no way to tell how long she'd been out either. Maybe she could still get back to the ship. Even if it was too late to warn them they must have noticed she wasn't back by now.

Although, maybe they hadn't. Quill wouldn't miss her, she knew that. Nor Jack—maybe he'd regret the chance to order her around and turn her tail into a good luck charm but that was it. Some of the other crew had made it plain they didn't care for her either.

The captain? Would he even realise? Sometimes it was like he didn't know who anyone was, beyond that he was captain of the *Tantamount*. Except the skipper—he always remembered the skipper. The skipper would realise something had happened to her. But would she care? Violet had let her down, and, after all, the skipper had never wanted her aboard the *Tantamount* in the first place.

The door opened with a suddenness that shocked her, a wall of blinding light that turned the world to white. Violet threw her arms up to cover her face even as she heard heavy footsteps enter her room. Straw was kicked into the air and her visitor made sounds of disgust.

"And aren't you the pretty wee thing," he said. The voice was familiar but Violet couldn't place it.

"They say tails like yours are good luck," her unseen visitor said, like Korrigan Jack had. "Guess it didn't do you no good. Hope the next owner does better."

Violet couldn't make out more than an outline—big, bulky, again reminding her of Jack.

"Pretty though," the voice from the shadows said. She felt a hand along her tail. "Gonna be such a waste."

Violet curled up into a ball instinctively. She knew who the man was now, could almost make out his features around the smudges in her vision. She heard him laughing and the hand started to rise higher up her tail. Violet thought of the skipper then, thought of what she'd do. Violet could barely lift her arms and legs, encumbered as they were, but she could still move her head. So that was what she threw forward as hard as she could.

Violet almost blacked out again from the impact, felt a thickening swimming sensation but her actions had resulted in a string of curses from the man. He wasn't touching her tail anymore but a second later he put a hardened boot into her stomach. Violet screamed and curled up again.

She might have been hit again, it was hard to tell. Her darkened world was in danger of slipping out of her grasp. She heard someone moving away from her and caught snatches of conversation.

"What are you looking at?"

There was a reply, words she couldn't make out.

". . . care. Put her in with the others."

As the door slammed shut Violet could make out the outlines of other people, just out of sight. One was familiar to her—she'd seen that silhouette plenty of times before. A Kelpie like Quill. That thought made her unbelievably homesick.

She curled up into a tighter ball, wrapping her arms around her knees and hugging them to her chest. Wrapping her tail over her arms. Something about that gave her pause. She reached down a hand, hesitantly, to her tail. What she found made her eyes widen in the dark.

When had that happened?

The *Tantamount* resembled a monster's playground. Shaky scaffolding framed her skin, a slapstick arrangement of poles and boards that hung together like a house of cards, the only thing holding it upright was its interlocking self. What was more incredible to Nel was the steady stream of troll labour that clung to the scaffolding like spider-monkeys, hammering boards and caulking fittings into the hull. Piper stood on the dock where he could oversee the whole operation and bellow orders to his work crew. His instructions were incomprehensibly repeated by the ever present Bandit, who found himself at home in the tangled scaffolding. The trolls ignored the loompa in the same way as they ignored Piper. Completely. They had their own way of doing things and weren't about to let a monkey or a human tell them differently. They caulked seams and fitted joinery, worked wood with an almost reverent, percussive therapy. Most importantly they had finally removed the mast from the ship's flank.

And Nel had to admit, they did good work. The trolls had references from Troshka, a trollish word, or whatever their language was called, which translated to something like "road of bridges." The group spanned multiple worlds and primarily dealt in bridge building, as their name suggested, but they had branched out into other engineering projects. Boat repair was evidently a lucrative sideline.

Horatio wasn't convinced. He ran this way and that, from the stern to the bow of his beloved ship, stressing every time a troll's hammer struck the hull and pulling at his stringy hair. He was liable to go bald at this rate.

"Cargo's coming," Nel said in an effort to distract him. She pointed at the line of golems marching toward the dock, each steaming construct pulling a travois loaded with crates from Ebon's warehouse. The Vodyanoy sauntered along beside the lead golem, short legs moving briskly to keep up.

"Your repairs seem to be coming along well now," Ebon called once he was within speaking distance. Nel and Horatio met him at the foot of the gangway, the latter almost hopping at the sight of the golems.

"Not on my ship!" he declared. "Not on my ship, not at all, I won't have them. Huge, ugly, loud, noisy, heavy . . ." The list went on, Ebon's brows rising incrementally with each adjective. By the time the captain finished his whiskers were wriggling as well.

"If golems had feelings," Ebon said when the moment arose to interject, "you would have hurt them."

"If golems had feelings they could feel me boot them off my ship."

"They're not on your ship," Nel reminded him. "Captain."

"And they're not getting on it!"

Nel considered the golems. Horatio had a point—each golem probably weighed close to a ton and their stance was wider than the gangway itself. The constructs would have to crab sideways just to get aboard. And that was without taking the cargo into consideration. Some of the crates were big enough to weigh in at several hundred pounds themselves.

"He's right," she said. "No golems on the *Tantamount*. That's a rule."

"A new one?" Ebon asked sceptically.

"Old one," Horatio snapped. "Very old one. Sacred. Sacrosanct, in fact. No golems on the ship. Bad luck."

"They'd never make it up the plank," Nel pointed out. "Just have them pile the crates over there and we'll use the cranes to get it aboard."

"Some of these are fragile," Ebon said. "Delicate, require careful handling. Is your crane operator competent, or should I put one of my people on it?"

"You're getting one piece of shifting ballast aboard my ship, Ebon, that's it," Horatio said. "One passenger. No golems, no crane operators, no one else! No one!"

Nel chuckled. It was nice when she and the captain agreed on things.

Ebon shrugged. "Fine," he said. "But I'll be watching. Any damage to my property and you'll be up for it."

"You're the one who used steam-powered golems to haul his fragile, cold storage cargo to a construction site," Nel reminded him.

Ebon did not look impressed with her logic.

"Where's your bill of lading?" Nel asked.

"Oh, that won't be necessary," Ebon said.

"Won't be necessary," Nel repeated him, deadpan. "It won't be necessary for us to sign off exactly what cargo we received and in what condition we received it in."

"No," Ebon said, "it won't. My associate has the bill, she can inspect the cargo and accept responsibility for the condition it arrives in."

And if Ebon didn't have her and the captain over a barrel Nel never would have agreed to something like that. The deal was getting worse already.

"Let's just get this over with." Nel waved up to the deck of the *Tantamount*. No surprise, there were idle crew members hanging around gawking at the golems.

"Someone get Quill out here, let's get some use out of him!"

Word had spread about the situation and the obligation the ship was under. There had been amusement first at the fake papers, weariness over the captain indebting them yet again, this being the third time in as many years, and then finally resentment at the idea of being saddled with an unwanted passenger. There were odds, a book being compiled, a sweepstake on who would be the one to do the excess baggage in. Rumour had it Korrigan Jack was already sharpening a knife and Quill's name would be top of the polls as well. Nel had considered whether to put a stop to it or not, and she'd decided to wait until she met the woman. If she turned out to be trouble, or a threat to ship or crew, Nel would be the first in line to pitch her overboard.

That was in the books too. Good odds.

"Quill's missing."

That was Cyrus. Probably had his money on Quill.

"Quill," Nel muttered darkly. "Always bloody Quill. Where the hells is he?"

Nobody volunteered an answer, which meant they didn't know. Or didn't want to say in front of Ebon.

"Did you know about that?" she whispered under her breath to Horatio.

"I haven't been here. Didn't you leave Quill in charge when you came ashore?"

"Last time I do that."

"Is there a problem?" Ebon called. He'd taken a seat atop one of his crates, despite his warnings about their fragility. The golems had already built up a substantial pile. The ship was going to be heavy going out.

"No," she said. "No problem."

She waved for the cranes to start loading. Crew came down to handle the dockside work, helping load the crates into the harnesses. A quick jog took Nel up the gangway. It wobbled even under her weight—it would never have survived even a single golem.

"Where's Quill?" She grabbed Cyrus's arm. "Where the hells has he got to this time?"

"I don't know." He shook his head. "Sharpe is gone too, Skipper. Someone said Quill may have gone after him."

Sharpe. If there was one person who irked her more than Quill, it was him. And in the time since she'd last seen him she'd managed to put him completely out of her mind. Out of sight, out of mind, only now he was full front and centre on her thoughts. She'd assumed he would have finally got the hint and jumped ship. Now that it seemed he finally had, her navigator had chosen to go after him?

"Hells," she swore. Sharpe she could do without—he wasn't crew—but not Quill. The ship wasn't going anywhere without its navigator. Most ships the *Tantamount*'s size carried two or three navigators, Quill was the only thaumatic they had capable of navigating. Right now Nel was cursing that fact.

"Skipper," Cyrus said hesitantly.

"What?"

Cyrus winced. "We've got another problem. That cargo, it's not all going to fit."

Nel grimaced. She'd already worked that out for herself. They were already carrying a near to full load with their current payload. Even running empty it would have been a tight squeeze.

It was a problem.

"That's not a problem," Ebon said when she told him.

"How so?" Nel replied suspiciously.

"You can leave your cargo here, under my auspices," he grinned. "It will give you another reason to live up to your side of our bargain."

Horatio fumed over that. But they didn't have a lot of options. Not with a half dozen golems squatting alongside their ship and no navigator to speak of.

"Where's this associate of yours?" Nel put it to Ebon. "I want to know who I'm working with."

"Patience, my dear," Ebon said. "She'll be here. It'll give you time for the rest of your crew to turn up."

Nel glared at him.

"Your crew talk," Ebon said calmly. "Hard not to overhear."

"I'll bet."

"It's ironic really. It just so happens my friend could help us both out," Ebon said.

"They a navigator?" Nel folded her arms at the apparent convenience.

"Something like that." Ebon shrugged. "Could manage a ship your size easily enough."

"You're right," Nel said. "That's ironic. And convenient."

The deal got worse and worse. She didn't like the idea of having anyone's paid man or woman aboard her ship, let alone them being the only capable navigator. That'd be giving Ebon far too much leverage over them. She had to stop herself thinking down that road though, it was only going to be a problem if Quill didn't show up. She wasn't ready to count him out yet.

"Ah." Ebon peered. "Here comes my friend now."

Another golem had appeared at the back of the assembly line that was still carting medical crates to the dock. This one was different from the steam belching wooden constructs that did manual labour on Cauldron. It was jet black stone, obsidian, volcanic glass polished to a mirror finish. The flaring torches set along the dock at regular intervals sent bouncing light off the finished surface. A geyser gushed up in the distance, a pillar of fire that reached twenty feet into the air, lighting up the golem with a cascade of reflections. This wasn't some cheap workhorse, this golem. This one was a masterpiece of craftsmanship, something someone very skilled had put a lot of work, likely years, into forging.

Silently Nel braced herself for the coming storm. She folded her arms across her chest, waiting for Horatio to explode.

"That?" Horatio pointed at the oncoming golem. "That's what you want to send with us? That thing? On my ship? No! Never! Never, ever, ever! I won't have it on my ship! I won't!"

As the golem came closer Nel could see it was not as large as the other golems, not much taller than Piper, though much bulkier. The golem's arms were thicker than Nel's waist and it had no neck to speak of. And it wasn't alone. A woman walked along beside it, small but lithe, red tinted and gold framed glasses perched over a button nose. Straight black hair fell behind her shoulders, held back by an ochre band. The cut of her clothes was fine but with a hint of practicality—men's style, no dresses or skirts for this lass. She had a matched pair of wands riding low on her hips. They might look ornamental but would no doubt be fully functional.

Shifting ballast, Nel had called their passenger. She was already shaking her head at the reference. And it seemed Ebon would be getting two people aboard the ship after all. She elbowed Horatio in the ribs. It wasn't necessary; his tirade had already been cut off.

"Scarlett, so good of you to join us." Ebon waved expansively to the woman. The woman, Scarlett, nodded cordially to Ebon, and pushed her glasses up a fraction of an inch as she looked the *Tantamount* over. She didn't look impressed.

"Which one of you is the captain?" she addressed Nel and Horatio. Her voice had that haughtiness Nel had always associated with the moderately educated, or people who automatically assumed themselves smarter than those they were addressing. She didn't hold out high hopes for liking her newest passenger.

"A curious point," Ebon murmured.

"I am." Horatio thrust himself forward, taking Scarlett's hand in both of his before she could pull it out of reach. She managed a strained smile as Horatio made the handshake last longer than was necessary.

"Horatio Phelps, my dear lady, Captain Phelps, that is, captain of the *Tantamount*, at your service."

Nel shook her head, caught the attention of Piper who had come down to inspect the new arrivals, and grinned. Horatio fancied himself a ladies' man and he could be charming enough, to be sure, but she figured him out of his depth with this one.

"Captain Phelps," Scarlett started to say.

"Horatio, my dear, no need to be so formal if we're going to be travelling together. No need at all." He appeared anxious for a moment. "Uh, Ebon, she is the one you're sending with us, yes?"

"Yes," Ebon confirmed, to Horatio's relief. "Unfortunately, Scarlett, we seem to have a problem."

"What problem?" Scarlet asked, her tone suggesting whatever the problem was it was clearly beneath her notice.

"Well, several problems actually. First, it seems our good captain's navigator has been mislaid somewhere."

"That's not a problem," Scarlett said dismissively, plagiarising Ebon's earlier statement.

"No," Nel said firmly, already feeling annoyed at this

woman. "It's not. Our navigator will be here by the time we're ready to leave."

Or, she thought, *I'll skin the scaly runabout myself.*

"The other thing, Scarlett," Ebon said rather heavily, "is that our good Captain Horatio Phelps here was just telling me about a most inconvenient situation they have aboard the *Tantamount.*"

"What situation?" Scarlett asked.

"They have a strict 'no golems' policy. I'm afraid Onyx here," Ebon reached out and rapped his knuckles on the obsidian golem's shiny surface, "won't be able to go."

"That is a problem," Scarlett said quietly. She turned to Horatio, the poor man wilting under her attention. "Tell me, Captain, is this a deeply entrenched tradition aboard your ship? This discrimination you enforce against my friend here?"

"Friend?" Nel muttered under her breath. No one seemed to hear her.

"Deeply, deeply entrenched," Piper said in his deep voice, to Horatio's consternation. "It is a very old rule, a sacrosanct rule."

"Piper," Horatio squeaked.

"Such things are to be respected," Piper went on to say. "Besides," he added, "golems are bad luck."

Bandit had come down as well. He hovered around the feet of the golem, inspecting it. One of the golem's feet lifted up slowly, covering Bandit under its shadow.

"Bandit!" Piper called. The loompa's head came up but he seemed unaware of the massive weight descending on him slowly. Piper moved with considerable quickness for a big man and scooped Bandit out of harm's way. Nel wasn't fooled—she'd seen the golem, Onyx, moving much quicker when it was coming down the docks. Someone, either Scarlett or Onyx itself, was making a point.

Which brought up one in itself; was Scarlett directly responsible for controlling the golem, or did it have something resembling a personality of its own?

"Bad luck," Piper reasserted. "Bandit could have been

crushed underfoot."

"This is too bad," Scarlett said. "Ebon, we'll have to rethink our arrangement. I don't go without Onyx."

"Well, that's not a problem at all," Horatio blurted out. "Not at all, simple really. That rule, silly old thing, never really even on the books. Old wives' tale, nothing to it. Rescinded in fact, just this morning. Yesterday, maybe even the day before. So there's no problem, no need to think . . . I mean rethink anything. Onyx is quite welcome, won't be discriminated against at all. Except maybe by Quill. But he's not here, so that's not a problem either."

"But you said . . . ," Piper started to say.

"I know what I said!" Horatio interrupted shrilly.

"You said 'no golems on the ship,' Captain," Piper continued.

"Exactly!" Horatio exclaimed. "No golems, plural. Plural Piper, plural, as in more than one. No more than one golem on the ship at a time. And there's only one of Onyx isn't there? Singular, an individual, one of a kind, like his lovely friend here, Miss Scarlett."

"Scarlett. Just Scarlett," the woman said.

"Of course, my dear, of course," Horatio gushed. "Anything your heart desires is my command. Uh, you are singular, of course?"

"I don't have a twin sister, if that's what you're asking," Scarlett said warily.

It wasn't what Horatio had been asking. But now that she'd put the idea in his head he seemed crestfallen that there was only one of her.

"Leave it alone, Piper." Nel put a hand on the big man's arm, recognising a lost cause when she saw it. She appraised the golem, sizing it up. It was small, for a golem anyway, but would still test the gangway.

"We'll have to use the crane to get it aboard," she said. "That all right with you . . . Scarlett?"

"Yes, that'll be fine," the woman said. "I should have some other things around here as well. You can see that they're stored with him."

Nel raised an eyebrow at that but didn't comment. Time enough to lay things out for this woman once they were away from Cauldron. Assuming Quill ever turned up, that was. She was starting to wonder if she was going to have to send people out after him. First things first though. They had a ship to finish loading.

Alone in her cabin for what felt like the first time in days, Nel hefted her wand in one hand. Opposite her was a target, three concentric rings marked in chalk, rubber, and tar against the stern wall of her cabin. The wall was pitted with scorch marks from past target practice. She added another one with a flick of her wrist, slightly off-centre.

The sight brought a grimace to Nel's face. It had been a long time since she'd practiced with any serious intent. The wand in her hand was almost fully charged—the only time she'd used it in the last few months was back on the dock against Ebon's giantess. She checked and found half a dozen charged crystals in a chest under her hammock— the ammunition for her wand. There were other weapons aboard, kept locked and secured in the armoury below decks. Only she and the captain had keys to the armoury. And only the officers were allowed to regularly carry weapons and only Nel regularly did.

She wondered what Scarlett would do if Nel told her to put her weapons aside while she was aboard. The problem was that it didn't matter. Even if she agreed she still had that golem, which by now was nestled snugly in the hold amidst Ebon's cargo. The thing was a walking weapon, solid as . . . well, as a rock, heavy to boot, unable to feel pain, forearms that had protruding blade-like fins. The glass came to such a fine point it'd accidentally sliced through the harness, almost dropping the construct when it was being hoisted by the crane.

Nel grimaced. She was little closer to finding and putting her crew back together. She had her captain back but had lost her navigator. And she still had no idea what had happened to

Violet.

"Skipper!" Banging accompanied the call.

"Sharpe is back," Piper said without preamble once she opened the door. "And he is alone."

"Violet?" Nel asked quickly, not quite registering his words. "Is Violet with him?"

"No." Piper shook his head. "Just Sharpe, no Violet, no Quill."

"Hells," Nel swore. She was going to get to the bottom of this right now. "Where is he?"

"The captain's cabin," Piper said.

"Good." He wouldn't get very far with the captain, not with two crew members missing and a woman the captain had no chance with aboard. If Sharpe thought he was going to slip into a berth on the *Tantamount* on the back of two disappearances he was in for a shock.

Nel burst into the captain's cabin without knocking—the door was halfway open in any case. It was already crowded with three people inside, and Nel and Piper made five, six if you counted Bandit. Horatio looked up, startled at her sudden entrance, knocking over a carafe of wine. It spread out quickly, a dark purple stain on one of his charts, tacked to the desk. Nel didn't recognise the chart but the wine was some of Horatio's good stock. His supposedly depleted stock. Not even off the docks and he was pulling out his best moves already—not good.

"Nel!" Horatio squawked, staring at her. "What's going on? Are we being boarded?"

Nel stared at him before remembering she was still brandishing her wand in one hand. She shoved it angrily into her holster. Out of the corner of her eye she noticed Scarlett was unobtrusively sliding her own weapons back from their half drawn state. The woman was quick.

"No, we're not," Nel said, not feeling inclined to explain further. "You." She turned on Sharpe. "You owe me some answers."

Behind her she heard the door swing shut with an

ominous thud. Piper. At least he was reliable.

"Answers about what?" Sharpe asked, hands in his pockets, looking innocent for all the world.

"For a starter, where the hells is my navigator? Where's Quill?" Nel demanded.

Sharpe blinked slowly, considering the question. He gestured. "Like I was just telling the captain, Quill is back in Cauldron. He's waiting for us."

Hoatio nodded in confirmation. "That was what he was just telling us, Nel."

"Why is Quill in Cauldron?" Nel demanded.

"Because he followed me there," Sharpe said. "Now you're going to ask me what I was doing there."

"Seems a relevant question, seeing as you told me you wanted a berth on this ship," Nel retorted. "Skipping out to find your pleasure in that slum is a strange way to go about it."

"This sounds like an internal affair," Scarlett interrupted them with a theatrical sigh that was too contrived for Nel's liking. "If you don't mind, I'll take my leave, Captain."

"Oh." Horatio's disapointment was obvious. "Well, yes, of course, my dear. Piper, would you show our guest to her quarters? There's a good man. We'll see you later, of course. High tea at the captain's table. I insist."

"High tea?" Nel muttered, but not taking her eyes off Sharpe while Scarlett and Piper were leaving the room.

"Nel," Horatio said, his voice coming clearly and firmly for a change, "you need to hear Sharpe out."

There was a satisfied gleam in Sharpe's eyes. Given his opening, he didn't wait to be asked twice. "I can get your missing girl back."

I can. Your girl. As if Nel was the one who had lost her and Sharpe was the only one who could get her back. There were lots of other ways he could shave said it; I know where she is, I know what happened to her. But no, he'd said he could get her back, him and only him. Which meant there'd be a price attached. Nel didn't have to ask what that was going to be.

"The ship's headed to Grange," she said. "That's not the

same as Marching. Don't think we're going to be making any special detours for you, whatever you've got to say about Violet."

"The two are very close really," Horatio commented. "Easy enough to board a trader heading that way."

"I'm from Grange, originally," Sharpe said. "Grange is fine."

"Then what were you meant to be doing on Marching?" Nel said.

Sharpe rolled his shoulders. "Visiting."

"Visiting," Nel repeated. She didn't buy it but would worry about it later. "Tell me where to find Violet."

"We have a deal then?" Sharpe asked.

Nel swore, not caring about the look on Horatio's face at her language. They hadn't even finished taking on the last deal they'd been forced into, a deal she could connect back to Sharpe with only a little mental gymnastics and here she was about to agree to another one. What were the odds they happened to be headed so close to where he was desperate to go?

"If you were any kind of decent person you'd just tell us about Violet," she said.

"But I'm not," Sharpe said with a crooked grin. "And this isn't any kind of decent ship and crew. I need to get home, and I'm offering you help in exchange for that. That's as fair and decent as this gets."

"Are you sure that's all you're offering?" Nel growled.

"Nel," Horatio said with a frown on his face. He was focused today, Nel realised. One of his better days. Not enough to catch all of what was going on but enough to realise he was missing things.

Sharpe gave that guarded smile of his again. "We could sweeten the pot, if you prefer, Skipper."

Nel snorted. "You've got nothing else I want. Tell me where Violet is and you can have your berth. But if you want to eat you'll pull your weight on the voyage."

"I might be safer not eating." Sharpe pursed his lips.

"Quill is still going on about being poisoned."

"Where are they?" Nel said with finality.

Sharpe became serious, putting the games aside. "There's a slum house on the far side of Cauldron. They're expecting a delivery to go out tonight, hired some extra muscle to make sure it went down smoothly. Quill and I are part of that muscle."

Nel was sceptical. "How'd that happen?"

"We asked. They offered."

"And the cargo?" Nel asked.

"Violet is the cargo," Horatio said.

They both stared at him. His face was sombre.

"I'm right, aren't I? They're running people—women, children," Horatio concluded.

"And anything exotic," Sharpe agreed. "And a Kitsune girl is definitely exotic. That's why they snatched her."

"And this has nothing to do with Ebon and his crew?" Nel asked.

"Are they involved in the slave trade?" Sharpe asked.

"Not that I've seen," Nel said grudgingly.

"Then no, it really doesn't. Just another independent gang running out of Cauldron."

"They might be cutting the Web in," Horatio mused. "Have to be some reason they haven't come down on them. Slaving is bad for business, makes people nervous when people just go missing like Violet did."

"I got the impression it was a very mobile industry," Sharpe said dryly.

Nel sighed. "Not a lot of kids like Violet in places like Cauldron." She should have known better than to let the girl out, certainly better than to let her wander around alone.

"But she was there and now they have her." Sharpe shrugged. "So let's get her back."

"You have a plan?" Horatio asked.

"I'm sure I saw a golem down in the hold when I came aboard. That springs to mind," Sharpe suggested. "Big bruiser like that we could just about walk in through the front door."

"And if they are cutting the Web in that's going to start a bigger fight than we can handle," Horatio said. "Something subtler is called for here."

Nel agreed with the captain. And using the golem assumed, a big assumption in her opinion, getting Scarlett's co-operation. They were indebted enough as it was.

"Will they have noticed you're gone by now?" she asked Sharpe.

"Doubtful." He shrugged. "That's why Quill stayed behind. He's the more visible of the two of us."

"All right," Nel said. She glanced out the back of the ship, through the stern windows at the end of Horatio's cabin. Outside she could see the steam rising from Cauldron's vents, swirling around some of the higher structures. And Old Smoky right in the middle of it all.

"This is what we're going to do," Nel said. "Horatio."

The captain blinked at her.

"I'm going to need you to work some magic."

"Of course, Nel," he said.

"On Scarlett."

The look on Horatio's face was priceless.

CHAPTER 5

In the end Nel and Sharpe left the ship alone, just the two of them. Nel considered taking Piper or even Jack with them, but neither was inconspicuous and her plan depended on discretion. She left Horatio to follow through with his part, trusting in his own nature and a temporary lull in the fog the captain usually lived in. Ebon watched them leave—there was no way they could have avoided that—but he said nothing. She didn't care what he made of their last minute expedition.

Sharpe led the way through Cauldron's twisted streets, taking them off the roads Nel would have taken by herself, away from the main trading districts of Cauldron and into the seedier back alleys where the locals lived. Locals that might spend less time in the area than visiting ships spent at the docks.

And Nel could see why. Cauldron wasn't the most inviting place. Its allure was twisted up in that very fact, that no honest merchantman would set foot on its surface and no official groups operated out of it. And that was where the slavers came in.

There were all sorts of people in the universe. Not just the obvious human, Kelpie, Brood, or any of the diverse peoples Nel had met in her travels. In fact, if there was one thing she detested it was those who categorised people into neatly defined boxes with traits and tendencies. She'd yet to find two

135

people she could define that way, let alone an entire group. People, they were varied. And if there was some sort of scale that could be used to define people in general the slavers came down near the lower end of the scale. But not at the very end, Nel conceded. No, that end belonged to the people that gave slavers and their like purpose. The hedonists and the sadists, the perverse and degraded individuals or masses. The ones who were never satisfied, who always craved more at the expense of others. They were the ones who would go into excess to satisfy themselves. It might be physical or material, psychological or immaterial, it never mattered. They wanted what they wanted, when they wanted it, and that inevitably came at the expense of others.

With this in mind, Nel kept a watchful eye on Sharpe. It had occurred to her that Sharpe could have been setting her up, intending to line his pocket by tacking her onto the end of a slaver's train. Possibly Quill had already undergone the same fate, though Nel pitied anyone stupid enough to purchase the malcontentious Kelpie. Was it a likely scenario? There was a simple way to test those waters.

"Are you setting me up, Sharpe?"

He turned towards her slowly, mildly amused. "Would I do that, Skipper?"

"Don't call me that," she rebuked him.

"What am I supposed to call you?" he said in exasperation. "You have this childish self-loathing for your own names, you've made it clear I'm not on your crew, so calling you skipper is out. And you're not in the Alliance anymore so any sort of rank you might have had is out. Why did you leave the service anyway? You could have made captain by now."

"None of your damned business," Nel snapped.

But Sharpe wouldn't let it drop. "You did more than your compulsory service, stayed on after you earned your voting rights. You were set on the career track. And then you left. Sounds wrong to me. Whose ship did you rig the wrong way to end up here and now?"

Someone on the *Tantamount* had loose lips and Nel didn't care for it. Her past wasn't quite black listed, it was just none of Sharpe's business.

"I had issues with my captain," she said shortly. "No desire to be one myself after that. And weren't you the one mouthing off about the past not being important?"

Sharpe rolled his shoulders in a shrug. "Just curious as to why such a rising star as yourself should change course. The Alliance needs people like you. It's a nasty universe."

"I have a younger brother who was more than happy to fill the void," Nel muttered. A younger brother who came at the opposite end of the scale Nel had been trying to place Sharpe on. All righteous indignation and cynicism was her sibling. But it was the lower end of that scale Nel had to contend with now. Her brother could have the Alliance.

"Here they come," Sharpe lowered his voice.

The further people came down the end of that scale the more excessive, the more depraved their needs and tastes became. And watching the pathetic line of dejection marching through the last of the alleys, Nel could witness the extent of that depravity.

The slaver's line was heartbreaking, a procession of wretched individuals who could be boxed together. They were all broken, physically and spiritually.

From the safe recess of a building overlooking their route, Nel and Sharpe watched the procession. At the back of the line one of the slaves staggered and fell, face down in the dirt. The slaver standing over them cracked her whip without hesitation, not at the fallen slave but at the next one in line. Nel saw blood fly on the air, ripped from the shredded skin of the slave's back. She heard the scream but refused to let herself feel it. The line started to move again, dragging the fallen link with it.

Sharpe shifted to face her, his own face hidden in the falling shadows. This far from the docks the only illumination came from the vents. Those were close enough to Old Smoky to be covered in a thick cloud of smoke and ash.

"Do you want to save them?" he asked, his voice as carefully controlled as Nel felt her face was.

It wasn't a question she could allow herself time to think about. "I'm here for Violet," she said. "The rest of them aren't my concern."

"It's a hard person who lets themselves think like that," Sharpe said.

"It's a hard universe," Nel said bluntly.

"I'm surprised at you," Sharpe commented, studying her. "I expected this to bring out the heroine in you. All this pain and suffering. Are you the same person who dived across the void to save a stranded sailor?"

"I came for my crew, Sharpe. No one else."

"Quill told me a story, about you."

"Then you can tell it to the marines, Sharpe."

"They wouldn't know this one. It was about a bar fight. All the best stories have them."

Nel glared at him.

"This one started with a young boy getting knifed in a fight. No reason for it, just in the wrong place at the wrong time. Maybe said the wrong thing. Except his skipper jumps in to try and stop it happening. This story ends with Quill dragging you out. It's not a happy ending."

"What's your point, Sharpe?" Nel said coldly.

"You can't save everyone, Skipper. And I think maybe that's what you're afraid of. But we can save Violet, we just have to wait for her to turn up."

"I haven't seen her yet."

"Patience is a virtue," Sharpe said. "In a place like this virtues should be cherished. Wait. If we don't see either of them soon, we can try another spot."

The waiting chafed at Nel. Partly because of the memories Sharpe had dragged up. But she'd long since made her peace with that, buried it deep down inside. Her thoughts strayed once to a sandy haired boy who'd once followed her around but she put it out of her mind. There was nothing she could do for him. She was here for Violet. And Quill.

She'd told Horatio to give her two bells, which was what she'd worked out to be the minimum safe time to finish loading Ebon's cargo and get the *Tantamount* ready for flight. Ebon was meant to have taken care of their docking issues, everything bought and paid for, though by now their original cargo was on its way back to his warehouse, a security deposit holding up their end of the bargain.

Once those two bells were up the *Tantamount* would set sail. If Quill wasn't back aboard by then, it would be Scarlett doing the piloting. The port authorities would help with the launching, but once the *Tantamount* was airborne a single navigator could manage the traversing of frictionless space. They only had until then. The halfway mark had already been and gone.

Sharpe grabbed her arm, his fingers digging into her bicep painfully. "There." He pointed towards an intersection below them. The guards had been positioned regularly; Quill was the last to make his presence known, bringing up the rear of the column.

"He looks edgy," Sharpe muttered. "Going to give us away."

"Quill always looks like that," Nel replied, relieved to see Quill for once. "Damned Kelpie can't sit still. Nervous habit. You're sure Violet's down there?"

"We saw her," Sharpe said.

"That was then," Nel hissed.

"And this is now. I'll head down and clue Quill in on the plan, you just be ready with your part."

"Trust me," Nel said dryly, catching Sharpe's eye as he started to make his way down. He paused, but only briefly. Pity.

She watched Sharpe unobtrusively join the line of guards, keeping pace with the slave train. He moved as if he had every right to be there, quietly and confidently, not hurrying nor taking his time. Few of the guards gave him a second look—chances were they'd seen him earlier when Quill and Sharpe were ingratiating themselves into the organisation.

What was his game, she wondered. There was too much cloak and dagger here. He was going to an awful lot of effort just to secure himself a ride. True, he'd seemed fond of Violet, but that didn't seem enough. And the way he'd talked before, he seemed almost disappointed in her unwillingness to act heroically stupid.

Sharpe made his way ahead of the line to where Quill was stationed, again moving as if he was supposed to be there. He leaned easily against a convenient wall, making what looked like small talk with the Kelpie. Quill didn't appear to react much to what Sharpe was telling him, but Nel could spot the telltale lashing of his tail. He got it under control soon enough but it was there to be seen.

Now they needed Violet. They couldn't rescue her if she didn't put in an appearance. And maybe it was because of Quill that Nel was watching, but she saw one of the prisoners in a second upcoming train dragging something behind them. Seconds later she realised it was a tail, ragged and dirty, but a bushy foxtail nonetheless, and the tail was very much still attached to her cabin girl.

Looking to see if Quill and Sharpe had noticed Violet yet, Nel found Sharpe had done his disappearing act again. Quill was still manning his post for a change, she thought ruefully, and Violet was approaching his position.

And that was where the problems started. In the time since she'd been taken Violet had been traumatised. The girl became hysterical, shrieking and running towards Quill as if she were actually happy to see him. Quill looked every bit as shocked as Nel felt, unsure how to deal with the situation. Violet was yelling his name, desperately trying to get his attention. She succeeded in getting everyone else's.

This stage of the plan had called for Sharpe to be the one to get Violet free and away from her captors. That was all torn now. Nel grabbed her wand and started to make her way down towards the ruckus. She saw weapons appearing among the guards: clubs, naked steel, a few wands. Quill backed up helplessly as the slaver guards converged on him. But Quill wasn't helpless—Nel could see the moment when Quill made his decision. Never the pacifist and more than content to settle his affairs with violence, Quill acted, his tail stopping to a slow wave and one clawed hand coming up. The first of the guards went flying, thrown bodily from the scene by whatever loose debris Quill had latched onto.

That settled it for Nel too. She leaned out as far as she dared over the precipice above the streets and rained fire down on the people who had kidnapped Violet.

From that distance the charges from her wand had mostly dissipated by the time they struck their targets, kicking up dirt and dust, singeing skin and hair but not doing any real damage. One man took a charge to the shoulder and spun, tripping over his own feet and falling. But the assault had the desired effect. More than half the guards turned in reaction, convinced they were under some sort of coordinated attack. Wand charges flew towards Nel's position, forcing her to duck back into cover. The people out there had a much bigger punch than Nel's lonely wand. They'd work that out and come for her soon. She leaned out to fire off another quick barrage before bolting for the stairs.

Her flight took her down to the first floor above street level. Cauldron's lean towards sprawling growth worked to her advantage—a running leap took her into the next building at the cost of just a few bruises. She worked her way to the window, to where she thought she should have a view over the intersection.

A shootout was in progress. Quill had thrown loose rubble around, giving himself some meagre protection in addition to the doorway that sheltered him. He was steadily depleting his protection as he pitched rocks at anyone he got more than a look at. The slave train, with Violet in the middle of it, cowered on the far side of the street, opposite Nel's vantage. She couldn't do much for them from here, so where the hells was Sharpe?

She got her answer when one of the slavers went down, wand requisitioned and comrades set upon. Thaumatically charged static flew, kicking up more dust, and another slaver went down. Sharpe stood a dozen feet from the train. Somehow in the confusion of the fire fight he caught Nel's eye, gesturing with familiar signs toward the slavers down the street from him. Before she realised what she was doing, her wrist flicked out, sending charge after charge down the line. Rocks fell from the sky as Quill added his own ammunition. Their position gave them a three point covering, a standard Alliance tactic for attacking a concentrated position. The enemy had three targets to split their fire on, they had just one. It was a tactic Nel hadn't thought about in a long time.

Sharpe had Violet free now. She clung to him as he pushed her along ahead of him, bent low and keeping close to the edge of the street. They reached Quill and kept going, the Kelpie pitching one final rock at the slavers before following them. Quill didn't run well, his backwards folding legs and tail meant he had to stoop low to make up any speed, something he found humiliating, but he still managed to trail the other two.

Nel almost emptied her wand at the slavers, trying to keep their attention from focusing too closely on the escapee. With any luck they wouldn't be that eager to pursue. With any luck they'd stay still and count their losses first. There were reasons Nel didn't believe in luck. The wand felt light in her hand, the charge almost depleted. She eyed the slave train with something gnawing at the pit of her stomach. Sharpe had gotten Violet out of her shackles. She could see them either broken or picked, lying in the torn up street. The chain that kept all the remaining slaves tied together still ran the length of the train. Knowing she was wasting time she took careful aim. The last of her wand's charge made the distance, hitting the chain with a shower of sparks.

She was distracted before she could see if it had made any difference. Someone had made it into her redoubt. She heard the impact of their feet hitting the ground after the jump, heard someone else storming the stairs behind her, felt the air pressure as they charged towards her.

Nel dropped her shoulder, shifting her weight and

driving up with her legs. The man who had been looking to crush her against the wall ending up going over her head and out the window, a shriek followed by a thud as he hit the street below. Between those two sounds Nel saw a familiar face. This time she recognised the oiled hair and pale eyes, though they struck her as odd, upside down and falling as they were. The petty mouth was open wide, meaningless sound gushing out of it. If Nel had had any more charge left in her wand she would have emptied it again straight into that mouth.

But before Brawn hit the ground though, she had already moved to deal with his friend, ducking under outstretched arms and turning back to forcefully introduce him to the wall, the same way Brawn would have done to her. Another body slid limply to the floor—a Kelpie this time, she noted. Some of its teeth had chipped against the wall, crumbling white fragments littered the floor.

No one else seemed to be coming for her yet. She ran, out another window and through the close-knit streets, the route she and Sharpe had worked out ahead of time. How long had it been now? Too soon or too late and this could all fall through.

She found the others at a place she and Sharpe had agreed on. They wouldn't have waited for her had she been late, not that she expected either Sharpe or Quill to have considered the notion. The Kelpie at least seemed in a good mood. Violet, wide-eyed, clung to Nel at first sight. Sharpe was silent, calm. Nel didn't care for that.

"I'm out," she said, holding up her wand, gently extracting herself from Violet's clutches.

Sharpe held up the wand he'd liberated earlier. "Never did like these things." He gave it a tentative shake. Nothing. Not a spark. "Can't rely on them."

"Discuss your affections later," Quill said. "If my ship . . ."

"Your ship?" Nel interrupted.

"You let someone else . . . ?"

"If you didn't keep leaving your damned post!"

"Hey!" Sharpe called. They both turned to look at him. He pointed. "Company."

"We need to move," Nel said, taking Violet's arm. She stopped suddenly. "Violet?"

Violet gave a helpless little shrug, glancing over her shoulder. Where there had been one, there were now two tails. "It's not my fault."

"Later," Nel said firmly. "Move."

They hustled further towards their target. Old Smoky leaned tall against a black pincushion backdrop. The closer they got to the peak the hotter the air became. By the time they reached the base they were drenched in sweat. Nel could feel rivers running down her arms. Only Quill seemed to find it easy going. *Damned cold-blooded Kelpie* was all she could think. With the sounds of their pursuers approaching she didn't take the time to voice her thoughts.

"Now what?" Violet asked shrilly.

"Up," Sharpe told her. This close to Old Smoky the air was filled with ash and soot. It stuck to his skin, leaving trails of black where it met sweat. Caked in ash, Sharpe took on the appearance of a tribal savage, something he wore well. Nel pushed Violet ahead of them and they started climbing.

"Rock," Nel yelled to Quill as he clambered along beside her. "We need a rock." The air was burning in her throat and lungs. She had to spit out a mouthful of soot every few feet.

Quill hissed. A rock bigger than Nel lifted up into the air just in front of them. Quill took a step and the rock sailed back down the way they'd come. There were cries of alarm and pain from within the smoke.

"What'd you do that for?" Nel turned furiously to Quill.

"It was in the way," he said. "So were they."

"You weren't supposed to throw it, you stupid lizard. We needed that rock!"

Quill blinked, once, twice, both sets of eyelids. "Why?"

"You didn't tell him?" she demanded of Sharpe.

Sharpe was helping Violet gain another few feet. "I was busy!"

"Find another one," Nel snapped at Quill.

He looked around the craggy landscape. "How challenging."

They hit the summit, a narrow lip abreast of the billowing crater. It was almost impossible to see with the smoke so thick. Nel could still hear wands discharging below them. It was just pot-shots now, they couldn't possibly have a clear line on. If this worked it wouldn't matter anymore, and if it didn't, then likely it wouldn't matter for long anyway.

"And now what?" Quill rasped. Seemed the heat and the grimy air were getting to him now as well.

Nel held up a hand. "Listen."

"For what?" the navigator cried. He flinched as a stray discharge shattered a rock, showering them all with stone chips.

"Listen!" Nel repeated angrily.

And there it was: ship's bells, chiming away like nobody's business, loud and clear in the smoky air of an otherwise barren rock.

"That's our ship, Skipper!" Violet cried out, her voice chiming like the bells.

"She's flying!" Quill said indignantly. "Without us! Without me!"

"Get over it, Loveland," Nel said.

"Now what do we do?" Quill demanded.

"We get back on board," Nel said.

"How?" Quil spat soot out of his mouth. "They can't lower a bubble inside this envelope!"

The forces present in an actual atmosphere and the turbulence around Old Smoky would smash a fragile bubble to glass splinters. They'd never find a rope or a ladder in all the smoke. But Nel had nothing so impractical in mind.

She grinned. "You're going to fly us out of here, Loveland."

The Kelpie and the Kitsune both turned to stare at her with wide-eyed sooty faces.

"Fly?" Violet said.

"Pick a rock, any rock," Nel told Quill. Then almost as quickly, "A bigger rock!" when he floated a rock about the size of her head into the air.

Quill found a bigger rock, roughly the size of a cart, honeycombed from magma bubbles. He frowned when Nel and Sharpe both jumped atop it.

"Climb up here, Violet," Nel said. Sharpe reached down and pulled the girl up with them. The three of them looked down at Quill from their floating platform.

"I fly the three of you up, yes," Quill concluded. "And what? You throw me a rope?"

Nel shook her head. "Just get on the damned rock, Quill, the *Tantamount*'s not leaving without her navigator."

Awkwardly, trying to keep his concentration focused, Quill put one foot on the floating rock.

"Lower it, Quill," Violet suggested. The Kelpie gave her a dark look for the practical suggestion but let the rock drop a few inches. He stepped on, his clawed feet finding purchase, and Nel and Sharpe pulled him up.

"What's the matter?" Sharpe asked him. "Not stable enough for you?"

Quill bared his teeth, clenched tight against each other. He dropped, clutching at the rock with clawed hands.

"It's different," he managed to say. "Not used to . . . not from here."

"Can you do it?" Nel asked him, feeling a moment of anxiety. If Quill couldn't do this . . . she hadn't thought about that.

"Of course I can do it!" Quill snapped. "Just . . . a moment!"

"There." Sharpe pointed to a dark shadow emerging from the cloud of ash hanging over the cone. "Now or never, Quill. I suggest now!"

"Be quiet!" the Kelpie snapped.

The rock lifted off, faster, erratically. The underside of the *Tantamount* loomed above them, maybe a hundred feet. Then fifty. Thirty.

Nel staggered, a feeling of light headedness striking her. The air was getting thinner—they were nearing the edge of the envelope. Cauldron's air was only truly breathable near the ground, up here it was thin and cut with smoke. A hand steadied her, making sure she didn't tumble off the rock. Sharpe again. He was holding onto her and Violet, feet planted wide to ground himself.

"Hurry, Quill," Nel said, waving Sharpe off and crouching down beside her navigator. He didn't answer but the rock closed in on the *Tantamount*. Twenty feet. Fifteen. Ten. Eight. Five.

Nel looked at Sharpe. He had a good grip on Violet and signalled that he was ready. She took a hold of Quill, shaking him. He started in surprise, his concentration broken. The rock slowed. If they'd timed this better it would have been a simple jump and step onto the deck of the ship. They hadn't. The smooth underside of the hull was barely within reach, without a single handhold in sight. Seizing Quill under the arms, Nel threw both of them at it, pushing against the rock with every ounce of strength in her legs. She felt gravity grab the makeshift platform and start to pull it back down to Cauldron.

For that moment she and Quill hung in the air, it felt like they would be caught between Cauldron and the *Tantamount*. There was nothing below them now but open air and a certain death fall to the ground below. She could almost reach out and touch the ship, her arm outstretched, tips of her fingers scratching at the curved wood, searching for anything to hold onto. There was nothing.

Until the ship's envelope caught her, pulling her against the underside of the ship. Quill grunted as he smacked into the ship beside her. Sharpe and Violet arrived a moment later. The girl grinned over at her, the smile nearly splitting her face in half.

There was another thump. Nel rolled over onto her back, a bizarre experience to now be looking down at Cauldron, with nothing between her and it to keep her from falling. Except the ship's own envelope.

The thump was Piper, looking like a mountaineer with a rope tied around his waist and Bandit perched on his shoulder. He walked across the hull towards them, at an almost right angle to all of them.

He ducked his head at Nel. "Skipper."

"Quill."

The Kelpie was slow in facing her, carefully finishing whatever calculations he'd been making over a chart before he acknowledged her. Professional, still annoying. The Kelpie hadn't been happy at all to find someone else flying his ship. He'd insisted vehemently on taking over the navigation to their next port of call. Scarlett hadn't cared, Nel suspected. She was still on the bridge. Nel had persuaded Quill to let the handover bide until Quill had completed his planning. Nel made a mental note to track the woman down later, to thank her. They were going to be stuck on the same ship for a while. It wouldn't hurt to keep things civil, and technically Nel owed the other woman.

"What?" Quill said eventually.

"What, Skipper," Nel corrected him pointedly.

"What . . . Skipper," Quill repeated grudgingly. She knew the word didn't mean much to him, that was why he so often forgot to use it. To Quill, actions spoke louder than words; the fact that he did what Nel and the captain told him to do, most of the time, was all the respect they were ever likely to get out of the navigator.

Which was what made his sudden camaraderie with Sharpe so puzzling. The two had been almost friendly before. Things like that made Nel suspicious. When things like that involved Quill it made her downright paranoid.

"Violet," Nel said without elaborating.

Quill chuckled. "That was entertaining."

Nel's paranoia flared. "Tell me what happened. How did you find them?"

"You wouldn't rather ask the girl? Maybe Sharpe?" Quill grinned, revealing sharp, dagger-like teeth.

"I'm asking you. Don't make me beat the answers out of you, Quill, I'm in the mood for it."

Quill chuckled again. "The mood suits you, Skipper."

There was no sarcasm attached to the word this time. "You should indulge yourself more often."

"Tell me what happened before I go find my skinning knife," Nel warned.

Quill shrugged. "Sharpe left the ship. I followed him."

"Was this before or after Ebon Masaius tried to board us?" Nel asked.

"After," Quill confirmed.

"So he didn't leave the ship 'til then?"

Quill frowned, a subtle and hard to read expression on his scaly face. "Possibly, maybe . . . I don't know. I didn't see him until he told us about the boarding party. He could have left."

Not very helpful. Nel steered them back to the subject of Violet.

Sharpe had already told Nel his side of the story. But she trusted Quill's word more than she ever would Sharpe's. The Kelpie didn't lie. He just didn't care whether people believed him or not.

"So you followed Sharpe. And he led you to Violet? Did he have something to do with—"

"No," Quill interrupted. "He did not." Again that chuckle— Nel was getting sick of it. "He sought out a man, a fixer, claiming he was looking for work. They attacked him."

Nel folded her arms. Better. "How did he handle himself?"

"Well, Skipper." Quill nodded approvingly. "Very well."

"So he didn't need any help?"

Quill shrugged. "I helped, he didn't need it."

Nel sighed. "What sort of work was he looking for?"

"The sort that would get him off-world. Whether he intended it to be in the same fashion as the fixer had in mind . . ." Quill shook his head ruefully.

"What?" Nel pushed. "What happened?"

"The fixer liked what he saw. Sharpe was after work, his new friend arranged it. He had someone take us to the stocks, said they were going to move some cargo to a private port on the far side of Cauldron. Part of that cargo was your cabin girl." Quill snorted, even now he didn't seem to regard Violet as of any particular importance. Which made his actions all the more puzzling.

Quill said, "We put on quite a show for Sharpe's new friend. His friends thought to do well out of us."

"As guards," Nel concluded.

Quill chuckled, a rasping sound from deep in his throat. "As trade goods."

"As slaves?" Nel was genuinely surprised. "They tried to take Sharpe?"

"Tried to take both of us," Quill said dryly. "I helped, remember. I should have known better."

Nel saw red, hand clenching around her wand. "When we go back to Cauldron to pick up our cargo you're going to point the rest of these people out to me, Quill."

Quill shrugged. "You would have cared?"

"You're my crew, Quill," Nel said bluntly. "Nobody touches my crew. You know that better than anyone."

A moment's awkward silence.

"Yes, well," Quill's tongue flicked out, "they were spending so much time congratulating themselves on how much money they were going to make out of us they were slow to actually restrain us. Sharpe," Quill hissed with mirth, "Sharpe said that in a situation like that, you always kill the mouthy one who bleats out his plans before enacting them."

"You killed them then?"

"One or two," Quill said. "No one who would be missed if we had to go back to Cauldron."

"How many were there?" Nel asked.

"One or two."

Nel snorted. "Of course. Both mouthy?"

"Very," was Quill's dry response. "In any case I went back, took my place as a guard. Sharpe went to get you."

Nel stared. "You went back? After they tried to capture you?"

Quill shrugged. "It might have been the two mouthy ones' own plan. If it wasn't . . . likely they would have hesitated before trying a second time, at least until they found out what happened to the first two."

"That was risky," Nel said.

"We didn't need long. Just long enough for you to come and play at being a hero, Skipper."

"Hells, Quill." Nel shook her head. "You did as much to rescue Violet as I did. You and Sharpe."

Quill looked annoyed. "We killed the mouthy ones. The rest was coincidence."

"You took the biggest risks. You're a hero."

An angry hiss. "Enough."

"Can you imagine what the rest of the crew will say?"

"The rest of the crew do not need to know."

"That you rescued Violet? The girl you claim to despise?"

"That is not funny."

"Don't worry, hero," Nel chuckled. "Your secret's safe with me."

Quill gave her a level look, his tail thrashing violently behind him. "Humans," he snorted in disgust. "Worthless, ungrateful gutter trash. You should be locked up and put down, the lot of you."

"That's never going to happen, Quill." Nel grinned. "Not with people like you around to look out for us ungrateful humans."

"It was unintentional," Quill snarled. "Sharpe was not out looking for the girl, it was pure chance we happened across her. He was looking to find the first ship off-world that would take him. Serendipity fell into his lap."

"I knew that," Nel said. "I just wondered if you did."

Quill stared angrily.

"Sharpe came back to get me because you were there, otherwise we'd never have heard. You pricked his conscience. So really it's all because of you."

"Maybe I intended to go with him," Quill growled. "Escape this vermin infested ship."

Nel grinned. "I doubt that. You might not care for the vermin, but you do care for the ship."

Quill shook with barely restrained frustration. "This is not funny."

"No, it's heroism," Nel said as her parting words.

Quill called out after her, loud enough for most of the ship to hear. "This is not funny! This was never funny!"

A small, dishevelled person threw themselves on Nel, wrapping limbs around her. Violet was all arms, legs, and tails. Nel had to pry her off. It took her a few moments.

"Violet," she said, giving the girl a quick look. She was dirty, with a few ugly bruises she hadn't had this morning. Someone had made a half-hearted effort to clean her up and comb her hair, probably Gabbi as Nel couldn't see Jack bothering. But her eyes were still bright and she . . .

"Violet," Nel repeated, "do you have more than one tail now?"

Violet twisted, peering over her own shoulder. Yes, Nel could see the girl had two tails now, two bushy fox-tails doing laps, chasing each other.

Violet shrugged self-consciously. "It happens."

Did it? Nel hadn't known that. Was it stress related, a maturity thing? Was it temporary? One more thing to look into—Kitsune physiology wasn't her strong point. Besides, she had other things more pressing.

"What happened to you, Vi?" she asked.

"Sorry, Skipper." The cabin girl's face fell. "They got me."

They. The memory of Brawn's face as he fell away from her returned. Brawn, who had met her and Violet at that checkpoint. She hadn't thought anything of his crass remarks about Violet at the time, anything more than the usual gutterside trash talk she'd expect on the docks at somewhere like Cauldron. Had he taken an interest then, or was it just opportunistic of him later on, finding Violet alone and vulnerable? Even worse was the nagging guilt that he might have done it as a way to get at her. But when had Brawn become involved in something as degenerate as the slave trade anyway? She'd been at a low point that night she'd first met him, no denying that, but had her judgement been that off?

"Skipper," Piper's voice interrupted.

Nel saw Piper and Sharpe had come up.

"I'm wondering," Sharpe opened. "Who brought the big rock? The one stowed down in the hold that's all bright and shiny."

"Personal cargo, belongs to our newest passenger," Nel said.

"Impressive," Sharpe commented. "Wish I had a rock that big. But I thought I was your newest passenger. This ain't the easiest ship to book passage on."

"We had a deal," Nel said. "That's the only reason you're here."

"Because I brought your stray puppy back." Sharpe grinned at Violet. "Earning my keep so far, aren't I? What'd the big rock's owner have to do? De-barnacle the keel? Volunteer to taste the soup first every night?"

"The soup is fine," Piper said. "Though there could be more of it."

"Let's hope the big rock doesn't want any then," Sharpe said.

"Rocks do not eat soup," Piper told him pointedly.

"No, they probably drink it like everybody else does," Sharpe agreed. "Have you ever tried sticking a fork in soup? Very messy."

Piper considered this. "You are a very strange little man."

"I'm not little, you're just big. Too much soup." Sharpe poked Piper in the belly with one finger for emphasis.

Violet laughed. Even Nel shook her head ruefully. Piper, despite his quirks, was easy enough to get along with, Violet impressionable, and the captain delusional. But even Quill seemed to have warmed to their marooned stray. And if there was one person on the *Tantamount* she could depend upon to dislike every other person it was Quill. The only thing he seemed to like was the ship and navigating it.

"Has Quill laid in our course, Skipper?" Piper asked, as if he could read the tangent of her thoughts.

"Yes," Nel said. "We're on a direct course. No more stopovers. Now how are the repairs holding up?"

"Well, Skipper," Piper assured her. "Trollish guarantees. But I still want to inspect them some more, ensure there are no leaks." He nodded to each of them, patted Violet on the shoulder, an affectionate gesture that made the girl's knees buckle, and left for below decks.

"Like trolls themselves," Sharpe commented. "Not pretty but durable. And damned hard to get rid of. Just as well you didn't let any of them hire on."

"You did not hire on," Nel reminded him.

Sharpe grinned. "The pleasure of your company is all the payment I require, Skipper." He winked at Violet as he spoke. "So, next stop is Grange then?"

"Grange," Nel confirmed.

"Grange?" Violet echoed. "Where's that?"

"That's where I'm from, little one," Sharpe said with a gleam in his eye. "The stories I could tell you . . ."

"Later," Nel interrupted. "Violet, you've got duties. Get to them."

She made to go herself.

"Vaughn."

Nel stopped, head half turned, already grimacing at the sound of her name.

"She's Guild," was all Sharpe said.

Nel paused. "You're not talking about Violet."

"No."

"And how do you know Scarlett is Guild?" Nel asked over her shoulder. "Until a moment ago you didn't even seem to know we had any more passengers." She turned to face Sharpe.

Sharpe blinked slow, unassuming eyes at her. "She is."

Nel hesitated. "I know."

The unspoken question hung there between them, neither quite willing to offer up the source of their recognition.

"I served in the Alliance," Nel said. "I worked with the

Guild sometimes."

Sharpe raised an eyebrow. "The Alliance only asks for Guild help if they can't avoid it. They consider it a last resort. An embarrassing one, at that."

"It's been known to happen."

"On unlisted, secret missions, certainly." Sharpe nodded. "What exactly did you say you did for the Alliance?"

"I was a sailor. And I never said."

"A sailor who worked with Guildsmen?"

"Even the Guild can't sail the void on their own. Someone has to fly them to where they're going."

"True enough." Sharpe shrugged, letting the issue bide.

"So why does a beat up ship like mine running a mercy load of medicines to a backwater warzone rate a Guildswoman, Sharpe?" Nel folded her arms.

"That's funny," Sharpe said. "I was going to ask you the same thing."

"How did you make her as Guild, Sharpe?"

Sharpe stared at her, still smiling. "Keep an eye on her, Skipper. You can never tell with the Guild."

Nel glared at the small of Sharpe's back as he walked away from her. Murderous thoughts flashed through her mind, briefly, but she considered it a good thing for Sharpe that she didn't have a knife on her person at that moment. Sharpe was doing it to her, just as he'd done it to the rest of her crew. Getting her to open up. And she was ready to throttle him for it.

Nel found Scarlett descending the stairs from the bridge, having relinquished the helm to Quill. Behind the woman, Nel's navigator fussed over his territory, brushing imaginary dust and smudges from fixtures. He paced from one railing to another, suspicious, no doubt, of what had happened to his ship in his absence. He gazed critically up at the *Tantamount*'s bulging sails, easing the pressure on some, intensifying it on others.

"Your crewman doesn't seem to like me much," Scarlett said dryly.

Nel shrugged. "Quill doesn't much like anyone. Quill likes ships, this one in particular. Far as he's concerned no one else could ever do right by her."

"Typical sailor," Scarlett agreed. "You'll explain to him this was a one time arrangement?"

"He wouldn't have it any other way."

"Good."

"A moment." Nel stopped her from turning away. The woman regarded her though tinted glasses. That irked Nel for some reason—she couldn't tell what colour the woman's eyes were. Was that where she took her name from? The rose tinted glasses, though the colour was darker than that in fact. Or were the glasses a play on her name, an affectation?

"I appreciate you helping out. It means something, to myself, the captain, and the crew, that we were able to leave Cauldron with all the souls we landed with."

Scarlett considered, pursing thin lips. "Suppose I hadn't been at hand to navigate the ship. What would you have done?"

The question took Nel by surprise. "Improvised."

"Improvised," Scarlett repeated thoughtfully. "How so?"

"I won't leave my crew behind," Nel said. "Not in a place like Cauldron, not ever."

Scarlett seemed to accept her answer. "I can admire your dedication to that." She paused. "I hope you'll show the same resolve in the rest of our dealings."

Nel felt her brow furrow at this. "We'll get you to where we're going, you can feel assured in that."

"Good," Scarlett said. "I'm going to retire now. We can speak later."

She left Nel pondering. Nel was still pondering when Horatio wandered past, a bottle of brandy in one hand, a pair of goblets in the other.

"Nel, there you are," he said. "Where have you been?"

"Busy." Nel frowned at the bottle. She'd thought the captain almost out of liquor. He must have restocked on Cauldron. If he'd run true to his usual tastes he'd likely run up another sweat-inducing debt to do so.

"Busy?" Horatio thought about that, then brightened. "Violet, how did that go? Did we get her back?"

"Yes, Captain."

"Excellent, capital. Give her my regards, will you? Or should I do it? I could do it. Where is she? We did bring her along this time, didn't we? Wouldn't do to have left her in Cauldron after all that. Didn't feel right at all, launching the ship without you and the others. Especially Quill. Imagine flying a ship without a navigator, who knew you could do that?" Horatio marvelled, looking down at the bottle he was holding.

"Seen Scarlett, Nel?" he asked, still looking at the bottle. "Was thinking I'd offer her a drink, now that she's done flying the ship. Wouldn't touch a drop before, sensible woman, don't drink and fly, terrible things might happen. Might as well let the golem fly. Ugly thing, isn't it? Still, it comes well recommended. Knows how to keep quiet too—some people around here could learn from that."

"Captain," Nel hesitated, reluctant to say anything. "I need to ask you something."

A flash of irritation crossed Horatio's face. Instant suspicion.

"About Scarlett," Nel said.

"What about her?" Horatio was almost hostile.

"Captain," Nel said. "We almost didn't make it to the ship. If we'd missed—"

"Nel," Horatio interrupted. "You never miss."

Nel smiled. "But if we had . . ."

"We would have turned right around and come got you, of course. Silly question, girl. What did you think we would have done?"

"With Scarlett flying the ship . . ."

"My ship," Horatio corrected. "I'm the captain of this ship, the captain of the *Tantamount*. She goes where I tell her. And she doesn't go anywhere without her skipper and her navigator." He eyed the bottle again; remembered something. "But even so, I must offer Scarlett a thank you libation. Ta-ta for now, Nel. We'll talk later."

"Skipper," yet another voice interrupted Nel's thoughts as the captain left to pursue his hopeless romantic leanings.

"What?" she said roughly to Quill's coarse inquiry.

"We have work to do," the Kelpie navigator reminded her. "The ship needs us."

Chapter 6

"So now you have two tails?"

Violet was torn between a sigh and a grin. "Yes, Piper, now I have two tails."

"Will you . . ." Piper hesitated and inclined his head at Bandit who was hanging above them in the stacks of cargo under the hold. His eyes caught the light of the glowstones. "Bandit . . . wishes to know . . . will you be getting more tails?"

"Bandit wishes to know?" Sharpe raised an eyebrow from his reclined pose amongst sacks of grain.

"Bandit is curious," Piper asserted. "Neither of us have seen creatures with more than one tail and we have travelled to many places."

"Met a lot of Kitsune, Piper?" Sharpe asked him.

"Not with so many tails, no."

"Well, how would you know? When she wraps them up like that you can hardly tell there's two of them."

"You are saying many foxes have many tails then?"

"Would you two stop talking about me like I'm not even here," Violet said crossly.

"Sorry, you're right," Sharpe apologised. "So how many more tails do you need before you go home?"

Violet scowled at him.

"That's why you don't see Kitsune with more than one tail,

Piper," Sharpe explained. "All the grown up ones go home."

"We do not," Violet told him, annoyed at the way Sharpe was lecturing her about her own people.

"So says the voice of age and experience?"

Violet aimed a kick at Sharpe's foot. He just laughed and pulled his legs out of the way.

Piper stopped moving cargo around. He was checking the caulked seams in the bottom of the hull. "If you are growing up then will you be leaving us soon?"

"Leaving?" Violet made a face. "Piper, it's not like that."

"Course it's not," Sharpe agreed. "She's not going anywhere. Not 'til she grows up and takes over being skipper of the *Tantamount* herself."

"Oh, shut up," Violet said. It was one tail. One! Back home there were decrepit elders with as many as nine. Nine tails and full of their own misguided self-importance. She was in no hurry to be like that, even less of a hurry to be back home. One day, maybe, but not now.

"Do you?" Piper asked, distracting her.

"Do I what? Piper, I'm not going anywhere. This ship is my home."

Bandit chirped at her from up in his perch.

"Bandit says he wants to be the skipper next," Sharpe translated.

"No," Piper said, "he said he hopes Violet is not the next skipper."

"Bandit!" Violet exclaimed. Bandit flinched and fled to Piper's shoulders as she jumped to the skipper's defence.

"The skipper is a good woman," Piper said, reaching up to comfort Bandit. "A good woman but maybe not a good example. Not for you."

"Interesting." Sharpe sat up. "What makes you say that?"

"Yeah," Violet said heatedly. "What makes you say that?"

"The skipper is a hard woman," Piper said slowly, considering each word before he said it. "She does what needs to be done. She does what the ship needs to be done."

"What's wrong with that?" Violet asked. The way Piper

said it made it sound like there was something wrong with it.

"Ah." Sharpe nodded. "I see."

"See what?" Violet said.

Piper rolled his shoulders uncomfortably. "This is not a good topic," he said, looking away.

"I've heard a name since I came aboard," Sharpe said. "Thyme."

Piper sighed, louder.

"Before me," Violet said quietly. "People don't like to talk about it."

"The skipper does not like to talk about it," Pipe corrected her. "Quill will not talk about it. The captain . . ."

"What happened to him?" Sharpe asked. "Seems I've never heard that part of the story right."

"I was not there," Piper said.

"But you know, don't you, Piper?" Violet said. "If the skipper would tell anyone it would be you."

"I do not," Piper said firmly.

"Three people went into that bar," Sharpe said. "Two came out. The two the ship needed most."

"What are you saying?" Violet turned quickly on Sharpe. "The skipper wouldn't . . . she . . . she . . ."

"Is a hard woman." Sharpe glanced at Piper.

"That wouldn't happen," Violet said angrily. "The skipper wouldn't. She came back for me. She didn't leave me on Cauldron."

"As did Quill," Piper reminded her.

Violet hesitated. That . . . had surprised her.

"So who made a decision, back in that tavern?" Sharpe said aloud. "Quill or the skipper?"

"It does not matter," Piper told them both, with a sense of finality. He rose, further indicating the discussion was over.

"You," Piper placed a firm hand on her shoulder, "are part of the ship. The skipper's crew. She does whatever she needs to do for her crew. The skipper is a good woman, Violet. But she is not someone you should try and be like."

"I thought you were her friend, Piper," Violet said, not

believing what she was hearing.

Piper sighed. "I am. And sometimes she is my friend. But the rest of the time she is the skipper just as the captain is the captain."

"What about the captain?" Violet said.

"All of us," Piper pointed to Sharpe as well, "are here because of the captain. Even the skipper is here because of the captain. But the captain is a better captain when the skipper is around."

"And that's the moral of this otherwise depressing story," Sharpe said brightly to her. "Have you grown another tail yet from all this wisdom?"

High tea. Nel had thought the captain was simply being grandiose to show off in front of Scarlett. It turned out he had every intention of following through on his words. Gabbi had muttered dark things under her breath about the extra work, enough that Nel had taken her aside for a quiet word of her own, not wanting a repeat of whatever had happened with Quill. She was relieved she had done so after the captain insisted she attend. Quill was tasked with running the ship, a situation he was only too happy with once he learned that Scarlett would be out of the way—the Kelpie navigator was still irritable about having another thaumatic aboard who could fly the ship.

Not as irritable as one Korrigan Jack, who had been drafted to serve the courses. Or even as much as Nel, who found herself seated alongside Sharpe and opposite Scarlett, with Horatio taking the head of the table. Four was seemingly the minimum for High Tea. The captain was dressed in his official best and Sharpe seemed to have begged, borrowed, or scrounged a clean shirt from someone more or less his size. Nel still wore her work clothes, her form of silent protest against being included in the affair and having come straight from her watch.

Awkward conversation also appeared optional. It was

left to the captain to fill in the long silences.

"We'll be passing through the Caleuche Lane on our way to Grange," the captain commented, swirling his drink in idle thought. "The stretch is notorious for ghost ship sightings. More than the rest of the surrounding sector put together."

Nel groaned as she reached for her drink. "Not with the ghost ships again, Captain."

"They're not uncommon," Sharpe leaned over to say. "Plenty of ships keep drifting even after their crew abandons them. Some places do it deliberately, set ships out on the long voyage as part of a festival or funeral."

"I don't like the term," Nel muttered after a mouthful of liquor. "Gives the wrong impression."

"Hid out on a ghost ship once," Jack rumbled as he deposited a platter of cheese and breads, most not even mouldy yet. "Air gets stale on them after a while. Was stuck there 'til this salvage group came by."

"Then what happened?" Sharpe asked.

Jack stared at him. "What do ya think happened?"

"We appear to be missing the soup, Jack," Horatio pointed out.

"Soup's coming, Captain," Jack said. "I only got the two arms."

"No soup for me," Sharpe said quickly.

Jack gave him another look before going to fetch the soup.

"You don't like soup?" Horatio asked.

"Heard some things, Captain, and your man Jack worries me some," Sharpe admitted.

"Jack?" the captain repeated. "Jack is harmless. Anyway, as I was saying, the Caleuche Lane, marvellous place. Most interesting stories come out of it. I'd think you'd be quite interested, Castor, seeing as how we came about you yourself."

Sharpe craned his neck the way Jack had gone. "Maybe I will have some soup," he declared.

"Found adrift on an Alliance frigate," Scarlett spoke for the first time, looking up from pushing a morsel around with her fork. "Seems to me I haven't quite heard the whole of that story."

"Not much to tell," Sharpe said. "Missed most of it myself, truth be told. Asleep in my bed at the time, next thing I'm being rescued by our gallant skipper here."

"Asleep. That's interesting," Scarlett commented, studying Sharpe.

"Fact is I'm a bit of a layabout," Sharpe admitted. "Lazy and unproductive, that's me."

"That's what the crew say," Nel agreed. "Never around when duties are handed out."

Sharpe gave her an injured look, but didn't try to argue. He did have a reputation for being scarce when there was work to be done, though so far his reputation from Cauldron was holding him up. Nel didn't expect that to last much longer if he kept shirking his turn at duties.

"I heard a rumour once." Scarlett leaned back as Jack returned with the soup, allowing him to deposit the steaming bowls amidst the diners. "About a ghost ship."

"Silly things, rumours," Sharpe said. "Never trust them myself."

"Depends how they get started," Nel said. "Please, go on."

"It was about a ghost ship, the likes of which the captain mentioned. It may even have been from this area, but I remember it wasn't like others. Unlike other ships that drift forever through the void this one would twist and turn, it would shy away from other ships like it had a mind of its own."

"So it was a living ship?" Sharpe asked. "That's different." He took up a spoon, looking suspiciously at his soup. Once Jack had left, he whispered to Nel, "Is this safe to eat?"

"You don't eat soup, you drink it," she said dryly.

"Funny. Swap bowls with me?"

"No."

"I remember hearing about a ship like that," Horatio mused. "A ship with a mind of its own. Very difficult to steer it was."

"Not quite like that, Captain," Scarlett dismissed his

fancy. "This ship had a crew, as ghostly as the ship itself. A crew that seemed to want desperately to avoid all others. But every once in a while another ship would get close enough to see across her lines."

"And what did they see?" Sharpe took a cautious sip from a spoonful of soup.

"They saw the crew," Scarlett said. "And they were all dead."

"Dead?" Nel repeated.

"As in ghosts?" the captain asked.

Scarlett shrugged. "Something like that."

"Wouldn't that be something." Horatio sighed, glancing out through the open doorway. Nel found herself following that look, seeing the miasma and stars surrounding the *Tantamount.* "I can think of worse things than spending forever out here."

"Can you?" Sharpe's eyes came up. "Like what?"

Jack stuck his head through the doorway, holding a kettle in his meaty hand. He looked sternly round at the patrons of the High Tea.

"Who wants coffee?" he asked.

Sharpe covered his cup with his hand reflexively. He had the decency to look abashed when Nel shook her head at his reaction, but he kept it there all the same.

"No coffee," he said. "Not for me."

"I'll take some, Jack." Nel held out her mug, grinning at Sharpe as Jack poured and steam rose from the vessel. She raised the hot drink to her lips as Sharpe cringed.

One down, Nel thought. She turned her attention to her other passenger. Something she'd intended to ask since the woman came aboard. "That friend of yours in our hold is one of a kind, Scarlett. Never seen the like before."

Scarlett sipped at her drink, not responding. Nel leaned forward over the table, planting one elbow. "Something that pretty must have cost a bit. Where'd you find it?"

"Maybe," Scarlett took a moment to polish her glasses, "he found me."

"I'd be interested in hearing that story some time," Horatio said. "Surely a fascinating tale, don't you think, Nel?"

Nel didn't answer, considering Scarlett. The woman stared right back at her, replacing her glasses with delicate attention. Scarlett and Sharpe, both reminded Nel of the other, both had that damned annoying habit of avoiding personal questions in wild chases that led nowhere. Nel wasn't prepared to bite this time. They had secrets, fine, neither could have anything that could do any harm to the ship or its crew out here. And once they reached Grange both of them would be off her ship. Until then she'd watch them.

A noise to her side distracted her. Sharpe poked at his food with a fork, pushing it around on his plate. Nel shook her head ruefully. At least she'd found Sharpe's weakness—she'd never seen a pickier eater.

A loaf of bread tucked inside her shirt, Violet found herself scaling the rigging again to the heights of the *Tantamount*. There were no sailors to wriggle past this time. The sails were set to Quill's exacting specifications and were unlikely to need much adjusting any time soon. The *Tantamount* had a long run to Grange, but they were fortunate that it didn't require a lot of deviation around obstacles or through highly trafficked lanes.

None of which comforted Violet as she climbed the last few feet and rolled herself into the crow's nest, landing in an ungraceful tangle inside. Looking up, she found Sharpe huddled against the nest railing, looking miserable.

"I feel awful," he told her, just to confirm it.

Violet gave him an equally miserable look. She hated being in the nest. "I brought you some bread." She pulled the loaf out and tossed it half-heartedly towards him. It landed next to him and Sharpe rolled his head to stare at it.

"I'm not hungry anymore."

Violet made a face. "You made me climb all the way down and all the way back up."

"It's not my fault the skipper stuck us here," he protested.

"It's not my fault you won't eat anything Jack's had a hand in," Violet said.

"I don't want to get poisoned," Sharpe said groggily. "That would be bad."

"And this is better?"

"Poisoning is . . . less better?"

"I hate you," Violet said. She crawled to the edge of the nest, throwing her arms over the side. It was harder to breathe up here. The air was thinner and didn't pull you down as strongly, all of which combined to make her feel queasy. She barely noticed when Sharpe joined her.

"There's Jack there." He pointed. "Why do you lot call him Korrigan Jack, anyway?"

Violet gave Sharpe what she hoped was a withering look.

"It's like saying Kitsune Violet or Kelpie Quill."

"That sounds stupid."

"My point exactly."

Violet groaned. "If I get sick, I'm blaming you," she said.

"If I get sick, I'm going to aim for Jack," Sharpe confided.

"You'd hit Gabbi too." Violet pointed at the two of them walking across the deck. "You don't want to do that. You really don't."

Sharpe turned his head to follow them. "Ever notice how everyone on this ship is paired up? Gabbi and Jack, the skipper and the captain. Bandit and Piper."

"That should be Piper and Bandit."

"I wonder if Piper really thinks he can talk to Bandit," Sharpe mused.

"Of course he can't really talk to him," Violet said.

"But do you think he knows that? It's the same with the skipper and the captain. They can both pretend, but it's just for show."

"Pretend?" Violet asked.

"About who's in charge." Sharpe smiled.

Violet thought about it. "Which one of them is Bandit?" she asked.

Sharpe chuckled. "There's Scarlett," he pointed.

Violet laid her head down on her arms. "Which one of them is in charge?"

"Well, she wouldn't get on the ship without the big rock, what does that tell you?"

"I don't know," Violet said, her stomach heaving as the ship listed to one side. She put a hand to her mouth and willed herself not to throw up.

"Think about it then," Sharpe said. "Take your time."

The last thing Violet wanted to do was think about it. She was sick of thinking, thinking made her feel sick and she just wanted her stomach to stay put.

"That leaves you and Quill," she said when she felt it was safe to talk again.

"Hardly," Sharpe said. "Quill and the ship from what the skipper tells me, but not Quill and me."

"You and who then?"

"You and me, obviously, little princess."

Violet covered her mouth, her stomach rising again.

"And after I rescued you," Sharpe grumbled, misinterpreting her response. "I hope you and your tails are very happy together then. Just remember who sat up with you and held your hair back when you were at your worst."

"I am going to be sick," Violet moaned. Leaning further out over the nest she felt a hand by her head, holding her hair back. And below her she saw Jack making his way back along the deck.

"Two ships pass each other in the night sky, faceless and blind to each other, unawares of the other voyager in the midnight miasma."

"That, Piper," Nel said, "is why we have signallers." She hefted the main forecastle signaller atop the bow mounting, grunting with the effort. The contraption was heavy but too awkward for more than one person to heft. The muscles in her arms, one heavily tattooed, the other bare skin, shook with the effort. Once the signaller was in place Violet reached in and hit the striker, trying to light the gas flame inside.

"Have to open the valve first," Nel pointed out to her. "Otherwise the gas can't get out. Not all the way, just a little."

They were a week out from Cauldron and had sighted another vessel out in the miasma. Ships traditionally ran lights when the miasma was thick. Space was vast but there was always the chance of colliding with another ship, particularly along the more travelled lanes and nearer the busier systems. But it wasn't unusual to go for weeks or even months at a time without encountering another ship. The path Quill had planned out to Grange wasn't expected to carry heavy traffic so the crew had been slow to react to the sighting. The signaller hadn't even been put back into place since their repairs at Cauldron and had to be dug out from deep in the hold.

"The odds of meeting kindred souls in such vast blackness," Piper mused.

"It's just another ship, Piper," Violet said. "You needn't be so grand about it."

"The little one does not appreciate the fortuitousness of such chance meetings," Piper said, gazing out at the other ship. It was of a comparable size to the *Tantamount*, probably another independent trader. Since there weren't a lot of other systems out towards their heading, apart from Thatch, there was a good chance the other ship had been there. It was good sense to exchange news and tidings when meetings like this occurred.

"You looking to find your soul mate on her, Piper?" Nel grinned at the third mate. It was rare to see him without Bandit. She didn't know where the rodent had got to but at least it was away from her. With any luck he would get caught trying to pilfer stores and get himself skewered by Gabbi. Likely he'd end up pitched over the side or served up as Quill's dinner after such an encounter.

"Destiny brings what it may, Skipper," Piper said, his words coming just as the pilot light caught, dividing the forecastle into red and green coloured halves. The white face of the tricoloured signaller was pointed out towards the other vessel.

"They already hailed us," Nel said to Violet. "Invited us aboard. Signal them that we accept and start prepping a bubble."

Violet worked the signaller, Piper prompting her when she hesitated for too long. She was still struggling to remember the colour coded signal language used between ships. To graduate from cabin girl to a fully-fledged crew member she had to become fluent in that language. And that was only one of the things she had to master. Nel restrained herself from laughing at all the work Violet still had ahead of her.

"Was that right?" the girl turned to her and asked.

"Close enough," Nel said. "Quicker on the short flashes next time."

Violet nodded intently. She grinned at Piper. "Skipper says I got it right."

"The skipper said you were close," Piper corrected.

"Close enough," Violet countered.

"Am I missing something?" Nel asked.

"Piper said if I got it right he'd tell me what his tattoo means."

"Which one?" Nel chuckled.

"The one with the bare-chested fish woman," Violet said.

"Fish woman?" Nel repeated, looking at Piper. She knew the one Violet was talking about and knew it to be found on Piper's left calf, normally hidden out of sight. She also knew the story behind the tattoo—it was not one Piper would be comfortable relating to the cabin girl.

"Keep it clean," she told them both. "I don't want to hear otherwise when I get back."

Nel made her way to where other crew members were prepping one of the bubbles for use, leaving Piper to talk his way out of the hole he'd dug himself. The *Tantamount* carried three of the glass constructs, one for each side mounted crane and one spare. It was only in emergency or extreme situations, like coming across another wrecked ship, that all three were deployed at once. Only one was going to be used to take Nel, and whoever else she chose, across to the other ship.

Sharpe leaned over the rail, studying the other ship. He stood a short distance away from the crew readying the bubble. "What do you think?" he asked her without turning. "If it came to a fight, could we take her?"

"And why would we need to do that?" Nel asked, her hand unconsciously straying to her wand. She'd been wearing it since they left Cauldron, an old habit that had been finding familiarity with her again.

"There is such a thing as pirates, Skipper," Sharpe reminded her.

"That is not a pirate ship," Nel said, drumming her fingers along the haft of her wand.

"Because they're not flying the colours? What self respecting pirate would?"

"She's laden—look at the way she's moving. Pirate ships run fast and light. They don't shift like they've got golems dancing in their hold," Nel explained.

"Yes." Sharpe grinned. "I noticed that too. But there's always the exception. Or a rogue that's already carrying a prize cargo."

"If they're carrying a prize they're hardly likely to start a fight with us," Nel said. "Pointless to take a risk like that if you can't fit the gains away."

"Maybe they're looking to pick up another ship. That'd be a prize in itself."

"Unlikely. Sharpe, do you honestly think that's a rogue out there?"

He shrugged. "No. But you didn't answer my question. Could we take her?"

"Ship to ship, we're both loaded to the gunnels, packing light cannon. We could take pieces off of one another all day without doing serious damage. We're both slow, it would be a tug race before someone got away."

"And up close and personal?"

"We have a golem on board." Nel shrugged. "They'd be hard done to beat that."

Sharpe's gaze focused on a point above and behind Nel. When she turned, she saw Scarlett on a higher deck. Like Nel she carried her weapons in full display. Like Sharpe she was engrossed in studying the new arrival. And it was hard not to notice how the rest of the crew avoided her, the hustle and bustle flowing around some invisible envelope centred on her. The veneer of appreciation hadn't taken long to wear off their passenger. Scarlett had been aloof from the crew and made it plain she had no interest or intention of cultivating friendships. The *Tantamount* was a means of transportation, her only concerns rested within its hold.

"Scarlett's got twice as many wands as you and a golem," Sharpe commented in that same musing tone. "Could you take her?"

"She's on my ship," Nel growled.

Sharpe chuckled. "Alliance teaches their marines to treat everyone as a potential opponent. That sort of training never goes away."

Nel glared at him. She didn't care for what Sharpe was implying. "And what sort of training might you have, Mister Sharpe?"

"Castor."

"I prefer Sharpe," Nel replied. "It's less personal."

He grinned. "But you're asking me personal questions. You should at least use my first name."

"I'll use your first name when I know the first thing about you, Sharpe."

"Well, then." Sharpe straightened up.

"Skipper!" Cyrus called from down the ship, near the crane. He'd be operating the bubble. "We're ready for you. Anyone else coming?"

Nel glanced at Sharpe. Tempting as it was to put him in his place by dragging him along, she didn't fancy being in a confined space with him. She thought briefly about taking Violet as part of her continued education, but decided against it.

"Jack," she replied to Cyrus's query. "Someone go find him and tell him to get himself down here."

"Aye, Skipper," the answer came. Swift footfalls on the deck told her someone was double timing it to find Jack.

Jack made his appearance shortly, not looking too happy about it either. She remembered then that he wasn't too keen on bubbles. Not a phobia, something more manageable. Which Jack wasn't when it came to him doing things he didn't enjoy. If looks could kill, Jack's would have cracked the bubble.

"I don't want to." His voice was morose and petulant.

"Too bad," Nel said firmly. Jack was hired muscle. There were plenty of people she would have happily sailed without, but Jack was the only one of her crew who gave her chills. Maybe it was his prison markings or his cold and unusually small eyes. Maybe it was just that he was almost undeniably psychotic. He liked Gabbi, so he worked with her, mostly did what Nel said. Beyond that . . .

What was it that Sharpe had said about sizing everyone up as a potential opponent? Nel had been doing that to Korrigan Jack since he first stepped foot on her deck. The fact that Jack did what Nel told him was likely because he assumed Nel would come out on top in a fight. Ncl had a feeling that if she ever backed down in front of Jack, ever let him get his own way or push her around, she would stop being the biggest, toughest dog around in his eyes. All assumptions went out the window at that point.

"Get in the bubble, Jack." She slapped his shoulder in passing, moving ahead and climbing into the bubble first. It was a deliberate challenge. If she'd waited for Jack to go first she'd effectively put him in charge. Go first and he had to follow or admit he was afraid. More afraid than his skipper. That wasn't allowed in Jack's world. And so he followed her into the bubble. Cyrus joined them inside and closed the hatch behind him.

Compared to the last time Nel had ventured out in a bubble, the trip was almost pleasant. At least there were no floating corpses and debris to worry about this time. Nothing more than banks of miasma that seemed to wrap themselves around the bubble. Cyrus steered them towards the other ship, getting close enough to make out the name.

"*Jeopardy*," Nel read aloud. "That mean anything? Anyone recognise it?"

Cyrus shrugged. "Can't say as I do, Skipper."

"Jack?" Nel asked.

"Naw, just another fancy name to me," Jack grumbled. He held tight to a wheel, trying to keep his feet planted on the floor of the bubble.

Nel nodded, tracing the intricate letters through the glass with one finger. There was no reason the name should have stood out, she would have been more concerned if it had. There were thousands of ships out there. Infamy was not something one often desired.

"Bringing us into formation, Skipper," Cyrus informed her.

Bringing a bubble aboard another ship was slightly more complicated than docking with its own mothership. It essentially meant linking the two vessels with the cable attached to the bubble. While it was possible to detach the bubble from the cable and hose, it was hardly desirable. The *Jeopardy* would winch them in with their crane, Nel and Jack would disembark, and Cyrus would stay with the bubble, trailing alongside the *Jeopardy* a short distance away to prevent their trailing lines from getting snagged. An awkward system, but it worked, and that was what counted.

Nel shuddered as they were pulled into the *Jeopardy's* envelope. She made herself stand still as gravity returned and the crew worked to equalise the different pressures. Her ears started to hurt and a moment later she felt them pop. Finally, the hatch opened, and she and Jack climbed out.

The ship's captain met them immediately. A middle-aged man with dark hair down to his shoulders, or it would have been if it hadn't been tied back in a seaman's ponytail. His face was weathered, suggesting he'd spent a fair bit of time in harsher climates.

"Captain Demetri of the *Jeopardy*," he introduced himself. "We've just come from Leopard, on our way to Eden."

"Nel." Nel shook the offered hand, finding it firm and solid. "First mate of the *Tantamount*. This is my crewman Jack. We're on a course for Grange, most recently out of Cauldron."

"Cauldron?" Demetri's demeanour changed. "Odd choice of port for an honest trader."

"Not so odd as necessary," Nel reassured him. "Our ship hit some debris a few weeks ago. Cauldron was the only port we could safely make for repairs. It wasn't a scheduled stopover on my captain's part."

"Captain . . . ?" Demetri probed.

"Horatio Phelps," Nel supplied. Demetri acknowledged this but without recognition. No alarm bells from her ship or captain's name. It was a pleasant change.

"I'm surprised at your last port of call," Nel said. "Leopard to Eden is hardly a common route. Not on the line you're on."

"Yes," Captain Demetri said. "I was about to tell you, since you're headed to Grange. You're aware there's a war going on?"

"I am," Nel said. "We were contracted to deliver medical supplies there in fact."

"Noble," Demetri said approvingly. "The trouble is there's an Alliance blockade around both Thatch and Grange. We were carrying food stores for Thatch and they turned us around."

"Why both? Grange and Thatch?" Nel asked. "I thought Grange was the one at war."

"At war with Thatch," Demetri said. "Odd that you didn't know that, being contracted into a war, as you are."

"It was a last minute arrangement," Nel muttered. "What else can you tell me?"

"Not much," Demetri admitted. "We tried to negotiate with the Alliance but they wouldn't budge. No one gets in or out until the conflict is resolved."

"I didn't know either of those two had Alliance connections," Nel admitted.

"They don't," Demetri said distastefully. "The Alliance is

looking to expand."

Nel chewed on her lip. It sounded like they were walking into a complicated situation. While personally she wouldn't have cared if they were turned back at the border by the Alliance she doubted Ebon would consider that acceptable. And he had his inside woman on Nel's ship, Scarlett and her pet golem. That might not go down so well either. She'd have to talk to Horatio about it when she got back. They had some thinking to do.

"What else can you tell me?" she asked the captain of the *Jeopardy*.

"The war's been going on for a few months." Nel gestured at a map showing the disputed territories. It didn't make a lot of sense. There was Thatch, a backwater planet if ever there was one. Rural, pastoral, the type of place that would drive Nel to drink just to pass the time. She couldn't imagine the planet having anything else to offer.

Grange wasn't much better. In fact it was a smaller version of Thatch, a satellite colony orbiting the planet, probably survived on mining or some other primary industry, exporting compressed impossible-to-find-elsewhere bits and pieces.

It would be some rare or exotic substance found only on that particular planet, or perhaps more depressingly, some more common but still essential product. Ether came to mind—there was always a market. It was needed for ships and centres like Cauldron, for weaponry like wands and cannons. If there was a profit or even a potential for profit there would be some ragtag, frontier group willing to try for it. How many times had Horatio hired out the *Tantamount* to haul cargo for groups like that? Nel had lost count.

"What started it?" Horatio looked up from the map. "The war?"

"No idea," Nel said. "Probably something minor, some local issue that flared up. Important to them, no doubt, pointless to the rest of us."

"It must have been something." Horatio frowned. "There aren't a lot of people out this way, not according to these charts, anyway. Thatch, Tribute, and Pale. A few thousand people between them. There's Marching and a few other settlements not worth the names planet-side on Thatch and out in the Rim. And Grange. Everybody out there is probably somebody's cousin."

"Inbreeding doesn't generally lead to great thinkers, Captain," Nel said.

Horatio grimaced. "Family squabbling doesn't usually lead to war, either."

"Doesn't it? I can think of any number of times that historically it has," Nel said pointedly.

"All right, fine," Horatio huffed. "But not out back in parts like this. Grange and Thatch probably can't even survive without each other, Grange for a certainty. There's no way a settlement like that is self-sustaining. Have you talked to Castor about this? He was on his way to Thatch when we found him."

"Aboard an Alliance ship, who we now find are blockading the system. You don't find that at all odd?" Nel asked.

"Should I?" The captain folded his arms. "What are you getting at, Nel?"

"I don't like this," Nel stated. "It all feels wrong to me."

"You're just being silly, Nel," Horatio dismissed her concerns, fussing with his hat. "We'll arrive in a few days, make our delivery, and be on our way back to Cauldron to pick up where we left off. A few weeks late but there's no help for it."

"And the blockade?" Nel asked. "Suppose they won't let us through?"

Horatio's forehead wrinkled, the captain's confusion causing the pit of Nel's stomach to drop. It was happening again. Horatio traced constellations on the maps spread out between them with his finger. "Blockade?" he said. "No, that shouldn't be a problem, shouldn't be a problem at all."

"Captain?"

"You'll see." Horatio smiled brightly. "It'll all work out, Nel. All work out. You'll see. Just be patient, have a little faith."

Nel sighed. "Aye, Captain." She started rolling up the maps. "I'll take these back to Quill before he comes looking for them."

"Yes, yes, of course. You do that, Nel. I should get to work. Paperwork, always some to do, isn't there?"

"Aye, Captain." Nel sighed again. "Always some."

She took the charts and left the captain's cabin, closing the door behind her. She took a moment to steady herself, leaning back against the outer wall with her eyes closed.

"Not a good day, Skipper?"

Nel opened her eyes, saw Gabbi. The stout woman inclined her head towards the captain's cabin.

"No, not a good one," Nel admitted.

"Yours or his?" the cook asked.

Nel didn't answer.

"Ah," Gabbi exclaimed. "One of those."

"I need to get these to Quill," Nel said, holding up the charts. "He'll have a fit if anything happens to them."

"All right," Gabbi said. "If you see Jack send him my way and tell him I said fresh. He's meant to be making stew and I still can't work out where he's put some of our stores. All the stuff in the hold seems to have moved."

"Fine," Nel agreed. She climbed the stairs to the bridge, where Quill was on watch. He'd been pulling longer shifts lately, still trying to make up for someone else having launched the ship from Cauldron. It meant shorter shifts for the other watch-standers, so for once Quill was finding favour with his shipmates.

"Here are your charts." Nel held them out. Quill took them stiffly, with a quick glance for any damage they might have incurred. They were swiftly stowed in a cylinder that went into a satchel draped over his shoulder.

"You're welcome," Nel muttered. "Seen Jack?"

"Below," Quill said.

Likely he was getting Gabbi's stores then. Still, Nel had rounds to make and that included below decks.

"You look perturbed," Quill commented

Nel snorted. If Quill was getting concerned about her, she must really look a sight.

"It's nothing," she said. "How long 'til we reach Grange?"

"Two days, possibly three to the planet itself," Quill said. "I won't know its orbit for another day yet."

"Good enough. Carry on."

"Skipper." Quill inclined his head.

Nel made her way below decks, pausing to let her eyes adjust to the reduced light. She moved slowly at first, thinking the layout had changed since her last rounds. It shouldn't have changed throughout their entire trip but sometimes cargo shifted. The only obvious difference was where their foodstuffs were stored, the pile gradually diminishing as the bells tolled. Still, some things seemed different this round.

She passed Onyx, the golem nestled amongst their cargo from Cauldron. The golem was directly under the lattice, crisscrossing, dappled lights patterning its upper body, the lower remaining shadowed. The golem, as far as Nel could tell, hadn't moved at all since it had been hoisted onto the ship. Whether it was waiting for the journey to be over, some command from Scarlett or something else entirely, the construct appeared entirely lifeless and inanimate now.

"You must have stories," Nel said quietly, standing in front of the golem, studying it. The light danced across its polished hide as her crew went about their duties above deck. "The tales you could tell me . . ."

She started at a sound, half drawing her wand as she turned. She heard cursing, recognised Jack's voice. Nel glanced at Onyx, half expecting the golem to have become alive, as if her misapprehension could cause it to spring into action. But it hadn't. If the golem had triggers, her safety and concern didn't seem to be amongst them.

"Jack!" she called out angrily.

"Yeah?" the big man replied. "That you, Skipper?"

"What in the hells are you doing?"

"Banged my knee," Jack complained. "It hurts."

"Take a light, that's what they're there for," Nel said. "Gabbi was looking for you. Supplies for tonight's stew. She can't find them."

"'Cause I ain't got them yet," Jack grumbled. "Where's Bandit?"

"Bandit?" Nel shook her head. *Everybody's looking for someone today.*

"Yeah, he was just here. Where'd he get to?"

"Jack, why are you looking for Bandit?"

"I wasn't," Jack grunted. "Was looking for meat to put in the stew."

Nel snorted. "Don't let Piper hear you say that. Or Quill. You'll give him ideas."

"What ideas?" Jack glowered at her.

Nel shook her head in resignation. There was no talking to Jack. "Never mind, Jack. Grab those supplies and get topside. Gabbi's waiting on you."

"I know she is," Jack growled.

"And she said to tell you only fresh stores. No poisoning the crew."

"I know," Jack grumbled. "That's what I'm doing."

Nel shook her head as Jack fumbled his way towards the stairs, leaving to make the rest of her rounds.

Violet had found a seat at the forecastle, legs dangling over the edge as they passed a nebula. Passing was a relative term, Violet conceded, as the nebula was an unfathomable distance away. In fact it was only a break in the miasma surrounding the ship that let her see it now. Looking out at all the mist made her glad she didn't have Quill's job of navigating through it.

"Move over," the skipper told her, shuffling Violet aside when she didn't move fast enough to suit her mood.

"Pretty," Violet commented.

"Such an understatement." The skipper shook her head. "Infinity above, eternity below, us just stellar dust on a solar wind. I've heard it said that nebulas are the artwork of gods on the canvas of the void. You're looking at something vaster than I can even comprehend, something divine. And you call it pretty."

Skipper's stealing Piper's best lines. Lucky he ain't here to hear.

"Very pretty, then."

The skipper chuckled. The woman's mood made Violet think she might get away with a question.

"What do you think of Scarlett?" Violet asked.

Something in the way she said it made the skipper sit up and take notice.

Not good thoughts then.

"What do you think of her?" the skipper asked instead.

"Sharpe watches her." Violet shifted, holding onto the rails tighter. *Sharpe watches everyone.* "I don't think he trusts her."

The skipper hesitated—maybe it was the reference to Sharpe. *She has never liked him, not since he came on board. Didn't stop her on Cauldron though, just like Piper was saying.*

"You know Scarlett is Guild?" the skipper said suddenly.

"Guild?" Violet repeated. The name was familiar, with some dark connotations.

"Sharpe didn't mention that part then," the skipper said.

"No," Violet said. "What do you mean Scarlett is Guild? What's the Guild?"

"The Guild is . . ." The skipper hesitated, seeming to struggle for an explanation. Violet expected her to dismiss it as another too complicated subject but she pushed ahead. "The Guild is a contractor. A specialised one."

Violet frowned, confused. "Like us?"

The skipper grimaced and shook her head. "Imagine you have a job that needs doing, you want something retrieved from the other side of nowhere. You want something made but have no idea how to make it, what you need, or how it's done.

Imagine you have a problem and the person to solve it just doesn't exist. That's what the Guild is."

Violet nodded slowly. It made sense. A very vague sort of sense.

"The Guild is who you go to when something needs doing," the skipper said. "The harder the job, the more complicated the problem, the more likely it is to end up at the Guild's doorstep. They don't come cheap, but they get things done."

"So Scarlett is part of this Guild?" Violet craned her neck, looking around the deck.

"Yes."

"So what sort of problem is she solving on our ship?"

The skipper chewed on her lower lip. "Everyone uses the Guild," she said. "Alliance, free traders, local governments, everyone. They'll work for pirates, for mercenaries, for the town barber if he has the right job and the right coin."

"So she could be working for anyone?" Violet asked.

"She could be," the skipper said. "That doesn't mean she is. The Guild will work with anyone, but not always. They have their own rules, the gods only know what those are. Anyone can hire them, but they still have to agree to work with you."

"Skipper," Violet said, "what do you think Scarlett is doing on our ship?"

"If we're lucky," the skipper said, "she's just here to make sure the cargo gets through."

"And if we're not?"

"I want you to keep an eye on her for me," the skipper said, avoiding the question. "Nothing overbearing, Vi, I don't want you hiding under her bed. Just keep an eye on her."

Violet lowered her voice. "Like Sharpe does." *And like Sharpe was saying I should. He and the skipper got more in common than they'd both like.*

"Right." The skipper nodded, not happily though. "Like Sharpe. If you see her do anything that seems wrong you come tell me."

"What if there's no time?" Violet asked. "What if she wakes up that golem and it tries to kick a hole in the ship?"

"Then it'll fall out and you come tell me about it," the skipper said. "Promise me?"

"I promise, Skipper," Violet said earnestly. "You can count on me."

"I know, Vi." The skipper ruffled the girl's hair. "I know. Now," she said, "about that tail of yours."

Violet craned her neck. "Which one?" she asked with a sigh.

The skipper pointed. "The second one."

"What about it?" Violet dropped her head, concentrating, 'til her tails untangled. They tended to twine if she wasn't conscious about it.

"Two tails is one too many. I don't like greedy crew members on my ship, Violet."

"Skipper?" Violet didn't see where this was going.

The skipper pulled a knife from a sheath attached to her boot. "I think we should get rid of one. I'll let you choose which."

"Skipper!" Violet yelped, jumping to her feet, flinching when the steel caught the light, putting her back against the railing. The skipper pointed the tip of her knife towards Violet, her eyes flicking between Violet and her tails. Her sides shook and eventually a smile cracked her face.

"You're hateful, Skipper," Violet said, sliding down the railing.

"Violet, really?" The skipper shook her head. "You really thought I would?" She slid the knife back into its sheath.

"Jack would've," Violet muttered. "He's always going on about how Kitsune tails are good luck."

"Well, Jack does need all the good luck he can get," the skipper agreed. "And he could do with a new belt."

"He can get his own sodding tail," Violet said grumpily.

"Does that mean you won't be getting any more then?"

"I hope so." Violet sat down again. "But not for a while at least."

"So it's supposed to happen?"

Violet gave the skipper an exasperated look. The skipper had the grace to look embarrassed.

"How many tails are we talking about here?" the skipper asked.

"Nine, eventually, maybe," Violet said. *Though that ought to be a long, long time away.*

"So you grow more tails as you get older?"

"No." Violet screwed up her face. "As we grow up."

The skipper frowned, not following. "Isn't that what I said?"

"Not quite, Skipper," Violet said, amused to be on the other end of the explanation for once. "Everybody gets older, not everybody grows up."

The skipper chuckled. "You've been spending too much time with Piper, Vi."

"He reminds me of folks back home," Violet said. "Always got some story about everything."

"Piper does like to talk," the skipper agreed. "If he doesn't have a story he probably makes one up. Don't hear you talk much about home though."

Violet looked out over the railings into the mist, resting her head on her hands. "Home's out there somewhere, Skipper. One day I'll go back."

"One day?"

Violet smiled. "One day, when I'm all grown up." She turned to look at the skipper and was surprised by what she saw. Misery.

"Skipper?" she said quietly.

The skipper shook herself, a forced smile on her face. "It's nothing, Vi," she said quickly. "Just be glad you've got a home to go back to someday."

The skipper got to her feet. "You've got galley duty tonight. Go help Gabbi out after the next bell."

"Aye, Skipper." Violet agreed, half raising a hand in salute. The skipper was already gone though, leaving Violet on the forecastle. She cast a last look out over the stars, some with planets.

Wonder which one is the Skipper's? And why she can't go back.

Chapter 7

"Now that," Gabbi marvelled, "is a big ship."

And indeed it was, a massive all big gun Alliance vessel, a dreadnought, with two smaller frigates in attendance. The frigates alone out massed the *Tantamount*; the dreadnought, a hulking behemoth blocking out more stars than the miasma, was so much overkill it seemed almost ludicrous it had been pulled in for blockade duty.

"Skipper?" Gabbi said. The three of them, Nel, Gabbi and Horatio stood on the bridge—it was Nel's watch and the captain had come to join her for the end of it. Nel had sent Violet off to fetch Quill, as it was likely they would need to heave to soon. One of the frigates had already altered course to intercept them.

"Big," Horatio muttered. "Stupidly big, isn't it? I mean look at it, a floating shed, ridiculous. It couldn't wallow its way out of a nebula, let alone chase down a blockade runner. What is something like that even doing here? Really."

"Presence," Nel said, squinting at the incoming frigate. "Something big and scary to make the locals think twice."

"And the tourists," Gabbi commented. "If they tell us to turn around, are we really going to argue the point?"

"That's the idea," Nel admitted. "Does anyone have a spyglass?"

"What for?" Horatio grumbled. "I can see all I want to of that lugger. Oversized tub. What do you think the captain is compensating for? I'll bet he's a small man. Tiny. A midget. Has to be."

"I'm more interested in the frigate about to cut across our bow," Nel said. She plucked Horatio's spyglass out of his belt. "Thanks."

Horatio didn't appear to notice.

Nel fixed the glass on the incoming ship. It took her a few tries to find what she was looking for; inky black space and whirling miasma made for poor reference points.

"That's not good," she muttered once she could make out the name of the ship.

"What isn't good?" Quill asked, having come up the stairs to join the bridge crew. Violet was trailing after him, practically stepping on his heels. He was none too pleased about it.

"Alliance," Quill noted the blockade, annoyed, unimpressed. "Typical."

"Hardly unexpected," Gabbi reminded him, for which she received a near miss lashing from Quill's tail. "What's the issue, Skipper?"

"Read the name of that frigate, the closest one," Nel said.

"I can't make it out from here," Gabbi said.

"Violet." Nel handed the girl the spyglass. Violet skipped to the edge of the bridge, bringing the telescope up to her eye.

"*Loneliness*, the *Killing Loneliness*, Skipper," she called out.

Gabbi shrugged. "That's an unpleasant name. But hardly cause for alarm."

"Loneliness is not such a bad thing," Quill said. "At least it would be quiet for once."

"Go stuff your mouth, skink breath." Gabbi raised her voice as she spoke.

Quill hissed angrily.

"The issue isn't the name, but the type of name," Horatio

said unexpectedly. The crew turned to look at their captain. Except for Nel—she already knew what he was going to say.

"The Alliance follows a specific pattern for naming their ships," Horatio explained. "See the floating beast out there? Even from here you can see the name, *Mangonel Falling*."

Mangonel Falling, in garish, gilded Alliance calligraphy ran along the length of the ship.

"Sharpe's ship was the *Falchions Rise*," Violet chipped in.

"Exactly, Violet," Horatio told her. "Alliance ships are named after weapons, bigger weapons for bigger ships. The names have two parts, the weapon and another word, usually a descriptive one."

"What of it?" Quill said. "I couldn't care less what the Alliance scrawls on the side of its boats."

"Pay attention, you cold-blooded crow bait," Gabbi told him spitefully. "You must have spent too much time down in the chiller."

"Insolent meat puppet," Quill muttered, seeming more interested in exchanging insults than following the thread of the captain's words.

"The other frigate is the *Distant Morningstar*," Violet called out, peering through the spyglass.

"Even the youngest meat puppet on this ship catches on quicker than you," Gabbi taunted Quill.

"That's quite enough," Horatio said, forestalling another round of bickering. "The point is that the frigate that just signalled us isn't an Alliance vessel."

"But they're part of the blockade," Gabbi objected. "How does that work?"

"Likely they're a privateer," the captain said. "Contracted to fill a gap. Either the Alliance can't spare adequate resources for a full blockade or is still waiting on reinforcements. It's not unusual for them to use auxiliary resources in a situation like this."

"Mercenary scum," Quill spat, earning a disapproving look from his captain.

"Are we going to let them board us?" Gabbi asked, looking

nervously at the approaching ship.

"Of course we are," Horatio exclaimed. "With that monstrosity out there? It's as much to keep the hired help in line as it is to scare away everyone else. If you can only commit a few ships to a situation like this you might as well make one of them a big one. None of which changes what an eyesore it is."

"They're here," Nel announced, watching the *Killing Loneliness* pull up alongside the *Tantamount*.

The navigators on the other ship—Nel could make out two on the bridge, both obscured by the blue lightning circling them—crabbed the frigate in sideways, very slowly. The air distorted visibly where the envelopes meshed, a difference in pressure, not a massive one given the difference in size between the two ships, but enough that the navigators were content to let the excess bleed through. If the procedure had been done quicker or more forcibly, such as in a combat boarding, the ship with the lesser pressure would take the full onslaught of the differential.

That was what had happened to Sharpe's vessel—the smaller ship always came off worse. Nel for one was happy to let the other crew take their time. Even so, the timbers near the meshing creaked and an artificial breeze stirred the loose rigging.

The sight and sound made Nel wince—this just from a ship their own size. The *Mangonel*'s envelope would have ripped the *Tantamount* apart, the same way as Sharpe's ship had been.

Nel followed Horatio down the stairs to where most of the crew was gathered. She saw Piper and Jack down the far end, looking large and intimidating compared to the rest of their shipmates. She was glad they were together, trusting in Piper to keep Jack from acting too belligerent. Who else was likely to make trouble? Sharpe came to mind—she spotted him leaning against the mainmast, ill at ease as he studied the new arrivals. Something was bothering him. Odd, the ship they'd plucked him off had been Alliance, but he seemed none too pleased to see them again. Though it could be just the privateer element. As Nel watched he turned and descended into the hold. Content to sit out the meeting or eager to avoid any face to face encounters? Something to ponder.

Scarlett was the last person Nel searched for. Their plan for dealing with the blockade centred around the Guildswoman. She was seated atop a water barrel, one of her wands laid across her lap, polishing invisible dirt from the weapon with a square of silk. Her eyes were diverted the way Sharpe had gone, but with no discernible expression that Nel could read. Still, interesting.

Gabbi tugged on her arm. "Look, Skipper. Quill might have some friends after all."

The crew aboard the frigate were one and all Kelpies. They made for an intimidating bunch, all teeth, scales, and tails. The sight of them made Nel glance back to the *Tantamount*'s bridge, where Quill had retreated. As she suspected, he didn't look happy to see his kin at all, if the lashing of his tail was any standard to go by. In fact, there were small telltale bolts barely visible around his clenched fists.

"What's his problem?" Gabbi asked, seeing the same signs.

"He's old-fashioned," Nel muttered, glancing at the other Kelpies. They were a mean-looking bunch, but either they hadn't noticed Quill or weren't paying him any attention. Their spokesperson was the first one aboard, darting across the planks bridging the gap between the two ships, followed by a dozen or so others, all of them armed. Most carried wands, a few even had the larger, more powerful staff variants. Nel eyed one with the weapon slung casually over their shoulder, clawed fingers beating a rhythmic tattoo into the shaft.

"Hells. Dammit," Nel cursed when she got a closer look at the lead Kelpie. The bottom of her stomach dropped, a fair imitation of how she felt when she got into a bubble.

"What?" Gabbi asked. "Ex-boyfriend?"

"Ex-captain," Nel told her grimly. She found she was clutching her wand again.

"Skipper?" Gabbi said incredulously. "You sailed under a

Kelpie privateer?"

"She wasn't a privateer back then," Nel said. "Come on."

"She?" Gabbi whispered as they got closer. "How can you tell? I don't see any . . . um . . ."

"She told me," Nel said tersely. "Now be quiet."

The Kelpie captain stood slightly shorter than her crewmates, not because she was female—as Nel could tentatively identify the group of Kelpies as a mix of genders—but because Heathen had always been shorter than average. At full height she would have towered over Nell but like all Kelpies she walked and stood with her legs bent, folding at the knee, and her head sloped forward. It gave Heathen and the other Kelpies a poised, attentive stance. Like a coiled spring to Quill's barely restrained, taut bowstring.

Heathen's tongue flicked out, sampling the air aboard the *Tantamount*.

"Where is the captain?" she asked in her race's oddly stilted tone.

"Here," Horatio said, stepping forward, one hand in his ship's coat, the other nervously stroking his moustache. "Captain Horatio Phelps of the *Tantamount*."

"Captain Heathen of the *Killing Loneliness*, currently under the Alliance colours." Heathen rested her hands on the belt around her waist, a belt with an Alliance wand holstered. A wand that was issued to captains on their first commission.

"This is restricted territory," Heathen informed Horatio, speaking loudly for the benefit of the crew. "Until the present hostilities are settled all traffic to and from this area of space is under embargo."

"Which hostilities would those be?" Horatio asked.

Heathen eyed him, perhaps considering whether he was being flippant. "There is a war going on between Grange and Thatch."

"Neither of which are vassals or members of the Alliance," Horatio was quick to say. "What right have you to place planets in the Free Lanes under an embargo?"

"The violence was beginning to spill over beyond the conflicted territories," Heathen said. "Action became necessary."

"What spill?" Quill interrupted, pushing his way through the crew. "There's nothing but open space for thousands of leagues in any direction. What possible reason could you," the word was laced with heavy sarcasm, "have for a blockade?"

Heathen barely glanced at Quill, keeping her attention on Horatio.

"That's my navigator, Quill," the captain of the *Tantamount* said, a hint of steel entering his voice. "He asked you a question."

"I don't care to know the name of one as delusional as he," Heathen muttered. "Nor do I care to answer his question."

"Then you'll answer mine," Horatio snapped. "What right has the Alliance to impose a blockade?"

"Trade was being disrupted," Heathen told him. "Traders, captains such as yourself, were being waylaid, their cargo taken as fuel for the war. Both sides were guilty of such actions. The Alliance has the right to instigate action in such a situation."

Horatio didn't look satisfied and opened his mouth to argue further.

"I recognise some of your crew, Captain," Heathen cut him off before he could do so. "Some of them served in the Alliance. I recognise a former officer of mine, in fact."

"Hells," Nel muttered to Gabbi, "here we go."

She strode forward, uncomfortably aware that the attention of two crews was fixed upon her. Maybe it wasn't the best idea given how Heathen had reacted, but Nel found herself coming to stand alongside Quill. The navigator shifted his weight at her presence but didn't show any other signs of emotion. He could be grateful or annoyed or just plain indifferent.

"Captain," Nel nodded to Heathen. "Strange, seeing you out of uniform. Last time I saw you it was more than just Alliance colours."

A sawtoothed grin. "Makes me a reliable contractor. Of course, the last time I saw you, it was skipper, not captain. And . . ." She glanced around and reconsidered her words. "Perhaps not. Not now."

Nel took a breath and let it out slowly. She trusted Heathen's discretion, she just didn't like reminders of her past life.

"You sail under this man?" Heathen cocked her head towards Horatio.

"I do."

"Hmm." Heathen considered. "Seeing you here, Vaughn, makes me recall things. But it changes nothing. This area is still under martial blockade. You know Alliance rules as well as I do. We have followed them to the letter in the past, we will do so again here."

"We're carrying a relief cargo," Nel said. "Medical supplies, meant for Grange. Nothing that would violate a mercantile or arms embargo. Nothing that could be used in terms of war, no munitions or supplies. The cargo is purely charitable."

Heathen's double lidded eyes held Nel's. "You will not object to us verifying this?"

Nel motioned behind her. "Gabbi, take them below."

"Aye, Skipper," she heard the cook answer. Two of Heathen's crew detached themselves from the boarding party. The rest remained with their captain, hands never far from weapons.

"Even a benign cargo is not grounds to bypass us, Vaughn," Heathen advised Nel. "You could be carrying information, coded messages, intangible things, things our search would never reveal. We cannot let you through."

"Is that what you think?" Nel was getting annoyed. "Have I fallen that far in your eyes?"

"In my eyes?" Heathen considered. "No, you have not. I remember you serving under me. But it matters not what I think . . ."

Quill snorted.

"Quill," Nel warned.

"Let him," Heathen said dismissively. "His opinion is as

irrelevant as his beliefs."

"He's my crew," Nel said, adding under her breath, "even if he is striving for galley duty."

"Captain," the call came from the returning search party. They hadn't been gone more than a minute. Heathen conferred briefly with her crew, turning back to Nel.

"What?" Nel folded her arms defiantly. "There's nothing down there but medical supplies."

"And a golem," Heathen said, her words having an immediate effect upon her crew. Weapons were drawn, prompting an outcry from the *Tantamount*'s crew. "You said you had no war materials. Explain that to me."

Quill stepped forward. "I would love to discuss the matter with you." A wave ran through the *Tantamount*'s crew—with weapons drawn on their deck some were clearly tempted to take Quill's side. That couldn't happen.

"Quill, no!" Nel barked, drawing her wand and pointing it at her navigator.

"You," he growled. He gestured at her. "You point that at me? On our ship . . . with them here!"

"Don't make me use it," Nel said. Quill stared at her down the length of the wand, furious.

"Stand down, navigator," Nel said, mentally pleading with him to do so. If it meant stopping an escalation she'd do it. She would shoot Quill, in front of the crew. Her crew. Her captain. Her former captain.

Stand down, Quill, she thought as hard as she could.

For the longest moment Quill just stared at her. She had his full attention now, had taken him by surprise, derailed his private crusade against his kin. And Nel watched as some sort of emotion passed over her navigator's hard face. Complication or confliction, it was hard to say, so brief and then it was gone, hidden away.

Quill stood down, refusing to meet Nel's eyes anymore. He took a step back, fading away into the crew. For some reason that made Nel feel even worse about it.

"The golem is private property," Nel said to Heathen,

lowering her wand. "It's not cargo."

"Yours?" the Kelpie captain queried her suspiciously.

"Mine." Scarlett stepped forward. She moved with an easy sway into a tense situation. Despite being the most heavily and visibly armed person amongst the *Tantamount*'s crew, she didn't draw as much attention as Nel had only minutes before.

Heathen regarded her suspiciously. "And you are?"

"Scarlett."

"Your rank, affiliation?" Heathen asked stiffly. Her eyes narrowed, straying back to Nel. Heathen clearly suspected she was being played somehow. And she was right.

Scarlett smiled. "Guild."

A shudder went through the Kelpie crew, whether fear or frustration it was hard to tell.

"You have proof?" Heathen demanded, but in a more subdued manner.

Scarlett did. She showed it. Nel scowled at that. It was only the day before when Scarlett had fronted with her credentials to her and the captain. Confided her plan for bypassing the blockade. Confirmation of what they'd already known, but it irked Nel that Scarlett had kept quiet about it. And now they were depending on her to get them through the blockade. An altruistic cargo wouldn't get them through, but one accompanied by a Guildswoman would be harder to reject. They were betting on it being too hard for the Alliance to justify.

Heathen studied Scarlett's identification soberly. Both sets of eyelids blinked, one then the other, crossing over each other.

"Guild authority," Horatio said what everyone was thinking, "trumps your blockade, Captain. We'll be proceeding."

"Yes," Heathen said, handing Scarlett's effects back. She glanced over her shoulder, in the direction of the Alliance dreadnought drifting out in the miasma. "As far as Rim."

"What?" Nel growled.

"Rim," Heathen repeated. "The outermost port before Grange. That's as far as your Guild pass gets you."

Nel glanced at Scarlett. The woman only shrugged in response. "Even we have our limits."

"Rim is a staging post," Heathen informed them. "You can drop your altruistic cargo there. It will have to make the remaining journey alone. Any further progression will be seen as a violation of the blockade and treated as such. This is the only warning you will be given. Attempt to land on Grange, or Thatch, and you will be treated as a hostile."

"Rim will be fine, Captain," Scarlett assured her. "We'll be returning from there shortly."

"That's good to hear." Heathen narrowed her eyes on the Guildswoman. "Perhaps I should have been addressing you this entire time. It could have prevented misunderstandings."

Scarlett shrugged. "Perhaps."

Typical Guild, Nel thought. *Take all the credit and leave them wondering. Another secret, another question. Another smug Guildsman leaving twisted arms and bruised egos in their wake.*

"Perhaps I should leave some of my crew on board," Heathen suggested.

"Not necessary," Nel said. "Particularly given the way some of my crew might react to their presence."

Even to her the words sounded hollow, a cheap attempt to get back on Quill's good side. Quill's mood got even uglier, if that was possible, and Nel wished she hadn't bothered. Quill stalked off to vanish into the still edgy crew as Heathen gave Nel that toothy smile. The one that said how little she cared if Quill didn't play well with his own kind.

"Since you have a Guild representative aboard, and given our own history, Vaughn, I'm prepared to let you sail freely to Rim. I trust you won't make me regret that."

Nel gave her former captain a chill smile. Heathen had never had any intention of putting crew aboard the *Tantamount*. She'd just thrown out some bait to see what sort of reaction she might get.

"A moment of your time," Heathen said to Nel, drawing her away from both crews.

Her former captain studied her for a moment, taking a measured glance around at the *Tantamount* and its misfit crew. "You travel in difficult company."

Nel felt her eyes narrow at the implication. "That's my crew you're talking about."

"Not them," Heathen corrected. "The Guildswoman. I believe a large part of your reason for leaving the Alliance was a longing for a simpler, less conflicted life."

Nel turned her face aside, reluctant to recall a time when she had addressed Heathen as captain. "That was a long time ago. And that woman is not on my ship by choice."

"Then things have not changed much then, have they, Vaughn." Heathen looked again to the Alliance dreadnought, weighing up something. "This is a difficult situation. An Alliance vessel has already been lost. There may be a retaliation."

Nel felt her heart start to race at her former captain's words. Reasons for leaving the Alliance came flooding back to her. "Dammit, tell me that's not why you're here," she whispered, grabbing her former captain's arm. It felt like catching a bolt from a wand with her bare hands. Nel jerked her arm back quickly, stung. She shook her hand, trying to get the feeling back into the fingers, cursing. She knew better than to lay hands on a thaumatic who didn't want to be touched.

"It may . . . may come to that." Heathen regarded her coolly. "Control your temper, Vaughn, and your feelings." The Kelpie looked past her, to the crew of the *Tantamount*. "Think of your crew, Vaughn. They are your concern, your priority. Deliver your cargo and get away from this place, forget you were ever here."

"That sounds like a threat, Captain," Nel said.

"A warning," Heathen corrected. "I would not see you or your crew drawn into the mess this conflict has become. Look after your crew, Vaughn, that's all I ask of you."

"That's all you ever asked," Nel muttered.

Heathen let her crew finish searching the *Tantamount*; they weren't quick. When they were satisfied there weren't any more golems hiding under the floorboards, they took their leave. The frigate pulled away, the separation of envelopes causing the two ships to bob unsteadily, like they were at sea. Nel didn't care for the sensation.

"Don't see a lot of thaumatics make the jump up to captain," Horatio commented, watching the ship draw away.

Nel flexed her fingers. They were still numb. "Not many like her, Captain."

"She's strong, isn't she?" Horatio tapped Nel's hand. "I remember you saying, when you first signed on . . ."

"Yes," Nel muttered darkly.

Horatio nodded. "Funny who you run into out here sometimes. Carry on, my girl."

"Aye, Captain."

"A word with you," Scarlett's cultured voice drew her attention. Nel found the woman standing not far away and was immediately annoyed at herself for not having noticed Scarlett earlier. She must be more rattled than she'd thought.

"I've a question you can answer," Scarlett continued.

"Heathen was my captain in the Alliance," Nel said, not wanting to belabour the question. "Five years ago."

"I'd gathered as much," Scarlett said. "That wasn't my question."

"What was then?" Nel was surprised.

"Your navigator. His opposition to the other crew seemed fundamental, not personal."

"Why don't you ask him yourself?" Nel suggested.

"Because he's in a violent mood." Scarlett's tone was dry.

Nel thought about it and decided there was little harm in talking about it. Quill's strife was hardly a secret, nor even unique.

"You're familiar with Kelpie religion?" she asked.

"Some," Scarlett said dryly. "Hardly the most enticing theology."

Nel chuckled sourly. "The deities you're familiar with are the new gods, sprung up maybe a hundred years ago. The cult took off like wildfire."

"Interesting." Scarlett considered this bit of cultural information. "What happened to the old Kelpie gods?"

"Killed off, for the most part."

Scarlett raised one elegant eyebrow at that revelation. "An impressive statement for the upstart newcomers, assuming you believe in such things."

Nel shrugged. Other than the occasional oath she was happy to leave gods, particularly other people's gods, well enough alone and could only hope they did the same for her.

Scarlett mused aloud. "So let me surmise, Quill follows one branch of the religion, the blockade captain and her crew the other."

The Guildswoman was quick, Nel had to admit. "Pretty much."

"Presumably such an association is perfectly obvious, if one knows what to look for."

Nel shrugged. "Probably is."

"Dangerous habit, worshipping dead gods," Scarlett noted.

"Way Quill tells it his lot were much more frightening."

"Dead all the same."

"Maybe so." Nel shrugged again. "Wasn't there myself."

The ghost of a smile flickered across Scarlett's face. "Hopefully we'll hear no more about it. Thank you, Vaughn."

"My pleasure," Nel said dryly.

"We'll be heading for Rim now, correct?"

"Once Quill stops seeing red, yes."

"I'd like you to signal the *Mangonel Falling* of our intentions." Scarlett watched the dreadnought floating out against the backdrop. Even from a distance it blotted out much of the horizon. "Specifically that we intend to deliver our cargo to Rim. And be sure to state the nature of our cargo."

Across the ship's flank the *Killing Loneliness* was still

pulling into formation with the Alliance ships.

"That seems a little redundant," Nel said, watching the manoeuvrings.

Scarlett pressed her lips together. "I'd like it done anyway."

"You don't think the *Killing Loneliness* will pass on our intentions," Nel said.

Scarlett shrugged. "I'd prefer there were no misunderstandings in this matter."

"As you like," Nel said slowly. "I can have Violet relay the message before we set sail."

"She's competent? With a signaller?"

"Aye, she is," Nel said, not willing to admit otherwise to the Guildswoman.

"I'll talk to her then," Scarlett said. The Guildswoman left Nel alone to consider the odd request. Again she found her attention drawn back to the privateer frigate. Sometimes the past just wouldn't stay away, no matter where one went.

"Let me try," Sharpe uncharacteristically volunteered after one look at Violet. The poor girl had ended up wearing most of the soup she'd taken to Quill. Nel had been moments from taking her wand to the Kelpie's backside but had ended up dabbing at Violet's face with a wet cloth instead. Fortunately for her and Quill, the girl had escaped any serious burns. It was only Quill's latest outburst since they passed through the blockade, but Nel was through letting him get away with it.

"Why is every place like this called Rim?" Violet complained, looking out at the dreary staging outpost unhappily as Nel tended to her.

Like Cauldron, it had an artificially created envelope, though by the simplest of means. A raft of ships that would likely never fly again, dry docks and planking nailed together to form a floating platform. Ships the size of the *Tantamount* could pull right up to the station without disrupting the envelope too much. Larger vessels, ships the size of the *Mangonel Falling*, of which there were none presently, had to ride out beyond the station's envelope and wait for the ferry craft to transfer their cargo. A tedious and inefficient exercise. In more peaceable times any larger ship would have made the journey further in to Grange itself. Rim would have been nothing more than a brief customs stopover, if that. Most planets had a Rim, an outer edge where the bare minimal amount of trading and such was carried out. Sometimes it was a moon, an asteroid, or a barren rock. Often settled by the dregs of planetary society, they made for a trash ridden landscape, like a city slums with inhabitants to match. Nel was hoping their visit would be a short one.

"Tradition," Sharpe told her helpfully when he returned from soothing a savage Kelpie navigator. "Saying you're a Rimworlder is like saying you're a peasant."

"In what way?" Violet twisted her face away from the washcloth. Nel grabbed her chin and held her, wiping firmly at the girl's grubby face.

Sharpe shrugged. "It's all anybody will ever see you for, or want to." He turned around in a slow circle. "I haven't been here in years. Doesn't look like anything's changed."

"You used to live here?" Violet made a face at Sharpe. "It smells terrible!"

Sharpe gave her a pained look. "We can't all grow up in fairy tale castles, little princess. Some of us have to start at the bottom."

Violet's head came up with wide, curious eyes. "What was that like? Did you ever join a Lane gang? How did you get out? Did you stowaway on a ship like I did?"

Sharpe gave Nel a helpless look.

"You got her started," she told him unsympathetically, bundling the cloth into a ball and pitching it down the length of the deck. "That's as clean as this one will get. You deal with her now."

"I didn't actually say I was one of those people," Sharpe told Violet. "Just that some people are. A lot of them in fact, but I'm not one of them."

"One of the seething, stinking masses," Quill called derisively, having come forward to squint at the layout of their destination.

"Exactly," Sharpe called back. He'd learnt to be quick when Quill started baiting him. The comradeship was wearing thin as Quill's usual nature took over. The Kelpie had been short with all of the crew since the run-in with his kin, Violet just the latest victim. Even the captain had been on the receiving end of his forked tongue lashing. That hadn't gone down well.

"Just a regular human, that's me," Sharpe agreed.

"Close enough," Quill spat. "Cursed humans. Filthy vermin, all of you."

"Quill!" Violet objected. The earlier lesson was apparently lost on her, despite the soup still matting her hair. "Watch your mouth! Or that's the last soup you're getting from any of us."

"It will be a pleasure not having to find fur in my soup, runt," the navigator told her. "You are no better than the rest of this crew. A human with a tail, more or less."

"More, rather," Sharpe commented. "Two tails in fact, if we're counting."

Nel glanced at Violet's backside. It was hard to tell she still had two tails. The bushy extensions poked through a flap in her breeches but wrapped around each other in an interlocking corkscrew.

"We are not," Quill retorted.

"No, *we're* picking another fight," Nel interrupted. "And *we* are likely to be assigned to clean up the galley slops if *we* don't get our scaly mouth muzzled and minding its own business. Consider yourself relieved. Go find your bed, navigator. You're not helping yourself today."

"Helping," Quill muttered as he stomped past them all on his way below deck. "I miss Cauldron already. At least the vermin there gave us excuses to exterminate them. Here we are supposed to . . . help."

"And we all know how much you love to help your fellows, Quill," Nel told him not so quietly as he passed. The comment cut deeper than any barb she could have thought of. Quill's look had daggers in it and the obscenities grew more colourful as he made himself scarce.

"It comes back to haunt you sometimes," Sharpe said.

"What does?"

"Your style of command, Skipper. Whatever happened to all that Alliance discipline instilled in you? Floggings, kissing the gunner's daughter, that sort?"

"Captain doesn't approve," Nel said.

"Captain doesn't run the ship." Sharpe folded his arms. "Humour me. You let this crew get away with things that would see them whipped bloody on other ships. Why?"

Nel hesitated. Her encounter with her former captain was still fresh in her mind. "You sailed on the *Falchions*?"

"Aye, saw the bosun raise his cat more than once, too."

"And the whole crew watched and said nothing."

"Of course they did. That's part of what discipline is."

"That's the part I don't like," Nel said. "I don't want my crew to have to stand there. If they think I'm wrong I want them to tell me."

"Quill thought you were wrong."

"His argument wasn't good enough."

"You're a complicated woman, Skipper."

"Are we going to look around, Skipper?" Violet asked, fidgeting at the rails. "It's been a long time aboard."

Nel had almost forgotten the girl was there. "The last time I took you off-ship you got yourself kidnapped."

"I didn't get myself kidnapped," Violet objected.

"That's true, she had help," Sharpe agreed.

"And Sharpe's been teaching me some stuff since," Violet said.

"Teaching?" Nel growled. She glared at Sharpe. "What have you been teaching her?"

"Nothing," he protested. "Well, all right, not nothing. But nothing you need to worry yourself about."

"Don't tell me what I worry about."

"Just things to look for, Skipper," Violet assured her. "What to watch for, who to watch for, same as you do."

"Same as you do." Sharpe couldn't keep the smirk off his face. "See?"

"Don't compare yourself to me," Nel said. "And Violet, don't you be getting confused about whose lessons you ought to be following."

"Aye, Skipper," Violet said, trying to sound serious.

"Aye, Skipper," Sharpe echoed, waving a mock salute.

Nel looked at them both critically. "Fine, we're going in. The three of us."

"The three of us?" Sharpe repeated. "Including me? Wait, why? You never want me to come along."

"This is your backyard," Nel reminded him. "Maybe you'll be useful."

Sharpe nodded. "That makes sense."

"And maybe I can find someone to take you off my hands."

"Ah," Sharpe sighed. "Your ulterior motive. I'm crushed."

Violet nudged him in the ribs. "Don't be giving the skipper any ideas, Sharpe."

Sharpe stared. "Good point, little princess," he conceded. "Good point."

"You told me you'd been practicing." The skipper had that disappointed sound in her voice again. Violet sighed.

"I have," she insisted. "Piper's been teaching me."

"Still not enough, it seems."

"Not his fault, Skipper," Violet defended her friend and tutor. "That message Scarlett had me send was hells hard."

"Shouldn't have been."

"There were seven breaks to it, Skipper. Seven."

"Seven?" the skipper repeated. "Seven breaks or it took you seven attempts? All you had to do was tell them where we were docking. How do you use up seven breaks saying that?"

Violet was about to repeat the litany of coloured flashes Scarlett had dictated to her when she caught sight of where they were. She stopped in her tracks.

"People live like this?" Violet whispered.

Sharpe stopped too. "Amazing, isn't it." His voice sounded ragged and he coughed into his hand. "Rim actually boasts a bad part of town."

"Sharpe, don't," the skipper's voice came from behind. Violet felt her hand on a shoulder.

"Don't what?" Sharpe asked her. "Look around you, Vaughn. I don't have to say anything, this is how the other half live."

They were in the slums, on the far side of Rim. Docklands warehousing where what Sharpe had bitterly called the "subsistent" population made their homes. There was no weather to speak of in places like Rim—it lacked even the basic thermal activity of Cauldron. Some of the buildings Violet had seen didn't even have roofs, others had walls that were in the midst of falling down.

Every now and then on the journey over they had come across bridges of ships. Old mothballed vessels that had become part of the town, wrapped up in reused planking and gantries until it was hard to tell where the ships ended and other buildings began. Near the edges of Rim the ships were more recognisable as former sailing vessels. Still clinging to their identity, as if they might breakaway at any moment for one last voyage.

This was no way for a ship to go out, the skipper had said, so quietly Violet didn't think she meant herself to be heard. Violet agreed, but it was the people she noticed more than the ships. The people who'd cannibalised those ships for planks and sails to scrounge together a home. Tarps and tent-like structures made up those dwellings, crammed with people who stared at the well-dressed, well-fed trio strolling through their community.

Up until then Violet had never thought of herself that way. But here she was uncomfortably aware that she was insulting these people just by parading around in their world. She didn't belong and everyone knew it.

"This isn't living," Violet said quietly. "Even home was better than this."

The skipper frowned at her words. But the skipper didn't know there were reasons Violet and those her age left home—to stay was to be forced to compete with those above her. Better to return when you had levelled that field. But here . . .

"No, you're wrong, Violet," Sharpe corrected her. "Bad as this is, this is still living. It gets worse than this. When you see carts hauling the dead and the not-quite dead away, then you'll understand what . . ."

"Sharpe!" the skipper snapped, stepping up until she was right in his face. The man chewed on the ends of his words, obviously wanting to keep spouting.

It was the most upset he'd ever acted around Violet. During his rescue, during her rescue, he'd been an ocean of calm. Here something was getting to him. From the time he'd come onto the ship he hadn't seemed to take anything seriously, buying into the rough house camaraderie aboard the *Tantamount*. Now he exchanged heated words with the skipper, words Violet couldn't hear as they were in hoarse, strangled whispers. Sharpe gestured around them expansively and the skipper put her hand on his chest, grabbing a handful of shirt. A warning, a threat, the skipper being the skipper.

"There are so many of them. Why are there so many?" Violet gestured around them. She saw families but there was something wrong with most of them. There were people missing from the basic units. Too many children and not enough adults.

"Refugees." Sharpe stepped away from the skipper, his shoulders slumped. "Fleeing the war. But this is as far as they can get. A pathetic little station on the backside of nowhere. Past here they run straight into that blockade, and no one here has the kind of coin to buy passage past that."

The more Sharpe talked the deeper the lines on the skipper's face got. Violet saw the woman take a long look around them.

"Skipper." Violet tugged at her hand. "Is there anything we can do for them?"

"We brought the medicine, Violet," the skipper reminded her. "That's a lot by itself. We are helping."

"You really don't care about anyone outside of your ship, do you?" Sharpe said.

The skipper's eyes narrowed to slits. "Stay here," she said to Violet, grabbing Sharpe's arm and pulling him away again. Violet turned away but strained her ears to catch what was said this time.

"Whatever your problem is, stow it."

"Doesn't it bother you, Skipper?" Sharpe's voice was bitter, resigned. "Look at all the misery around you. Can't you feel it?"

"It's not my problem. I've got my own issues, this isn't one of them!"

"I figured you for better than that."

"Then you figured wrong."

"Your old captain was right, Vaughn."

"Right about what?" The skipper's voice rose. "Hells, Sharpe, you weren't even on deck when she was. I saw you run and hide when they came aboard."

Violet heard a scuffle behind her and risked a look. Sharpe had pulled the skipper close, her face inches away from his. He wasn't bothering to keep his voice down either. "She was right. That medicine we brought, that you brought, you think the likes of these will ever see a drop of it? Think it won't go straight to the war effort, never mind the people who might actually need it?"

"I didn't start this war." The skipper pulled away. "Don't expect me to try and solve it."

Sharpe grabbed her shoulder. "The ship's bursting at the seams. No one would miss a single box, even several."

"Keep your voice down," the skipper hissed, pulling him close again, enough that their faces were practically touching. "The last thing I need is you . . ." She whispered the rest, half looking to see if Violet was looking. Violet tried to look like she wasn't.

"I get that you're angry," Violet heard her say, "but this isn't something we can fix. Coming out here was a mistake, we're heading back to the ship. I'm getting Scarlett, her golem, and this hells-damned cargo off my ship and then I'm turning her back to Cauldron. Now. Violet!" she called loudly. Violet jumped.

"Back to the ship," the skipper told her. "Stay close, no running off."

"Yes, Skipper," Violet said. She turned around and started the long walk back towards the docked *Tantamount*.

"This is just Rim," Sharpe said as he walked past her. "Can you imagine what it's like on Thatch and Grange?"

"Ignore him, Violet," the skipper said, catching up. "He's just bitter."

He has reason to be, Violet thought.

"Castor!"

The man who ran up to Sharpe was as ragged as everyone else they'd seen. Even in a place made of recycled ships and wooden planking there seemed to be an excess of dirt, much of it on his face, and an absence of clean water with which to wash it off.

The man staggered to a stop, hands on his knees, hair falling over his face. His shoulders heaved up and down but he didn't seem to be breathing hard. "You're back."

Sharpe stiffened, a spasm that ran down his back and he glanced at Nel and Violet before facing the man.

"Not for long," Sharpe said. "This is just . . . passing through."

"Passing . . . yeah, of course," the man said, "why would you want to stick around this place?"

"How long have you been here?" Sharpe said. "I thought you were all on Grange still."

Violet missed what was said next. Something brushed her arm, causing her to turn. Grey flesh, hanging ragged and dry, met her eyes. She looked up into that face and screamed, falling back.

She heard the skipper swear before her scream had finished echoing, felt someone's arm wrap around her, Sharpe's. He was between her and the creature now, hugging her close to him.

"Don't!" he called, holding a hand out. But it was the skipper that open palm was thrust towards.

"I wasn't going to. It's just a Draugr."

A Draugr, like the one's from Sharpe's ship. Supposedly harmless. It didn't look it. Violet felt a whimper escape her, something incoherent.

"It's okay," Sharpe soothed, stroking the top of her head. He turned to look at his friend, the one who'd originally stopped him. "This isn't a good time," he said firmly. "You should take him back."

"Back?" the man frowned. "Not a good time?"

"You scared the girl." Sharpe sounded angry. "Take the . . . Draugr home."

"Yeah," the man said slowly, "guess we'll be going. Come on, you." He motioned to the Draugr to follow him, setting off without waiting to see if it did.

The Draugr wasn't quick to do so. It looked down at Sharpe and Violet, like it wanted to say something. Could Draugr talk? No one had ever said, not that Violet could recall.

Sharpe scowled up at it and jerked his head in an obvious command.

The Draugr reached towards Violet and Sharpe, hesitating when Violet flinched, wanting to bury her head against Sharpe's chest. She saw something when the Draugr's sleeve pulled away, coloured skin, some sort of marking.

"Leave," Sharpe told it firmly.

The Draugr stared at Violet for a long time. It could, she realised, have been someone she knew. It looked like a person, the same way the ships at Rim looked like *Tantamount*. And it almost looked hurt by the way she stared at it. Finally it withdrew the withered hand and shuffled off, following the same route Sharpe's friend had taken.

"That was odd," the skipper commented.

"Just scared her, that's all," Sharpe grunted, brushing himself off. "You can probably put that away now." He pointed at the skipper's's wand, which she held drawn and loose in one hand. The skipper did so, but slowly.

"He startled me," Violet apologised, ashamed at how she'd overreacted. "He . . . I'm sorry."

"Don't be," the skipper said. Then to Sharpe: "Who was your friend?"

"Wasn't a friend, just someone I used to know."

"You knew the Draugr was his," the skipper said.

"Had to be someone's."

"Bit unusual for someone in a slum to have their own Draugr."

Sharpe sighed. "Draugr get cast-off too, Skipper, same as people. They get used up and broken and lost. They end up in places like this same as regular folk and someone has to tell them what to do. Usually turns out to be whoever's nearby."

"Did you notice the brand on his arm?" the skipper asked him.

"What brand?"

The skipper grimaced. "Never mind then. Violet, you all right?"

Violet nodded through a shuddering breath. "Can we go back to the ship now?"

Sharpe put a hand around her shoulders. "Come along then, little princess."

He held her as they walked, talking quietly to her the whole way back to the *Tantamount*.

Violet was in a bleak mood on the return to the *Tantamount*. She withdrew into herself, refusing to be drawn in conversation. Sharpe kept close, talking softly to her, words just out of earshot. Her mood seemed to rub off on Sharpe eventually, or perhaps he was still mad at Nel. Maybe he really did care about the plight of the refugees.

Nel's mind kept flashing back to the Draugr. She'd called the markings she'd glimpsed a brand, like some mark of ownership, and in a way it was. Unconsciously she rubbed at her right arm, tracing the designs and the memories inked on her skin. It didn't feel any different, raised and rougher in some places but for the most it just felt like normal skin. That was her though, her life, her past, her stories. The rope around her wrist and palm when she'd first signed up, the winged compass when she'd made her first solo navigation, others that wandered along her arm from shoulder to wrist. Some were common to sailors but most were only found on those who'd served in the Alliance navy. Nel's fingers brushed across a cannon, wrapped in barbed wire. She recalled that one vividly, when she'd hailed under Heathen's watch. A routine patrol, herself still green and naïve, reports of piracy, the chase, the roar of cannons, the confusion when they'd boarded the other ship. An Alliance symbol to remember one's first battle, ship-to-ship warfare.

The Draugr had the same marking.

The crane was operating, hoisting cargo from the bowels of the ship onto the dry dock. Nel saw the captain leaning over the railing. On the docks hulked the golem, Onyx, finally free from its lair in the ship. The golem was as still as ever, it hadn't moved the entire trip. Its master was down amidst the unloaded crates, walking with one of the dock officials. By Nel's reckoning about a third of their cargo had already been unloaded.

"Violet, go ask Scarlett what her plans are." Nel nudged her cabin girl. "If we're offloading then we can start making plans to head back to Cauldron and get back to our original run."

The words came with only a hint of bitterness. They were weeks behind their scheduled delivery—the *Tantamount*'s and Horatio's reputation would be in shreds. Horatio might protest otherwise, he might even believe his own speeches, but that was the cold, sobering truth. Horatio's reputation was the *Tantamount*'s reputation; and with it the livelihood of all her crew.

"That load looks too heavy for the crane," Sharpe mused, looking up at the next payload. "What's Jack thinking? He's overloading it."

"What?" Nel glanced up and saw Jack hauling an ominously large crate towards the crane. She frowned. "It's big, but not . . ."

Sharpe pointed. "And the other three next to it?" He shook his head in disapproval. "He must be overloading the crane, how else could he have got so much of this off already? I'm going to go talk to Jack. Before he breaks something."

Sharpe jogged up the gangway towards Jack. Nel shook her head that Sharpe had chosen now to become a productive member of the crew. At least he seemed to be in less of a mood. Much as she hated to admit it, she preferred the flippantly shallow, self-centred Sharpe to the bleeding heart version.

She made her way over to Onyx. The golem gleamed in the glare of oil-fed lanterns, the light collecting on the curves of his body. Shoulders, forearms, his rounded head. There was no gleam of awareness in the golem's face, at least not now. Nel wondered, her gaze straying down the smooth curvature of the golem, at its construction. It had no discernible gender and she'd not once heard it speak but it seemed more natural to think of the golem as male. In the same way Nel knew the *Tantamount* to be female, a lady of dubious virtue maybe, but one who made her life on the high and free.

"Seems like you'll be leaving us soon," Nel remarked, hearing someone coming up behind her. From the elongated shadow she guessed it to be Scarlett.

"They're not happy about letting the ship go any further," Scarlett admitted. "We'll need to make arrangements to take the cargo the rest of the way in on domestic runners."

"This is as far as my ship can go," Nel reminded her. "So this is as far as my crew goes. There's no point in us lingering in these parts. Captain's already had the ship patched once. Hanging around a warzone isn't healthy for ship or crew."

"Scarlett's mouthed pressed together in a lipless line. "You were given a job to discharge your debt.”

“Fraudulent debt,” Nel corrected. “In a rigged game.”

“Horatio is almost proud when admitting both sides cheated.” Scarlett tossed her hair back disdainfully. “The fact stands you have an obligation to see this delivery through to the end.”

Nel was about to retort when both women heard a crashing sound come from the *Tantamount*. Nel couldn't see Jack or Sharpe near the crane. The crane itself was still empty.

“What the hells was that?” she said out loud, glancing at Scarlett.

The woman looked fierce. “Your man Sharpe,” she demanded, “where is he?”

“My man Sharpe?” Nel echoed her. “Why?”

The golem, so briefly before inanimate and lifeless, lit up like a harvest festival tree. At least its eyes did, smouldering fires at the back of two pitch black caves. A thin layer of dust, accumulated during the voyage, shifted from its body as the golem stirred itself awake, creaking like a stuck gate at first.

“No.” Scarlett held herself back, shaking her head. “No. On the ship, damn it. Damn it!”

Nel stared at her for a moment then bolted for the ship, taking the gangway in long strides. Her wand was in her hand by the time she cleared the railing.

“Captain!” she called, looking around for Horatio.

“Nel!” Horatio replied shrilly, descending down a level to meet her. “That noise, it came from below deck.”

“The hold,” Nel said, hearing another crash, the sound of breaking wood and a scream of some kind.

“Who was that?” Horatio gasped, wide eyed.

“Not who,” Nel said grimly. She recognised Bandit's panicked shriek. He only made sounds that piercing when . . .

“Piper,” she said, already running towards the centre of the ship, towards the screaming.

“Piper?” Horatio called after her. “He was down in the hold, helping load the cargo.”

The wooden grilling to the cago deck had been removed but inside it was still pitch black. She couldn't see anything. Certainly not Piper.

"What's going on?" Jack had come up beside her, peering down suspiciously into the unknown black maw of the ship.

"Where the hells have you been?" Nel growled at him. "Wait, never mind," she cut him off, seeing the chargrilled haunch in his own meaty hand. "Where's Sharpe?"

"Down there." Jack gestured with the meat towards the hold. "Said he needed to check something."

Another yell from below, this one definitely not Bandit.

"Hey, that sounded like Piper," Jack growled. "What's he doing?"

"Nel." Horatio grabbed her arm, worry creasing his face. "We need to get down there."

"I know," she agreed. "Jack, swing the crane around. Quickly."

"Aye," Jack muttered, lumbering to the machine. He wasted little time in rotating the hoist round and over the open hold. Nel reached out and grabbed a hold, hooking one foot into the netting. She waved with her wand for Jack to lower her.

Nel's eyes were already partially adjusted to dim light but it was difficult to make out more than vague shapes and darker shadows. Inside the hold the dark felt thicker, all around her instead of just looking in.

Something dove at her out of those shadows and Nel lashed out with her wand instinctively. Her aim was off but the flare-like burst was enough to light up the hold briefly. Enough to see that it was Bandit diving at her like a crazed bat, if the raking claws clinging to her arm and shoulder weren't enough to tell that.

"Get off me," Nel hissed, trying to shake off Piper's pet. But the loompa was plainly terrified—he clung to her fiercely and refused to budge.

"Damned rodent," Nel said. "Fine. At least be useful. Where's Piper? Piper?"

Bandit just shook on her arm, his mouth making small

chittering noises.

"Piper," Nel repeated, softer.

Bandit's head turned, chattered. Was he being useful? Either Piper was that way or whatever had spooked Bandit. *Likely both*, Nel mused. And only one way to find out.

She took a step deeper into the hold, trying to pry the loompa off her wand arm but had to concede it was a lost struggle and settled for switching her wand to her other hand. She'd missed Bandit from close range, her aim could only improve.

"Piper?" Nel whispered when she finally found her third mate. The big man was lying motionless in the space formerly occupied by Scarlett's golem. Fearing the worst she reached down to touch him. Bandit chirped quietly but refused to relinquish his hold on her, not even with Piper so obviously hurt.

Her hands didn't find the sticky and liquid evidence she'd feared. She felt warm breath on the back of her hand so Piper was still alive. That made her breathe her own sigh of relief. Her fingers found and traced the contusions on his shaved head. He'd been hit and hit hard.

A light flared into life ahead, just a few feet, an oil lamp. Nel winced, shielding her eyes.

"That's far enough, Nel," Sharpe told her. "Don't come any closer."

"Sharpe," she growled, gripping her wand tighter. "What in the hells are you doing?"

"What I came to," Sharpe said quietly.

"And what's that?"

Sharpe moved the lamp slightly, bringing his face into view. Only half of it showed, the other half was hidden away from the one sided light. It was enough. Nel fired.

She had enough to time to register the ghost of a smile on Sharpe's face as he swung the oil lamp into the path. Liquid fire exploded across the hold, showering the innards of the *Tantamount*.

Nel panicked, wondering insanely if their cargo was

flammable. Then reason took over and she cast about for a way to smother the flames. Nothing came to hand or mind. Fire was a nightmare risk during a voyage and not much better in a place like Rim. All she could do was escape and gather the crew to fight the fire. She'd already lost track of Sharpe—he could be gone or trapped behind his own conflagration for all she knew. Bandit was gone too. The loompa had scarpered at the sight of flames.

"Hells," she said to herself, looking down at Piper's dead weight bulk. This wasn't going to be easy. She manhandled him into a sitting position, his big head lolling uselessly against his chest. Getting her arms under his, she linked her hands and pulled, straining the muscles in her arms, legs and back to move his weight. She managed to drag Piper a few feet but between the heat of the growing fire and the sheer effort she was already sweating.

"Skipper!" Korrigan Jack's booming voice barely precluded his entry. He arrived in a stomping flurry, squinting beady eyes to try and make out what was going on.

"Jack!" Nel yelled to get his attention. "Help me with Piper."

Jack looked down at Piper, not moving. Nel thought he was going to argue, going to be difficult, but he stooped and levered Piper up onto his shoulders, hefting the big man up, grunting with the effort. Piper's arms dragged on the floor but at least he was moving.

Nel trailed Jack out of the hold, casting about for any sign of Sharpe. There was none. She thought he must be long gone until she heard the ruckus above decks.

"Jack, move!" she yelled, trying to push past him on the stairs. But Jack's bulk added to Piper's made for an impassable barrier. She had to wait for Jack to plod his way up the stairs before she could find out what was going on.

There was a battle raging on the *Tantamount*'s deck. Smoke rose through cracks and slats in the deck. Nel could only see a dozen feet, if that. People ran to and fro. She saw what could be weapons clutched by silhouettes, and thought she heard wands being discharged. Something came whizzing out of the smoke, a kettle. It nearly took her head off.

"Gabbi!" she yelled into the smoke screen. It had to be Gabbi, none of the other thaumatics on the ship would be throwing kitchen stock around.

Nel found Gabbi standing over Sharpe. The latter was bruised, bleeding, but still very much alive and defiant. He was caked in white powder—flour. It wasn't hard to deduce what had happened. The half empty sack, burst at the seams, lay beside him.

Gabbi turned to Nel, then caught sight of Jack and his cargo. "Oh, Piper," she whispered. Rounding furiously on Sharpe, she raised a hand, a hand bright with writhing electricity.

"Gabbi, no!" Nel lunged and locked her hand around her cook's wrist. A jolt ran up her arm. It went numb to the shoulder and she couldn't hold back a gasp, but she didn't let go, forcing Gabbi's arm upward. Again Nel found herself staring at the stark angry eyes of one of her crew.

"I want to talk to him," Nel said levelly, surprising herself at how steady her voice sounded. Her arm shook uncontrollably, the charge from Gabbi firing the nerves in her muscles. She felt the spasms start to move further into her body.

"He hurt Piper," Gabbi said stubbornly. "He attacked us, he set fire to the ship." There were tears in Gabbi's eyes. "He . . . he went after the captain, Nel!"

Nel's breath caught. She couldn't see the captain—maybe someone had hustled him off—but it explained why Gabbi was in such a state. And all because of Sharpe. The ship was burning, the crew injured, because of him.

The spasms moved across her chest.

"I need to know why," Nel whispered to Gabbi.

All the current running through her body suddenly died like Gabbi had flipped a switch. The tension went out of Gabbi's arm, lowering to her side, and Nel was able to let go. Her fingers refused to close again afterwards. The tattooed sleeve that ran the length of her right arm seemed to writhe and dance, the markings moving with an anarchistic freedom beyond her control.

Gabbi held her eyes level with Nel's. "And when he doesn't want to talk?"

Nel felt her features harden. "Then I make him talk."

The expression that came over Gabbi's normally soft face was not a nice one.

Nel clapped her friend on the shoulder with her left hand. The right one was still numb. "Go help with the fire, save what we can."

"Aye, Skipper," Gabbi said automatically. She ran off, apron flapping about her knees.

"You too, Jack," Nel said over her shoulder. "Get Piper off the ship and go help with the fire."

"Right," Jack rumbled, looking down at Sharpe, considering. Piper seemed a forgotten thing on his shoulder.

"Now, Jack," Nel ordered.

Jack shrugged with one shoulder but started towards the dock, Piper's head and arms swinging carelessly behind his back.

Chapter 8

Water was being pumped from the dry dock onto the *Tantamount* and it was going to cost them. Water was expensive out here on the Rim. But then fire was more expensive. Damn Sharpe.

"Why?" Nel demanded, kneeling down in front of Sharpe. He rolled his head to look up at her. Expressionless. Arrogant. Blood oozed sluggishly from a cut above his eye, turning his coat of flour into a gooey paste. But he didn't say anything.

His eyes rolled back in his head when Nel slugged him in the jaw. She stood up, rubbing her knuckles. Turned out there was some advantage to not being able to feel them.

It took them a time to bring the fire under control. By smothering the fire inside the hold it was starved of air and killed itself off. Scarlett found Nel shortly afterwards on the dock.

"Some of our cargo is missing."

Nel stood up from the rigging she'd been going through, wiping a soot stained forearm across her brow. The rigging was spare from the hold and was spotted with burnt fibres. It would have to be cut down to salvageable lengths and re-spliced to become usable again. And it was hardly the only damage to contend with.

"It went up in smoke," Nel said bluntly. "There's nothing we can do about that."

Scarlett made a face, like it was a personal failure on Nel's part that it had happened. "Not from the fire," she said. "From what was already offloaded onto the docks."

"What about it?" Nel scowled. The cargo had been the last thing on her mind. The *Tantamount* had been wounded, again, and Nel felt that injury like it was her own. The soot stains on her hands might as well be blood. She hadn't even had time to check on Horatio yet, nor investigate the inside of the ship.

"Someone took it," Scarlett said coolly. "Your girl."

"My girl this time?" Nel said. "What in the hells are you on about?"

"Violet," Scarlett said the name distastefully.

"Violet?" Nel said. "Don't waste my time. Our ship was on fire, there's no way she was ransacking your precious . . ."

"She did," Scarlett told her. "Onyx saw her. She took a box of the medical supplies and ran off into town."

Nel remembered the look on Violet's face in the Rimward slums.

"I need those supplies, Vaughn," Scarlett said. "Too much was lost in the fire as it was."

"One box can't make that much difference." Nel grimaced, knowing she was quoting Sharpe.

Scarlett's face was set. "You need to find her. Now."

"It's not my problem and this is a damned charity run," Nel reminded her. "A mercy mission. Violet's going about it the wrong way, but she has the right intentions."

"Plough her intentions," Scarlett snapped. "If I wasn't afraid of what might happen here I'd get the supplies back myself. And there wouldn't be enough left of your girl to fit into the box they came in."

"Don't threaten my crew," Nel said, letting her hand drop to the hilt of her wand. "Not now, not ever."

"You're forgetting who's in charge here," Scarlett said.

"I don't forget, Scarlett."

The two stared at each other, deadlocked.

"Fine." Scarlett looked away, her eyes becoming distant for a second. "I'll find her myself."

The dock shuddered, Onyx looming over Scarlett's diminutive form. When Scarlett spoke, she did so towards Nel, but there was no confusion over who her words were meant for.

"If anyone else touches the cargo . . ." She let the tension build for a moment. "Kill them."

Nel swore. She glanced hurriedly at the golem. It had already settled back into its passive state, looking like a harmless statue. One that would shortly be without a master to rein it in. Scarlett had already left, not waiting to see Nel's reaction.

"Dammit," Nel fumed. "Jack! Don't let anyone touch the damned cargo. I'm going after Scarlett."

Smoke rose from the docks. Violet watched it curl away and spread out into a mushroom where it met the envelope around Rim. Minutes went past and the column became a cloud, hanging over the docks where the *Tantamount* lay.

The box of medicine she'd taken from the ship, medicine shipped all the way from the seedy, smoky underbelly of Cauldron, lay forgotten at her feet. Something had happened to the *Tantamount*, she felt that in her gut.

Violet didn't hear the locals coming up. Didn't notice when one of them opened the box. It wasn't until someone grabbed her shoulder and spun her round that she came back to the real world.

"You was with himself, weren't you?"

Violet took a step back from the man, suddenly realising she was surrounded. Her heart skipped a beat at the sight of the hungry eyed crowd. As a group they made Korrigan Jack look doe-like.

The man held up grimy hands to show his good intentions. "Easy, lass, ain't nobody gonna hurt you." He glowered at the folk around them. "Hold your horses, folk. Give the girl a second here."

Violet drew a short breath. "You know Sharpe, right?" she queried.

"Aye." The man chuckled, displaying a row of yellowed teeth. "Himself. Said someone would be coming back. Didn't figure it for such a little one." He shrugged.

"Where's your friend?" she asked, searching the crowd. "The Draugr? Where's he?"

"You didn't seem too taken with him last time, lass."

Violet flushed. "Felt bad, wanted to say so."

"Yeah, well Wallace ain't here, lass. Sorry, you'll have to make do with me. Name's Grouse. But what you got oughta make up for it. Got something for you back, lass."

He held out a leather tube. It was worn but still too clean to have come from the slums.

"What's this?" Violet took it, still eyeing the crowd. Several of them crowded round the box she'd brought, enough that she couldn't see what was in there.

"From himself." Grouse shrugged. "Said it was for your captain. Didn't say other than that. Other than you should keep it close."

Violet stared at the package. A small voice in her head told her to run now. There was more going on here. And somehow she knew it was all going to be her fault.

"Who are you?" she asked Grouse.

"Who put you up to this?"

"Put me up?" Scarlett was amused enough to stop. They'd been searching through the slums for almost half a bell now. For someone whose legs were so short Scarlett could set a pace when she had the mind.

"All our troubles have come from your crew, not me," Scarlett reminded her.

"Not that. This run. Who cared enough about a backwater brushfire to put a Guild contract on a bunch of medical supplies?"

Scarlett shrugged. "Someone who could foot the bill.

Beyond that I don't care."

Nel didn't buy that. Not at all. "You seem bent on seeing this through. Ebon must have made it worth your while."

Scarlett gave her a withering look. One that said Nel was wasting her time fishing.

"Charity runs like this must make you feel good," Nel went on anyway. "Must make up for some of the damned nasty things you people do with the rest of your time."

"You know what will make me feel better?" Scarlett commented, picking up the pace again. "Dealing to that girl of yours."

Nel's hand gripped her wand tightly. "I warned you about threatening my crew."

Scarlett's voice was starkly cold. "You have your priorities, I have mine. If you're concerned, then start praying she hasn't done anything with that box she stole."

"Those medicines are meant for the needy," Nel said. "Plenty of folks here need them, just as much as those further inward."

Nel scowled when she realised she was echoing the arguments Sharpe had made earlier. She could have done without the irony that they'd had some influence on her after all.

Scarlett snorted. "Medicine isn't some plug you can shove in a hole to stop a leak. You give it out without thought it'll just make things worse. Besides, nobody cares about the wretches out Rimward."

Then why the trip in the first place, Nel thought before giving voice to her concerns. "I'm surprised that anyone cares about any place this remote."

"I certainly don't," Scarlett muttered. "Though it seems your man did."

Nel stopped. "What's that supposed to mean? That's the second time you called Sharpe my man."

"I didn't have to explain who I meant, did I?"

"Try explaining what, then," Nel challenged her.

Scarlett shrugged. "He's part of your crew, that makes him

your man." She didn't wait for Nel, kept up her quick pace.

"He's no more part of my crew than you are, Scarlett, and that wasn't what you meant by it. Was it?"

"You're wasting your time trying to figure out what I mean and what I think, Vaughn. The way he watches you could be taken any number of ways."

"What way?" Nel snapped. "And what watching?"

"Like he's expecting something," Scarlett said. "And since we both know he's not really one of your crew, why don't you tell me this. Do you even know who he is?"

"Do you?"

Scarlett smiled. "Let's just say I recognise him." The Guildswoman stopped. "There. That's her."

Violet was ahead, surrounded by Rim slum folk.

"She still has the box," Nel observed. "Doesn't look like she's done anything with it yet."

"Good."

Nel had been watching Scarlett. The woman was ice, that much was obvious. All business and no heart. So when Scarlett went for her wand, Nel went for hers. Nel was faster. She had the tip of her wand under Scarlett's pointed chin and her hand around Scarlett's wrist before the Guildswoman could draw it back. Nel squeezed hard until she felt the joint flex under her fingers. Scarlett gasped in pain and dropped her wand.

"Go for the other one and I'll really hurt you."

"You'll regret this." Scarlett grimaced as Nel forced her chin up higher.

"I told you not to threaten my crew," Nel reminded her. "You didn't listen."

"You're a fool," Scarlett said bluntly. "You've no idea . . ."

"Skipper." Violet was almost underfoot now, the stolen box in her hands.

It was empty.

"What did you do?" Scarlett snatched for the box, oblivious to Nel's wand. She shook it, peering inside. There was nothing to be seen. A look of fear came over her face—

it was almost enough to make Nel lower her weapon. Almost.

"You little fool," Scarlett whispered, holding the box. "What did you do?"

Violet drew away from her. "I gave it away."

"To them?" Scarlett gestured around, indicating the Rimworlders.

Nel could see Violet biting down on her lip, confused and frightened.

"This whole place," Scarlett said, throwing the empty box away. "This whole place is going to burn . . . because of you."

"What do you mean?" Nel demanded. She stepped around Scarlett, grabbing Violet's arm.

"We'll never get them back," Scarlett told her. "They'll disappear into these slums. Rimworlders, refugees. You couldn't get them back if you wanted!" Fierce determination lit Scarlett's eyes. "We need to leave this place."

"We're leaving." Nel pushed Violet behind her. "You're not getting back on my ship."

"Don't," Scarlett whispered, "be so sure about that."

Violet screamed. Nel dove to the side, something dark rushing past the space where her head had been, whipping displaced air until it shrieked. Nel turned as she fell, lashing out with her wand, kinetic force discharging at whatever had attacked her.

The charge burst on Onyx's obsidian chest, splaying outward. It didn't seem to bother the golem. It raised one arm, the sharpened protrusions catching the light.

Nel rolled. The dock was reduced to kindling splinters instead of her. She attacked with her wand twice more, scraping a few flakes of stone, but little else.

Something in the corner of her eye caught her attention and she dove again. Twin charges shot past her—Scarlett had regathered her wands and joined the fray. Nel tried to put Onyx between them but a few shots across her bow put paid to that idea. Scarlett was showing her talents now and all Nel could do was duck for cover.

Nel flicked off a shot at Scarlett, then dodged behind a

shack. She didn't see where Scarlett went but Onyx's oversized fist demolished the corner of her chosen building. Demolished it and then froze. Nel stared, confused.

"Skipper?"

Cautiously, Nel emerged from the demolished shack. Violet stood over the Guildswoman, a brick clutched in her hand. Scarlett lay sprawled, wands kicked out of reach.

"Good work, lass," Nel said after a moment.

Violet dropped the brick. On Scarlett, of course.

Nel stared at Onyx. The golem remained frozen, as always. The same way it had during the voyage. That was . . . odd. Nel could freely admit she didn't know much about golems but it seemed to her that the golem should have at least finished carrying out Scarlett's instructions. Instead its animation seemed to be tied to the Guildswoman herself. And her being conscious.

Nel eyed the golem suspiciously. Behind her she heard a moan. The golem twitched, creaking. Violet kicked Scarlett in the head and the golem stopped moving. So did the moaning.

"Weird," Nel muttered. She took aim and fired off a shot at the golem, aiming for what should have been its kneecap. The shot ricocheted off. Nel flinched even though the charge went skyward.

"Have to remember that, Skipper," Violet said, glancing up at the fast vanishing charge.

"Hope we don't have to," Nel said, eyeing the unconscious Guildswoman. The thought to do something permanent about at least one of her many problems had occurred to her. No more than that though.

"Don't think this gets you off the hook, lass," she said sternly. "We're going to have a long talk about what you did."

Violet wilted under her glare. "I was just wanted to help," she said weakly. "To do . . . something." She clutched a hand to her chest, head downcast.

What was the worst that could happen? Scarlett had

certainly been afraid of something.

"What was in the box, Violet?" Nel asked her.

The girl gave a helpless shrug. "Medicine?"

"What did it look like?"

"I don't know, like medicine. What should it have looked like?"

"Forget it," Nel sighed. "We need to get back to the ship." There were more supplies still on the dock. She could check them over herself and see what all the panic was about.

She glanced at Scarlett's prone body as they left. The right thing to do would be to take her with them, the golem notwithstanding. Anything could happen if they just left her lying there. But it was just a thought. After all, it wasn't her problem.

"Skipper . . ." Cyrus deflated at the sight of Nel as she stormed past him, kicking her way through the cargo. Violet trailed after her, a meek little shadow in her footsteps. The *Tantamount*'s crew pulled away from them, exchanging nervous glances with each other, faces and bodies still marred by soot from the fire and clean up.

Nel sank down beside her captain. His face was grey, a large, purpling contusion lending the only colour to his skin. Strands of stringy hair were brushed back and Gabbi was wiping him down with a rag that was crusted with grime and blood. The ship's cook didn't look up.

"He looks worse than he is." Gabbi sounded like an automaton. "They both do."

The other was Piper, laid down beside his captain. His big chest rose and fell steadily though his jaw hung open and slack, a small trail of drool running down his cheek.

"Is he gonna be all right?" Violet crouched down alongside Piper. She took his burly, tattooed hand in her two smaller ones, holding it close.

"Knock like that may have done him some good," Nel muttered. She searched the crowd. "I don't see Quill."

"He was on the ship," Gabbi said tonelessly.

That did not surprise Nel.

"Would somebody like to tell me," she raised her voice so the whole crew could hear her, "where in the hells my damned ship has gone?"

All her crew found ways to avoid meeting her eyes. She could see for herself the frayed ends of guide ropes, floating just outside the Rim's envelope. They'd been torn free, either given way under pressure or held and their contacts ripped out. There was no sign of the *Tantamount*.

Nel ran a hand through her hair in frustration. "Is anyone else missing? Was anyone else aboard the ship?"

"Everyone seems to be here." Gabbi was morose. She brushed the captain's hair again. She didn't seem to know what else to do.

"Where's Bandit?" Violet asked. "I don't see him. Wouldn't he be with Piper?"

Gabbi shrugged.

"Brilliant," Nel muttered. Her ship was gone, her navigator with it and with him her only crewmember capable of launching a ship. So unless Quill had finally seen fit to follow through on his longstanding threat to leave them all and take the ship with him she needn't look far for her culprit.

Sharpe.

He'd come to, freed himself, found the ship otherwise deserted and managed to somehow suborn Quill and make him take the ship out.

She frowned.

That didn't make sense. What had Sharpe been trying to accomplish? He'd set fire to the ship with himself inside it, now he'd made off in that same fire-damaged ship. The irony was there if she could stand to look at it, and granted things hadn't gone the way Sharpe had likely hoped. But still, it struck her as too convenient that all of Sharpe's actions had left the ship unloaded, unmanned, and sent both her and Scarlett running off to the other side of Rim.

Even if the golem hadn't come running after its master, Onyx wouldn't have been able to get back on the ship to stop Sharpe. He was too heavy.

Hang on, Sharpe's actions . . .

Nel glanced at Violet. The girl still clung to Horatio's hand like a drowning man clung to a rope. There was a fervent desperation to the girl's behaviour.

"Violet," Nel said, kneeling beside the girl and speaking in a low tone. "When the fire broke out, why didn't you stay to help?"

Barely restrained tears made the girl's eyes bright in her face. "I wasn't here, Skipper. I . . . I'd already . . ."

Nel nodded. It confirmed what she'd already suspected. That made more sense to her than how Scarlett had put it.

"The box you took," Nel kept her voice calm and steady, "was that your idea?"

Violet's stricken look was all the answer Nel needed. The tears started to flow freely. Violet knew too.

"Sonofa—" Nel lashed out at nothing angrily, stalking away from Violet lest she take her frustrations out on the girl.

"Nel!" Gabbi's voice cracked across her tantrum, bringing her round. She stared at her friend, still furious, but it was a cold anger now.

"He played us, Gabbi," Nel said. "He played us, he played me for a fool. Gods only knows how long he was setting us up for. Since the start, maybe."

"It's not your fault," Gabbi said, but the response sounded automatic to Nel.

"He's got my ship, Gabbi. Quill . . . Quill . . ."

Gabbi shook her head. "I don't think he was in on it, Skipper."

Nel snorted. "You really think Sharpe bullied him into flying the ship out? Quill could have pitched him overboard."

"Can't throw people, Skipper," Gabbi reminded her.

"He would have found a way," Nel retorted. "Hells, I can't believe you're standing up for Quill. He couldn't stand any of us, the only person he even remotely liked was Sharpe.

Sharpe!"

"He liked you, Skipper," Gabbi said quietly.

No, Nel thought. *Not anymore.*

Not after what happened at the blockade. He was mad and had every right to be mad. Mad enough to . . . to what? Mutiny? Or just run off with the ship when opportunity presented itself?

"Sharpe found a way to get to Quill, Skipper," Gabbi insisted. "He must have."

Sharpe now. Not Castor.

"Maybe." Nel wasn't convinced. She couldn't think of any way Sharpe could have persuaded Quill to launch the *Tantamount* against his will.

The *Tantamount*. Her ship.

She wanted it back. She was going to get it back.

"Do what you can for the captain and Piper," she told Gabbi. "I'm going to need to talk to them as soon as they come round. Violet." Nel nudged the girl with one booted foot. The fox girl looked up through teary eyes.

"Start getting the rest of the crew together. I want them ready."

"Ready for what?" Violet dashed tears away with the back of her hand.

"I'll let them know when they're ready." Nel jerked her head. "Move, girl."

Violet got to her feet shakily, but moved with purpose, flitting from person to person of the crew. Nel caught the eyes of one of them and beckoned them over.

"We needs another ship, Skipper," Jack grumbled as he lumbered over.

"I want mine back," she said.

Jack grunted. "Sharpe's got it. Don't think he wants to give it back."

"Didn't much plan on asking, Jack."

Jack grinned at her, a collection of stained, broken teeth. "What am I doing, Skipper?"

"Finding me a ship."

"Not our ship?" he clarified.

"Something small and fast," Nel said. "A ferry, a runabout."

"Those aren't fast."

"It only needs to get us to our ship, Jack."

"Right. I'm with ya now. You want me to buy it then?"

"Rent," Nel said.

That evil grin again. "Negotiable?"

"Don't steal it, Jack," she warned.

"I wasn't gonna." He laughed. "You really likes our ship, don't you, Skipper?"

"More than I like you, Jack," she told him honestly.

More laughter. Jack flexed his muscles, cracked some knuckles. His small, dark eyes were already squinting in consideration of how to go about his task.

Nel moved to head him off. "Take some others with you, Jack."

His face darkened. "I don't play good with others."

"You don't have to play with them," she assured. "They'll just make you look scarier."

Jack thought about that and nodded in approval. "Okay."

"Don't be long, Jack."

He grunted in response, casting a speculative look out into space, past where the *Tantamount* had been docked. "Sharpe's a strange one, isn't he, Skipper?"

Nel raised an eyebrow questioningly.

Jack shook his head. "Daft man. Set fire to the ship, then he stole it. Daft."

Jack, of all people, had put his finger on another of Nel's concerns. Giving it voice had brought it to the crux of her thoughts. Why had Sharpe set fire to the ship in the first place?

Obviously his intent had been destructive. What were his potential targets? The ship, of course, but since he'd gone and stolen it afterwards that didn't seem likely. There were Nel, Horatio, and the crew, but again she couldn't think of a reason that justified that. He had nothing to gain from them dying in a fire. That left Scarlett, but as far as Sharpe had known she hadn't even been aboard. She'd been dockside when Sharpe had started his conflagration. He'd walked past her and her pet golem on the way to the ship.

Which only left the cargo itself. Half of which had been unloaded on the docks. Nel paced, thinking. Why would Sharpe care about a cargo of relief medicine, one destined for his own home?

Was that it? Did Sharpe not want those supplies getting through? It hardly seemed worth it for a delivery of medical supplies.

Assuming that was what they were delivering.

Scarlett had almost lost it when she found out what Violet had done with that one box. Nel turned, looking at the stacked cargo spread out over the dock.

What in the hells were they really carrying?

Piper sat back on his haunches, considering the contents of the box he'd opened. He hadn't said anything since coming round and Nel had explained the situation. He'd taken it upon himself to go through all the remaining cargo; the foodstuffs and the medical supplies. Horatio hovered nearby, peering over and around Piper's shoulder and generally getting in the way, having seemingly taken on the role of filling in for Bandit until the loompa reappeared.

Nel had the impression both men were annoyed at having been unconscious for most of what had happened. Piper wasn't talking and the captain was doing his best to pretend it had never happened. Both had taken to their tasks with unexpected zeal.

"Well?" Nel drummed her foot. "That's the last box, Piper. What are we dealing with?"

Piper and Horatio exchanged a long measured look. Horatio's fuzzy eyebrows somehow managed to rearrange themselves into a sage expression; one of wisdom hard acquired through years of rough living and travelling. Piper's face was like when he was at his most philosophical. A number of facial expressions passed between them, a silent communication until they were ready to explain. They turned to her as one.

"We have no idea," Horatio said.

"None," Piper confirmed.

The assembled crew drew back in trepidation.

"So what," Nel growled, "have you been doing for the last bell?"

Piper shrugged. "Being thorough."

"Yes, being thorough," Horatio said shrilly. "And don't you take that tone with me, young woman." He shook one bony finger at her. "As long as you serve on my ship don't you take that tone with me."

Nel glared at him flatly. Horatio shook, but didn't look away.

"I want my ship back," he whispered so only Nel and Piper could hear. "Get her back, Nel. Get my ship back for me."

Nel sighed, unable to hold the glare.

"I'll get her back, Captain." It was all she could say.

"Skipper," someone called. "Jack's back."

Nel turned to greet her scarred crewman. He was alone.

"Where are the others?" she asked immediately. Worst case scenarios flashed through her mind.

"With the boat," Jack said, like it should have been obvious. He held up his hands. "It's not very big."

"What isn't very big?" Horatio asked. "Eh? Speak up, boy. Now's no time to mumble."

Jack sized the captain up in annoyance. Nel could read his thoughts plainly. To Jack you were either top dog or you weren't. Without a ship to command Horatio had gone down in Jack's pecking order.

Time to draw his attention to her. "What'd you find, Jack?"

"It's a tug," Jack said, adding "Skipper," almost as an afterthought. "Won't fit many of us."

"How many?" Nel pushed.

Jack shrugged. "Not many."

Great, Nel thought.

"Piper," she said, "you're coming with me."

"With us," Horatio said huffily.

Nel hesitated, then nodded reluctantly. Not a battle she had the energy to fight right now.

"Gabbi," she called, "keep an eye on things 'til we get back."

"That gonna be long?" Gabbi asked.

"I'm getting my ship back. Takes as long as it takes."

Gabbi wheeled on Piper and the captain. "You two be careful. I didn't patch you both up so you could go and get the stuffing knocked right back out. You hearing me?"

Piper and Horatio exchanged another of those looks. "Never argue with the cook," was Piper's solemn comment.

"Indeed." Horatio agreed, eyeing Gabbi warily. "We'll be careful," he promised.

"You'd better," she warned them.

Nel took Gabbi by the shoulder, leading her away. "Keep an eye on Violet," she told her friend. "Keep her here, make sure she doesn't try and follow us."

Gabbi glanced at the Kitsune girl. She was seated glumly on a crate, but watching everything intently. "You think she might?"

Nel squeezed the woman's shoulder in an affirmative. "Given half a chance, yes. She's feeling guilty. Don't let her do anything too stupid."

"No, I'll leave that to you and the captain," Gabbi drawled.

"Watch your mouth, cook," Nel admonished.

"Aye, Skipper, watching it."

Nel snorted. "Fine. Be that way. I'll be back with our ship."

"Good. Don't bother with Quill though. Damned Kelpie's not worth the sweat."

"Fine, you can push the sails then," Nel said. Gabbi made a face like she'd sucked down an extremely sour lemon.

"Watch yourself, Skipper," Cyrus said as she went to rejoin Jack and the others. "Just sighted one of those blockade ships coming in."

Nel hesitated. "One of the frigates?"

Cyrus grimaced. "No, *Mangonel,* the big one. Still a ways out, can see the big tub from leagues off."

What was the *Mangonel* doing headed this way? Nel put it to the back of her mind. *Worry about it if it becomes a worry.*

"Nel," Horatio called to her from across the dock. "I've been meaning to ask you. What happened to Scarlett?"

"You're kidding me," Nel said. "That's the best you could find?"

The best had turned out to be not much more than a longboat, a glorified tub, the hull lined with a threadbare layer of ether, just enough to snag a breath of air when it left the Rim's envelope. They wouldn't get far in it. Maybe a few miles outside of Rim. They could go further but wouldn't have enough air to get back. Not a pleasant thought.

"That was all they had," Jack growled.

"He's right, Skipper," Orim, one of the crew who'd gone with Jack, chimed in. "We tried everywhere, you shoulda seen the stuff we didn't go for."

"No, she shouldn't," Aldy, the other crewman, added.

"Hells," Nel muttered, pacing round the boat. Jack hadn't been exaggerating, it wasn't fit to be called anything else, it barely even qualified as that. Her pacing didn't take long. The boat wasn't much longer than she was tall.

"This isn't going to work," she said.

"Course it will," Horatio said. "Just has to get us to the *Tantamount.*"

Nel glanced out at the cold, empty expanse surrounding Rim. Blackness and miasma, no sign of the *Tantamount* or any other ship out there.

"We can't all fit in that thing," she said.

"Well, I'm not staying behind," Horatio said emphatically. "I won't hear of it."

"It can take two," Piper said speculatively. "One to work the winches and one other."

The boat had the same hand operated propulsion as a

bubble. It just didn't have the ability to operate for as long away from an actual envelope. There wasn't even enough ether to keep the passengers grounded. Instead there were straps to tie them down to their seats and stirrups to mount their feet in.

"You and me then, Piper," Nel said.

"I said I'm going!" Horatio insisted.

"I ain't staying either," Jack growled. "Not on this heap."

"This isn't up for a debate," Nel said.

"I'm the captain," Horatio screeched, doing a madcap dance and waving his arms. "I want my ship back!"

"Yeah," Jack grunted, folding his beefy arms. "He's the captain. He tells you what to do, Skipper. So he goes and I go."

"Eh?" Horatio paused, looking Jack up and down.

No, Nel thought immediately. There was no way she could let that happen. Out there in the miasma, she didn't trust Jack with the captain. Not alone, not one bit. Hells, the way he was acting she wasn't even sure she trusted him here. She glanced at Aldy and Orim, saw the same uneasiness. They weren't the smartest sailors on the roster but they'd spent the last bell with Jack, had noticed the way he was acting.

Korrigan Jack was crazy. Nel had never doubted that. But crazy by itself didn't bother her, half the crew had some sort of mess they were forever hiding or trying to work around. Jack worked to some set of rules unknown to anyone but him. Sometimes there was a twisted kind of sense that could be found to fit his actions, but with the ship gone some of those rules seemed to have changed. Nel did know one thing though, Jack was not someone she could ever back down to.

"Captain," she said, "the ship was taken on my watch. Getting her back is my responsibility. Besides," she added, seeing her words start to have an impact, "you didn't even bring your wand."

Horatio patted his belt, looking concerned.

"Piper and I will be going," she said this last to Jack.

Jack didn't answer her. He was watching the captain frisk himself, a calculating look on his face.

Hells, Nel cursed inwardly. *He wouldn't dare.*

Would he?

"Skipper," Piper said loudly. She glanced at him. "You should take Jack. I am . . . not myself." He pointed to his head and the signs of his last run-in with Sharpe. "And I would spend some more time looking for Bandit. I am concerned for him."

"Bandit's missing?" Horatio piped up. "Well, we can't have that, Piper. Can't have that at all. Bad enough we've got a missing ship out there without losing any more crew along with her."

Nel caught Piper's eye. He nodded imperceptibly. He'd noticed the way Jack was acting as well. Enough to move to ensure the captain wouldn't be left alone with him. And the captain was . . . well, the captain was the captain. Some things never changed.

"Get in the boat, Jack," Nel ordered. "Aldy, Orim, launch the damned thing."

"Aye, Skipper." The two jumped to it.

"Did I ever tell you about my cat, Piper?" Horatio was saying as they made to cast off.

"No, Captain, you did not," Piper rumbled.

"Damnedest thing. No idea what happened to it."

In Nel's mind the boat had ceased to be anything that could even be dignified as such. So from the prow of the dinghy, she watched Jack turn the crank that worked the propeller. Jack watched her too. In between watching each other they searched for the *Tantamount*. It wasn't there to be seen, so they spent more and more time looking at each other.

Surrounded by banks of miasma deeper than the thickest fog, Nel considered her situation. It wasn't good. If Horatio had been out here she suspected Jack would have already made his move. Because it was her, he hadn't.

Nel sat with her feet tucked into stirrups set into the flooring, hands resting on knees, wand tapping against the palm of her hand. From the weight, slight though the difference was, it remained about half charged. To fix that she needed crystals and the crystals were in her cabin, aboard the *Tantamount*. If she had to use the wand on Jack, in a vessel this small, at this range . . . well, it would deal to him. And likely her as well.

Jack stopped, tensing. Nel did the same.

Was this it?

His head moved, not looking at anything she realised, he was moving his head to try and locate the direction of a sound. In the miasma there was almost no sound and no perspective to give it reference. The only thing that made sound was the rumble of something massive, an envelope cutting through space and fog.

A ship, in other words.

Nel rose to her feet, swaying in her stirrups while Jack twisted in his seat, both trying to see better. The movements were unconscious and didn't accomplish much. The miasma was too thick to let them see anything until it was uncomfortably close. They could make out the beacon lights of Rim, blazing in the mist, but nothing else.

Nothing until the mist turned dark, giving way to what could only be the *Mangonel*, the massive hull close enough that Nel should have been able to make out individual nails and planks. But all she saw were silhouettes and lines, coloured signal lights and vague disturbance where the envelope began.

Jack grunted, leaning back. "How'd we miss that?"

Nel sat back down, reaching out to hold both sides. Jack's weight alone was enough to rock the boat.

They must have gotten badly turned around to get between the Alliance dreadnought and Rim. It didn't make their chances of finding the *Tantamount* look any better.

"What are we doing out here," Nel said. She didn't mean to make it a question but Jack interpreted it as such.

"I like the quiet," Jack said.

"Why's that?" Nel asked, for lack of anything else to do.

"It ain't quiet in prison."

Nel eyed him. Jack's face was blank, hard.

"You never asked me," he said.

"Never asked you what?"

"About what I was in for." He rubbed the shiny scar tissue bracelets on his wrists.

Her hand might have tightened on her wand, but Nel looked Jack right in the eye then. "I don't care who you were, what you did, why you did it. That's the past. On our ship the past stays out of it. You don't bring it aboard and I won't ask about it. You're part of my crew now."

"Yeah."

Talking with Jack was frustrating. He didn't respond like a normal person. Every time Nel said something to him it felt like she was checking a box, taking them down some course of action. The problem was she had no way of knowing what the course was, and until she checked the right boxes, or enough of the wrong ones, Jack wasn't going to act.

His head came up. "There's another ship."

Nel got halfway to her feet before the boat rocked wildly under her feet.

The envelope, she thought, *we must be meshing. The other ship's too close!*

The boat rocked again, one foot came loose, and Nel felt herself falling, pitching over the side. Felt the icy rush of the void as she hit the miasma. Her wand dropped from suddenly frostbitten fingers as she flailed desperately with both hands, seeking a purchase. There was none. Her other foot came loose of its binding and there was nothing left anchoring her to the boat.

Except Jack. The ex-convict Korrigan lunged over the gunnels of the boat, clamping one meaty hand around her ankle. They hung there, freezing in the void, Nel outside the envelope, Jack straddling it. Nel stared at Jack, saw the confusion in his face.

Jack had just saved her.

And just as suddenly he let her go.

Nel gasped, not in shock—she was beyond that—but in pain. She fell, but only a short distance, hitting something solid and unyielding before she fell too far. She groaned, wanting to curl up into a ball, but resisted the urge. Above her, Jack and the boat he was still in floated down gently to settle at her feet, canting to the side.

Nel sat up, bare hands and feet finding wooden decking under them. She recoiled at that touch, her toes and fingers burned from the cold. That made her angry and drove her to her feet. The boat in front of her rocked unsteadily as Jack stood and tried to climb out of it, forgetting he was still strapped in.

A familiar voice broke the silence. "Skipper, if I didn't know better I'd think you were following us."

Sharpe. If Nel hadn't lost her wand she would have used it. Her cold snapped limbs weren't fast enough to catch him but she gave it her all, chasing Sharpe across the deck as he ducked and weaved away from her punches.

"You ploughing, gutter trash snipe!" she yelled at him, narrowly missing his head. "You attack my crew, set fire to my ship, steal my ship . . . "

She couldn't talk anymore, she was too angry. Sharpe, it seemed, had had enough too. He reached out and grabbed her wrists, holding on tight. She fought him, trying to throw him, break free, but he held her firm. So she kicked him in the knee. The knee buckled and he went down and she hit him higher. But when she threw a punch meant to connect with his face, she instead connected with a barrel that hadn't been there a moment ago. Nel howled in pain, dropping to her knees and clutching her hand.

"Amusing as watching you two monkeys beat each other is, we have other concerns."

"Quill," Nel growled up at him, following the sound of his voice. "You slimy, snake-skinned bast—"

"Yes, yes," Quill snapped irritably. "We are all that. All of us, illegitimate spawn the lot of us. Educational as your vocabulary can be, may we move on?"

Nel glared at him.

"Quill!" Sharpe yelled in warning.

Quill turned, throwing up a hand. The oversized harpoon nudged aside, barely missing him. *Careless of Quill to leave something like that around for Jack to throw at him*, Nel thought.

Jack appeared peeved that his missile had failed to do its job. He set about correcting the issue, this time with a heavier object. Having nothing else at hand he reached for what was — the boat. Grunting and roaring with the effort, he awkwardly lifted first the end, then the whole length of the dinghy off the deck and swung it like a club at Quill.

Quill stopped him, though he didn't make it look easy. The more surface area he had to work with the stronger Quill could push on an object. Having something work against him made it harder, not normally a problem in the motionless, frictionless void when he was merely pushing massive sail cloth, but Jack seemed up to the task and for a moment the two seemed evenly matched.

"Call him off!" Quill demanded, voice cracking with the strain. "Call him off now!"

"Why should I?" Nel staggered to her feet, cradling her injured hand. It really hurt now, after smashing it into Quill's improvised shield.

"I saved your miserable skins," Quill growled.

"From what!" Nel demanded. "The only danger was when you pulled us aboard!"

With a yell Quill ripped the boat away from Jack and pushed it over the edge of the ship, out into the void. Part of the tiny boat stayed in Jack's hands, splintered handfuls of timber he stubbornly refused to let go of. He glared at the Kelpie resentfully, but didn't try anything else. *Put in his place then*, Nel thought.

"Good riddance," Sharpe said, reminding Nel he was still there. "I can't believe you made it this far out in that thing."

Nel glared. "Somebody stole my damned ship!" She whipped back to Quill.

"That can be explained," Quill shrugged, adding, "Skipper."

Nel seethed. "Setting fire to it? Attacking Piper and the captain?" An explanation wasn't going to cut it here.

"That's a bit harder," Sharpe admitted.

Nel walked until she could look at them both at once.

"Talk," she said. "Talk fast and make it good. Really good."

The two exchanged a look.

"Actually now's not the best time," Sharpe said. Quill left the conversation to him and stalked back to his position at the helm.

"We were following that behemoth out there." Sharpe gestured out into space. "Almost ran into it coming out of Rim. So we were sticking to its blind spot, down below. We saw you almost get taken out, thought we'd pick you up on the by. But while that monstrosity is docking at Rim we've got somewhere else to be."

"And where's that?" Nel said, wishing again she hadn't lost her wand. That was going to hurt, more than the freeze burns, when she had time to stop and feel it.

"Grange," Sharpe said. "I'm going home. To whatever's left of it."

Chapter 9

It hadn't been hard to slip away from the crew. The skipper might have told Gabbi to watch her, but when the *Mangonel Falling* arrived that had stolen everyone's attention. The dreadnought emerged from the miasma cloaking Rim, blotting out the horizon as it drifted alongside the station. The *Tantamount*'s crew, the dock workers, and more were all drawn in, watching as landing parties made their way towards Rim. But Violet wasn't watching the *Mangonel*, though she found her eyes were continuously drawn back to it.

It was Scarlett that had her attention. Scarlett and Onyx. The golem supported Scarlett, half-carrying the woman as they skirted the edge of the docklands. Blood crusted the woman's hair and one side of her face. Violet felt a pang of guilt over that, until she remembered what the woman had tried to do. That memory was only reinforced when Scarlett cast one long look towards where the *Tantamount* had been docked.

Violet trailed them, keeping as close as she dared. The Guildswoman's intentions were obvious even to her—she was going to meet with the landing party from the *Mangonel*. It was a rendezvous Violet arrived at after the Alliance group.

From what Violet could see the landing party was heavily armed. All carried wands at their belts, nearly half carried the heavier staffs. They cut a formidable picture, grim-faced men and women of different peoples, bonded under a common blue and white livery. One stepped forward to meet Scarlett some distance from the main group. They appeared cautious, but not unduly threatened by the Guildswoman and her golem.

Violet couldn't hear the words that were being exchanged. Taking a deep breath she darted closer, moving from cover to cover. She expected a shout of discovery any second from some sharp-eyed Alliance watchman. But none came. She crouched down behind an empty stack of shipping pallets, close enough to catch parts of the conversation but not to see the speakers.

". . . overrun with Draugr," Scarlett was saying. The woman's voice was patchy, hoarse.

"We went to extreme lengths to keep Rim isolated."

Violet missed Scarlett's reply.

". . . what you were brought in for. You've made the situation worse."

"The situation has escalated." Scarlett sounded angry.

". . . not acceptable," the officer was telling her. "There are hundreds of people on Rim."

"Were."

There was a long pause, long enough that Violet thought to risk a look. She saw the officer's face. He was conflicted.

"The first step is to secure the remaining supplies," he told Scarlett. "Will the crew be a problem?"

"No."

It didn't take the Alliance long after that. Violet heard orders barked and before she could think about moving they were gone. They moved swiftly and directly, leaving a small group to tend to their vessels. Violet thought to get back to the captain and the others but the Alliance was between her and them. She could only watch as they closed in around the *Tantamount*'s crew. She waited, heart hammering in her chest, but there was only quiet. There was no sound of weapons being discharged, no yells or screams. Violet let herself believe that the crew were still safe.

A glance over the top of her cover told her that the remaining Alliance sailors were watching. Too risky to move yet. Violet put her back against the pallets, forcing herself to wait. Her heart was still pounding. She put a hand to it and it almost stopped.

There, under her shirt, was the package Grouse had given her. Grouse, the man from the slums who'd known Sharpe. The man Sharpe had asked her to take a box of the *Tantamount*'s cargo to. He'd given her the package in exchange but until now she hadn't checked inside it. She'd forgotten.

Now, with nothing to do but wait, she had the time. She pulled the package out, a leather tube bound in twine. The sort papers and letters were kept in. Violet studied the tube, turning it over in her hands. It felt smooth to the touch but there were indentations around the body that could have been made by fingers. Handled often and gripped tightly.

Violet tugged at the twine 'til it came loose, popping the top off and upending it. Rolled parchment slipped out into her hand. She set the container down and unrolled the parchment in her hand.

Intricate calligraphy covered the top third of the parchment, pillars and ivy sketched in colourful ink. The writing began further down. Letters were not Violet's strongest suit but she'd learnt them on the *Tantamount* alongside her other lessons. Sailors depended on charts and references. And letters were nowhere near as difficult as numbers and the calculations needed to navigate the *Tantamount*. But at first Violet's eyes refused to reconcile the letters she was looking at.

It was the deed to the *Tantamount*.

Violet's fingers shook as she re-rolled the parchment and sealed it back in its container. She held it tight against her chest. Sharpe had taken the deed, that was the only explanation. He must have passed it to Grouse in the slums. Sharpe had played her, manipulated her. She realised that, didn't need the disappointment in the skipper's eyes to know that. But what had been the point in separating the deed from the ship? Had there been another plan in the works or was delivering the deed just a kick to the crew when they were down?

Somehow she had to get the deed back to the captain. It was the only way she could start to make things up.

Which meant she had to move. It could be disastrous to get caught by the Alliance sailors, but staying here made that just as likely. Violet started to move, foot by shaking foot, still expecting to be discovered at any second. But she wasn't.

When she had cover between her and the Alliance landing party she started to circle back around towards the *Tantamount*'s crew.

A month ago Violet would have screamed when the hand closed around her upper arm. Screamed into the hand that wrapped around her mouth precisely to stifle such a scream. But now she bit down hard on that hand, twisting and writhing in the grip, tangling up in her attacker's feet, sending them both tumbling. She lashed out at where she guessed her would-be abductor's face was.

"Hey, hey! Leave off, girl! It's me!"

Violet could taste blood in her mouth and hear it pounding in her ears. She pulled back only to cast around for something she could use as a bludgeon. And it was only out of the corner of her eye that she saw her attacker uncurl feebly from a foetal position, peering at her from behind shakily raised elbows.

"Grouse?" she demanded.

"Aye, the same," the other confirmed weakly.

Violet stared at Sharpe's friend. Then kicked him hard in the stomach. "What in the hells are you doing, grabbing me like that? And this, you've got some nerve nicking this off my captain!" Violet brandished the leather holding the *Tantamount*'s deed.

"I didn't nick nothing!" Grouse objected, staring at the bloody teeth marks in his hand. "I just gave you what Sharpe gave me. Damn, girl, but you've got some teeth in that foul mouth of yours."

Grouse flinched when Violet narrowed her eyes at him and spat out a mouthful of his blood. "What are you doing, grabbing me?" she repeated.

"Was trying to help you!" Grouse complained. "Won't be doing that again. Alliance just rolled through your ship's camp, you was headed right for them."

"So what's that to you if I am?" Violet lowered her voice at the reminder of the Alliance.

"Sharpe said to watch out for you."

"Sharpe? After he stole the captain's deed? After he stole the captain's ship?!"

"You're an angry wee one, aren't you?"

Violet shook her head in disgust. She was, she realised, starting to understand how the skipper must feel all the time. Reluctantly she held out a hand to Grouse, which he accepted with his good one and let her help him to his feet.

"Seems you and I had the same idea," he said, eyeing her warily.

"And what's that?" Violet asked.

Grouse jerked his head in the direction of the Alliance landing party. "Finding out what the boys in the pressed white and blues are up to on Rim. And I reckon you had an earful of just that."

Violet shrugged.

"I don't think the Alliance would have hurt your crew, lass, but they did scatter them good. If they've any sense, they'll head in towards the shanties. We can talk there. If you tell me what you know, I can help you look for them."

Violet looked at him, saying nothing. She thought it over. Grouse began to fidget as her silence went on.

"Well?" he asked her. "What do you say?"

"I'll think about it," Violet said.

Hidden away in the slums of Rim, Violet sat on a crate that was acting as her seat in the back of a dusty shack. Her hand kept straying to the front of her shirt, fingers tracing the lump that was the deed to the *Tantamount*. She'd searched but hadn't seen any of the crew. Not the captain nor Gabbi nor Piper. And it could only be her imagination, but the longer she held on to it, the hotter the deed felt under her shirt.

Fixated as Violet was on the *Tantamount* and its crew though, she hadn't missed the activity that was running through the shanty town. She watched Grouse's Draugr, whom she had since learned was called Wallace, haul in a bundle of tarps. They were the same tarps, mostly old sails, she'd previously seen acting as roofs for the ramshackle buildings of Rim.

There was already a bundle of tarp and cloth piled high in one corner of the shack. Wallace dumped his addition atop that and turned to leave. The Draugr stopped though, catching Violet's attention fixed on him. He stared back at her with disturbingly dry eyes.

Violet squeezed her hands together, uncomfortable under that stare. It reminded her of the way she'd over-reacted her first time in the slums.

"I'm sorry I screamed," she said.

Wallace kept staring at her. Violet wasn't sure if he understood her or not. She still didn't really understand Draugr herself. It was impossible to tell what was going on behind that weathered face.

"What are you?" Violet said aloud, jumping off the crate and taking a step towards Wallace. The Draugr's head moved slowly to look down at her. He was built solidly with corded muscle that still flexed and bulged when he moved. She ran a hand across the biceps of one arm, watching his face for a reaction. The Draugr stared at her touch but gave no other response.

Does he understand me?

Under her hand the skin was dry and cold, like wood. It didn't yield to her touch the way normal flesh should. Her fingers traced the contours to the marking she'd seen on his arm during their first meeting. She realised now it was a tattoo.

"My skipper has a tattoo just like this," she said. "From when she was in the Alliance."

It wasn't her imagination. The Draugr smiled at her. Just before turning around and walking out of the shack.

Grouse came back not long after, a loaf of day old bread in his hands. He tore off a hunk and handed it to Violet. She took it, realising she was famished.

"My captain?" she asked between swallows. "My crew?"

"Ain't found them yet," Grouse said through a mouthful of bread, crumbs slipping out of his maw.

"Did you look?"

"I said I would, didn't I? They'll end up here, lass, ain't nowhere else for them to go."

Violet said nothing to that, focused instead on chewing the bread. It was tough and gritty but palatable. She'd had worse.

"There was a Guildswoman on our ship." She anticipated the question Grouse opened his mouth to ask. "She was talking to the Alliance about Draugr. About being overrun with them."

"Overrun?" Grouse repeated.

"Wallace has an Alliance tattoo."

"Eh?" Grouse frowned. "So?"

"Did he used to be in the Alliance?"

"Why? He say he was?"

Violet scowled, not sure if Grouse was making fun of her.

"So he's got some Alliance ink, so what?" Grouse shrugged. "Sometimes scratchers like to practice their work on Draugr before the real thing."

"Who was he before?" Violet asked.

"Draugr don't talk much about before. Don't talk much about anything usually. What else did you hear?"

Violet sighed. "Not much," she admitted. "They talked about the situation escalating, about how there were hundreds of people here on Rim." She hesitated, remembering. "No, Scarlett said there *were* . . .

"We need to find the captain," she said urgently, feeling a tightness in her chest suddenly. "We need to find him now."

"What? Why . . ." Grouse turned his head as they both heard

yelling outside. Beneath that Violet heard the pounding of feet hitting the wooden ground. Men and women in Alliance colours crashed into the shack.

"Two more in here!" one of them yelled back through the doorway as wands were brandished at the two of them.

"Are they Draugr?" another asked, staring at Grouse suspiciously.

"I ain't no bloody Draugr!" Grouse yelled back, taking a step forward. It was enough. One of the Alliance soldiers lashed out at him with a wide sweep of his arms. Sparks flew from his wand and brightly coloured light struck Grouse at close range, throwing him back against the far wall. He landed softly amidst the tarps and sails Wallace had piled but his neck was twisted at a horribly impossible angle. Violet gave a small cry at the sight.

"What about her? She's no Draugr either."

"No loose ends," someone replied. "Finish it."

Violet turned. Braced herself. She didn't see a way out. The Alliance soldier who'd fired raised his wand again.

He went down, taking the other two with him as Wallace and a mob of others crashed into them. Shouts filled the air and through the open doorway Violet glimpsed a crowd of people rushing past. She ran outside, jumping over the pile of bodies in front of the door. One of the Alliance soldiers made to rise but someone beat them down again.

Outside there was smoke. A fire burned and ash rose on the air. The noise was deafening as a mob surged around her. She saw flashes of Alliance colour but mostly it was the people from Rim. They were attacking the Alliance, viciously, with whatever came to hand. And Violet found herself swept along in that rush.

It should have taken them almost two days to make the trip from Rim to the inner system, to Thatch and then Grange. And with only four people crewing the ship it should have taken them even longer—the ship was barely manageable, not meant to be handled by so small a complement. Nel was amazed Quill had managed to launch it with only Sharpe to help him. The Kelpie's thaumatic abilities were even more skewed towards large scale than she'd thought. The polar opposite to the way Gabbi's talents worked actually. Quill could launch the *Tantamount* but couldn't lift something as small as a spoon. Perhaps that had something to do with why the two clashed so often.

Nel had learned it wasn't going to take them two days to reach Grange. Sharpe knew a shortcut, the kind of route Nel had taken before but had never been entirely comfortable with. Quill, on the other hand, relished what was coming.

"Why doesn't everyone use this corridor?" Nel turned away from looking over the shortcut.

Sharpe shrugged in response. "The locals all know about it. Young sailors cut their teeth on this stretch."

"And how many broken ships are littering this stretch?" Nel asked.

"A few," Sharpe admitted.

"And you're sure you can do it?" Nel directed the question to Quill.

"Of course," Quill hissed. "Certain."

"And you ain't gonna break the ship in two?" Jack eyed Quill suspiciously.

"No, Jack," Quill dismissed his concerns. "I will not break the ship in two."

"You better not," Jack growled. He prodded Nel with an elbow, lowering his voice. "Gabbi told me I was to flatten Quill if ever he did anything to mess up her kitchen."

He hefted a battered frying pan suggestively. The cast iron rim was dented in several places and wouldn't lie flat on a stove. One too many of Gabbi's temper tantrums.

"Hold that thought," Nel advised him, to Quill's annoyance.

She took another good look at the corridor they were about to embark down. A corridor was a stretch of space littered with ether. The concentration of so much dispersed ether usually came with additional debris, like asteroid fields or planar rings.

What it created was a field or expanse of space littered with pocket envelopes, each with their own gravity well. In this particular case the field was longer than usual, a corridor stretching almost from Rim to Grange.

The plan was for Quill to guide the *Tantamount* through that corridor, whipping from one envelope to another, picking up speed much like a ship cresting a wave might. Only the *Tantamount* wouldn't slow down after any of those whips. There was a real danger, as Jack had mentioned, of Quill breaking the ship in two. Even if he managed to avoid crashing the ship into another stellar object they could get caught up in the field of another envelope, or the sheer acceleration itself could damage the still smouldering ship.

Both Quill and Sharpe had been dismissive of this. Their cavalier attitude had motivated Nel to ransack Horatio's cabin until she found an old duelling wand. There were others locked in the armoury but this one was a match for the crystals in her own cabin. It wasn't the same as having her own weapon back but it was close enough to feel comfortable.

"This had better be worth it," she found herself muttering to Quill from atop the bridge. "And it had better work."

"It will work," Quill insisted stubbornly. "Have some faith in me, Skipper. I've no liking for fool's errands."

Nel snorted. "This doesn't count as a fool's errand?"

"This is our trade," Quill replied. "Plying rough waters, maybe, but hardly uncharted or impossible. Have faith."

"You keep saying that. You haven't done a lot to make me have faith in you lately, Quill."

Quill faced her, a hard to read expression on his hard to read visage. "You speak of lately. I speak of all the years we have known each other, sailed under the same master, on the same ship. Does that, does all of that, weigh less than . . . lately?"

Nel stared at him, unable to answer.

"Thyme," he said. One word. Brutally. For a moment Nel

hated him for that cheap, underhanded blow.

"I know. I . . . I haven't forgotten," she said at last. "I've never heard you talk like this, Quill."

Quill looked away, breath hissing through his lips. "Yet you talk as many of my people do."

"What do you mean?"

"You talk like Heathen," Quill said.

Nel grimaced. "She was my captain, once. That doesn't make us the same."

"You echo her beliefs nonetheless. Your memory is short and your faith is weak."

"Quill . . ."

"Do you know why Heathen and the others abandoned the old ways, Vaughn?" Quill said. It was hard to miss the appellation he used. Quill might not like referring to Nel as skipper but he'd never argued the point. And as far back as she could remember he'd never once used her first or given name either. Until now. It was rare for him, she suddenly realised, to call anyone by name.

So Nel waited, knowing Quill wouldn't be satisfied until he'd vented whatever was bothering him to her.

"Gods are like parents," Quill muttered, speaking almost to himself. "Someone to look up to, to aspire to be like, someone to look out and protect you when you're young and know nothing better. But sooner or later the guiding hand has to step back. Those like Heathen, those before her, they were indignant at the lack. They sought attention elsewhere, forgetting all the times before. Like you, they remembered only the . . . lately."

Quill said this last bitterly.

He went on. "A parent who smothers their child raises a weak and pathetic thing, unable to think for itself or even to stand unaided. That or a bitter and resentful spawn who defies them merely for the sake of it. So it is with parents, so it is with gods."

"That's a harsh way of looking at it," Nel said.

Quill snorted. "Once over brandy you told me of a resentful

girl child who flouted her parent's laws under their own roof. Just because she could. And then ran away to sail distant skies, against her parents' wishes. Remind me again who that child was?"

Nel flushed. *Damned brandy*, she thought. *One day I'll learn.*

Quill didn't pursue the matter though. He was too fixated on reliving his own past. "My people resented the cutting of the apron strings. They found . . . others to cling to. New gods, to replace what they perceived as abandonment. Ones more suited to their own upstart, resentful temperaments."

"And what did you perceive it as?" Nel asked. "If not abandonment?"

Quill was a long time answering. "Faith."

"Isn't that just another word for ignorance?" Nel muttered.

"It is close, sometimes similar. It depends on the person."

Nel touched a hand to the wooden rail of the *Tantamount.* Something solid, dependable. Reliable. Something she did have faith in. "The way I remember hearing it, your old deities didn't do so well against their upstart competition."

"There was no competition," Quill said.

Nel frowned in confusion. "What do you mean?"

"Ask me," Quill said, staring out into the void. "Ask me how they died. Ask me how you kill a god."

Nel looked out into the darkness, trying to see what Quill saw. The Kelpie was making her head hurt with his home-brewed philosophy. She wasn't sure she wanted to ask the question. All she saw was the corridor. The one Quill said he could navigate.

"Faith."

Nel jumped at the interruption, swore under her breath. Sharpe grinned at her as he came up the stairs. "Forgot I was here, didn't you? That'll teach you to ignore me."

Nel didn't answer him. Then aloud, "Damned Kelpie."

Quill smiled.

"Take us in," Nel said tightly. "Though so help me, if you break my ship, I'll string you up by your tail and fly you as my new personal flag."

"Aye, Skipper." Quill turned to do what he did best.

The ship started to move, slowly at first, a massive weight being levered onto a downhill slope. And just as inexorably it picked up speed. Nel clutched at the bridge's railing 'til her hands went numb, watching as the first envelope loomed.

It was small, this first one. A small tidal pool in an otherwise featureless ocean void. But it was just the first shoal of many. Concentric rings shimmered I in the space around it, oily and only visible if looked at just so. Of course Quill knew where it was, he could see them, sense the thaumatic push and pull of ether. That was why he was the navigator. He took them straight in, smooth as butter and then caught the outermost ring, the ship leaning to the side as Quill rode the curve of the envelope, arcing the ship straight into the corridor.

Nel swallowed as she felt the ship's speed increase. There was little to measure it against—the painted backdrop of stars didn't give perspective, but already she could see the second envelope, frighteningly close. Were they that close or was the ship going that fast? Quill caught the spin again, and the *Tantamount* whined a little in protest, blackened timbers creaking under the strain. They went through a third, then a fourth, before Quill straightened the ship's line. His lips were pulled back in a grimace, the effort starting to show.

"Now what?" Nel asked.

"We hold this course," Sharpe said. "A few bells, half a day at most. Until we get to the end of the corridor."

"No more pockets?" she asked.

"Some." Sharpe didn't look worried. "We should avoid most of them though—the pockets are mostly clustered around either end. The ones in between Quill should be able to use to keep our course steady. The far end is where it gets difficult."

Nel knew what awaited them at the far end. The reverse of what they'd just been through—a half dozen or so envelopes of densely packed ether, only this time Quill would use them to slow the ship down. Their present speed was too fast to let them mesh with a planet's envelope and too fast for Quill to slow them down on his own. He needed an external force to work with and that was where the danger lay. With the ship battered as it was, the stress from the rapid deceleration could rip it apart at the seams.

"So there's nothing to do 'til then?" she raised her voice.

"Little," Quill called back with a shrug.

"Good," Nel said. "Then I want a word with my navigator. In private."

Sharpe's reaction was little more than a raised eyebrow and a shrug. He left the two of them alone, clapping Quill on the shoulder as he passed.

"Start talking," Nel said once Sharpe was out of earshot.

Quill regarded her with his cold, lizard eyes. He didn't speak.

"You left us at Rim. Took the ship," Nel stated.

Quill nodded.

Nel went on. "If I had another navigator, I'd have you hung from the mainsail and used your tail as the noose."

"You do not have another navigator," Quill pointed out. He spread his arms wide. "And you will not likely find another one out here."

Nel tracked Sharpe's movements further down the ship. The man wandered aimlessly. Clearly he had nothing to do to pass the time. "Sharpe turned you."

"Turning would imply he steered me from another course," Quill muttered.

"Didn't he?"

Quill shrugged.

"You left us. You left me." Nel discovered it hurt to say that aloud.

Quill hesitated. Much to her surprise he appeared troubled. "It was," he said slowly, "for your own good."

"How?"

"It was safer," Quill said.

"Safer? How is being left at Rim with backwater natives and warzone refugees safer? And that's not even mentioning the ploughing golem and its Guild handler!"

"Ah," Quill mused. "The Guildswoman is not pleased then? No doubt concerned about the state of her cargo?"

"Dammit, Quill, what do you know?" Nel demanded. "What were we carrying? Who in the hells is Sharpe? Is he part of the Guild too?"

"I don't know," Quill said. "At least not about Sharpe."

Nel shook her head in frustration. "Then how did he get you to work with him?"

"He offered up something I wanted."

"What?" Nel demanded. "What did he offer you?"

"A chance, the sort of opportunity I often dreamed of but never truly expected."

Nel stared, then cursed. The gods-cursed Kelpie wasn't going to tell her anything. He was too wrapped up in his own private revelations, whatever they were. She was going to have to wait until they got to Grange to find out what secrets Quill and Sharpe were keeping from her. She already knew she wasn't going to like them. And she hated waiting.

So did Jack. She found him in the galley and, of all things, tidying up. He had maybe half the kitchen in order; most of the pots and pans were swaying on their hooks, stores and ingredients packed away. The room didn't seem to have taken any damage from the fire. There were scorch marks on the ceiling and benches, but they'd been there before Sharpe turned the hold into an oven.

"Jack," she called, "what are you doing?"

"Gabbi don't like it when her kitchen's out of order," Jack grunted. "Stuff is in the wrong place. I'm putting it right."

Nel was bemused. "But why?"

"'Cause it ain't right," Jack said. "I'm making it right."

"But Gabbi's not even here," Nel reminded him. "She's back on Rim with the captain and the rest of the crew. There's nobody here but us."

"Still ain't right," Jack insisted stubbornly. "But it'll be right when Gabbi sees it."

Nel found herself smiling. Jack had more than a soft spot for Gabbi—like a child looked at its mother, always trying to please her. Maybe it was because Gabbi was the ship's cook—they did say the way to any man's heart was through his stomach. Or maybe it was just Gabbi herself. No, had to be the food.

"Just remember to use fresh stores," Nel said.

"Yeah, I know, that's what Gabbi always tells me. I ain't stupid. Hey, where have you been all this time?"

"Me? I've been on the bridge with—"

"Not you, Skipper," Jack interrupted, though he pointed towards her. "Him. Where's he been?"

Nel turned, came face to face with black eyes and furred face. She swore, flinching. Bandit squawked, retreating up into the racks, setting the pots and pans chiming.

"Where've you been?" Jack repeated like he expected an answer. "Slacking off, hey?"

"Of all the ploughing hells," Nel muttered. "You knew he was on board?"

"Had to be, didn't he?" Jack said. "Wasn't back on the docks at Rim, were he?"

"What's going on in here?" Sharpe called, sticking his head through the galley doorway, arms braced against the frame.

"What was all that noise?" he said, looking at the clanging pans Bandit had taken refuge in. The loompa saw him too, still entrenched in its perch. And launched itself at Sharpe, landing on his face, striking with sharp claws and something else. Sharpe recoiled, falling back out onto the deck with a cry.

"Jack, stop!" Nel yelled when the big man ran out after the battling pair, a meat cleaver in hand. He didn't seem to hear her, so she raced out after him.

Sharpe was rolling across the deck, back and forth, clutching at the loompa, which had a firm hold on his face with three grasping limbs. The fourth held something like a flail that the creature was pummelling Sharpe with.

Quill got to the brawl before Jack. Nel hadn't seen him arrive though he must have come down from the bridge. He snatched Bandit, plucking the loompa off the helpless Sharpe, suspending the struggling rodent in one clawed hand. Bandit writhed in that grasp, windmilling arms and legs, squawking rage and indignation.

"Oi, Kelpie, that's my helper there, you let him go!" Jack called out, advancing on Quill with the meat cleaver raised.

Quill looked between Jack and Bandit. "The ship's slop monkey has a rodent for his helper? This explains much."

"Eh?" Jack grunted, looking confused by the wordplay. "You gonna let him go or what?"

Quill laughed. He tossed Bandit in Korrigan Jack's general direction. Jack fielded the catch in one beefy hand, the loompa clinging to his arm and scampering onto his shoulder, spewing angry noises in Quill's direction. He thrashed his make-shift weapon as well and for the first time Nel got a good look at what the loompa had assaulted Sharpe with.

Sharpe chose that moment to sit up with a groan. He touched his face, raked with long bloody gouges. He pawed at his mouth, spluttering.

"What was that about?"

Nel snorted. "That," she said, "was for Piper."

Sharpe grimaced in confusion, then realisation dawned. "Ah, yes. Possibly I had that coming then."

Quill chuckled.

"Oi," Jack snapped his fingers at Bandit, "give it here."

Still squeaking angrily, the loompa handed over his prize. Jack held out the wharf rat by the tail for Quill to see.

"How you like your meat, Kelpie?" he asked. "This one's been nice and tenderised for you."

Quill's eyes narrowed. "Where did that filthy thing come from?"

"Must have picked it up at Rim," Jack said. "Ain't seen none since before Cauldron, and I would have 'cause Bandit would have caught them. Best ratter this ship's ever had, he is. So how do you want it?"

"I do not," Quill snapped. "It's vermin."

"Yeah?" Jack shook the dead rat. "Ain't heard you complain none before now. When'd you get so picky, Kelpie?"

Quill stared hard at Jack. "You," he hissed, his voiced shaking with rage, "you have been feeding those . . . things to me!"

Hells, Nel thought. She could already see the charged air starting to gather around Quill.

"Fresh meat," Jack grinned, inflaming the situation. "Fresh, just like Gabbi always says."

"Hells," Nel swore aloud. "Jack, shut the hells up. Just shut up."

Quill took a step towards Jack, one hand raised. Sharpe shot to his feet, putting himself in front of the Kelpie. Nel did the same to Jack.

"Get back in the galley, Jack," she said. "Get back in there now and finish cleaning the damned thing up."

Jack looked past her and chuckled. "Sure," he said. "I could do that."

"And throw the damned rat over the side too. The same for any more your helper catches."

Jack scowled. "Waste of meat, Skipper. Waste of meat."

"We're going to talk later, but for now don't argue with me, Jack," she growled. "Get back in the galley before I beat you half to death myself."

Jack took a long look at her, evidently deciding she meant it, which at that point she did. She waited 'til he was back in the galley before turning to deal with Quill.

She could hear a low, steady stream of curses coming from the direction of the bridge. Quill was gone. Sharpe remained, shaking his hands ruefully.

"Shocked me," he explained. "He was right worked up there for a bit."

"Don't expect any sympathy from me," she said, remembering what it had felt like when she'd grabbed

Gabbi's arm.

"Wouldn't dream of it." Sharpe shook his head. He gagged, pawing at his tongue.

"Uh, rat hair."

"Skipper!"

"What?" Nel turned to the bridge. Quill stood there, arms raised, and it almost hurt her eyes to look at him. Quill's body absolutely writhed with incandescent energy. He raised his arms, preparing.

"Oh hells," Nel whispered. "Grab on to something!"

Sharpe stared for a moment before grabbing for a line. He was just in time—the whole ship shifted, timbers screaming horribly as Quill attempted to turn the course at breakneck speed. There was a yell from the galley as all of Jack's cleaning came crashing down. Threats of murder streamed out the door.

"What happened?" Sharpe yelled, looking as unsettled as Nel had ever seen him. She didn't answer him, twisting to face the tumbling rock that rolled leisurely past them, just outside the *Tantamount*'s envelope. As it passed it blocked out the miasma horizon. Even Jack, emerging from the galley, was sobered into silence.

"Hells," Sharpe echoed Nel's thoughts when he caught sight of it.

"You said this corridor was clear." Nel turned on him, clenching her teeth to keep from yelling.

"It was. It was!"

"You said it was clear, gods damn you!"

"Skipper," Quill descended from the bridge. He was unsteady on his feet, leaning against the brightwork for support. "That . . . was not supposed to be there."

"Quill." Nel held out a hand to steady him. "Well done, you . . ."

"That rock was not supposed to be there," Quill repeated. "There are no others like it here."

"Then where'd it come from?" Jack demanded suspiciously.

"We can worry about that later," Nel said. "We need to get out of this corridor, before we find any more like it."

"As you say, Skipper." Quill studied her. "As you say."

Chapter 10

The golem made it look effortless, hoisting the grey skinned Draugr off his feet. Violet and the rest of the mob watched in horror as Wallace flailed at the golem's arm. Onyx wasn't just lifting the Draugr, the golem had impaled him. And with a negligent toss threw him away.

A circle formed around the obsidian construct. The mob of Rim's refugees and slum dwellers had pushed the Alliance all the way to where they'd first landed on the docks. Where the golem had been waiting. But even that display wasn't enough to break them. Not yet. It took the arrival of the rest of the blockade ships to do that.

Fresh boarding parties crossed from the frigates, timbers creaking and twisting where the ships had forced their meshing. Uniformed Alliance sailors and cold-eyed Kelpies met the Rim mob in a rush. Then the mob broke, crying out in panic and splintering into small rushing groups and individuals.

Violet ignored them as best she could, kneeling by the fallen Wallace. She lifted the Draugr's hand in hers but wasn't sure what else she could do. There was a massive hole in the creature's chest. It didn't seem possible it could have survived, but it had.

Wallace's eyes found hers. There was something there in the

cloudy visage. The Draugr smiled.

"I'm sorry," Violet whispered.

A shadow fell over them. The golem. And behind it the Guildswoman, Scarlett.

"You!" the woman mouthed, lips twisting into a grimace. Onyx's fist came smashing down. It would have crushed her if Wallace hadn't shoved her out of the way. Violet scrabbled away, crabbing back on hands and feet as the golem extracted its fist from the timber ground. It exposed something that sent Violet's heart into palpitations. There was nothing beneath them, nothing under the thin planking but empty space and the longest fall imaginable.

The golem raised its fist again, but hesitated when something struck it. A rock. Followed by crockery, claw plates, and bowls that shattered ineffectually against its skin.

It didn't take Violet long to figure out that was Gabbi hurling projectiles. Her heart lurched when she saw the cook and the captain, the latter brandishing his wand at the golem. Scarlett saw them too and seemed to be weighing who to set the golem on first.

Wand-fire from the captain bounced off Onyx just as it had for the skipper. All it did was provoke the golem to advance on the captain and Gabbi. Gabbi threw more rocks, but Onyx didn't even slow.

"Scarlett!" Violet yelled to them. "You have to aim for Scarlett!"

Gabbi didn't hear her, or at least she didn't change her tactics. The cook continued to pepper the golem with every makeshift projectile she could rip up. Rocks, crockery, discarded food from rotting refuse piles. The golem lowered its head, preparing to charge. But the captain had got the message. His wand littered the air with bolts, forcing Scarlett to duck for cover.

Whether self-aware or acting on instructions, Onyx changed course, putting itself between Scarlett and her attackers. The captain darted forward, flicking his wand in wide, sweeping arcs. He grabbed Violet's arm and pulled her to her feet with surprising strength.

"Time to go, my dear," he said, pulling her towards Gabbi and the rapidly vanishing crowds. Behind Onyx more Alliance sailors were appearing, armed and as stone faced as the golem. The tide had well and truly turned.

"Wait!" Violet wrenched her hand free from the captain. She ran back, towards the golem and Alliance, to the captain's cry of dismay. She saw wand fire shoot past her as he did his best to cover her mad rush. She skidded to a stop next to Wallace, tugging at the fallen Draugr.

"Get up," she said. But the Draugr just stared blankly at her.

Hells. He has to move, I can't lift him. I can't leave him, neither. The skipper wouldn't leave no one.

"Get up," Violet snarled. "Move your hells damned carcass, sailor! Move!"

And to her complete amazement the Draugr complied. One hand pressed to the gaping hole, Wallace somehow made it to his feet, letting Violet drag him along towards the captain and Gabbi.

Violet caught a last glimpse of Scarlett as the captain pulled her away, standing near her golem. The women's face was dark, with eyes that promised blood.

Coming out of the corridor wasn't as rough as Nel had feared. She worried Quill might take his frustration out on them and the ship, but she should have known better. He guided the ship out smoothly, wrapped in cotton wool and goose-down, decelerating through the final turns of ether pockets. From there it was a short run to Grange. Whether by luck or design they'd come out near to the closest point of the moon's orbit in relation to the corridor. According to Sharpe there was only the one settlement on Grange, and before long it came into sight.

There was a harbour, deep enough to moor or dock the ship, but at Sharpe's urging Quill set the ship down in a dry-dock cradle. Then he led them into the centre of town.

"This isn't possible," Nel said.

She'd promised herself if Sharpe and Quill didn't show her something monumental, something so important it made up for all the drama they'd caused her, she was going to bait the pair of them on the ship's anchor and trail them out for the rays.

And damn them they'd gone and done it.

Quill was sullenly silent. Not so with Jack. He grumbled and complained, he didn't understand. He said as much.

"Shut up, Jack," Nel told him shortly.

Her crewman growled. "Somebody explain it to me."

"You wouldn't understand," Quill said. Jack turned on him, but Quill didn't seem to notice. Maybe he didn't care. Nel could understand that.

"It's a lot to take in." Sharpe sounded sympathetic.

Nel swallowed. A lot to take in. Sharpe had a flair for the understatement

"I don't get it," Korrigan Jack said, getting louder.

"They're dead, Jack," Nel said quietly. "They're all dead."

The whole township, all of Grange. For as far as the eye could see, dead bodies filled the town. Men, women and . . . no, not children. The children were still alive, as far as Nel could see. But all other ages. Whole generations, almost entire families. Some had been dead a long time, bodies decaying and rotting, barely holding together. Others . . . others it was harder to tell.

Jack took a step forward, looking around at one corpse, then another. There was practically steam coming out of his ears as he struggled to wrap his mind around what he was seeing.

Nel had seen towns filled with bodies before. Towns and bigger communities besides. She knew Jack had seen his share too. This one was different. No fires, no smoke obscuring the view, no miasma hiding the grisly details. It was all present and on show. There was none of the hallmarks of destruction, just death. She waited for Jack to accept what they were seeing.

It turned out he wasn't going to.

"You're wrong," Jack stated. "You're all wrong."

"Jack," Nel started.

"You're wrong," he repeated stubbornly. He pointed, stabbing with one thick skinned finger. "Dead is dead. That ain't dead. So they ain't."

The crowd of dead people exchanged long looks with each other. It was hard to tell on some of the slack and withered faces, but they might have been amused.

"You," Jack pointed, "what's your name?"

"Hazel," the man responded. His voice sounded slurred, gravelly. Just like Nel had expected it would sound.

"There," Jack grunted. "Dead people don't have names. They get headstones, if they're lucky. But they don't answer questions and don't tell you who they is."

Quill muttered something.

"What was that, Quill?" Nel said tiredly.

Her navigator struggled, agonising over some inner turmoil. Then came the shocker. "He has a point."

"What did you say?" Nel asked incredulously.

Quill gestured, taking in the whole settlement. "You can see the ones who fought, the ones who don't talk."

He indicated the shallow graves on the edge of the settlement. The graves were recent, the ground freshly disturbed and piled up. Makeshift markers stood out, piles of stone, pieces of wood nailed or lashed together. A few dozen altogether.

"The first, they are the most far gone, you can see how ravaged they are," Quill rasped, looking at the most decayed walking dead. They replied back with gruesome rictus smiles, teeth and rotting gums peeping through holes in cheeks.

"Others look like ones you might see elsewhere. And some," he paused, "some it would be hard to tell which side of the line they walk on."

"What about the children?" Nel said, thinking of Violet. "They don't look . . ."

"What?" Sharpe asked her. "Infected?"

"Dead," Nel said shortly.

"They're not," he told her. "They hid the children after it became clear what was going on."

"We tried," Hazel said. "Maybe we did keep them safe. Maybe they were too young, were never in danger in the first place."

"Are you saying none of the children were affected?" Nel asked.

Hazel nodded. "None."

"There could be something to that," Nel said, taking a few steps outward. She looked around. Sure enough all the walking dead were safely out of childhood. Safely, that was the wrong word to use.

"I've seen plenty of Draugr," she said. "They have them on Alliance ships."

"Not just ships," Jack said. "Saw some on Cauldron too. But these aren't like them. Stiffs on Cauldron didn't move and talk like these folks."

"On Cauldron?" Nel said.

"Yeah, when we got the stores. Delivered them too. Gabbi didn't like them much. They upset her."

"She didn't say anything," Nel said.

"They upset her," Jack repeated.

"The High Lanes are built on the backs of Draugr labour. What's the official Alliance line, Vaughn?" Sharpe asked her. "What do they tell you marines these days, where do baby Draugr come from?"

"There is no official line," Nel said. "Just rumours. That they're golems made flesh, that they witch Alliance dead to come back and keep helping out. That it's what they do to the enemy dead to keep punishing them.

"But," she said, "I've never seen a Draugr that could talk, least I never heard one. Nor act without instruction, beyond the most basic tasks."

"You've never seen anything like this," Sharpe told her. "Not many people have."

Nel took another look at the settlement full of dead people. Except for the children. What was it doing to them? Seeing their parents, friends, family, brothers and sisters, walking around as rotting corpses?

"That blockade out there," Sharpe went on, "it's not just to keep people like us out. It's here to keep people . . . like this, in."

The Alliance blockade. And Nel hadn't forgotten that when she first found Sharpe it was inside the wreck of an Alliance ship, one that according to him had been bound for Marching, on Thatch. And the Draugr on Rim with the Alliance tattoo.

Sharpe shrugged. "What do you know about Thatch and Grange?"

"I didn't know this," Nel said.

"Come with me," Sharpe said. "It's time for us to talk."

"What do you know about Grange and Thatch?" Sharpe asked her again. They'd retreated into Horatio's cabin on the *Tantamount*. Quill and Jack had remained ashore—both actually wanted to mingle with the locals. Nel didn't waste any energy pondering why, she was focused on Sharpe. If he was finally ready to come clean she wanted to hear it.

"Nothing like this." Nel glanced over at the wall. There were no windows or portholes to see through but it was hard to forget the scene outside.

Sharpe grimaced. "This isn't indicative of Grange, or even Thatch."

"Then this is part of the war?" Nel asked. "It's . . . cold. Even for an act of war. I've never heard of anything like this before."

"No," Sharpe said. "This isn't because of the war. The truth is there is no war."

Nel frowned. "Then how do you explain what we saw out there. How do you explain what we saw on Rim?"

Sharpe leaned forward over the table, pouring both of them a glass of Horatio's ice brandy. "Rim is just Rim. It really is that bad—you just saw what you expected to see, the cost of war. Doesn't take a war to do stuff like that."

Nel bristled under that. "And out there?"

Sharpe sighed. "No one gets local politics. Everyone forgets them. We see a planet, we think of it as a single, homogenous group. We forget people have their own differences. Places like Cauldron should remind us of that, but people have short memories."

"You could say the same about civil wars. People fighting amongst themselves," Nel pointed out.

"I told you, there is no war. At least not right now. There's been conflict in the past, but it's not internal. Grange is completely independent of Thatch, always has been."

Nel raised an eyebrow. "Really?"

"Really," Sharpe insisted. "They were colonised by two different groups. Thatch mostly waves of Seltic Brytons and Grange by Fomor Nemedians."

"Should those names mean anything to me?"

"Two sides of the same argument. Everyone likes to put a name on it. But no, their names aren't important, trying to keep them straight usually gives one a headache. It's an old story, usually involves religion, a different idea of how things should be done. The names are the only parts that ever really change."

"So what happened?" Nel took a sip from her brandy. It was cold, but burned after she swallowed.

"People happened. You put the last two people in the void on the same rock, they could be twins and they'd still find something to fight over. People are just like that. Thatch started to expand, tried to push Grange's way, moved a ton of their own people out here."

"When was that?"

"Few hundred years ago," Sharpe grinned. "It goes back and forth, never really got settled. Maybe folks prefer it that way. It does flare up now and then though."

"That's what happened then? A flare up?"

"No, that's not it at all, Skipper. What do you know about Draugr?"

"You already asked me that." Nel was annoyed. "And I

already told you."

"But do you have any idea how they come about?"

Nel thought about the question. It was a subject often speculated about at Alliance schools and academies. Speculated on but not much more. She heard all sorts of ideas at one time or another. One theory popular outside the ranks said Alliance crew signed a pact written in their own blood; service for so many years, to be rendered even after death. She doubted that as she'd never been asked to sign anything like that during her service, nor did she know anyone who had. It wasn't as if coming back as a Draugr were some selective, elite distinction. There were tens of thousands of the creatures.

"Nobody knows," Nel admitted. "Not that I've met."

"Somebody knows," Sharpe said. "Somebody has to make the things in the first place. They don't breed—gods below I just gave myself an image of that," he shuddered, "—but there's always more of them. So they have to be coming from somewhere."

"And you know where?" Nel leaned back, folding her arms sceptically. She glanced outside as she did so. "It's not here, is it? This isn't some sort of farm?"

"You're closer than you know, with that." Sharpe swirled his ice cubes as he spoke, watching them move around the bottom of his tumbler. "No, in this case the where isn't as important as the what."

"What?"

"Exactly."

"Quit messing me around, Sharpe," Nel growled.

He gave her the small, irritating smile. "Suppose someone were to stumble on the secret behind our friends in the Alliance. To Draugr."

Nel's eyes narrowed, closing on Sharpe. It went unsaid the potential for wealth associated with such a secret. Particularly if one were able to somehow get their hands on the secret.

"Some months ago," Sharpe continued, "a ship was passing through this part of the void. On that ship, was just such a secret. A formula, part of the process in creating Draugr. Not the whole process, not the whole secret. But an important part, maybe the most important part.

"So," Sharpe said, "this Alliance ship is out here, all alone, carrying such a valuable prize. Dangerous, you might think, except no one knows about this prize. Someone attacks the ship, right above where we're sitting. It all goes wrong, the ship crashes onto the moon, Grange, right outside this settlement in fact."

"I didn't see any sign of a crash when we came in."

"Because it's not there to see anymore. The raiders came down, found the wreck picked clean, the survivors hidden. They did . . . terrible things, Vaughn. They wanted what was on that ship, wanted it bad. And it didn't bother them how many people they had to kill to get it. They'd already slaughtered the better part of an Alliance vessel, they weren't going to baulk at a few backwater locals. And then things got worse."

Sharpe chuckled, dry, amused, bitter. "The dead started rising, Vaughn. You saw the graves outside, they weren't filled for very long. The first ones to go were the strongest, the most defiant, those who tried to fight back. Their families buried them, they rose on the third night."

"How?" Nel said. "You said before whatever the ship was carrying wasn't the whole secret."

"But I did say it was the most important part. You see, these Draugr aren't like the ones you know, they remembered who they were, how they died. They weren't docile, they didn't take orders. And they wouldn't die a second time. The raiders could cut them and beat them but they couldn't stop them. So they fled."

"How?" Nel repeated. "Was it contamination from the crash? Did the Alliance survivors do it, were they that desperate? Did some village idiot think it was a good idea to chug down whatever moonshine he looted from the crash?"

"Vaughn, it really doesn't matter," Sharpe said impatiently. "It happened. The raiders fled. That might have been the end of it, except that it didn't stop there. People who died afterwards . . . they came back too. Some were sick, one fell off a roof, another drowned in a trough leaving the pub. It didn't matter, they all turned out the same. Whatever they'd started they couldn't stop. And then the Alliance came."

"The blockade."

"The blockade." Sharpe nodded. "Somebody sent word to the Alliance, they arrived to find one of their own ships downed, a small planet starting to teem with uncontrolled Draugr. So they blockade Grange, blame it on the loss of shipping, a local war flaring up, try to figure out what to do about the situation.

"Something like this cannot get out, Vaughn. You were in the Alliance, think of the damage something like this would do. That's the first thing anyone in authority thinks. Somebody makes the decision that Grange has to be wiped clean. But everybody who dies just comes back and because it wasn't done right from the start they all have this annoying thing called free will. What to do, what to do?" Sharpe rose to his feet. "Come on, I want to show you something."

Sharpe led her swiftly to the hold, still reeking of charred timber and smoke. He picked up a box of the medicine they'd been carrying, the one intended as relief. It was little more than burnt packaging now.

"The decision was to let the contamination run its course, even accelerate it. Ensure everyone on the planet turned and then make any necessary . . . adjustments. This," he gestured, "was meant to have been the final dose to let that plan run to fruition."

Nel felt cold. Icy sweat under her clothes that made her twitch in her seat.

"No," she whispered. "There's no way, the Alliance would never have let us run something like that. That's mad, to bring in another party in a situation like this. Why not use an Alliance vessel?"

Sharpe shrugged. "The Alliance, for all that it is, does have morals. Somebody made this decision, that doesn't mean they expected everyone to agree with it. Those ships in the blockade,

I expect they're close to the extent of the Alliance who actually know what's going on out here. And only because they were already here, had already seen. So when you have an impossible situation that needs handling without awkward questions, what do you do?"

"You use the Guild," Nel muttered. "Gods below, Scarlett."

"Your friend Ebon Masaius too. All they needed was someone to move the cargo for them."

"Us," Nel said bitterly.

"Helps when the first officer happens to be ex-Alliance," Sharpe said quietly. "Makes you reliable. Predictable even."

"Watch it," Nel warned him, annoyed.

"More so when the captain has a gambling problem," he added.

"But why didn't they take it off us when we passed the blockade?"

"It wasn't the Alliance that boarded us, Vaughn," Sharpe reminded her. "What did you think that beast of a ship was heading to Rim for? It was because of us."

"Hells," Nel groaned. "Horatio and the others are still back on Rim." She leaned against a post, forehead on her arm. "I need to get back there."

"They should be fine," Sharpe assured her. "The Alliance isn't going to want to bother with them, they only want the cargo."

"Scarlett," Nel said grimly. "I left her lying facedown in a Rim gutter. She's going to seethe when she wakes up."

"Scarlett? What happened?"

"Violet hit her with a brick," Nel admitted.

Sharpe looked startled at that. "Violet? Our Violet?"

"My Violet," Nel growled at him. "I'm still not sure where you fit into this."

Sharpe cleared his throat, accepting that. "Here, this is what I wanted to show you."

He moved aside a crate, revealing a trollish patch, a repair where the *Tantamount* had been holed. Nel watched as Sharpe, with some effort, levered the whole patch out.

"That should have been caulked properly." Nel was unimpressed. Piper had assured her with regards to the labour he'd hired. "If we'd set down in the harbour we'd be hip deep in water by now."

"It was done properly." Sharpe grimaced. "Damned well too, it took me days to work it loose."

"Sharpe," Nel said quietly. "You are really testing my patience."

"Here." Sharpe handed her the patch, ducking halfway through the breach in the hull. He braced himself on his knees and pulled back, holding up a box similar to the burnt ones Piper and the captain had examined on Rim.

"You hid this on the outside of the hull," Nel said as she took it from him. It was undamaged and heavy in her hands. Full.

"And more besides." Sharpe confirmed. "I got the notion from when we rescued Violet. Scarlett had no idea."

Casually Nel dropped the box into Sharpe's waiting hands while he was still down on his knees. She had her wand drawn and levelled at him before he could react.

She glared down at him. "You talk too much."

"I've been told so." He didn't look concerned about the thaumatic weapon, but he didn't make any sudden moves either. Carefully setting the box on the floor, he sat down, pulled his knees up and waited.

"Why would you tell me all this?"

"Because I want you to understand." Sharpe shrugged. "I need your help."

"I'm not helping you steal Alliance property," she said through gritted teeth.

"Why? Because it's wrong?" Sharpe grinned.

She hit him, a lash across the cheek with her wand. His head whipped to the side and was slow in coming back.

"You stole and hid this cargo," Nel said. "You set fire to my ship and ran off with it. You think you can use me, use my ship and my crew like this?" she said. "And you're stupid enough to show me how you did it?"

Sharpe stared, then started laughing. "You think it was me? You think I'm the one who attacked the Alliance ship in the first place?" He rose to his feet, laughing. "Oh, Chanel, now that's funny."

Nel hit him low and hard this time. He doubled over but didn't make a sound, only looking up with a dribble of blood leaking out of the corner of his mouth from her earlier hit.

"Don't call me that," she said.

"You called me much worse than that," Sharpe said, wiping blood off his chin. "But if it makes you feel better, go ahead, hit me again, it's not like I can feel it anymore."

"What?" Nel glared at him.

"Go ahead." Sharpe spread his arms wide. "Hit me."

Nel was tempted, gods below was she tempted. But she didn't. Sharpe lowered his arms.

"I sailed as part of the *Falchions Rise*," Sharpe said.

"That was the ship we plucked you off," Nel retorted.

"It was the same ship that crashed here, six months ago. I survived the crash, Vaughn," Sharpe chuckled, "wasn't so lucky with the rest of it."

"No." Nel shook her head. "No, you can't be. You sailed on my ship, you couldn't hide something like that."

"Didn't you wonder when you saved me from the wreck?" Sharpe pressed. "We were all dead men sailing on that ship, it was wrecked but we got it to fly again, we tried to get away, to get help and you saw how far we got. The others froze in the void, I survived because of that scrap of an envelope you found me in. But only because I was already dead."

"Then how . . . this . . ." Nel gestured at him. "You look fine, you look normal. You ate in my galley, alongside my crew. How come you haven't rotted away like the rest out there?"

"That stuff." Sharpe nudged the medicine with his foot. "It's incomplete, like what the *Falchions* carried. It doesn't preserve us like normal Draugr. But keep taking it and it stops the rot. I had some with me, all that was left when we set out. Picked up some more at Cauldron, courtesy of our friend Ebon."

He gestured. "Vaughn, those people out there need this. They're not just dying, they're actually, literally wasting away. This can help them, give them time."

"Time to what?" Nel took a step back, waving both arms. "Where do you go, where do you go from this?"

"Away," Sharpe said, his voice firm. "Some of my crew stayed. They've been teaching them how to sail. All we needed was this," he kicked the box at his feet, "and all we need now is the ships to sail."

"And then what? Where are you even going to get ships?" Nel snorted.

"There's a place. We just need to get there."

"And how will you do that, Sharpe?" Nel shook her head. "How will you get there?"

Sharpe gave her his trademark grin. "Vaughn," he chuckled, "why do you think I had to get everyone off the *Tantamount*?"

"I'm surprised at you, Quill." Nel leaned vambraced forearms on the bridge railing, looking out over the deck of her ship. Below them the people of Grange filed onto the *Tantamount*. Nel had been adamant that there was no way they could fit everybody onto the ship. Surprisingly it had been Jack who had come up with an answer. Since the Grange-Draugr didn't need to eat or move, possibly not even to breathe if Sharpe were telling the truth, then they didn't need normal accommodation. Korrigan Jack's solution had been predictably simple. Stow them.

He'd been down in the hold for half a day, packing the people of Grange in like silver spoons, one atop the other, in every nook and cranny he could find. They fit, but only barely. Any more and Jack would have started stacking them on the outside of the hull. The only ones they really had to make room for were the children, half a hundred stoic faced runts that made Nel pine for Violet. These were broken, hardened beyond their years. It wasn't right.

"How so, Skipper?" Quill asked, joining her at the railing.

"Look at what you're letting onto the ship," she explained. "Filthy doesn't begin to describe it."

Quill chuckled his sibilant laugh. "Launching the ship may prove a challenge with this many."

"You said you were up to it." Nel turned quickly, alarmed at the idea.

"I am, but it will still be a challenge. I enjoy a challenge."

"Why did you go along with Sharpe in the first place?" Nel asked him. "Are you ready to tell me that now?"

"Why are *you* going along with him now?" Quill countered.

"I didn't want to argue with a planet full of hungry shambling corpses," Nel snapped. "It seemed like the prudent choice."

"I will enjoy telling Jack the passengers are hungry." Quill had a gleam in his eye. "Perhaps if I am lucky they will eat his ridiculous rodent helper."

Nel restrained herself from making any rodent jokes. Quill would have a fit.

"Why'd you do it?" she said instead.

"Revenge is a petty thing." Quill shrugged. "No less enjoyable for that."

"And who are you getting revenge on today, Loveland?" Nel asked, watching as a half dozen figures in tattered Alliance uniforms made their way up the gangway. That would be the last of them, the "surviving" crew of the *Falchions Rise*.

"Didn't Sharpe tell you who his captain was?"

Nel was about to answer that he hadn't when one of the Alliance crewmen called out to her. "Captain?"

"Captain Horatio isn't with us right now," Nel said, descending to meet them. "I'm Nel Vaughn, first officer."

"You call her Skipper," Quill told the corpse.

"Aye, Skipper, I know that one." The man saluted in traditional style.

"You're a midshipman?" Nel deduced from what was left

on his uniform.

"Aye," he confirmed. "Midshipman Stoker, at your service."

"You're the highest ranking officer left then, Stoker?" Nel asked.

"What's left of me, aye, Skipper," Stoker grinned. It was ghastly, but at least the man still had his sense of humour. Nel nodded appreciatively, heard the chuckles from the other men. It sounded like the inside of a cutter's tent. All hacks and coughs.

"Rest of the deck officers shipped out with pretty boy himself there the last time." Stoker gestured across the deck to Sharpe. "Weren't a lot of us left by then anyway."

"We're short on crew, lads," Nel told them. "Think you can handle her?"

"Aye, Skipper, we can handle her," Stoker said. "She'll be heavy, but she's in better kit than our last girl. Long as your man there can get us up, we'll get her to where she's going."

"Oi, Kelpie," Jack bellowed, pushing his way through the Alliance sailors. He didn't seem at all bothered by their appearance. "The children are hungry."

Quill stared at him. "So?"

"So?" Jack grunted. "So what do I do about it? What do children eat anyway?"

"Why are you asking me, imbecile?" Quill grated. "What does the pest-child Violet eat? Feed them that."

"Violet ain't no kid," Jack said. "She's crew, crew ain't children. Can't be. Wouldn't be able to crew, would they?"

"Then feed them that damned rodent." Quill turned to Nel. "How is this my problem? Why is he not asking you about this?"

"Bandit?" Jack shook his head. "That won't work, he's looking after them. I cook him and Piper'll get mad at me. Gabbi too. And I won't have nobody to catch the rats, then what're you going to eat, Quill?"

"You—" Quill clutched at the railing furiously.

"Let it go, Quill," Nel said.

Quill muttered choice insults under his breath as his claws

gouged deep grooves in the railing.

"Besides, I get rid of Bandit then someone else has to look after the kids. And I'd have to do it cause you're too ugly, Quill." Jack shook his head some more and glanced over at the Alliance sailors. "You lot, what do kids eat?"

Stoker gestured to one of his men. "Go help the cook find something for the children to eat."

"Assistant cook," Jack grunted. "Gabbi's the cook. But she ain't here right now."

Stoker pondered this. "I don't even remember what happened to our cook."

"Resigned," said one of the other sailors. "On account of no one was eating his muck no more."

"That his idea or ours?"

"I forget. Could have been ours."

"Sounds too smart for us."

"Ain't so smart. Look at us. We ain't been eating right."

Nel chuckled. Some things never changed.

"The rest of you go man the lines," she said. "Stand by to cast off."

"Aye, Skipper," the five remaining sailors chorused with mismatched salutes.

"You ready, Quill?" Nel asked of her navigator.

"Aye," the Kelpie nodded. "It'll take us longer to get back to Rim. We can't try the corridor with this much weight."

"Is that practicality I hear from you, Loveland?" Nel asked.

"I like my ship in one piece," Quill said dryly. "And I'm eager to see our dear captain again."

"So am I," Nel admitted. "Wait, why?"

"He owes me money," Quill grinned. "I won the bet."

"What bet?" she asked suspiciously.

"Why, about you . . . Skipper." Quill's grin was malicious now.

"Me?"

"You. And Sharpe."

"What about Sharpe?" Nel said, feeling her voice drop to

a threatening range.

"The captain took a liking to the man, he wanted him to join the crew. As he always does. I believed you had had your fill humouring the captain on this matter. Thus, a bet."

"Damn you, Quill, how long have you and the captain been putting bets on me?"

"A while." Quill shrugged. "Since before you joined the ship, if you must know."

"What?" Nel spluttered.

"Remember the state the captain found you in? The captain believed he could make a decent officer out of you."

"And you bet against me?" Nel derided him.

"Aye, I did," Quill said. "You did not impress me at first."

Nel paused. "At first?"

"And once you did I wondered why you stayed." Quill shrugged.

"Why do you?" Nel retorted.

"Where else would I go?"

Nel glared. "Cast off, you gods-damned Kelpie. Get us back to Rim so I can bludgeon our captain."

"Aye, Skipper, as you say. I had coin on that as well."

Violet pressed a wet cloth to the captain's brow, covering the swelling. He looked up sheepishly as she placed his own hand against the cloth and held it there.

"What happened?" he asked her.

"You hit your head, Captain," Violet told him, leaning back on her heels. She studied the captain with some concern. He had taken a toll in the last while.

"How?" the captain grimaced, sitting up. "How did it happen?"

"You were trampled."

"Trampled?" Horatio grumbled. "That's embarrassing. Humiliating. Why'd I do that?"

"You don't remember? Wallace carried you back."

"Who's Wallace?"

"Him in the corner." Violet pointed to where the Draugr was sitting. Wallace had kept up with them after they'd fled the docks, then ended up carrying the captain after he got caught up in a press of panicking locals. And he still had a sizeable hole in his chest where Onyx had stabbed him. Violet had tried stuffing it with rags but the Draugr didn't bleed, didn't seem bothered much at all. He'd had no problems carrying the captain after Horatio had been run over by the panicked people of Rim.

Horatio grumbled some more and tried to stand. Violet pushed him back down. "Gabbi said you weren't to do that. That you're to lie down and stay put."

"I'm captain, I tell Gabbi what to do, not the other way," Horatio complained.

"Never argue with the cook," Violet reminded him.

"What about arguing with the captain?" Horatio complained. "Cabin girl telling me what to do, whole chain of command is upside down. I want my ship back."

"The skipper will bring her back, Captain," Violet said. "Won't be long now."

The captain squinted at her, reaching to explore the back of his head with his free hand. He winced at what he found. "You're starting to sound like her, Violet. Like Nel."

Violet shrugged.

"Yes," Horatio sighed. "That's what she'd say too."

Violet cast her eyes down to her fingers, twisting them around each other. Like her tails. It took a deliberate effort on her part but she untwined the pair of them, curling them round to where she could see both.

"Still just the two, Violet?" the captain asked her.

Violet nodded. Still just the two.

"Good," the captain declared. "Wouldn't want you growing up when I wasn't looking. Children do that sometimes. Very distressing, makes me think about how old I must be getting."

It didn't feel right. She didn't know what to do with the second tail—if she didn't keep them both wrapped up tight they'd bang into stuff or trip her up.

Two tails, growing up, hells, I'm not growing up. Can't even stop from needing to be rescued all the time. If it ain't the skipper, it's the captain. Or Wallace. She looked for Wallace, only to find the Draugr had left. She hadn't even noticed. But the captain was still there.

"You saved me, Captain. You and Gabbi."

"Good. Need to do something useful now and then. Remind everyone why I'm captain."

"Why'd you do it, Captain? Why'd you take me on?" Violet asked.

Horatio eyed her thoughtfully. "You never asked me that before."

"Quill asks all the time. Jack too, sometimes so does the skipper."

"All crew like to talk," the captain dismissed that. "Wouldn't be crew if they didn't think they knew better."

"I stowed away on your ship. Why didn't you throw me overboard? Why not leave me at the next port?"

"You think I'd do that, Violet?" The captain's look was piercing now, clear-eyed despite the twinges of pain in his face.

"I know you wouldn't, Captain. Just don't know why."

"You never did know Thyme, did you, Violet?"

"No, Captain." Violet shook her head at the unexpected mention of her predecessor. "Don't think you would have let me stay if he'd have still been alive."

Horatio sighed. "Nel took that boy's death hard. Wasn't anybody's fault, that fight, but they got caught up in it all the same. Quill was there too, did you know that?"

"No, I didn't."

"Nel saved Quill's life. Or maybe he saved hers. I'm not even sure, I wasn't there. Always wondered if either of them were able to let it go. Felt guilty, maybe. The skipper needed something to take her mind off of Thyme. Needed to do something useful. And there you were."

"And Quill?" Violet asked, feeling a dryness in her throat.

"What about Quill?"

"Do you think he felt guilty?"

The captain looked at her. "When he gets back with my ship we can ask him." He frowned. "What? What is it Violet?"

Wordlessly Violet reached into her shirt and removed the package she'd hidden there, holding it out to her captain. Horatio took it with a puzzled look, opening the case and pulling the deed out. His eyes widened as soon as he unrolled it, grey eyebrows climbing up his face.

"Do you know what this is, Violet?" He peered over the top of the parchment to her. Violet nodded mutely.

"Did you read it? All of it?"

Violet shook her head.

"So you didn't realise it's a fake?"

Violet felt her own eyes widen.

"Sharpe had something to do with this, didn't he?" the captain said shrewdly.

"I . . ." Violet didn't know what to say. "I think he stole it."

"Strange boy." The captain tucked the deed away in his coat pocket. "Why do you think he'd steal a fake, Violet?"

"He can't have known it's a fake," was all Violet could think to say.

"Oh, he knew," the captain assured her. "We talked about it, often, after Cauldron. He asked me where I kept the real one a few times. Subtly, of course. I didn't tell him, not that it would have mattered. He couldn't have stolen it."

"Why not?" Violet couldn't help asking. The captain regarded her with a sly grin and a twinkle in his eye.

"Ah, let's just say I have my moments, lass. Brilliant, it was, even if I do say so myself. Not what Nel says, of course, but she's just worried about the day she has to put on the captain's hat.

"Of course," he said, tapping the deed, "that can't happen so long as I have this."

"Captain." It was Gabbi, who peered anxiously at their captain, scrutinising his condition. She didn't appear satisfied with what she saw but made no comment. "You should come see this."

Horatio extended a hand to Violet. "Help me up, my girl. Let's go see what's about."

"I see smoke, Skipper." Stoker pointed. Ahead, barely visible through the mist, was Rim.

"For a dead man you've got good eyes," Nel grumbled, holding a spyglass to her own. She rolled her shoulder, trying to throw Bandit off. The creature had transferred its affections from Jack to her and she didn't care for it. Everything she'd tried so far to discourage him had just made him dig his claws in deeper.

"I can't tell if that's mist or smoke from here," she said.

"It's smoke, Skipper," Stoker reaffirmed. He pointed to his eyes. "Far-sighted, always have been. Nothing's changed there."

"Good to know." Nel flattened the spyglass. "Now what does it mean?"

"Fire, probably, Skipper. Don't look like any kind of signal either."

"Then that's bad," Nel grunted. "Spread the word and keep an eye out for that Alliance blockade. I'll assume you're not going to have any conflicts over this?" She raised her brows at the former Alliance midshipman.

"Uniform's just for show now, Skipper," Stoker assured her. "I'd take it off but we'd all prefer I kept it on."

"You got that right."

"Good, 'cause the rest of what's been happening out here ain't been right at all. How many ships did you see in that blockade?"

"Three," Nel said. "Two frigates and a dreadnought."

"Dreadnought?" Stoker tried to whistle, found that he couldn't. He made a face instead. "We should be right flattered. Could get ugly though, Skipper."

Nel clapped him on the shoulder. "Then let's try and be gone before the beauty pageant." She was starting to like Stoker and his dry sense of humour. The man was a good sailor. Pity he was dead.

Better stop that line of thought. Quill and the captain could have the books on another bet otherwise. She was still intent on making them both suffer for that.

It had taken them just under two days to come from Grange to Rim. Quill had made good time though the strain was starting to show on him. Long trips suited him better than these short runs; he could take more time to rest and regain his strength. If they came through this, Nel vowed to seriously look into securing another navigator. If nothing else she'd be able to hold that over Quill the next time he thought about putting money on her.

"Tell me something," Nel said, tapping her spyglass against her thigh.

"Aye, Skipper?" Stoker turned to face her.

"Being like that." She inclined her head.

"Dead? Post mortis?"

Nel grinned ruefully. "Draugr labour is a big part of the Alliance. Keeps the High Lanes running. What you're doing here could be considered treasonous."

"We don't see it that way, Skipper." Stoker waved in his fellow sailors' direction. "Something bad happened and someone out in this blockade made a decision to do something about it. What happened to them on Grange, we couldn't stand by and do nothing, wasn't right with us." Stoker lowered his voice. "Don't mean we're gonna start looking at the Alliance as a whole any different though."

"If they'd have you back . . ."

"They can't," Stoker said. "That's been clear to us from the start. Too many awkward questions. Better for all of us if we just go our own way and disappear."

"There's a lot of Draugr out there," Nel said quietly.

"Thousands," Stoker agreed. "But they ain't like us."

"You don't think so?"

"We had a lot of time to think down there, Skipper. More

thinking than most of us have ever done before. And I don't think there's a whole lot of oppressed Draugr out there in the Alliance, if that's what you're getting at."

"If this was one of the old fireside stories, that's what would happen," Nel said. "You'd go after the villains, fight for your oppressed people, free the slaves, lead a revolution against the evil overlords."

Stoker stared at her. And burst out laughing, which turned into an almost hacking cough. He leant over the rail, spitting out phlegm and mucus. "Skipper, you kill me," he said, wiping at his mouth. "This ain't no fairy tale, I ain't no leader, and I've no interest in any revolution. Our ship, the *Falchions*, we did runs like this a lot. Carried that special sauce more than a few times. I know more than I want to know, way more than I oughta. There's no repressed slave population out there, most ain't no different from your average golem. Can't think for themselves because they don't think and they stopped thinking long time before they end up like this. And they got nothing else in common with me. The only people I got are the lads on this ship. You know how that is."

"I do," Nel agreed. "But what about the people from Grange? How come all of your crew didn't ship out on the *Falchions*?"

Stoker sighed. "Felt guilty, didn't we? Not their fault they got caught up in this. Them folks tried to help us, ended up like this because of it. Then there's them kids. Wouldn't be right to leave them, Skipper. Not after what Heathen did to them."

"What?" Nel's hand shot out, grasping Stoker by the neck of his tattered uniform, dragging his sagging face within inches of hers.

"What do you mean, what Heathen did?" she demanded.

Stoker looked confused. "Captain Heathen, Skipper, she was the one who took us down. I thought you knew, Sharpe said you . . ."

"Sharpe!" Nel seethed, releasing her grip. "No, to hells with Sharpe."

"He said you used to serve under her, was why you wanted to help," she dimly registered Stoker saying as she stormed the length of her ship, heading for the bridge.

"Quill!" she yelled out halfway along the breadth of the *Tantamount*. The ship lurched under Nel, almost throwing her off her feet. She grabbed at the rigging, righting herself. A dozen feet from her the air rippled—they were meshing with Rim. Glaring at the disturbance, Nel practically threw herself up the stairs to the bridge.

"Quill!" she yelled again, drawing her navigator's attention to her.

"We're heavily laden," he said, as close as he would ever get to an apology. "I couldn't slow the ship enough."

"You bilge swilling, gods cursed, cold blood Kelpie snake!" Nel spat every word.

Quill scowled back at her. "You are overreacting. The mesh was not nearly that bad." His tail flicked behind him, startled in spite of his words.

"You're doing this because of Heathen," Nel accused. "You stole my ship because of a damned religious argument."

"Ah," Quill breathed. "Someone told you who was behind all this."

"Listen to me, Kelpie." Nel kept advancing on her navigator, fists balled. "Horatio might not give a damn about your crooked past, but I do. Your past stays locked up in your damned cabin—you don't bring it out to mess the rest of us round. If your personal dramas ever affect this ship—"

"The captain is on the dock," Quill interrupted.

Nel glared. "We're not done, Kelpie. We'll finish this later, you mark my words."

Quill didn't answer and Nel didn't linger to watch his response. While Jack and the Alliance sailors were tending to the mooring lines she vaulted down to the deck, not waiting for the ramps to be lowered. She saw Horatio and the rest of the *Tantamount*'s crew. It hadn't escaped her attention that they weren't where they were supposed to be on the other side of Rim. They'd brought the *Tantamount* in on the near side of Rim, figuring it to be the most removed from any Alliance ships that might be moored at the outpost.

Several figures were sprinting ahead of the crowd towards Nel. Violet was the first, tackling her around the waist.

"Easy, lass, I need my legs." Nel tried to extract herself from the girl. "Where's the captain?"

"Nel!" Horatio answered the question. He was flanked by the rest of the crew, Gabbi and Piper trailing close on his heels. "Is that my ship? It is! Nel, you found my ship, you brilliant girl!" And from there Nel watched the captain's face change from exuberance to confusion. He raised himself up on his toes trying to get a better look.

"Who are all those people on my ship!?" he demanded loudly. "Those aren't my crew, they're all here." He looked back to confirm this. "And what's wrong with them? They look like they're all . . . Nel! Why are there dead people on my ship? No dead people on the *Tantamount*, it's a rule!"

"Skipper?" Piper queried. "What is going on?"

"And is that Sharpe?" Gabbi said angrily. "What's he doing on our ship? Skipper?"

"It's a long story," Nel said. "Captain, that cargo we were transporting, the medical supplies . . ."

"It turns people into Draugr," the captain finished for her.

"How . . . ?" She looked down at Violet. "That missing box, gods below. People here started turning?"

"No," Piper rumbled. "They did not."

"Then what . . . Piper, what's happened since I've been gone?"

"Sorry, Skipper," Violet whispered from down at her knees. "It's all my fault."

"No, it's not, Violet," Horatio told her firmly.

"Piper," Nel encouraged.

"After you went looking for the ship, the Alliance dreadnought arrived," Piper started to explain.

"The monstrosity," Horatio muttered.

"Please, Captain," Piper sighed. "Anyway, the dreadnought was too big to dock but they sent over landing parties. Scarlett met with them."

"She told them everyone on Rim was going to turn into Draugr," Violet piped up. "Said they all had to be eliminated."

"How do you know what she said?" Nel asked.

Violet hung her head.

"She was keeping an eye on Scarlett," Piper said, sounding reproachful. "Like you told her to."

Nel sighed and shook her head. One more long conversation to have later.

"All right," she said. "What happened next?"

"The Alliance sailors weren't happy, they argued with her," Violet said.

"She must have talked them round though," Gabbi said darkly. "They went out and attacked one of the slums."

"Maybe they were trying to take prisoners," Piper said, "it is hard to say. But it did not go their way. They did not have enough people ashore and they were driven back to the docks."

"They were driven back?" Nel shook her head. "Even with a golem?"

"The golem stayed at the docks, with Scarlett. Protecting the rest of the cargo we brought, they didn't fight 'til the Alliance had to retreat to the docks. Desperate, Skipper, the people here were very desperate. We thought the Alliance was going to try again, they started landing more of their people on the docks—after they confiscated our cargo I might add. The rest of their ships arrived, the *Morningstar* and the *Loneliness*."

"Heathen," Nel muttered.

"I didn't see her," Violet said. "But Scarlett, Onyx . . . they saw me."

Gabbi hugged the girl. "They almost got her too."

"Almost," Horatio snorted. "We convinced them to leave her alone. They chased us away from the docks after that."

"Thank you for that, Captain," Violet transferred her affection to her captain's bony frame.

Horatio patted her head awkwardly. "Yes, well, again you're very welcome there, Violet. Anyway, Nel, it looks like someone convinced them to pull out. They've been gone a while now. No way to tell what they're up to. We were the only ship that's been let through the blockade in weeks, apparently. There's nothing here that can fly. Which reminds me, what happened to that tug boat you and Jack took out? The owner has been asking."

"I know what they're up to," Nel said grimly. "Violet, go to the ship and find Sharpe and Quill, bring them over here. Get Stoker too while you're there."

"Who's Stoker?" Violet asked, puzzled.

"He's the Alliance midshipman. You remember the rankings? Good girl, get going."

"Alliance midshipman, Nel?" Horatio complained. "Who have you been letting on my ship? Gods below, just how many people did you let on? Look at them all! Hells, where did you put them . . . Nel, are they all paying passengers?" He brightened at the thought.

"No, Captain," Nel sighed, "we're not getting paid this time around."

"Seems like lately we never get paid," Gabbi muttered. "Won't be able to stock the ship at this rate."

"Jack's been finding all sorts of ways round that," Nel said.

"Huh?"

"Never mind, later."

Violet was back with the other three trailing behind her. Sharpe's arrival was met with thinly veiled hostility.

"We have a problem," Nel said brusquely. "The Alliance thinks people on Rim are infected, same as Grange."

"Ah." Sharpe blinked, considering this new information. "That is a problem."

"The locals threw them off Rim," Nel said. "They've gone to regroup."

"And what will they do?" Quill asked. He pointed to Stoker. "You are the Alliance monkey, you must have some idea."

"Your mate's a real charmer when he wants something, Castor," Stoker commented. "Can't say to be honest. Getting hard for them to contain the situation. If I was in charge I'd be starting to get worried. If things have spread to Rim, who's to say it hasn't got to Thatch as well."

"It hasn't," Sharpe declared firmly. "And there's no way it could have."

"You and I know that, mate." Stoker shrugged. "But frightened imaginations run wild."

"Hells," Sharpe muttered.

"Figure they'll start calling in more ships," Stoker added. "They'll have to, can't keep it bottled up on their own any more."

"Who're you?" Horatio pushed himself forward. "What were you doing on my ship?"

Stoker looked Horatio up and down, eyes settling on his hat. He saluted. "Captain Phelps, I presume? Midshipman Stoker, formerly of the *Falchions Rise*, Alliance Air-Corps. Pleasure to make your acquaintance, sir. Grand ship you captain there, made the trip from Grange faster than any I've sailed on. Was an honour to sail under her colours, sir."

"Oh, well, thank you, my boy, much obliged." Horatio faltered under the praise, unable to hide his delight. He tipped his hat at Stoker before leaning back and whispering to Nel, "This one has good taste, what did he say his name was? Never mind, get it later, I want to keep him."

Nel grimaced, shaking her head.

"We should have a little time before the Alliance floods this place with ships," Sharpe spoke up.

"You I don't like though." Horatio adjusted his hat so he could glare up at Sharpe. "Not any more. You're an ungrateful little bilge rat, after everything I did for you, assaulting me and my crew and setting fire to my ship."

"Aye, Captain," Sharpe sighed, bowing his head. "I'm all that. I'm sorry for the way I went about things. I needed your ship—I had a planetful of people to rescue." He pointed to where the people from Grange were still filing off the *Tantamount.*

"Really," he said, "it was all for the children."

"Children?" Horatio echoed.

"Aye, Captain, children," Stoker confirmed the story. "Orphan children, not a living parent amongst them."

Quill snorted derisively.

"Don't you start, Loveland," Nel warned him. "I can't believe I'm saying this, but his reasons were better than yours."

"Loveland?" Stoker repeated.

"What of it?" Quill snapped.

"Nothing," Stoker said. "It's a lovely name, rolls off the tongue."

"What reasons has he got?" Gabbi demanded, pointing at Quill. "He never does nothing for nobody."

"I have a bone to pick with you, chubby one," Quill glared.

"Chubby? You mouthy skink, that's the last meal you're ever getting out of my galley."

"For that I thank you," Quill hissed.

Gabbi scowled. "Thank me? Now I know I'm hearing things."

"Shut up, all of you," Nel said. "We don't have much time. Not enough for you all to be fooling like this."

"Why? What's going on?" Gabbi asked.

"Sharpe," Nel said. "Tell them what happened to the *Falchions*."

Sharpe's eyes darted from one person to the other. "We were rammed."

"We already knew that, Nel," Horatio said.

"By what?" Nel prodded.

Sharpe winced. "Another ship?"

"No," Nel growled, "try again."

"Hells," Sharpe sighed. "We were hit by a rock, an asteroid."

"That's impossible," Stoker retorted. "I knew those men, there's no way they'd get sunk by a ploughing asteroid. No way!"

"Well, we were," Sharpe told him.

"How?" Stoker demanded.

"Heathen," Nel said when Sharpe hesitated in his answer.

Stoker stared at her. "I don't understand."

"I do," Horatio said.

Nel had expected that. And in a way she was pleased the captain had been able to put it together, and fast. One of his better days.

The captain waved to her. "Nel, you tell them. I promised."

"Thank you, Captain," Nel sighed. Steeling herself, she spoke, "Heathen's a thaumatic."

"A navigator?" Stoker asked.

"No. Further up the line."

"How far?" Quill said, his eyes narrowing.

Nel met his eyes. "Far as they go, Quill."

"I'm still lost," Stoker said.

"She wasn't navigating the *Loneliness*," Quill ignored him, following the thread of the conversation. It was taking him longer than the captain to put it together but his reptilian eyes were narrowed in dark suspicion.

"Because she couldn't," Nel said.

Quill's fanged maw opened in a silent expression of shocked comprehension. "Her powers are skewed," he said to Stoker, raising his voice so others could hear. "Grossly. She could never navigate a ship, she'd rip it to pieces, even one like the dreadnought. But she could push something massive and solid. And, more importantly, she could steer it."

"Or aim it," Nel finished.

"Gods below," Stoker whispered. "Skipper, I've heard of people like that in the Alliance. There aren't many but . . . gods below, they call them . . ."

"Planet killers," Sharpe sighed. "We really need to leave. Now."

Chapter 11

Violet's legs ached. She'd been running messages over what felt like half of Rim since the skipper brought the *Tantamount* back. Now she was trailing the captain on his inspection of the ship. They'd fixed what they could, strengthened the rigging, reinforced burnt timbers, repacked what little stores they'd managed to salvage and scavenge.

It made Violet claustrophobic to think of all those people packed down in the hold together. Two days like that, barely able to move, all pressed up against each other. It would have driven her mad.

But it was a good thing Quill and the skipper had done, Violet realised. She'd seen the faces of the people they'd brought in. And looking at the faces of the children, the only ones still alive, she'd suddenly realised something. Why the captain was such an old man with all his lines and wrinkles.

It was responsibility that made you old. Responsibility for the ship and the crew. Their ship had carried that medicine that was responsible for what had happened to those folk on Grange, so in some ways they were responsible for looking out for them now.

It was what made the captain look so old sometimes. It made Violet feel old when she looked at those children.

If she wasn't careful she was going to grow another tail.

Couldn't have that. She'd be old before her time at this rate.

"She's a good girl," the captain said unexpectedly. "One of the best."

Violet blinked. The captain was fanning himself with his hat, looking around the hold. He was smiling.

"She's a fine ship, Captain."

"Aye, she is, lass. Breaks my heart to see her hurting like this," the captain sighed. "And I think we'll put her through more before we're clear of this."

"She can handle it, Captain," Violet said. "She's a hard one."

"Aye," the captain chuckled. "Just like her skipper. Speaking of which, I need a word with her. I think we're done here, Violet."

"You don't need me for anything else, Captain?" Violet asked.

"No, lass, not right now. Though I imagine there's someone else who does. That's why you're lurking around, Mister Sharpe?"

"Aye, Captain," Sharpe's voice came from behind Violet, making her turn. "I was wanting a word before we all parted ways."

"The last time you were on my ship you stole her." The captain frowned at him. "I trust there'll be no repeat of that."

"No, Captain," Sharpe promised. "Got my eye on another. Not as pretty as the *Tantamount*, but she'll do the job."

"We'll see," the captain said. "I'll be with Nel if anyone asks, Violet."

"Aye, Captain."

Sharpe waited 'til the captain was gone.

"You used me," Violet said before he could start.

"Aye, I did," Sharpe said. "I needed the distraction."

"Scarlett came after me. She tried to kill me."

Sharpe winced. "That was a risk. I knew it was a risk and I still did it. I'm sorry, but I had to. If I had to do it again . . ."

"You'd what?"

"I'd still do it."

Violet grimaced. She could appreciate the honesty. And after seeing the children from Grange . . . maybe she could understand. Maybe.

"You and Vaughn managed to handle Scarlett and her pet rock, I hear."

"Skipper's a hard woman." Violet shrugged. "She looks after her crew."

"Aye, she does at that."

"Why'd you steal the deed, Sharpe? Captain said you knew it was fake. Why bother if it wasn't the real one?"

"Have you seen the real one?" Sharpe replied.

Violet made a face. "I ain't even seen the fake one."

"Well, if you get the chance, make sure you read whose name is on it. I'll admit as I'm curious to that, but guess that's gonna have to wait. Captain keeps the deed close, couldn't get if off him if I tried."

"You should go," Violet said, turning away from him. "I don't think we've got anything left to say here."

"Aye, I'm going," Sharpe said. "You take care though, princess. Remember what I said about this ship, everyone's got a partner. Nel's going to need someone else to balance her out once the captain's gone. I hope you're up to the job."

Violet heard him leave but didn't watch him go. She kept her focus on what she was doing though her mind wanted to stray.

Captain ain't going anywhere, she thought. *The skipper neither. Not if I got any say about it.*

"I'd like a word with my first officer."

The captain stood in front of her, hands sheathed in the pockets of his jacket, hat perched and straightened over his stringy hair. His face was more deeply lined than Nel thought it should be, but his eyes were bright and alert.

"Captain," she acknowledged him, raising a hand to her forehead.

Horatio took a seat on a pile of planking, wooden debris in

the process of being pulled up. Stoker and Sharpe had set their Grange crews to work swiftly, putting their mad plan into action.

"You never salute me," he said. "Can't remember the last time you did."

"You told me not to, not long after I signed on."

"And since when did you ever listen to what I tell you?" Horatio chuckled.

"I always listen to what you say, Captain," Nel said.

Horatio snorted. "Nel, we put on a fine show but everyone knows it's you who runs this ship."

"You're the captain of the *Tantamount*, sir," Nel said. "The crew and I wouldn't have it any other way."

"Aye, you're a miserably stubborn bunch, aren't you?" The captain chuckled again. "Gods bless you for that. Do you remember Cauldron?"

"Hard not too, Captain."

"Ebon Masaius asked whose name was on the deed to the ship. Have you ever looked at it?"

"Captain," Nel said, "It doesn't matter to me which name is on some scrap of parchment. You're the captain, my Captain, that's all I want."

Horatio smiled, pleased. "Time was you had another captain."

"Time was I wore tight pressed whites and saluted every other officer." Nel shuddered. "You told me not to bring that stuff aboard the *Tantamount*."

"How long have you been with me, Nel? How long since I told you that?"

Nel smiled. "A while, Captain."

"You never talk about your time in the Alliance, not since you signed on."

"No, Captain," Nel sighed.

"Gods below, Nel, it wouldn't kill you to confide in someone once in a while. Get drunk some time, let it all out."

"You asked me to stop doing that as well, Captain," she said.

"I'm not going to be around forever, Nel," Horatio said.

"You got money riding on that, Captain?"

Horatio made a face. "Quill told you about that, then. Stupid thing really. I lost at cards to that big gorilla you ran into at Cauldron. What was his name? Brawn. Gods, it was years ago now. And there was you, fresh out of the Alliance and us needing a new officer."

Nel snorted, not trusting herself to say anything.

Horatio fidgeted with his hands. "Dammit, Nel, this crew bets on everything, you know that."

"But . . . Sharpe, Captain?" Nel gave her captain a pained expression. "Do you have to pick up every stray we come across?"

"I think they were in cahoots," Horatio muttered. "I'm sure Sharpe was in on it with Quill."

Nel shook her head in disgust. "Captain," she sighed.

"Captain," Horatio said loudly. "Dammit, Nel, you distracted me there. I came to talk to you about your old captain."

"What about her? She's out there, probably towing a big rock towards us as we speak."

"Nel, you know normally I don't like bringing up my crew's past."

"Normally our past doesn't throw giant void rocks at us, Captain," Nel pointed out fairly.

"True enough," Horatio conceded.

"So," Nel asked her captain, "what did you want to know?"

"Nothing," the captain told her. "You already told me everything when you signed on. I just wanted to tell you how proud I am of you."

"Captain?"

Horatio clasped her shoulder. "For getting out of the Alliance when you did."

Nel bit down on her bottom lip, hard. "Thank you," she whispered.

"Nothing to it, lass," Horatio said. "Now that we're done with the emotional stuff, why don't you tell me how in the hells we're going to launch a bunch of mothballed ships without any navigators?"

"We do have navigators." Stoker turned round to face Nel and the captain. "Leading seaman Loader is a certified apprentice navigator."

"And you can still push?" Horatio asked, squinting. "Aren't you a little bit dead?"

Leading seaman Loader had died young, possibly from a wand discharge if the blackened scorching under the neck of his uniform was anything to go by. He had the swarthy, cratered skin of those late out of adolescence, reinforced by swept back greasy hair. His skin was paler now, with a touch of grey, but for all that he didn't look as visibly far gone as many of his comrades.

A section of Rim's foundation, pried loose in the recent work, lifted off, hovering a few feet in the air. The weight was more than Jack and Piper could have lifted together.

"Aye, Captain," Loader confirmed. "Can still push."

"Lad hasn't sat his rating yet, but I don't think we'll be filing any reports over that," Stoker said.

"That's one," Nel said. She didn't add that one wasn't nearly enough. Sharpe's plan was mad and brilliant all at the same time. He wanted to break up Rim, use the derelict and decommissioned ships to fly the population of Grange out into the void. Jack's idea of stowing the Draugr had got them from Grange to Rim but it was no solution for the long term. They needed ships and lots of them. The problem was how to get them flying. It was possible to fly ships out in the void without navigators, barely, but solar winds and currents did exist. Launching them, that was the problem.

"Remember when you took us for a walk through the shanties when we were first here?" Sharpe asked.

"I remember you preaching a fair bit from atop a soap box," Nel recalled.

Sharpe ignored that. "Do you recall a friend of mine?"

"Thought you said he wasn't a friend, just someone you used to know," Nel said, though she hadn't believed it at the time either.

"He was," Sharpe said. "I was thinking of the one that looked like Stoker."

"Like me?" Stoker said.

Sharpe nodded. "Dead, like."

"Ah. Like that. You'd be meaning Wallace then," Stoker concluded. "Always liked him. Knew when to keep his mouth shut."

"Have I told you how much I dislike you, Sharpe?" Nel said.

"It's come up," Sharpe conceded. "Quill swears by it, in fact. So I hear. Wallace was one of the *Falchions'* crew. He stayed here when we passed through."

"Been making some contacts," Stoker informed her. "Squirrelling out thaumatics amongst the locals."

"You've been planning this for a while then," Nel said.

"Not planning." Sharpe shook his head. "This, this was never the plan. The plan was to get out on the *Falchions*. After that, the plan was swipe the cargo when we unloaded it at the dock."

"Not to set fire to my ship?" Nel said darkly.

"That damned golem really complicated things," Sharpe said, looking genuinely annoyed. "Having Violet run off with that one box was the only way I could get it away from the ship long enough for Quill to launch it."

"I can't believe you talked Violet into that." Nel shook her head. "You put her at risk. And you risked what happened on Grange happening here."

"Give the girl her due," Sharpe said, "she felt bad about screaming at Wallace. I meant for him to pick up the box from her and lead Scarlett and her pet rock on a merry chase. Turns out Violet is a better person than all the rest of us. She really did give the goods away. Made some friends, though. Wallace and the others got to the stuff in time, lucky for us."

"Then the locals have agreed?" Piper asked, speaking for the first time. "They will come with you on this grand exodus?"

Stoker and Sharpe exchanged a look.

"Some of them," Sharpe said.

"The ones originally from Grange," Stoker said. "Those who claim descent from Thatch . . . they don't want anything to do with us. They blame Grange for what's happened."

Horatio and Nel shared a look.

"How many altogether?" Horatio asked.

"How many people?" Stoker asked. He shrugged. "Don't know, I ran out of toes. The boys don't like it when I start counting on theirs. Have to take off their boots. Ain't pretty no more. Weren't much before but now it's worse."

"How many thaumatics did you find?" Nel clarified irritably.

"Seven," Stoker said. "That many I can count on my own."

"Seven is being overly optimistic," Sharpe said. "We have seven people we'd rate to push a tug boat through a decent fog bank, that's not the same as launching a dry docked vessel, especially the sort of luggers we're talking about here."

"Those luggers are part of the bulkheads keeping this place together," Nel reminded him. "Are you even going to be able to pull them out in the time you have?"

"No, we're not," Stoker said.

"The *Tantamount* is shipping out with all hands before Heathen and the *Mangonel* come back," Nel warned. "You do not want to be here when they arrive."

"Actually," Sharpe grinned, "we do."

There was a silence round the group as everyone processed that.

"You realise what Heathen is going to do?" Nel said. "She's going to slam a ploughing great rock into this scrap heap of a station. It's going to be ripped apart."

Sharpe chuckled. "I'm counting on it. Here." He took a nail, pried loose in the deconstruction, and etched a rough map against the boards of Rim's foundation. "We've found six hulks that suit our purposes. All located on the sunward side of Rim. But they've been here so long that Rim has actually grown up around them. So . . . Rim needs to go."

"You're going to wait for Heathen to smash her rock into Rim before you try and launch." Nel stared at him. "Gods below, Sharpe, you really are mad."

Horatio studied the crude diagram. "No," he said. "It makes sense. If they ran too early, Heathen and the Alliance would chase them down. If they wait until after, there would be a field of debris for the Alliance to wade through."

"If they're even able to launch," Nel said. "There's no guarantee, none at all, that you'll be able to pull those wrecks free when it all happens."

"Worried about me, Skipper?" Sharpe grinned.

"This isn't about you, Sharpe. And what about everyone else on Rim? The people from Thatch?"

"We're spreading everyone out on those six hulks," Stoker said. "Hedging our bets. The people from Thatch have until Heathen arrives to change their minds. If they don't . . . ," he shrugged, "they'll go down with Rim, same as they would anyhow. It's not their fault, but it is their choice."

"So that's the plan." Sharpe rose to his feet, chucking the nail away carelessly. "Unless anyone has a better one that's what we're doing. Skipper, Captain, it's been a pleasure."

"Mister Sharpe," the captain shook his hand gravely. "Midshipman Stoker."

"Captain," Stoker saluted. "Perhaps we'll see you again under less trying circumstances."

"I'll bring the brandy," Horatio promised.

"You're an idiot. You're all idiots. Let me tell it to you again, slowly so you can all understand. There is a thaumatic Kelpie out there with a case of scale itch to make a Draugr turn over in its grave and a warship bigger than this damned outpost. She is going to grab the biggest rock she can find and slam it right between your docks, just because she can. She is going to rip this place apart and there is not a damned thing anyone here can do about it. If you don't start running now, you're all dead.

There are ships, waiting, on the far side of Rim. But they won't wait long and if you don't go now you won't be around to complain about that. Forget about arguing, forget about packing, forget about everything except running. Because that's the only chance you have."

It was fun watching the skipper yell, Violet thought. Fun when she was yelling at other people. There was some shifting and restlessness amongst the crowd she was addressing but it looked like that mule-headed stubbornness was going to prevail.

The skipper thought so too. She turned away from the crowd in disgust, making her way back to where Violet and Wallace waited. This was the third group Violet had seen the skipper deliver her speech too.

"We're out of time," Nel said, looking past Violet to the direction the Alliance blockade ships were expected to come from. "Time to head back to the ship and weigh anchor. I'm not risking the crew or the ship over this. Not any more than we already have."

"You tried, Skipper," Violet said. The skipper turned away, hands turning into fists as she raked them through her hair in frustration.

"For all the good it did," the skipper said bitterly. "I got out of the Alliance because I never wanted to have to see this again. How the hells did Heathen and I end up here, doing this again . . . ?" her voice trailed off and she ground her teeth angrily.

"Why'd she do it?" Violet asked. "I mean back when you were in the Alliance . . . what . . ."

"It doesn't matter why." The skipper met her eyes. "The point is that she did it. The point is that she's about to do it again. And we can't be here when it happens."

The skipper looked at Wallace, who'd been standing there, quiet as always. "You need to go too. Get back to Stoker and the others, tell them to leave while they still can."

The Draugr turned to her. He raised his hand to his forehead, holding a salute. Nel returned it, adding a wistful nod at the end. Wallace came to Violet last.

"Goodbye," he said, voice little more than a whisper.

"Take care," Violet told him, feeling her eyes start to tear up. "Watch out for Kelpies."

Wallace smiled and turned away. He walked back through the crowd of refugees, pausing when he came to a small child. The little one was alone with no sign of parents, dirty, ragged, and following Wallace with wide, fearful eyes.

Wallace bent down and scooped the urchin up. Ignoring the rest of the crowd he marched towards where Stoker and the others were waiting.

"Better than nothing," Violet heard the skipper say.

The clicking of Quill's feet on the wooden deck echoed the length of the *Tantamount*. Nel could hear it all the way from the bow, punctuated occasionally by the whip-like cracks of air as the nervous Kelpie snapped his tail.

"Violet," Nel grumbled. "Go tell Quill to stop his damned pacing before I nail his miserable tail to the helm."

Even to Nel the threat was starting to sound old and Violet didn't seem to have even heard. Like most of the crew she was glued to the rails, watching the mist shrouded horizon for the Alliance blockade vessels. Rim drifted ahead of them, hopefully positioned between them and the incoming Alliance vessels. The *Tantamount* was running without lights, a dark shadow compared to Rim, which shone with hundreds of lights and torches against the mist. The Alliance ships would have to run with lights too, or else run the risk of crashing into each other, or worse, their rocky payload, amongst the mist.

"Violet!" Nel snapped. The girl's head jerked round in response.

"Skipper?"

"Go tell Quill to keep his peace," Nel lowered her voice, aware she'd drawn the attention of half the crew. They were all on edge, sitting here waiting. But none had voiced any complaint. Nel had been on her own in that regard.

"I couldn't live with myself, Nel," the captain had told her when she put her concerns forward. "Not knowing what happens here. We're involved already, so we're staying to see it through."

Nel's concern was the ship and the crew. This wasn't their fight, whatever their personal feelings might be. It made no sense for them to be drawn in any more than they already had. But privately, if she admitted it to herself, she was glad it wasn't her decision to make. She needed to know how it turned out as well.

"Heck of a run, hey, Skipper?" Gabbi commented, looking back at her.

Nel nodded brusquely.

"Feels good to be back on the ship," Gabbi said. "No golems or passengers shifting ballast, just our crew."

Nel glanced at her. "Thought you had your eye on Castor Sharpe."

"Man's too complicated for me." Gabbi waved a hand. "I like my men plain and simple."

"Explain Jack to me then," Nel muttered.

Gabbi frowned. "He didn't give you any trouble out there, did he?"

"I thought he would," Nel said. "I fell out of that damned rowboat when we found the *Tantamount*. Jack caught me."

"Told him he better keep you safe." Gabbi shrugged. "Jack's not so complicated as you seem to think, Skipper. He either likes you or he doesn't. Nothing more to it."

"Skipper," Piper called out from the other side of the ship. "Signal from Rim. They've seen them."

"Here we go, then," Nel muttered. Then, raising her voice, "All hands stand ready!"

The whole crew visibly flinched. The pall of silence cast over the ship broken, they stuttered back into life, moving to take up their posts with jerky movements that became smoother as familiar routines took over. There was no chance of any of the noise making it back to Rim, let alone the Alliance, and giving away their position, but that hadn't stopped the crew from clamming up as if it would. Back doing their jobs, that weight seemed to have been lifted. Nel could see them all sneaking glances towards Rim, hoping to catch first sight of the Alliance, but at least they were moving again, not frozen like gaping statues. Voices started to echo up and down the ship as she came alive again, sails hauled into position but not unfurled, winches manned, the sounds of the *Tantamount* stretching her muscles. Nel felt a moment of pride in the ship and its crew. Both were beat up and had been through rough weather, but stood ready.

"Movement at the ships," Piper announced, offering Nel a spyglass. He had Bandit perched on his broad shoulders again. Both appeared happy to be reunited.

She brought the spyglass to her eye. "I see it." She couldn't make out individuals but there was a lot of activity around the breakaway ships. "Looks like some of the Thatchers have decided to come after all."

"A prudent decision," Piper agreed sagely.

"They seemed bent on staying, wonder what changed their minds," Nel commented, lowering the spyglass.

Piper pointed. "That."

Nel watched as the mist started to boil, billowing and pushing out. Massive shadows started to darken the horizon as vast shapes moved closer to the edge of the bank.

"I've never seen the mist do that," Piper said to Nel.

"It's Heathen," Nel explained tersely. "She's making heat when she pushes on the rocks. Normally the envelope swallows the heat but those rocks don't have one. So the heat is evaporating into the mist, like when you breathe out on a cold day."

"Interesting," was all Piper said. "I thought she would bring one big rock. It appears I was mistaken."

Nel chewed on her lip. She counted three giant rocks tumbling their way free of the mist. Cratered and jagged, spinning relentlessly towards Rim, all were bigger than the *Tantamount*, one almost bigger than the *Mangonel Falling*. Following that realisation came the appearance of the dreadnought itself, emerging from the mist like some behemoth predator. Only the flanking lights let Nel make out the dimensions of the ship, reminding her just how massive it really was.

Heathen would be on that ship, she suspected. She needed the biggest possible anchor to brace herself against the forces she was manipulating. Who would she have left in charge of her own ship then? Some trusted deputy, no doubt, someone who wouldn't second guess her captain and argue with her over morality.

The thought made Nel bite down hard on her lip. She tasted blood in her mouth, spat it out over the side. As a captain Nel still respected Heathen. She was typical officer material; cold, unflinching, and carried her orders out no matter the course. And some of those orders . . . some Nel hadn't been able to look at herself in the mirror afterwards. This wouldn't be the first time she'd watched Heathen do something like this. It was just the first time she'd been near the receiving end.

Which she wasn't really, she thought, watching Rim with a strange sense of anxiety. The station was a hive of activity now, though most of the hive workers had retreated to the ships. Scaffolding and other structural debris had been cleared from around the ships but they were still firmly anchored to Rim, they were Rim. It was going to take some substantial demolition to free them. Demolition Heathen and her Alliance compatriots were going to provide.

"Any sign of the *Loneliness* or the *Morningstar*?" Nel asked.

"Both hanging back." Piper pointed. "Flanking the *Mangonel*."

"Staying clear of the firing zone," Nel reckoned. "They won't advance until after Heathen demolishes Rim. They're probably not even expecting to have to. They'll be looking for blockade runners before the hammer goes down. Nobody will be expecting to have to chase a whole damned fleet after the fact."

"One would hope so," Piper agreed. "Bandit thinks Sharpe is quite mad indeed."

"Did he also tell you about how he beat Sharpe black and blue with a dead rat?" Nel asked.

"He did not," Piper said, looking sternly at Bandit. "Bandit has been getting into fights? This is not good. There will be discipline over this. Bandit is too small to be picking fights with those so much bigger than he is."

Bandit started a stream of chatter that seemed to involve a re-enactment of the fight with Sharpe. Feeling malicious, Nel couldn't resist throwing another barb out there. "What about the fact that Bandit has been rat-catching for Jack, and those rats have been ending up on Quill's plate?"

"Bandit!" Piper sounded shocked. "Why would you do such a thing? Quill is our friend and Jack is . . . Bandit should not be associating with the likes of him. What must the skipper think of us? What must Quill think? I think I may be sick just from thinking of it. Rats? Bandit, I am so very disappointed in you."

The loompa's chatter died off, the creature hanging its head in shame. Nel felt an odd sense of satisfaction in that. The feeling evaporated into the mist when she looked back at Rim.

"Gods below," she mouthed as the first rock crashed into the station. It was the smallest of the three and Heathen's aim was slightly off, chipping the edge of the floating platform. The docklands disintegrated under the impact, vanishing into a storm of splinters as the rock drove through them like wet paper. It could only be her imagination, but Nel thought she heard screaming then.

What were the people on those embedded ships thinking now? Were they frozen solid in fear or had the desperation sunk in? If it were Nel, she would be taking an axe to anything tethering them by now. Maybe that's what they were doing. She refused to think about the people not on the ships. It was too late for them to change their mind.

"This is why you left the Alliance." Piper moved closer to Nel, putting a hand on her shoulder. "You witnessed this before?"

"I watched her kill a planet," Nel whispered. "I couldn't stop it happening. And I couldn't stay after that."

"This time will be different," Piper said simply.

"Maybe." Nel reached up and grabbed Piper's hand, squeezing it once.

"Now what?" Piper asked. "What will she do?"

"That was to get her bearings." Nel gripped the *Tantamount*'s railings with her other hand. The damage to the far side of Rim where the breakaway ships were still locked had been minimal. None of the encouragement being shouted up and down the *Tantamount* could make any difference to that. The chatter died, another hush descending as Heathen made her next attempt. The massive boulder she'd plucked from out in the void, the one rivalling the *Mangonel* in size, started to move. Tumbling slowly, a great ball gathering speed, it rolled towards Rim. Her aim was dead on but it wouldn't have mattered. The sheer mass of the missile spelt out the end of Rim.

To Nel, it seemed to happen in slow motion. The planet killer rock hit the edge of Rim and the station began to crumble. The rock dug in deeper, crashing through dead ships, timbers, pilings, shanty towns and warehouses. Nothing slowed it. Loose debris was swept up in a cloud, spreading out in an all encompassing herald ahead of the actual demolition. Now Nel was sure she could hear screaming. It didn't matter that it was all in her head.

"Go," she heard herself whisper as the breakaway ships remained locked to their stations at the edge of Rim. The giant boulder was halfway through Rim now and showed no signs of slowing. They weren't going to make it. All the desperation, all of Sharpe's madcap efforts, they weren't going to be enough. Had never been enough. She hadn't realised 'til that moment how much she'd actually believed he could pull it off.

"Dammit," she cursed, slamming a fist into the railing and turning away. She couldn't watch what was going to happen—screams were already ringing in her ears, she didn't want the images to go with those screams.

"Skipper!" Piper grabbed at her shoulder urgently, forcing her around to watch the scene. She tried to look away, tried to tell Piper she didn't want to see. He made her.

A whole section of Rim, a massive area around where the breakaway ships were encased, had broken away. Directly in the path of Heathen's missile the structure had broken clean away from the rest of the station, drifting only a few hundred feet away.

"They're pushing!" Gabbi ran up to the bow, shoving people aside to get a better look. Her round face was beet red, whether with exertion or excitement it was hard to tell. "I can feel them from here."

"Those ships are still locked together," Nel said, "they can't get away like that."

"I think they meant for that to happen, Skipper!" Gabbi said excitedly. "I felt them all push against that rock, just before."

"Are they trying to slow it down?" Piper asked. "That is a very big rock there."

"No," Gabbi rushed, "I think they weakened the structure around all their ships. Instead of pushing each ship they pushed against Heathen's rock. The pushback they got was so strong it ripped that section free and now it's keeping them away from it."

Piper and Nel shared a look. "Very clever," Piper approved.

Nel made a face. "Sharpe."

The free floating section of Rim was starting to edge away from the planet killer missile. They couldn't outrun it, but working together the seven thaumatics aboard managed to nudge themselves to the side, out of the path of rampant destruction. The rest of Rim was gone, a field of debris miles wide. None of it was recognisable, bits and pieces hung together, forming solid clumps that twisted slowly outward in the nether. Worst of all were the tiny stick figures of people who hadn't been aboard the ships, those that hadn't made it. There was something distinct and instantly recognisable about a body in the void, even at this distance.

The breakaway ships were finally doing that, starting to breakup and separate from one another. First to go were the ones on either end of the section, taking some scaffolding with them, but otherwise finally starting to look like real ships.

"Oh no," Gabbi cried out.

The Alliance blockade hadn't taken long to realise what was going on. The two frigates had set sail, one to each flank of the debris field, the long way around. As predicted, they were unable or unwilling to take the short, direct route through what had been Rim. Not so with the *Mangonel Falling*. The dreadnought would pass directly through the field, damning the consequences. Then Nel saw what they were really doing. The dreadnought swung wide, following one of the flankers the long way around, slow and ponderous, but frightening just to behold. What kept going straight through the remnants of Rim was Heathen's last missile. Smaller than the previous projectile it would nonetheless make short work of Sharpe's remaining ships if they didn't get clear in time.

Two more of the ships had broken free of their trappings, leaving two more still to escape. The last two were mired in the leavings of the previous four, unable to break away from their solid moorings.

Nel felt the ship list to the side momentarily—the crew's fault, they were all lining the rails watching the drama. She yelled at them, ordering them back to their posts as Quill steadied the ship. Some listened, mostly those who were meant to be in the rigging where they were afforded a better view.

As Nel and the crew watched, another ship managed to fight clear of the last remnants of Rim, sails unfurled and trailing flotsam and other scraps. It was the last ship to do so—the sixth and final vessel vanished in an expanding cloud as Heathen's rock did its job. Nel flinched back from the edge of her own ship, breath shuddering at what she saw.

"The other ships are scattering," Piper rumbled.

"Splitting up," Gabbi said.

Two and three, that was what Sharpe's rag-tag fleet had split into. If it was even still Sharpe's fleet—he could have died, again, on that final doomed ship. It was unlikely he'd have survived a second encounter of that kind. An Alliance frigate was pursuing each group, the *Mangonel Falling* further behind, but the sleeker frigates both threatened to close in on their targets. Nel had been impressed with Stoker and his fellows when they'd sailed with her, but whoever was crewing those hulks wasn't up to their standard. The ships drifted and turned sluggishly, their sails patchy; former tents pressed into a new lease of life by the looks of it.

"What's he doing?" Gabbi cried, leaning dangerously far out over the edge of the ship. Bandit squawked in alarm and grabbed onto the back of her shirt with two limbs, holding onto Piper with his back ones.

"Skipper!" Gabbi turned and called. "Look, one of them's turning back. Is he mad?"

"I see it," Nel said. "Guess that means Sharpe wasn't on that last ship."

Gabbi paled. "Gods below, what is he thinking?"

From the group of three ships one had done a swift about face, barrelling back towards the chasing frigate. The other two continued to flee.

"Dammit, Sharpe," Nel muttered. It was a sacrificial gambit, it had to be. As far as she knew none of the breakaway ships were even armed. She saw plumes of smoke as cannon fire left the Alliance frigate, joined by fluorescent trails as mounted wand weaponry joined in at closer ranges.

"All crew, stand to combat stations."

"What?" Nel whipped round to face the bridge. The captain stood gravely at attention at the top of the stairs, wand tucked under his arm like a parade baton.

Gabbi and Piper looked at Nel, stunned, but left to man their stations. Nel stared for a moment longer before racing to the bridge.

"First Officer Vaughn," Captain Horatio Phelps said to her formally. "Would you be so good as to take your key and open the small arms locker. See that weapons are dispersed amongst the crew against the chance that we have to repel boarders. After that if you would be so good as to take charge of our cannon."

"Captain," Nel said stiffly, "what the hells are you thinking?"

"Two of those ships will be cutting across our bow as they attempt to escape this area," Horatio explained. "They are being pursued by a hostile vessel. In this situation the two fleeing vessels qualify as non-combatant refugees. We have an obligation to assist them in any way we can."

"Obligation?" Nel blinked. "Against an Alliance vessel?"

"It's a little late for us to be splitting hairs," Horatio said. "Aware of our presence, the Alliance would likely treat us as hostiles. I prefer to make the first move."

"Sir," Nel forced herself to speak slowly, "I strongly advise against this course . . ."

The captain interrupted her. "Given that you have personal history with the commanding officer of an enemy vessel I give you permission to stand down and remove yourself to your quarters once you have distributed the small arms."

"Captain?" Nel stared.

"That's the *Killing Loneliness* out there, Nel," Horatio said. "I'll make this easy for you."

He held out one hand, open, palm up. "If you wish to remove yourself from the situation and retire to your cabin for the duration, simply relinquish your key to the small arms locker."

Nel's hand went to the key, tied on a leather thong around her neck and tucked away under her shirt.

"No, Captain," she said quietly. "I have no wish to retire from this situation."

Horatio nodded. "I see. I'd like you to hand over that key anyway."

Nel protested. "Captain, I already said . . ."

"The key, First Officer Vaughn!"

With shaking hands Nel drew the key over her head and dropped it in Horatio's outstretched hand.

"If that's all, Captain," she said stiffly. "I'll retire to my quarters."

"Hmm," the captain's eyes came up from the key. "Oh, no need for that, Nel. Here," he placed his captain's hat atop her head, "Acting Captain Chanel Dominica Vaughn, I hereby place you in charge of the *Tantamount* for the duration of this engagement. Don't lose my hat, I've only got the one."

He swung the key on its loop. "I'll see to those weapons then."

Stunned, she stepped onto the bridge, found the whole crew staring up at her. It was enough.

"Get back to your posts!" she bellowed at them. From behind her she could hear Quill assume his post as the *Tantamount*'s navigator. She turned on her heel to face him.

"And what are you looking at, Loveland?"

The Kelpie shrugged. "Better you than him. The captain knows nothing about combat."

"Don't remind me." Nel plucked the captain's hat off her head and stowed it in one of the lockers.

"Orders . . . Captain?" Quill asked, sounding amused.

"Head for the *Loneliness*," she ordered. "Full speed. We'll try and draw their attention away from the ships and lose them in the mist."

"That is your plan?" Quill snapped. He shook his head. "That is . . . ahh, never mind. Still better you than the captain."

Nel studied the *Killing Loneliness* as Quill took up the slack in the sails. The privateer had closed the distance on its prey but the *Tantamount* should still reach it before it closed the rest of the distance. She wondered what Heathen would say if she knew Quill, whom she'd so readily dismissed for his faith in his old gods, was steering the *Tantamount* straight for her ship.

Nel recalled an earlier conversation. "How do you kill a god,

Quill?" she asked.

"You ignore them," Quill answered without any hesitation.

Ignorance. Another word for faith, really.

Nel faced her navigator. "Ready to demonstrate what ignorance leads to?"

The smile Quill gave her was pure nasty. She'd expected nothing less.

"Fire!" Nel ordered, slashing down with one arm. There was a yell from the forecastle and it momentarily vanished in a cloud of smoke as half the *Tantamount*'s weapons battery opened fire on the *Killing Loneliness*. They'd taken them unawares, approaching low and from underneath the line of sight. They were still distant, both their shots going wide but they'd got the privateer frigate's attention and the enemy was in no position to return fire.

"Reload!" Nel shouted, leaning out over the bridge. She watched Jack and Piper heave shot into the smoking barrels of their two fore mounted cannon. Others hurried to refill the magazines and re-aim the weapons.

"Getting close," Quill muttered behind her. "They still haven't changed their course yet."

"Steady as she goes," Nel told him. She waited, counting heartbeats as the frigate loomed close. When she could make out figures on the deck above her she gave the order.

"Fire!"

One of the cannon rang true, punching a hole in the underbelly of the *Loneliness*. She saw something glittering with phosphorescent light stream away from the hull. Where it ran, mist gathered around it in a swirling cyclone. Ether. They'd gotten lucky, better than Nel could have hoped for, and holed the ballast. The privateer started to list to one side, her equilibrium stung.

"Reload!" Nel yelled. "Aim for that breach!"

Before her crew could do so, the *Loneliness* started to roll, bringing the ship's broadside around to bear on the *Tantamount*. Heathen's ship wasn't ignoring them anymore.

"Quill!"

"I see it!" Quill snapped. He rocked everyone aboard as he threw the ship away, pitching it down to dive under the *Loneliness*. A number of the broadside cannons fired sporadically, none hitting their mark. Over-eager gunners unable to wait for a proper line.

"Ready the stern guns!" Nel called out to the second teams of gunners. She'd positioned two of their four cannon at the stern of the *Tantamount*, wedged, strapped and sandbagged behind her and Quill on the bridge. Inevitably she'd known they'd have to run and turn their backs on the enemy.

"Hard to starboard, Quill," she ordered. "Make a run down their line so they can't draw that broadside onto us. One salvo is all it would take."

Beneath her she felt the *Tantamount* turn hard. She silently thanked the ballast in their own ship for keeping the plane level, no matter what angle they might really be on. Down was always down. Every ship had their own opinion as to what was up and down. It was easy to forget that there was more to naval combat than a level playing field. There was every other spherical angle to consider.

"Ready guns," Nel called out again. "Aim for the breach if you can."

The four cannons, stern and bow mounted, all tilted directly upwards. They would never have a better shot than the underneath of the *Loneliness* for a killing shot. Their cannon might be small, and the underside of the frigate would be solid and reinforced against such an attack, but at least they couldn't shoot back.

Or so Nel had thought. Looking up she was shocked to see the deck of the *Killing Loneliness*, the open deck topside of the frigate with all its crew and cannon. The frigate had rolled all the way over, making a mockery of perceived reality. The *Loneliness* had its own orientation and was making full use of it.

"Quill!" Nel called out desperately. "Dive! Get us away!"

It was their only chance. She could see the Kelpie crew above them angling the mounted weaponry towards the *Tantamount*'s deck, just as she'd intended to do. One volley and they were finished. At this range they couldn't miss. It all depended on Quill . . .

Nothing was happening. There was no lurch, no rush, no sense of movement from the ship. It felt clapped in irons; their wind had died.

Beside her Quill struggled, his scaly skin slick with perspiration. His eyes bulged in his head and his fanged mouth was open, gasping.

Looking up, she realised why. It was disorientating to look up at the deck of the *Loneliness*, but there was no mistaking the massive black form in the centre of the deck. And now that she looked she saw the diminutive form accompanying the golem, wrapped in its obsidian arms. That was all Nel had time to take in as the *Killing Loneliness* opened up, cannon and wand fire raining down upon them. Screams ran the length of the ship. A water barrel was hit, the contents geysering over the deck. Nel threw herself down, covering her head and squeezing into a ball, all she could do until the barrage stopped.

Ears ringing, she risked opening her eyes. Impossibly Quill still remained on his feet, wreathed in lightning now as he raged against another thaumatic, fighting to exert his influence over the *Tantamount*. The *Loneliness* was still above them, wreathed in discharged smoke and mist. And she could make out the obsidian golem and its mistress.

The pair began to fall, rising, she realised, towards the *Tantamount*. She heard a snarl from Quill, pure rage and frustration, and knew who had been fighting him. The golem and its payload flashed in the void as they passed between envelopes, spinning and shooting through the *Tantamount*'s envelope to come crashing down to the deck. Splinters flew, kicked up from the golem's massive weight and the ship shuddered. Next to her Quill was thrown bodily to the back of the bridge, the resistance he'd been fighting vanished as the source steadied herself on Nel's deck. The *Tantamount* lurched then, free to move again, throwing crew around like rag dolls. Above them the *Loneliness* moved off to resume its pursuit of the breakaway ships, content to ignore them again.

Nel clawed at the bridge railing, hauling herself up to see Onyx open his bladed arms on the main deck, Scarlett stepping out from them, wands clutched in both hands. Steam rose off her body, flushed from her exposed skin. The crew members around her were already battered and broken, too shocked to react to her presence.

Scarlett's arm whipped out, wand extended. A cascade of thaumatic charges flew from the shaft. Crewmen started to fall, started to scream, the deck turned into mayhem as people ducked for cover or scrambled to find weapons.

Jack was the first to react. One of his massive harpoons in hand, he charged the golem with a roar. The harpoon struck the golem's raised forearm, carving a gouge in the unblemished hide. Jack struck again, but the golem lashed out, snapping the weapon in two. A backhand caught Jack, lifting him into the forecastle. He rose again, too stubborn to stay down, swayed and fell forward onto his face. He didn't get up a second time.

As Nel watched, several of her crew attempted to engage Scarlett. One attacked her with a cutlass, recoiling as Scarlett caught the bladed weapon on crossed wands. The wands were thaumatically charged—touching them to metal was like grabbing a navigator's bare skin, more so since Scarlett was a thaumatic herself. The woman ducked and weaved her way through clumsy attacks, the golem advancing in her wake.

Nel reached back with her wand, drawing it past her shoulder and whipping her arm round hard. The concussive charge should have taken Scarlett in the head but something made the Guildswoman turn. She caught the charge on one wand, pivoted to her side and redirected it. It struck Cyrus, pitching him off the edge of the *Tantamount* with a shriek abruptly cut off once he cleared the envelope. Scarlett spun around, meeting Nel's eyes across the deck.

Violet crashed into the captain, tackling him around the knees and bringing him down to the deck. Wand fire flashed through the air where he'd been standing. The captain scrambled beneath her, clutching at his wand, trying to stand back up. He gave a squawk, echoed by Violet as the air was squeezed from her lungs, the cause being Piper as he dived onto the pileup to take cover from the firefight.

"Stay down, both of you," Violet yelled at them. Only Bandit seemed to heed her, burying his head under the captain's jacket. She risked a peek over the railing, enough to glimpse Scarlett and the skipper going at it, exchanging fire from opposite ends of the ship. She saw the golem and something that made her cover her mouth to keep from crying out. Cyrus.

Violet ducked down again, putting her back against what was happening. "Captain," she said, loud as she dared. "I've got an idea."

"Will it get that damned golem off my ship?" The captain climbed to his knees, brandishing his wand.

"Yes. Only . . ."

"Never mind that, Violet, just tell us what to do," the captain snapped.

Violet told them. Piper and the captain stared at her, then at each other.

"She has been spending far too much time with the skipper," Piper rumbled.

"And doesn't it show," Horatio agreed. "All right, Violet, get to it. But you need a distraction."

"I know. I need a few minutes."

"Leave that to me. No golems on the ship, should never have broken that rule."

Violet sucked in a fast breath. If she stopped to think about it she'd never do it. She rose to her feet, flinched at a near miss and ran for the side. And jumped, vaulting over the ship's railing.

Bandit squawked his alarm and darted after her. The two disappeared from sight.

Claws scraping against wood, snarling his frustration, Quill stood up beside Nel. "I do not like this woman," he hissed.

"I'm going to kill her," Nel whispered. Scarlett smiled in response, turning away as another crew member made a vain attempt against her.

"Good," Quill stated grimly. "I'll deal to that golem." He raised both hands, slamming them down and then wrenching them to the side. On the deck the golem shuddered, the boards under its feet cracking in protest, then Onyx was pushed towards the side of the ship. Scarlett looked up, raising one arm. The golem's journey stopped abruptly.

"Not so fun, is it?" Quill said through gritted teeth. "She's stronger than me . . ."

"No golems on my ship! It's a rule!" someone cried out. The captain appeared, gods only knew where he'd been. He had his wand in hand and promptly used it against Onyx, though the charges just ricocheted off like they had for Nel. Scarlett lined up the captain and dropped him with a clean shot to the head. It was done almost casually. The captain fell backwards, lay there motionless.

"Captain!" Nel called out. *It wasn't fatal*, she told herself. *He isn't dead, he couldn't be.*

Quill gave a triumphant cry and the golem slammed into the side of the ship, smashing through the timbers. Scarlett caught the construct just in time, hauling it back with brute force onto the deck of the ship. The golem reached out, taking firm hold on the nearby rigging with its rocky hands.

"Skipper!" Quill snarled. "Get her!"

Nel vaulted over the rail, down to the deck. Her ship cried out in protest at even this modest impact but Nel couldn't take the time for that. Too many of her crew were dead or dying. She stalked towards Scarlett, yelling for her crew to get out of the way. Those who were able staggered or crawled away, dragging those who couldn't. Nel whipped her wand from left to right, sending charge after charge the Guildswoman's way.

The first winged Scarlett's shoulder, startling her out of her reverie. A scowl darkened the woman's features. She started to flick aside Nel's incoming fire, redirecting it on her wands as she had earlier. Nel had never seen anyone do that before, didn't know it could even be done. But Scarlett's aim was indiscriminate now, she wasn't trying to hit anyone, her actions purely defensive. Nel kept closing the distance between the two of them.

She heard timbers creaking all around Onyx. The golem's body shook as it was pulled one way then another by Scarlett and Quill. Then Nel saw something that almost made her lose her own concentration. Piper appeared with a massive sledge hammer in his hands. She thought he meant to pummel the golem, maybe crack its obsidian shell, but instead he turned his attentions to the deck itself. He struck at the planking by the golem's feet. Strained and stressed by numerous hardships, the decking gave. Onyx crashed through to the bowels of the ship. Piper went with him.

A yell brought Nel's attention back to Scarlett. Free from distraction the Guildswoman directed her full attention against the skipper, lashing out at close range with both wands. Nel caught one blow on her own weapon, locking the wands hilt to hilt. The second hit she caught on her bracer. The hardened leather took some of the sting but she still felt the jolt of electricity run up her arm. Gritting her teeth, she twisted her wrist, catching Scarlett's own. Nel squeezed, refusing to let go even as the thaumatic grief poured into her. Keeping the other arm locked against her wand Nel forced the smaller woman towards the edge of the ship.

She felt Scarlett's arms shaking, struggling against a stronger opponent. Nel had been sailing most of her life—this wasn't a contest she would lose. Those same years taught her that desperation bred foul play. Nel slammed her forehead against the bridge of Scarlett's nose, staggering the woman, blood gushing from her face, her rose tinted glasses shattered.

Nel drew back her wand, ready for the final blow. She was hit by the dirty trick then, later than she'd anticipated. A crate, the remains of a barrel, some debris from the broken ship, whatever it was slammed into her side, throwing her against the forecastle. Her head spun. She saw Scarlett, bloodied, above her, wands raised.

Then something happened to her. The woman's eyes rolled up into her head, showing only the whites. Scarlett staggered, leaning against the railing. She grabbed at a hawser, looking dazed. Nel saw this, recognised the opening but couldn't find her wand. She reached, desperately searching the deck around her. Nothing.

A massive weight rushed past Nel, making the air squeal. It missed her, but not Scarlett, sweeping her clean off the ship. The woman didn't make a sound.

"The hells," Nel gasped, struggling to her feet. Her head was pounding, blood ringing in her ears. There was a trench carved through the *Tantamount*'s deck next to her. The edge of the ship where Scarlett had stood was gone, leaving a jagged hole in the woodwork. Nel clambered to that hole, grabbing hold of stray rigging to keep her balance.

"Do not fall." Quill grabbed her arm, steadying her. She clung to him.

"That's Scarlett," she breathed out, watching the figure tumble away.

"I hit her with the anchor," Quill explained. "It was still attached."

Sure enough there was the anchor, floating free and trailed by lengths of severed rope.

"It's hard to tell," Quill muttered, studying the mass of empty space surrounding the *Tantamount*, "but I believe that is the golem out there too."

"What?" Nel stared. *Damned Kelpie must be seeing things.*

"There." Quill pointed. "Against the mist."

"Maybe." Nel was dubious. She could make out the silhouette against the mist, far away and falling further. It could be the golem. "The hold. Piper."

She found her wand and, with Quill steadying her, made her way to the other side of the ship where Piper and the golem had crashed through the decking.

The hold was a mess, even worse than the deck. The golem had rampaged through here but there was no sign of it. Or of Piper. What there was, was a hole, all the way through the bottom layers of the ship. Black void and starlight on the other side, trails of mist swirling around the breach.

"The golem didn't fall straight through," Quill observed. "These holes are not aligned for such."

"Hells," Nel muttered. "Watch my back, Quill." She didn't wait for his response, kneeling down by the breach and swinging herself down into the hold.

It was dark inside but with the two breaches she could see well enough. Everything within reach was destroyed. Smashed or torn apart. The golem might have gone mad but there was still no sign of it and precious few places something that big could have hidden. Maybe Quill had seen it out in the void after all. She stepped up to the second breach. It was smaller and the timbers leaned outwards, like they'd given way. Nel leaned over.

A dishevelled, upside down head stared back at her. "Skipper!"

Nel flinched back, falling flat on her backside. "Godsdammit, Violet!" she yelled.

Violet's hands appeared at the edge of the breach, testing carefully for purchase. One of those small hands held a broadaxe almost as big as Violet herself. The girl swung herself inside the hull, making the transition from one plane to another look easy. She stood up with a rueful grin on her face. Bandit climbed up the girl's back, perching on her shoulder, chattering excitedly.

"It worked, Skipper," Violet panted as she spoke. Then she made a face. "Just like Sharpe said . . ."

"Sharpe?" Nel exclaimed.

Violet grimaced. "What he said when he first came aboard about being able to walk on the outside hull. The floor was already weak from what Sharpe did so when Piper brought the golem down into the hold it just needed a little work and it gave." Violet spoke in a long, breathless spiel, hefting the axe for emphasis. It was amazing she'd been able to swing the thing.

"Where did you even get that thing? Never mind. Piper. You two planned this?" Nel seized the girl by the shoulders. "Piper? Where is he?"

Violet craned her neck, looking worried. "Uh, I don't see him. Bandit? Go find Piper."

The loompa's head shot up, scanning the hold. After a moment's consideration he dived off into a dark corner.

"Follow him," Nel ordered.

They trailed Bandit through the wreckage of the hull. They found the spare bubble, stowed out of harm's way. It was cracked, a spider's web of cracks spreading across one hemisphere. There was blood, a thin, sticky trail that widened as they followed it.

Piper was by the stairs, one hand wrapped around his stomach, head resting on the third step. He raised his head when they approached, managing a bloodstained smile when Bandit fussed over him, pawing at his face, trying to clean the blood off.

"Hello, little one," he said to Violet.

"Piper," Violet's voice was very quiet as she knelt in front of the big man, taking his hand in hers. "We did it. We got rid of him."

Piper smiled. "Good, we did a good thing then." He spoke very slowly, measuring out each word. "The captain will be pleased."

"Lying down on the job, Piper?" Nel said, kneeling down beside him. She ran one hand down his face, pausing at his neck. His skin felt cold and clammy to her touch, the pulse sluggish.

"Apologies, Skipper," Piper said. "I will not be down here

much longer, I promise."

"You're going to be all right," Violet told him. "We did it, Piper. We did good."

"Yes, we did." Piper nodded gravely. "You did very well, little one. You too, Bandit."

Bandit chirped once in response.

"Violet, would you go check on the rest of the crew for me?" Nel said. "I need to know how the captain is doing."

"I . . . I want to stay."

"It is good that you do, little one," Piper smiled, "but I would like a moment with the skipper. We have things to say."

"Ok, Piper." Violet stood up, wiping at her eyes with one sleeve. "You'll take care of him, won't you, Skipper?"

"I'll stay with him," Nel promised. "Go find the captain. Take Bandit with you, he'll only get in my way."

"Come on, Bandit," Violet called, scooping the unresisting creature up. As they walked up the stairs together Bandit waved to Piper with one small, black hand.

"What are you covering up there, Piper?" Nel asked quietly once the sound of footsteps faded.

Piper moved his hand slightly, revealing the broken spar that had impaled him. The splintered length of wood had pierced all the way through his abdomen and out the other side.

"Oh Piper," Nel sighed.

Piper covered his wound again. The two were quiet for a moment, then heard footsteps coming back down the stairs. The falls were heavy and clipped. Quill.

"Ah." The Kelpie navigator took in the scene without need for explanation.

"Go away, Quill," Nel whispered. She didn't want to have to deal with Quill right now.

The Kelpie navigator shifted his weight from one foot to the other, but didn't leave. He met Piper's eyes. "You are not long for this world, are you?"

Piper bowed his head, his chin almost touching his chest.

The Kelpie hissed, letting his breath out slowly. "Is there . . . anything?"

Piper closed his eyes. For a moment Nel thought he was gone.

"We did a good thing today. I am glad it is you two . . . here." He opened his eyes once more. "You will look after the little ones?"

"Yes," Quill said.

Nel wasn't sure if Piper had meant to include Quill in his request but he looked pleased with the answer. Nel nodded her head as well.

Piper sighed, content. "My friends . . ."

And he was gone.

CHAPTER 12

"It's not over yet."

"What do you mean, Quill?" Nel asked tiredly. They were back above deck, both of them squinting against the change in light.

"I came to get you." Quill pointed. Sharpe's two breakaway ships, the two that had cut by them, chased by the *Killing Loneliness*, had been caught. Unable to match the speed of the privateer frigate, they were now within firing range. The *Loneliness* was finding its bearings, firing intermittent test shots as it closed the remainder of the gap. It was only a matter of time.

"What do you wish to do?" Quill asked.

Nel closed her eyes. "Dammit, Quill, we barely slowed them down last time. And look what they did to us."

"What would the captain say?" Quill asked.

"I'm acting captain," Nel muttered darkly.

"Then what does the acting captain say?"

Nel swore. "To hells with it, Kelpie. Make for the frigate."

"Excellent." Quill grinned. "Though with the ship as it is we likely won't make it in time."

"Go plough yourself, Kelpie," Nel snapped. "Just fly the damned ship."

Nel made her way to the forecastle where she'd last seen the

331

captain. She passed crew members still picking themselves and their comrades up. As she reached the forecastle she found the wounded laid out in a makeshift infirmary.

"Jack." She clapped the ex-convict on the shoulder, surprisingly pleased to see him up and about. Parts of him were wrapped up in cotton wool. He didn't seem happy about it, reaching under bandages to scratch at things.

"Skipper." His eyes were glassy, not quite focusing on her.

"Not helping with the wounded?" she asked.

"Gabbi told me not. Says I'm con . . . conus . . ."

"Concussion," Nel supplied. "Means you'll get dizzy easy."

Jack made a face. "Why didn't she just say that? Stupid woman."

"Sit down, Jack," Nel said. "Before you get dizzy."

"Aye," Jack grumbled, sitting down heavily. "I can do that."

"Good man," Nel said, moving onto the captain. Gabbi was leaning over him; so was Violet. Horatio pushed them away, sitting up as he did so. The concussive charge had fried his hair, the ends were slightly blackened and clumps stood out all over the place, and his eyes wouldn't co-operate with one another, determinedly staring in separate directions, giving the captain a manic, crazed look.

"Get off me, women," he cried. "I don't need attention, I need my hat! Nel, is the battle over, can I have my hat back?" He looked at her in concern. "Where's my hat? You haven't lost it, have you? I've only got the one."

He jumped to his feet. "Golems! No golems on the ship, sacred rule! Where is that blasted rock? Somebody find me a hammer. And a chisel!"

"Sit down, Captain," Gabbi said firmly, dragging the captain back down.

"It's not over yet, Captain," Nel said.

"Then don't call me captain." Horatio sounded annoyed. "You're captain 'til we get through this. Go find my hat!"

Gabbi caught her eye as she left, mouthing a name silently. Nel shook her head in a negative. Gabbi's eyes misted over for a moment, but she caught herself. Time for that later.

"Aldy," Nel said, hauling the man up by his elbow. "You hurt?"

"No, Skipper." He shook his head. "Just some scratches."

In Aldy's case that could mean anything. No time for that now. She had orders for him. "Grab whoever you need and stand by the guns. But don't fire 'til I give the word."

Aldy saluted, running off to collect whoever was still standing. Nel ran back to the bridge, breathing hard by the time she got there.

"Quill . . . ," she started to say.

"Look," he said.

Hells, she thought, *what now?*

Quill had brought the ship close to the running battle. It was one sided as before. None of the breakaway ships were able to return fire. They could have made the job easier by splitting up again, tacking and gybing, anything to make themselves a harder target. Instead they just ran, straight as they could, and it wasn't enough. Except . . . where there had been three ships, counting the pursuing frigate, there were now four.

"What is that?" Nel exclaimed. What she was looking at was not so much a ship as a collection of conglomerated flotsam and debris. There might be a hulk under all that but it was hard to tell. It hurtled at breakneck speed towards the frigate.

"Sharpe," was Quill's guess, though even he sounded unsure. "They came through the debris field?"

"Crazy sons of . . . " Nel shook her head in disbelief. "All that trash got caught up in their envelope."

"I think that was what they intended," Quill growled. He grabbed hold of the helm, throwing the ship wide. There were cries of alarm from the crew at the sudden, violent movement. The ship groaned in protest, joining in the chorus.

"Quill!" Nel yelled at her. He didn't answer her, his gaze fixed on the junkyard hulk.

The ship ploughed straight for Heathen's ship. The Kelpie

crew seemed to realise the danger it posed, the stern cannon began to fire on the incoming vessel. The assault had little effect, those shots that struck home seemed lost in the concentrated wreckage the ship had collected on its sojourn through the debris of Rim. The ship kept coming.

"Gods," Nel whispered. She saw the envelopes start to mesh but this was no gentle melding like was meant to happen. This was fast and explosive, the different pressures in the two envelopes creating a storm around both ships, a storm that found ample ammunition with all the debris Sharpe's ship had collected. Crew were ripped off the deck of the frigate, followed by rigging, barrels, and even cannon as the hulk drove directly over the top of them. The two ships disintegrated under the combined pressure.

"You said something, Skipper," Quill said, "about the risks of ignorance?"

Nel could only shake her head wordlessly. She didn't think she'd ever witnessed anything so brazen in all her life.

"Survivors?" Quill said.

Nel gestured. "Take us in, Quill. I'll start . . ." She turned and examined the ship. The bubbles were gone, all of them destroyed in the battle. "Just take us in, Quill. Any idea where that dreadnought got too?"

"It couldn't chase down a one-winged ray," Quill dismissed it. "You are safe to give the captain his hat back."

"Later," Nel said. "Take us closer."

He nodded. "Aye, Acting Captain."

"Just fly the ship, Quill."

Quill did so, taking them in close and beginning a slow circle of the wreckage of the two ships. It was already starting to expand, having been tightly contained at first by the combined ballast of the two ships. It drifted apart now, settling into minute envelopes that evaporated as they collided against each other. Bodies were easy to make out, that distinctive silhouette against void and mist. But from what Nel could see they were all Kelpie.

"Did you see any of your lot on Rim or Grange?" she

asked Quill.

"My lot?" Quill hissed.

"Kelpies."

"That does not make them my lot! Do you consider the Alliance monkeys out there to be your lot?"

"Godsdammit, Quill," Nel complained, "did you see any on Grange or not?"

"Not," her navigator said huffily.

"Well, me neither, so who was flying the other ship?"

"Skipper." Nel felt a tug on her arm and found Violet standing by her side. Bandit was still riding her shoulders, hands tangled up in her fairy-locks. "Is it over?"

"It seems to be, Vi." Nel pursed her lips.

"Was that Sharpe that crashed into the Kelpie ship then?" Violet asked.

"We think so."

Violet ran to the edge of railing, like always practically climbing to see over it. Bandit stood atop her shoulders, scouting. To Nel's surprise he immediately began emitting a series of shrill shrieks, gesturing insistently.

"That's not a Kelpie," Nel said, seeing what Bandit had. It was easy to miss, deep blue, with only scraps of white cloth showing up against a dark background. Drifting out on the periphery.

"Would you stop saying things like that," Quill hissed at her. He eased the prow of the *Tantamount* in, but soon slowed the ship to a halt. "This is as close as we go," he said, daring Nel to challenge him.

It's doable. Nel measured the distance. *Just barely.*

"What are you doing?" Quill said, as she started to run towards the bow. "Dammit, what are you doing now?"

"Violet, rope!" Nel ordered as she ran. She cleared the steps to the forecastle in a jump, throwing up hands to catch herself against the front of the ship. She could see the figure clearer now.

"What's going on?" Gabbi looked up in alarm from her patients. "What are you doing?"

"Tie this off somewhere," Nel said when Violet trotted up with the rope bundled in her thin arms. Nel grabbed one end, looping it around her waist and over one shoulder.

"Nel, what in the hells are you doing?" Gabbi repeated, eyes going wide. Beside her the captain pushed himself up again, staring about in confusion.

Nel clinched the knot at her waist, pulling hard to make sure it was secure. Then taking a deep breath, she backed up as far as the forecastle would allow. With all eyes on her she ran forward, taking the length of the deck in a few steps, up onto the bowsprit, pushing off at the last second as hard as she could.

She rose for a moment, the gravity of the *Tantamount*'s ballast plane insufficient to pull her back. Then she hit the edge of the envelope and passed through it and all she felt was cold. She didn't slow, there was nothing to slow her. Nothing to change her course. If she'd measured this wrong, misjudged the angle . . . but no, there it was, a blue clad figure in scraps of torn uniform, tumbling against a cold miasma background.

Nel reached out, her arms spread wide as they crossed paths. The impact stunned her, knocking what breath she had left out in an icy plume. Her arms closed around the body, hugging it to her. That was what it felt like, a body. Cold and stiff, frozen. Nel couldn't see anymore, she'd closed her eyes against the cold for what little it would do. The two of them spun around each other, tumbling in the void.

She didn't feel the tug of the rope, there were no other sensations than that numbing cold. But she felt it when they passed back through the envelope. The shock of air burned her skin, then gravity as they really did start to fall. She held on tighter, too numb to unclench her arms even if she wanted to, not even when they both slammed into the side of the *Tantamount*. Someone was pulling them up, then onto the deck. She felt hands on her.

"You idiot."

Nel opened her eyes to find Quill's maw inches from her own. The navigator was furious. An unending stream of curses spilled from his mouth, all directed at her. He ranted, raved, threw his arms around, lashed his tail, gnashed his teeth. He stopped, glaring at her. Then started again.

"You stupid, inconsiderate, selfish excuse for a captain," he growled at her. "How could you do something like that? How dare you!" He leaned over her again. "You will never do such a thing again, ever! You are not . . . not to leave me!"

"Quill?" Nel could only stare.

"With them!" Quill stabbed his clawed finger at Violet and Bandit, both keeping their distance from the enraged Kelpie.

"Are you all right?" Gabbi asked, kneeling down beside her. She rubbed at Nel's arms and shoulders, trying to get some warmth into them. "I've never seen Quill act like that. He tried to pull you back in himself. Didn't work of course, he just about hit us with the things he did grab though. I had to push it all away from the ship."

Nel laughed, then wished she hadn't. Her throat was raw and painfully dry. "He just didn't want to be stuck with the little ones."

"What little ones?" Gabbi scowled. "Never mind, are you all right? You look all right . . . apart from being frozen solid. You should be better in a few bells as long as I keep Jack away from you. And you don't do anything else so stupid," Gabbi admonished her sternly.

"For myself I'm glad she did what she did," said the person Nel had plucked from the void. He raised a hand, staring at the fingers. "Frozen solid, all right. Can't move a one."

"Stoker?" Nel said.

"I ain't the patron saint of good fortune," Stoker groaned. "Or if I is, I was a lousy choice."

"Skipper thought you might have been Mister Sharpe," Violet piped up.

Nel glared. "I did not, Violet."

"Sharpe? Just as well I ain't him, little girl. Was out there a while." With some effort Stoker moved his head to look at Nel.

"Gods below, Skipper, I need to thaw. Sharpe ain't dead like me, but he would have been."

"What?" Nel growled at that. She tried to get to her feet and stumbled. Violet steadied her, holding onto her arm. Nel leant on to the girl for support. "Sharpe said he was infected, same as the rest of his crew."

"His crew?" Stoker looked affronted. "Sharpe weren't part of our crew. I figured he was from Grange, never did know how he talked his way onto the *Falchions* after we rebuilt her though. But he weren't dead. Not like us."

"He said he was," Nel said.

"Which?" Stoker asked. "Said he was part of the *Falchions* or the other?"

"Both."

There was a thump, then a bitten off curse. Nel saw Quill clutching at his tail.

"Did you just bang your tail?" Violet asked.

Quill chose to ignore her. "Sharpe told me he was part of Heathen's crew," he said. "That he fell out of favour with her over the attack on Grange and the *Falchions*."

"Well, that don't sound right, neither," Stoker said. He grimaced, touching a frozen hand to his face. "Want to shake my head here, never realised how much you use your head when you're talking."

"Mister Sharpe said a lot of things," Violet said.

"Sharpe played us," Quill said through gritted teeth.

"Clever boy, wasn't he?" Horatio said. "Nel, my hat. You better not have left it out there."

"It's on the bridge, Captain," Nel assured him. "Violet, go get the captain's hat, it's in a locker."

"Where is Sharpe anyway?" Horatio asked. "Anyone seen him?"

"Wanted to visit some old friends on the *Distant Morningstar*," Stoker said. "We dropped him off on the way."

"You did what?" Gabbi exclaimed.

"Climbed into a barrel and Loader pushed him out there.

Said he was going to do for their navigators."

"By himself?" Quill asked suspiciously. "Himself, against a whole ship?"

"I asked him that too," Stoker agreed. "Said it wasn't the whole ship, just the navigators. Must have too, 'cause we saw the *Morningstar* drifting all over the place on the way over. Looked like a drunken donkey, she did."

"And what would you have done if not for this act of miracle working?" Quill asked him. "Rammed the *Morningstar* as well, I suppose?"

"Course. It was just me and the lads on the wreck. And Sharpe. We always knew somebody would have to play hare to the hounds. Figured we were the best ones for them to choke on. Sharpe jumping ship just meant we had a shot at both frigates. Glad it worked out this way, wouldn't have felt good about ramming the *Morningstar*. Might have known somebody on there and that would have felt all kinds of wrong."

Nel considered something. "Captain," she said slowly.

"A moment, if you please, Nel." Horatio beamed as Violet returned with his hat. He spent a minute fussing with it, getting it to sit just so. "That's better," he pronounced.

"Captain," Nel repeated.

"Yes?" Horatio turned to face her.

"What did Sharpe tell you about himself?" she asked.

Horatio froze, hands on his hat. "What do you mean?"

"He told Quill he was with Heathen and me he was with the Alliance. Stoker thought he was from Grange. So what'd he tell you?"

Horatio hung his head evasively, mumbled something under his breath.

"Captain," Nel's voice hardened.

"He might have mentioned something about the Guild," Horatio admitted reluctantly.

There were exclamations of dismay and disgust from those assembled.

Nel glared. "And you didn't tell me?"

"He asked me not to!" Horatio protested. "A captain's word

is a serious thing. Besides, I thought he was full of himself, never believed it for a second."

"Now why don't I believe that?" Nel muttered.

"Nel!" Horatio exclaimed.

Nel glared at her captain. "He said you were a lousy card player, you know that?"

"Lousy?" Horatio exclaimed. "He did not! I was teaching him how to play! How to spot tells and underhanded dealing . . ."

"And this was right before you lost the ship in a game?" Nel said.

Horatio spluttered, drawing himself up. "I'm insulted. And that's no way to speak to your captain. I'll be on the bridge when you've quite sorted yourselves out."

The captain strode off in a huff. Nel motioned for Violet to follow and keep an eye on him.

"So?" Quill demanded. "Who was he? What was he?"

Nel snorted. "Hells, I don't know, Quill. He could have been any of those things. Maybe none of them. Maybe he just liked telling stories."

She extended a hand down to Stoker. "Can you move yet?"

Stoker considered. "I can't feel my feet. That may or may not be a bad thing."

Nel stared at him, then, raising her voice, "Jack!"

They spent another bell circling the remains of the *Loneliness* and Stoker's ship. They found no more of his Draugr shipmates. Still running without lights, the *Tantamount* sailed at a cautious pace to a prearranged rendezvous point. They did find the four surviving breakaway ships there. There was no sign of the Alliance dreadnought, the *Mangonel Falling*. It was during the short journey that Nel finally had time to take stock of the damage to ship and crew.

The *Tantamount* was in a state, worse than Nel had ever seen her, but she would fly. The crew were worse off, seven dead, including Piper. Five bodies were laid out on the deck, wrapped in sail cloth, weighted with cannon shot. Two others had been lost overboard, gone ahead to see what awaited their former shipmates.

Nel knelt down beside Piper, easily recognisable as the biggest shroud on the deck. In her hand she held small chunks of obsidian, flakes of stone chipped off the golem during the fight, possibly by Piper. She liked to think so. She laid the black handful along the length of the funeral shroud.

"Look after the others, Piper," she told her friend.

Nel was the last to say her farewells. Once she stepped back the bodies were pushed down the ramp leading off the *Tantamount*. One at a time they slid feet first to the edge of the envelope, helped by the weights wrapped in with them. The result was a solemn line of white wrapped bodies, marching out into the void. The crew stood silent by the railing until the last body disappeared into the miasma.

"Where will you go?" Nel asked of the Alliance midshipman. He'd more or less thawed out though he still moved somewhat stiffly. There were similar funerals taking place on the other ships—not all of them had escaped without casualty. It seemed even Draugr could die, fail as it were, given sufficient damage. In spite of that, Stoker had insisted on staying for the funerals aboard the *Tantamount*.

"That ways," Stoker said vaguely. "We didn't really think so far ahead. Suppose we should be thinking about what's best for the children and such. I reckon we'll manage though."

Quill snorted at this, taking the opportunity to stomp his way back to the helm. "I'll be waiting," he said.

"Strange one, isn't he?" Stoker commented. "Skipper, it's been an honour. I'd shake your hand but I'm still trying to make mine work properly and I dunno how it would go."

Nel managed a smile for him. "Stay safe, midshipman Stoker."

"Aye," he sighed, "I'll do my best. Gods below, I can't believe I'm doing this. Where's the Kelpie with that barrel?"

Nel shook her head, wishing the man luck at finding an

intact barrel on the *Tantamount* right now.

"Well, Nel, ready to head back to Cauldron?" the captain asked her. He was hunched over to one side, the weight of Bandit on his shoulder bearing down on him. The loompa was still trying out different crew members for size and fit. She suspected Bandit would settle on Jack. She hoped Bandit would settle on Jack.

"You don't see any problems with heading back to Cauldron, Captain?" Nel asked.

"No, why?" Horatio said. "Should I? Nonsense, we've got a cargo to retrieve and deliver. Where was it we were going with that? Seems I should remember these things. Must check my log book. Captain's log, destination, bound to be in there. Bound to be."

Horatio squared himself, puffing out his chest. "How do I look?"

"Like the captain of the *Tantamount*." Nel declined to tell him he was in danger of losing his hat to the loompa. Piper had never worn hats. It seemed Bandit didn't approve.

"Excellent." Horatio beamed. "Just as I should. Well, then, First Officer Vaughn. Take us out would you?"

"Aye, Captain, I'll get right on that."

Nel shook her head, watching the captain with a slight smile on her face. Couldn't go anywhere 'til Quill got through shipping Stoker home anyway.

"Ready to head back to Cauldron, Vi?" she called, looking up at the girl. Violet was perched in the riggings, one arm wrapped around the rope while she played lookout. The other hand was pushing tangled locks of hair out of her face.

The girl looked down at her, pointedly. "Ready to start paying me, Chanel?"

"Watch your mouth." Nel pointed a mocking finger at her. "But keep our captain from betting the ship and I'll buy you your first drink."

"You're a hard woman, Skipper," Violet said. She checked so see who else was nearby, climbing down closer to the deck. "Who else knows, Skipper?"

"Knows what?"

"That the captain had the deed tattooed on his back. I saw it when I was looking after him."

Nel raised her brows. "It was Piper's idea."

"Captain says it was his."

"It was Piper's," Nel repeated firmly.

Violet smiled sadly. "I miss him. Piper."

"Aye, lass, I do too. We'll get you a tattoo to remember him by on Cauldron."

Violet looked sceptical at the idea. "Quill's coming," she said. "Must have finished flying Stoker home."

Nel laughed. "Tell him to take us out, Violet. We've got places to be."

"Aye, Skipper." Violet leaned far out of the rigging, hanging on with arm and leg. "Oi, Quill! Shift your worthless, milk drinking skink hide and get us moving!"

Nel looked away as the Kelpie's outraged response filtered back. The girl was learning.

Acknowledgements

If I acknowledged everyone I should the list would be longer than this novel. Instead let me try and cover most of them in one go. To the girl in question, thank you.

About the Author

Thomas J. Radford is a New Zealand author who wrote his first novel when he should have been studying for an end of year school exam.

After that he acquired a few qualifications relating to History and Film. Now he gets paid to watch Television but is banned from telling children this by their teachers and parents. *Tantamount* is his first novel.

He wants to know how the story ends as much as you do but lately the inmates seem to have taken over the asylum. And by inmates we mean characters and asylum we mean ship.